ROBERT K. TANENBAUM

HOAX

A NOVEL

$7.99 U.S.
$11.99 CAN.

COMPLEX, CONTROVERSIAL,
AND ALWAYS ON THE CUTTING EDGE. . . .
Read these Butch Karp novels in the "richly plotted
tough, funny crime series" *(People)*
from Robert K. Tanenbaum

RESOLVED
ABSOLUTE RAGE
ENEMY WITHIN
TRUE JUSTICE

Don't miss his chilling true-crime classics

BADGE OF THE ASSASSIN
and
THE PIANO TEACHER:
THE TRUE STORY OF A
PSYCHOTIC KILLER

All available from Pocket Books

Butch Karp is back in
Robert K. Tanenbaum's new thriller

FURY

Coming soon in hardcover
from Atria Books

50799>

EAN

"[Tanenbaum's] people and plots are more interesting than they have any right to be."

—*Kirkus Reviews*

ABSOLUTE RAGE

"Gripping. . . . Richly told. . . ."

—*The Washington Post*

"Absolute Rage [is] a champion. . . . Robert K. Tanenbaum's novels stand out as oases in a desolate waste: vivid, witty, unflagging, and zestful."

—*Los Angeles Times*

ENEMY WITHIN

"Tanenbaum makes his people complicated souls who live and breathe. . . . [He] has a wonderful way with instinctive throwaway lines, the sort you reread just to savor."

—*St. Louis Post-Dispatch*

"A fast-paced, suspenseful, tightly plotted, and morally complex legal thriller."

—*Tampa Tribune*

TRUE JUSTICE

"Intelligent dialogue, a well-designed maze of political and moral traps, and the charming and incendiary chemistry between Karp and Ciampi."

—*Publishers Weekly*

"Deftly handled. . . . Karp and Ciampi are smart, honest, and aggressive."

—*Los Angeles Times Book Review*

"Tanenbaum is one lawyer who can write with the best of them."

—Joseph Wambaugh

ALSO BY ROBERT K. TANENBAUM

ROBERT K. TANENBAUM

HOAX

POCKET **STAR** BOOKS

New York   London   Toronto   Sydney

A Pocket Star Book published by
POCKET BOOKS, a division of Simon & Schuster, Inc.
1230 Avenue of the Americas, New York, NY 10020

Copyright © 2004 by Robert K. Tanenbaum

Originally published in hardcover in 2004 by Atria Books

All rights reserved, including the right to reproduce
this book or portions thereof in any form whatsoever.
For information address Atria Books, 1230 Avenue
of the Americas, New York, NY 10020

ISBN: 0-7434-5289-5

First Pocket Books paperback printing June 2005

10 9 8 7 6 5 4 3 2 1

POCKET STAR BOOKS and colophon are registered
trademarks of Simon & Schuster, Inc.

Cover design by Carlos Beltran

Manufactured in the United States of America

For information regarding special discounts for bulk purchases,
please contact Simon & Schuster Special Sales at 1-800-456-6798
or business@simonandschuster.com.

To those most special,
Patti, Rachael, Roger, and Billy
and to the memories of my legendary mentors,
District Attorney Frank S. Hogan
and Henry Robbins

HOAX

In the beginning . . .

IT WAS ONE OF THOSE LOVELY EARLY JUNE EVENINGS
*in New York City when the new leaves on the trees were still
lime green, and the salt air was blowing in from the harbor
fresh and warm as a cup of espresso at the Ferrara café on
Grand Street.*

*Several blocks west of that hundred-year-old institu-
tion, Roger Karp stood with his twin sons on the sidewalk
where Grand crossed Crosby, soaking in the last rays of
the setting sun. Giancarlo had his face turned to the west
like a sunflower, smiling serenely behind dark Ray Charles
glasses. But Zak was obviously troubled, frowning and
kicking at the curb. Finally he said, "I still don't understand why that baby had to die. Why does God let good
people die and bad people live?"*

*The question caught Karp—Butch to all who knew
him, the current district attorney for the county of New
York—off guard. Several weeks earlier, the eleven-year-
old boys had surprised him by asking if they could study
for the bar mitzvah—the right of passage into manhood
for Jewish boys—and then he'd surprised himself even
more by agreeing to help teach their classes.*

*The whole family seemed to have embarked on spiritual
quests. His wife, Marlene Ciampi, and their daughter,*

Lucy, were trying to "find themselves" in the New Mexican desert, and now the boys. But he didn't consider himself to be on particularly good terms with God, dating back to the death of his mother when he was in high school. Yet, here I am, left to field questions from the twins that I don't know if I have the answers to, he thought.

At the last class, they'd discussed the biblical story of David and Bathsheba, in which God caused the couple's firstborn son to die because of their sins. The boys thought that was unfair to the baby, and he didn't really have an answer to their complaints as he thought so, too. He tried to show that it was a story about actions having sometimes unforeseen consequences, and thought he'd made his point.

However, Zak was obviously still troubled, and Karp wanted to say something meaningful. For some reason, the question had brought to mind his mother, her beautiful face thin and drawn by her battle with cancer, in pain and desiring the peace of death. It was the most painful time of his life, yet all that he would become had been determined then.

"I don't really know, Zak," he said. "All I can say is that there seems to be a sort of economy to the world, a sort of balancing act. I don't even know if there's a grand plan to all of it, or if that's just the way it is. But sometimes you have to wonder: What if we could change the past when something bad happens? Would that always be a good thing?

"For instance, what if that baby had lived? David and Bathsheba had another son later, you know. His name was Solomon, and he became the wisest of all kings. There's a story about how two women once came to his court, both of them claiming to be the mother of a baby boy. He listened to the women and announced that he couldn't decide who the real mother was. So he ordered his men to cut the child in two and give half to each woman."

"Oh great," Zak complained, "another baby gets whacked."

"Well, no, because one of the women pleaded with the king not to kill the boy. 'Let her have the child,' she said. And you know what happened?"

"No," the boys answered dutifully.

"Solomon said he knew that she was the real mother because she would rather have lost her baby than let him be hurt. So he gave her the child . . . it was a test."

"Pretty smart," Zak conceded.

"Yes, it was," Karp said. "But more than that were the larger concepts we got from Solomon that became part of the foundation of western law and civilization. In this case, holding impartial hearings to weigh the evidence in front of wise people in the community to settle disputes with justice.

"But getting back to your question, Zak, what if the first son of David and Bathsheba had lived and became the next king of Israel? Maybe we would have never even heard of Solomon. And would the first child have been as good a king? Would he have been fair and wise? Or would he have waged unjust wars, murdered innocent people, and made life-and-death decisions according to his whims? Would the world we live in today be worse or better?"

Karp paused. There was a time he didn't believe what he was telling the boys, and he wasn't sure of it even now. "So maybe in the economy of the world . . . ," he closed his eyes and tried to recall an image of his mother before the disease, her smile and laughter, ". . . maybe there is a reason why bad things happen to good people, even if it also hurts the people who love them."

He opened his eyes. The facades of the taller buildings in the Financial Center that faced the sun were anointed in a golden glow as befitted the financial capital of the world, the windows reflecting the ending of the day like newly minted bullion. Rising from the streets and sidewalks, the symphony of traffic, the underground rumbling of the subways, the laughter, shouts, and conversations of eight million people blended together into a constant hum as though the breathing of a single enormous creature. So full of energy and life that it had been able to absorb a wound like September 11, 2001, and, while vowing never to forget, became even more than it had been, stronger, better.

Karp loved his city, and yet he was grateful for the little harbor out of the storm that was Crosby Street, where he and his family lived in a loft on the top floor of a five-story brick building built around the turn of the century. He liked the look of his 'hood, as the boys called it, a throwback to another time.

Still paved with cobblestones, Crosby was almost more of an alley than a street, too narrow for delivery trucks to drive past each other without one climbing up on the curb. Rickety old fire escapes clung to the sides of the buildings like steel insects trying to look in the windows, and it wasn't hard to imagine the days before dryers when clotheslines filled with the day's wash would have been hung between them.

The street level and walk-down shops still retained some of the street's old flavor—like Anthony's Best Shoe Repair and Madame Celeste's Tarot Parlor and Piercing Studio (Free Reading with Navel or Nipple Piercing). Other businesses reflected the ever-changing ethnicity of the neighborhood. The bottom floor of his building was occupied by the Thai-Vietnamese restaurant supply store. And still others reflected the times. Down a block was the Housing Works Used Bookstore—proceeds of which were used to provide housing for people infected by HIV and AIDS—a favorite hangout of Marlene's. It was a great place to sit down in peace with an old book and a good cup of coffee that didn't come from one of the ubiquitous Starbucks that had sprung up all over the city.

Surrounded by the crowded sidewalks and heavy traffic of more famous streets like Houston, Broadway, Mott, and Canal, he and Marlene thought of Crosby Street as a haven from the more impersonal city "out there." They had remained in the loft even after they could have afforded to move to tonier digs. Then gradually others had seen the possibilities, and lofts like theirs were now going for a million and more, but the Karp and Ciampi clan wasn't selling.

He looked at his sons, both of them now standing quietly shoulder-to-shoulder as close as possible without actually touching, yet connected as only twins could be. A breeze ruffled the dark curls of their hair—a legacy from their Sicilian-American mother—and they laughed because they were young and alive. I wish they could have met you, Mom, he thought.

The reverie came to an abrupt end when a dark blue Lincoln town car pulled up to the curb and a large, muscular black man in a suit got out. Clay Fulton was the chief of the NYPD detectives who were assigned to the district attorney's office as investigators. The twins, who'd known him all of their lives, were delighted with his arrival and immediately started peppering him with requests for a tale about taking on the bad guys single-handedly. "Can't tonight, got to talk a little business with your dad," he said, making eye contact with Karp to let him know what he had to say wasn't for the twins' ears.

Karp sent the disappointed boys in to do their homework and turned to Fulton. They were both big men. The DA maybe a little taller at six foot five, most of it still in decent shape despite the debilitating demon—middle-age—and a bum knee from an old basketball injury. Fulton was twenty pounds heavier, though all of it was lean muscle as it had been back in his playing days as a middle linebacker for Penn State.

"What's up?" Karp asked.

"They've made an arrest in that quadruple homicide," Fulton said. "The rap star, ML Rex, and his buddy, from Los Angeles, plus the two hookers."

"Yeah?" Karp said. The foursome had been gunned down on a Saturday night ten days earlier while sitting in a limousine in East Harlem. It was a bloodbath that had all the earmarks of a gangland hit.

As a tone-deaf, rhythmless white guy who still thought the Beach Boys and the Animals were the beginning and end of rock and roll, Karp wasn't up on the rap scene. But the twins had filled him in on the particulars of gangsta rap and the simmering conflict between the East Coast and West Coast rap camps. Some sort of modern-day Hatfields and McCoys, he gathered, only this feud was conducted with assault rifles and semiautomatic handguns.

The media was all over the story, engaging in a little East Coast–West Coast rivalry of its own. The Los Angeles Times had flown in a team of reporters and photographers to Manhattan, as had several West Coast television news stations; the New York papers and stations had, of course, escalated to match. Nor was the story confined to the two cities. Karp had gone apoplectic when the National Enquirer *came out midweek with crime-scene* photographs showing the torn and twisted bodies that had been ML Rex, his manager, Kwasama Jones, and the Gallegos twins, late of Queens. The photographs—obviously sold to the tabloid by some enterprising police crime-scene technician—ran under the headline Bloody Rap War Erupts in the Big Apple. The accompanying story quoted a half-dozen anonymous sources who as much as said that the murders were committed by East Coast thugs and that more bloodshed was likely. There was even a line from an unidentified source that contended "the NYPD and DA's office are dragging their feet because ML was from Los Angeles, man."

One of the mysteries had been cleared up after a few days when the detectives finally tracked down the limousine driver, who'd been lying low in his apartment in the Bronx. Apparently he'd seen the killers approach and took off running, then was too frightened of retaliation to come forward.

As if Fulton knew what he was thinking, the detective said, "The chauffeur identified the suspect in a lineup. We're good to go."

Karp hoped that the arrest would at least stop the rumors. But it didn't explain why Fulton had driven over to tell him about it. Normally he would have called, or even left it for the morning at the office. There had to be something particularly alarming or sensitive about the latest development. "So who'd they collar?"

"Well, not surprisingly, the deceased seemed to make enemies wherever he went," Fulton replied. "But the best lead was that he had been involved in an altercation at a club on West Thirty-eighth Street the night before his *murder with a local rapper named Alejandro Garcia. Apparently the two exchanged death threats, and this Garcia is recently out of juvie for shooting some other Harlem gangster. The detectives who picked him up told me that he had a rep even before that shooting as a real hard case."*

Karp frowned. Alejandro Garcia—he thought he'd heard the name before, but couldn't place it. "Anything else?"

Fulton shrugged.

Good, Karp thought, maybe the press will move on to the next bit of bloody mayhem or sex scandal . . . hopefully, in someone else's town. But then he recalled an axiom he'd learned from Francis P. Garrahy, the legendary former district attorney of Manhattan. "It's the supposedly easy cases that get messed up," the old man had told him once when Karp was still a wet-behind-the-ears assistant DA. "It looks like a slam dunk, so everybody relaxes, gets sloppy—the cops, the prosecutors—then before you know it, the bad guy walks."

"Garcia lawyered up?" Karp asked Fulton. If the suspect invoked his right to remain silent or asked to see a defense attorney, it wasn't likely he was going to answer any questions.

"Nope," Fulton said. "But he hasn't said much, other than he had nothing to do with it like they always do. I thought you might want to try to talk to him."

"Okay, give me a minute to get the boys settled and let's go down to the Tombs and see if he'll chat," Karp said. He turned for the door but stopped when Fulton mumbled something about there·being "something else."

"Yeah? What is it?" It wasn't like the detective to beat around the bush.

"It seems that the twins, Zak and Giancarlo, were also present during the altercation at the club. In fact, they may have been in the middle of it."

For a moment, the city seemed to hold its breath. The traffic, the subways, the voices all stopped to listen as Karp swore.

1

Eleven days earlier . . .

THE AIR IN THE NIGHTCLUB PULSED TO THE REPET-
itive throbbing of a bass guitar as two spotlights swept
above the bobbing heads of the audience. With the recent
ban on cigarettes in Manhattan restaurants and bars, the
wraiths of smoke that danced to the beat in the glare of
the lights emanated from quick secret tokes on marijuana
pipes, giving the big room a smokey-sweet smell and a
decidedly outlaw ambiance.

The beams of light met at center stage and focused on
a pair of young men who had stepped from behind a curtain. The men—one black and one Hispanic—sauntered
to the center of the stage where they were handed micro-
phones by the master of ceremonies like eighteenth-
century duelists accepting pistols. But instead of "ten
paces turn and fire," they stood two feet apart, glaring at
each other and seemingly oblivious to the throbbing
music and the pumped-up crowd.

Six inches taller than his counterpart, black rap musician ML Rex was thin as a slab of bacon and wore a loose

muscle shirt to show off a bevy of thick gold chains and tattoos on his mocha-brown skin meant to impress "the bitches and the busters." His left shoulder bore a tattoo of the ornately drawn numerals 10-78, the police radio ten-code for "officer needs assistance." The inference was that he was a cop killer, though he'd never actually had the balls to shoot at someone who was ready to shoot back. Drive-bys and firing indiscriminately into crowds had been more his style back in his gangbanging days in the Watts neighborhood of Los Angeles. But the 10-78 tat went with the gangsta rap image he cultivated, as did the drawing on his right shoulder of a large-breasted and nude woman posing with a semiautomatic handgun above the inscription Guns & Hos.

The son of a hardworking grocer and a domestic servant, ML Rex had been given the name Martin Luther King Johnson. His parents had greatly admired the fallen civil rights leader, but that was all ancient history to "Marty," as only his mother still called him. His heroes were superstar athletes, rappers, and, especially when he was young, the OGs—old-time gangsters in the 'hood—because they had the money.

He'd insisted in junior high that he be called Mustafa Khalid Mohammed after a sudden growth spurt to six foot two had him fantasizing about a lucrative future career in the NBA, and he decided that an Islamic name sounded more sensational. However, his talent with a basketball did not grow with his body, and he'd had to look else-where for the attention he craved.

With both parents working long hours and little else to do away from the gym, he'd gravitated to the Bloods street gang that infested his neighborhood like the red-brown cockroaches that took over the house he grew up in every night when the lights went out. The gangs made life difficult, even dangerous, for any young person who might have had a mind of his own and dreams that included college or actually working for a living. But Mustafa was lazy and so he fit right in—selling crack cocaine and taking the occasional potshot at members of the rival Crips gang.

He might have ended up like so many of his friends—in prison or in a cemetery—but he'd discovered a talent for the violent, misogynist rhyming to music known as gangsta rap. Combined with a certain knack for getting his foot in the door and ingratiating himself with people who mattered, he'd found his ticket out of the poverty of his youth and away from the 'hood where a boy could get shot for the color of his clothes. He took the stage name ML Rex. Someone had once told him that *rex* meant king in some fucked-up European language—so he thought Martin Luther King, ML Rex, was pretty clever. Now, except for the occasional pilgrimage back to Crenshaw Avenue and 103rd Street to show that he was still a Blood at heart, he lived in a nice upscale apartment in Brentwood. Not quite Beverly Hills, he conceded to his envious friends, "but the same 'hood where O.J. kilt that white bitch, homes."

Despite the look of impending violence on his face as he stared down at the teenager in front of him at the nightclub, Martin aka Mustafa aka ML Rex was in a great mood. Some of that had to do with the two fat lines of cocaine he'd snorted immediately before leaving the dressing room backstage, the daylong use of which caused him to grind his teeth until his jaw ached. But his ebullience had even more to do with a business meeting he'd demanded that morning with his record label's executives.

His first CD, *Some Desperate S**t Fer Ya*, had been recorded in Los Angeles but produced by Pentagram

Records, the main offices of which were in the Penn Plaza building off Thirty-fourth Street and Eighth Avenue. A single from the CD *My Baby a Crack Ho'* had reached number six on the hip-hop charts for two weeks, and the CD had gone gold, but then it tumbled back off as quickly as it had climbed aboard. He was wealthier than he'd ever imagined growing up on the streets, but he was very disappointed not to have reached the elite status of rappers like Eminem and Snoop Dogg. The way he saw it, Pentagram's failure to pour more money into promotion had cost him a platinum record and his rightful place among the hip-hop hierarchy.

So he'd come up with the idea of forming his own record company. He was calling it, logically enough, Rex Rhymes. His business manager, childhood friend, and fellow Blood, Kwasama "Zig-Zag" Jones, had protested the move. He was worried that his own ride out of the ghetto was about to hit a brick wall, but his pleas fell on deaf ears. He wasn't much mollified when ML Rex explained that this way they'd cut out the middleman, pocket all the cash, and "we'll control our own des-tin-nees, dog."

ML Rex expected that Pentagram executives—a "bunch of white faggots in suits"—wouldn't be too happy with his declaration of independence. So he was surprised when he and Jones met with them that morning and the company president listened quietly and then merely asked if he was sure he had "thought this through carefully."

"Fuck, yeah," ML Rex said, adjusting his sunglasses with what he hoped looked like nonchalance and slouching even farther in his seat to demonstrate that his position on the matter was firm.

"Word," Jones added, adjusting his shades and slouching, too, in a show of solidarity.

"Well, all right, then," the executive said with a sigh and a shrug. "I'm sure we'll find some amicable way to resolve the fact that you're still under contract to Pentagram."

ML Rex scowled at this and prepared to tell whitey where he could shove the contract. But the man stood, held out his hand, and insisted that ML Rex continue to avail himself of Vincent, the bodyguard/chauffeur the company had sent to meet him at La Guardia. "We want your trip to New York to continue to be a safe one," the man said with a smile. "You never know . . . we might work together again sometime."

The executive's friendly response had at first unsettled the rapper, not to mention hurt his ego—he'd expected them to make a bigger fuss over losing a rising star of his caliber. "Fuck those muthafuckas," he'd told Jones as they left the building. "Fuckin' wit my head, thas what they tryin' to do."

"Word," Jones agreed.

Several hours and two grams of cocaine later, ML Rex was feeling better about how he'd "stood up to the man." Still, he was happy to retain the services of Vincent, "jus' call me Vinnie," a huge white man he assumed was some sort of mobbed-up Italian. Vinnie was nearly as wide as he was tall, and with a round, pink face so fat that his beady brown eyes nearly disappeared into the slits above his cheeks. The rapper assumed that the lump beneath the chauffeur's left armpit was a gun, which made him feel better as he'd been forced by airline regulations, and a previous felony conviction for distribution of a controlled substance, to leave his own heat at home.

Despite the brave show, ML Rex was a little nervous

about being in New York. He'd made his reputation by adding verbal fuel to the fire that perpetuated the West Coast versus East Coast rap wars that the general public had first been made aware of in 1996 with the murder of Tupac Shakur in Las Vegas, and then the shooting of Notorious BIG a year later in Los Angeles. Various truces had been arranged, but every so often someone would say something in a rap, someone else would take offense, and the bullets would fly. His own lyrics referred to the East Coast artists and males in general in numerous derogatory ways ranging from faggots to bitches to busters, and boasted about what he'd do to them if their paths ever crossed. Of course, that was safer to say when living large in LA on his own turf.

Still, he felt safe enough in the Hip-Hop Nightclub when Vinnie said he needed to stay with the limousine. "Bad neighborhood," he'd grunted. ML Rex figured he had Zig-Zag to watch his back, and it wasn't a bad idea to have his ride ready for a quick getaway should the crowd prove hostile. He looked over at his compatriot, who was standing offstage with his arms around the two hookers they'd procured for the night by calling an "escorts" ad in the back of the *Village Voice*. The girls were a couple of Puerto Rican sisters who, high on crack and sure of a big payday, gyrated their hips and shook their breasts to the beat as if they'd never been happier in their lives, which might have been true.

Yes, he thought as he glared down at his competition, life is good. In the morning he would consummate his business dealings in New York City by working out a deal with a national distributor to get his independent-label CD in stores for a percentage of the sales. Then in the afternoon, he would make the rounds of the big New York radio stations and sweet-talk the DJs (aided by gifts of cash and coke) into giving his forthcoming single plenty of airtime. He'd realized that to really make it big, he was going to have to move away from his West Coast–centric roots and go for a national audience. That was the reason he was going through with the appearance at the night-club arranged by Pentagram and had agreed to a round of "battle rhyming" against one of the local rappers.

Battle rhyming—essentially two opponents competing with lyrics to win over a live audience—was the roots of rap. It was part asphalt poetry—reflective of life in a ghetto—and part clever, and generally good-natured, put-downs. A way of establishing sidewalk supremacy without anything worse than someone's ego getting hurt. But what had begun as social commentary and competition branched into gangsta rap—the anthems of the violent, cocaine-financed organized crime cartels that supplanted the old neighbor-hood gangs—until much of the music was little more than death threats and boasts of cuckolding each other's bitches. This was the rap that shocked mainstream white America into assuming that all rappers were angry young black men with guns, and attracted white teenagers who, bored with their safe, middle-class suburban lives, wished they were black gangsters, too.

As a whole, the rap genre had lost much of its street sen-sibilities when record companies finally recognized that poor urban teenagers who couldn't afford to buy new laces for their Lugz would spend every last penny on the latest Wu Tang Clan CD. Slickly produced, with lots of bells and whistles, the commercialized rap had drummed the on-the-fly improvisation right out of the genre. Despite the success of Eminem's film 8 *Mile*, the story of a battle-rhyming, odds-beating white rapper, it was hard to even find the art form away from the amateurs on the sidewalks where it all began.

The Hip-Hop Nightclub, a formerly abandoned warehouse on West Thirty-eighth Street near the Hudson River, was one of the few venues left in the city. It had been open for two years, mostly struggling by in a neighborhood of boarded-up, graffiti-marred buildings. But slowly the club developed a loyal following of rap purists, and a reputation as the place for local would-be rap stars to catch the ears of record label scouts searching for new talent. Over the course of its existence, several rappers who'd appeared in the Friday night battles had been signed to recording contracts.

ML Rex couldn't have cared less about the history of his art. He was in it for the money and the prestige. Like most rappers, he got his start on the sidewalks and in gang hangouts, rhyming with his fellow Bloods while guzzling "40's" of Schlitz Malt Liquor. But for a star such as himself, battle rhyming was generally seen as beneath his status, and he considered his appearance at the Hip-Hop Nightclub to be slumming.

In fact, he'd regretted it as soon as he'd heard himself agree to "give the folks a thrill by participating in our little show," as the owner/MC had put it. He'd have much rather just been introduced, perhaps hyped the audience with a little taste of something off the new CD, then waved goodbye and gone on a little booty call with the hookers back at his expensive suite in the Waldorf-Astoria. But there was that ego thing, emboldened by the cocaine, and he couldn't back down once he'd accepted the challenge.

Backstage in the waiting room he'd insisted on for privacy, he considered a variety of options that would allow him to leave before the show without losing face. It had been a long time since he'd participated in a battle, and he wasn't thinking as clearly as he'd have liked. He was therefore relieved when he was introduced to his opponent, a short, stocky Puerto Rican teen who looked like he'd wandered in off the street. *If this little spic's what passes for a gangsta in New York City,* he thought, *I got shit to worry 'bout. Li'l muthafucka can't even dress hisself.*

The self-assurance, however, evaporated as he stared in his opponent's eyes while the MC worked the crowd into a frenzy. He didn't know what it was, but there was something about the other young man's gaze that rattled him. The teen seemed so . . . calm, or maybe it was confidence, or both . . . like he didn't need the bluster and bluff that defined ML Rex's personality. Thrown off his game, he broke off from the staring contest and smiled at the crowd. "Sheee-it, this li'l bitch the bes' ya'll got?" he shouted into his microphone.

2

ALEJANDRO GARCIA'S FACE HARDENED FOR A moment at the insult, causing the grin to disappear from the mouth of the black rapper, who quickly glanced back over his shoulder to make sure his manager was paying attention. But then Alejandro smiled—a wide, toothy Cheshire Cat grin that looked almost luminescent in the spotlight.

Eighteen years old, he was short and barrel-chested with thick shoulders. As his opponent noted, he dressed plainly in a baggy Xavier High hooded sweatshirt and a pair of old worn jeans that hung halfway down his butt and gathered in pools at his feet. His neck was circled by a thin gold chain upon which dangled a simple crucifix, and a gold hoop hung from his left earlobe.

Somewhere in the distant Caribbean past, Indian blood had mixed with Spanish and produced his handsome, bronzed, and angular face. Left alone, his hair would have been thick and black as coal, but he kept it shorn to a stubble that emphasized his soft, doelike brown eyes. Eyes that were shining with excitement onstage because this night was his big opportunity.

Pentagram Records had sent over one of its stars, asking to battle with him, and was said to have a scout in the audience. Not bad for an orphan who'd been born and raised in Spanish Harlem, most of it living with his maternal grandmother in a jaundice-colored brick warehouse, the James Madison tenements on 106th Street and Third Avenue.

As a child, he'd loved the neighborhood just a few blocks east of the northwest corner of Central Park. On warm summer nights, he'd wandered the sidewalks with his crew of boys, skipping to the beat of the blaring salsa music that serenaded each block from the open doors of cars parked in front of the buildings, as the tenants gathered to drink beer and discuss love, life, and the New York Yankees in rapid-fire Spanish.

Long before they noticed him, he admired the beautiful Latinas, with their dark shiny hair, flouncing along the sidewalks in their bright dresses, flashing smiles as they pretended not to hear the whistles and entreaties of the young men. They seemed to learn early how to move their hips in such a way as to drive all the Don Juans crazy. He also loved the smells that wafted from the tiny Puerto Rican restaurants—of carne asada with red rice and beans—and wished that he were old enough and had the money for a plate and a cerveza with lime.

It was a tough neighborhood, too, though it wasn't until he was older that he realized the rest of the world didn't live with early morning hours punctuated by gunfire, sirens, and screams for the "POLICIA! POLICIA! AYÚDEME!" echoing up and down the dark and empty streets. The police didn't like to venture into Spanish Harlem, and when they had to, they came angry, suspicious, and ready to bust heads or shoot first and ask for an interpreter later. So each generation learned to protect itself and its territory.

Drugs were rampant and the root cause of most crimes committed in Alejandro's neighborhood. The heroin junkies weren't so bad—they were usually half-comatose under the influence of the drug, and when awake were mostly just petty thieves trying to steal enough for the next high. The crack cocaine trade that arrived in the late 1980s, however, had changed everything. It was controlled by the street gangs—not the old kind, like in the movie *West Side Story*, rumbling over turf, girls, and insults—but the sort whose reason to exist was the proliferation and protection of the lucrative crack cocaine trade. Crack meant money, money caused envy, and envy created a need for bigger and better guns to protect the crack and the money.

Life was hard enough on girls and boys who came from relatively normal family lives. They saw too much, heard too much, experienced too much when they should have been allowed to just be children. But Alejandro's childhood had been rough even by those standards. An incident when he was a boy—a memory he'd buried as deep as a well—followed by his father walking out on the family, and then his mother succumbing to a heroin overdose a year later, had left scars that he still felt but had covered beneath a tough exterior.

He was fortunate to have his grandmother, Eliza Contreras, a tiny woman who had first come to the United States from Puerto Rico as a child to work in a sweatshop in the Garment District. She had married at fourteen to a twenty-one-year-old man who'd seen her on the bus and followed her home to ask her father for her hand. She had her first child, a boy, at age fifteen, but the infant died from measles within a year. A daughter, Alejandro's mother, had been born shortly afterward.

Eliza had grown to love her husband, who took his

responsibilities to his young family seriously and worked two jobs toward their dream of someday moving to one of the suburbs where they might own a home with trees in the yard. She had hoped for many more children, but her husband was shot and killed by a robber as he made his way home one night from his second job. Their dreams had bled into the cracked sidewalk where his assailant left him, and she never remarried.

Instead, she had hoped for many grandchildren when her daughter, Maria, married Alphonso Garcia, and Alejandro was born six months later. But Alphonso was no good, and her daughter was a slave to the heroin that eventually killed her. Alejandro was all she had left, and she'd done her best to raise him to be a good citizen. But he'd still gravitated to a gang—the 106th Street Inca Boyz—which provided the male role models, protection, and sense of extended family that he wanted.

By age fourteen, he'd earned the street name Boom for his willingness to use a gun to protect himself, his home-boys, and his neighborhood from all encroachment. Unfortunately, the attitude got him into trouble at age six-teen when a trio of older black boys from a rival gang made the mistake of leaving Harlem to the north looking for trouble. They found it in the alley next to the tene-ment where Alejandro lived. Believing that they had located easy targets to bully, the older gangbangers sug-gested that Alejandro and his childhood friend, Jose "Pancho" Ramirez, perform certain sexual favors or "git your punk asses kicked."

"Chinga tu madre," Alejandro responded, tilting his head back to look out from beneath the wide bandana covering his forehead to just above his eyes, Chicano-style. He then translated loosely. "Go fuck your mother."

One of the older boys reacted to the insult by reaching up under his New York Knicks sweatshirt as if he had a gun. The boy probably only meant to intimidate the younger teens, but he'd chosen the wrong pair to bluff.

Without hesitation, Alejandro stooped next to the Dumpster at the mouth of the alley. When he stood up, he was pointing the .45 caliber Colt Mustang he hid there every morning just in case. His antagonists took off running, with Pancho, who'd grabbed a slat from a wooden box, in hot pursuit. As one of his antagonists tried to scale the chain-link fence at the end of the alley, Alejandro let off a round. He was holding the gun sideways and not really aiming, so he was just as surprised as the other boy when the bullet hit the target in his butt, catapulting him over the fence and onto the pavement on the other side, where he lay screaming.

Alejandro tossed the gun into the Dumpster. Then he and Pancho ran inside the building to tell his grandmother what had transpired.

The wounded gangbanger managed to get himself to Harlem Hospital, where he promptly described his assailant to the police. "A short Puerto Rican mutha-fucka." Based on the location and his reputation, the cops went looking for Alejandro. But accompanied by his grandmother, he had already turned himself in. "I put a cap in some buster's ass," he confessed, and told the detective at the precinct house where to find the gun.

Even though he had admitted to the shooting, Alejandro still complained to his Eliza about the other boy breaking the code of the streets by reporting him to the Five-Oh, gang slang for the police, whose genesis was the old television police drama *Hawaii 5-0*. "What did you expect, *hijo?*" his grandmother replied. "The code of the streets is a lie. There's no honor among criminals, and, Alejandro, you are a criminal."

Eliza sighed as she wiped at the tears that filled the wrinkles around her eyes and from there spilled down her brown cheeks. She cursed the streets for their cruelty. She'd lost her daughter to them, but she'd had such hopes for Alejandro. Six days a week she caught the number 4 subway train down to midtown to cook and clean for a wealthy family to support herself and her grandson. He'd been such a sweet, smart little boy before he'd turned to the gang. Even then, he'd met her without fail every night at the subway station at 103rd Street to walk her safely home. But now the streets threatened to swallow his life. In despair, she'd called the man whom she trusted the most in the world, the priest who'd baptized Alejandro and the closest thing he'd had to a real father.

Michael J. Dugan of the Society of Jesus had known Alejandro off and on since he was a boy. He knew that the teen was not the semiliterate street thug he acted like around his peers, but the product of well-respected Xavier Catholic High School on West Sixteenth Street. The school was nearly a hundred blocks south of his home, which necessitated rising and leaving the tenement before the sun was up with his grandmother to catch the number 4, taking it to the Union Square Station. No matter what the weather—bitter cold, driving rain, hot and muggy—he rarely missed a day. The priest, brothers, and lay teachers who toiled at Xavier were tough but fair. They'd turned many troubled boys into fine young men, and Alejandro was another.

To Dugan, the boy's perseverance made him a cut

above his gangbanging peers, most of whom dropped out of school as soon as they could and looked no further into the future than the next day. In front of other teenagers, he spoke in the street vernacular, but when he wanted, he was articulate and well-spoken. At school, Alejandro had excelled in writing courses; the brother who taught the modern literature class (a closet fan of Allen Ginsberg's) raved about his talents as a poet.

When Eliza called, Dugan immediately caught a cab to the New York jail, a gray and dreary monolith appropriately known as the Tombs. Although he was usually more of a flannel-shirt sort of priest, he purposely wore his "official" black shirt and white collar, knowing its effect on the Irish Catholic cops and police officers in general. He was aware that they were not really supposed to let him speak with Alejandro; the law said he had a right to an attorney, not a priest. But he figured he'd get in with enough Irish blarney and benevolence—not to mention he was a familiar face at the Tombs—and he was right.

Even without his priestly garb, Dugan in his sixties was an impressive man physically. His crew-cut hair was the color of pewter but still thick as a hedge. The hair framed a thick, ruddy face that might have belonged to a hard-drinking Irish potato farmer, though in fact he was a graduate of Notre Dame University, where he'd run over opponents in a most un-Christian-like manner as a 230-pound blocking fullback for the Fightin' Irish. Famous for his temper if crossed, he was more likely to laugh; either emotion could make his blue eyes glint like icicles in the sun. Those eyes were angry when he sat down across the table from Alejandro and asked why he felt it was necessary to shoot the other boy.

"I wasn't trying to shoot him," Alejandro explained. "I was shooting at him."

"Yes, but bullets often find unintended victims, 'Jandro," Dugan replied. "The fact is, you pointed a gun at him and pulled the trigger. It would have almost been better if you were trying to shoot him; at least then you would have been thinking and not mindlessly spewing bullets around that could have just as easily struck a child or some other innocent not involved in your gang bullshit."

Alejandro shrugged. "You know as well as I do that if you don't stick up for yourself in the 'hood, everybody's going to think you're a pussy. And once they think you won't fight, they'll be all over you like pit bulls on a rat."

The priest sighed. He knew Alejandro's childhood secret and believed that it was a wonder the boy wasn't more jaded than he was. But Dugan was tired of the funerals, tired of visiting young men locked up behind walls and razor wire, tired of going to the morgue with grieving families to confirm the identity of another young victim of a drug overdose or gang shooting. "You say that if you don't shoot you'll be perceived as weak. But someday somebody's going to have to be strong enough to break the cycle of violence. Nobody ever said it was easy to do the right thing."

Alejandro scoffed. "The right thing? What's doin' the right thing ever got me? Remember when I was a kid and I tried to do the right thing? Where'd it get me?"

It was tough to argue with the boy's childhood, but Dugan did his best. "Sometimes it's not a matter of whether you gain anything from it, even if all you gain is comfort and safety. Yes, you deserved better, but sometimes you do the right thing because it's the right thing to do."

"Well, I guess I ain't that strong, Father," the boy

replied. "I ain't gonna turn my cheek so that somebody can slap the other one. I did that once before and it still hurts."

The interview ended with Dugan taking the boy's confession. "Forgive me Father for I have sinned," he mumbled. "I fornicated with Lydia Sanchez on Tuesday and again last night in her uncle's car. I called Panch a stupid, punk ass muthafucka and hurt his feelings. And I might have taken the Lord's name in vain a few times." He looked up hopefully, "And while I shot a punk, he deserved it and then he ratted on me, so maybe it makes us even?"

"No, Alejandro, it doesn't make you even in the eyes of God," Dugan growled.

"Okay, then in addition to those other sins, I shot a punk who deserved it," Alejandro grumped.

Despite his concerns for the boy, Dugan smiled. He was not going to change his gangster mentality just because he was scared and in jail. Dugan had mostly gone so he could call Eliza and say he'd seen Alejandro and that her grandson was all right—gangbangers had been known to meet with accidental bumps and bruises in the squad cars on the way to the Tombs. Maybe Alejandro, who despite his notoriety had never been arrested, would learn from this experience enough to save his life, but for now, all the priest could do was hand down spiritual penance. "Ten Hail Marys and ten Our Fathers . . . no more fornicating with Lydia Sanchez—from what I understand, she has been fornicating a lot and sooner or later is going to give you all the clap or worse. Panch *is* a stupid, punk ass muthafucka, but he is also a loyal friend and deserves better. Watch the swearing . . . and no more shooting punks, even if they deserve it."

• • •

The New York District Attorney's Office charged Alejandro with attempted murder. A court-appointed defense lawyer got the DA to go for reckless endangerment in exchange for a guilty plea and eighteen months at the Mario Cuomo Juvenile Corrections Facility in Rockland County.

Even before the boy was sent to Cuomo, Dugan had regularly visited the facility. Quite a number of sons from families he'd known when he was a parish priest in Spanish Harlem were there, and he'd made it a point to try to visit at least once a month. Many of them were uncomfortable confessing to the facility's official chaplain, figuring he probably went back to the warden and told on them, so Dugan's visits often lasted well into the evening. It was surprising how many sins they could commit even while locked up.

It was a long drive—two hours up and two back—in the old black Buick sedan he drove, but after Alejandro was sentenced, Dugan tried to double his visits, unwilling to lose another of the ghetto's best and brightest to the New York Department of Corrections. To keep Alejandro connected with his home, the priest sometimes brought special visitors—Eliza or some friend who the priest thought might be a good influence on his young friend.

One of these was one of Alejandro's oldest pals, Francisco J. Apodaca Jr. Francisco wasn't in a gang, but he'd never broken his ties to Alejandro and Pancho. He was bookish but too poor to attend a private Catholic school, so instead had to do the best he could at the run-down, quasi–war zone that passed for a public education in the neighborhood. Every day he had to pass a gauntlet of drug dealers and thugs—and that was just in the hallways. However, he did not let them quash his dreams.

Ever since he was a boy, he had insisted that he was going to college to become a doctor. So he'd put up with a lot of teasing, and sometimes bullying, from classmates. They resented that he sat in the front of the classroom, raised his hand to ask and answer questions, and committed the unpardonable sin of taking his books home to study. His life would have been harder except that the bullies knew that if they pushed too hard, they would have to answer to Boom Garcia and Pancho Ramirez.

During one visit to Cuomo a half year into Alejandro's sentence, he and Francisco were sitting on a bench talking when the latter asked something that had been on his mind as he watched teenage boys shuffle past in handcuffs and ankle shackles. "What are you going to do when you get out?"

Alejandro shrugged. "Don't know, 'Cisco. Maybe get a place of my own, then the same old same old."

"Same old same old," Francisco repeated. "You mean dealing crack and gangbanging?"

Alejandro smiled. "Whatever it takes, dog."

"But you know you'll just end up back here . . . or worse, some hellhole like Attica."

Again, Alejandro shrugged. "Nothin' much I can do 'bout it. I am what I am. Like the counselors say, 'a product of my environment.' The system is stacked against me, so I ain't gonna make it, unless I take it."

For one of the few times in his life, Alejandro saw the mild-mannered Francisco angry. His friend stood up and pointed a finger in his astonished face. "What the fuck is that, 'Jandro?" he shouted, amazing his friend as much by his unaccustomed use of the F-word as the vehemence with which it was hurled. "I'm a product of the same environment. But I don't sell drugs. I don't shoot people. I'm not in prison. Only poor fuckin' Alejandro, who the system has it in for."

Francisco reached out and grabbed Alejandro's face with a grip that was surprisingly strong for such a thin boy. "Look at me, 'Jandro. Look at me, *mi amigo*," he shouted. "Every time the bleeding hearts give someone like you an excuse to fuck up because 'he's just a product of his environment,' it's a slap in the face to those of us who actually work to make something of our lives. It lets the bigots think I'm a freak, an exception to the rule that all Puerto Ricans are lazy, no-good criminals. . . . You're as smart as I am, 'Jandro, maybe smarter. You could be someone in this world, but instead you're too busy blaming 'the system,' whatever that is, for fucking up. It's just an excuse, *hermano*, a bad one."

Francisco let go of his grip and, much truer to form, burst into tears. Alejandro's cheeks hurt but that wasn't the reason he rubbed his jaw. The truth was worse. He stood and hugged his friend. "I'm sorry, 'Cisco," he said. "I'm just talkin' big 'cause I'm scared. I'm just afraid that there's nothin' out there for me. I don't have dreams like you. All I see is bangin' or some menial job that will suck the life out of me until I'm just another washed-up nobody drinking beer out of his car on 106th."

"Find one, 'Jandro," Francisco said as they stood back from one another. "Find a place in the world and a dream to hold on to. You're a writer, a poet, so write . . . maybe you'll write the great Puerto Rican–American novel."

Alejandro smiled at the suggestion. "Yeah, maybe I will . . . Ernesto Hemingway," he said, and they both laughed. But the seed planted by Francisco took hold and sprouted, though not in a way either had imagined at that moment.

• • •

Almost a year after Alejandro's arrival at Cuomo, Dugan saw him one day sitting beneath a tree and writing in a notebook. The teenager tried to hide the material from him, but the priest insisted on taking a look. The notebook was nearly filled with handwritten poetry, or more aptly, rap lyrics. The work was raw and street-hard, filled with violence and despair. But it was also powerful because it was honest.

With Dugan's encouragement, Alejandro began trying out his material on his fellow inmates with Pancho providing the background percussion by sputtering an imitation of a bass guitar and slapping his thigh for drums. It wasn't long before Alejandro was attracting a crowd, winning over even some of his former enemies with words they all understood.

Alejandro's rap was the hit of the annual talent show that year. But his pride took a fall when he saw a pained look on Dugan's face after the show and asked what was troubling him. The priest tried to blow it off. "It's nothing," he said, feeling suddenly that he was too hard on the boy. After all, Alejandro had made good use of his time in Cuomo, going to school and getting his GED, keeping his nose clean. Let him enjoy his moment in the sun, he thought.

But Alejandro kept insisting that he say what was bothering him. Finally, the older man allowed that he was disappointed that Alejandro's message was not growing beyond the violent, demeaning language common to gangsta rap.

Hurt by the criticism, the teenager got defensive. "This is the poetry of the streets, Father. Ain't no bullshit sweetness and light on 106th and Third. Besides . . . ," he said, shrugging, "they're just words."

"Nigger isn't just a word, Alejandro," Dugan said softly. "It isn't all right just because a bunch of lowlifes, who have no perspective on the legacy of pain associated with that word, use it on each other. How can you expect whites to stop referring to black men and women that way if those men and women call each other 'niggah.' "

Alejandro tried to object, but the priest wasn't finished. *"Bitch. Ho.* They're not just words. They're demeaning to someone's mother, sister, girlfriend. Glorifying guns and drugs aren't just words. They're a perspective on how you see the world and they're poison to young minds."

"But nobody takes that shit seriously," Alejandro argued. "What do you want me to write about . . . some fuckin' crap like 'A Rose in Spanish Harlem'? There weren't any roses in my neighborhood, Father, just weeds."

The priest was having none of it. "Maybe your older listeners will know that," he said. "But little kids are listening to that gangsta shit over and over in their heads until they know it better than the Lord's Prayer. They start to think that it's okay to think of women as bitches and whores and that shooting people is a game. They hear you, or some other gangbanger they respect, rapping and think it's how you live your life, and they want to be like you."

Dugan sighed. *How do you get through to them?* "It's about taking responsibility for what you say, as well as your actions, and the effect it has on those who look up to you, Alejandro. They're not just words."

On that day, Alejandro stomped off. But Dugan noticed the next time he heard the boy performing, the N-word was missing from his vocabulary, as were derogatory references to women. And when he spoke about guns and drugs, it was with sadness for lives lost and families shattered. As disappointed as the priest had been before, he let him know how proud he was of him now.

"Thanks, Father," Alejandro said as they shook hands. "I think I've found what I want to do. Maybe things are looking up for me."

Dugan gave him a hug. "Maybe they are, son," he said, though he wondered what other obstacles might be laid in the boy's path to a brighter future. He didn't have long to wait.

A month before Alejandro's release, he saw Dugan walking across the grounds toward him. He was happy to see the priest and wanted to talk to him about getting a job and someplace to live when he got out. He also wanted to run some ideas past him about breaking into the music business, but his smile disappeared when he noticed the sadness in his friend's eyes.

Dugan led him to a bench where they sat down next to each other. "Son, I have some bad news for you," he said softly, placing a hand on the boy's shoulder. "Eliza . . . your grandmother . . . is dead."

For a moment, Alejandro just looked at him, blinking his eyes rapidly. Then a sob escaped from his lips, which released a torrent of tears. When at last he calmed down a bit, he asked the question that the priest had hoped to avoid. "How?" the teen asked, swiping at his tears with his shirtsleeve. "How'd it happen? Was it her heart? Did she forget to take her heart medication?"

Dugan shook his head. He wished it were that simple. "She was walking home from the subway after work," he began but had to stop to clear his throat. "It was supposed to be a simple purse-snatching, but you know your grandmother, she held on and wouldn't let go until the guy hit her and knocked her down. She struck her head on the sidewalk . . . ," he paused again, ". . . she never regained consciousness." As he spoke the last part, the priest had looked down at his own clasped hands and said a silent prayer, but he looked up in time to see the grief on Alejandro's face turn to anger.

Alejandro's dark eyes had turned darker still until there seemed to be no color, only blackness. "Who did it, Father? Who killed her?"

Dugan looked at Alejandro for a long moment, then shook his head. His eyes were still sad, but his voice was tinged with anger when he answered. "Why, Alejandro?" he asked. "So that when you get out of here, you and your gang can go kill him? Take another life and ruin your own?"

"Don't give me that shit, Father, the muthafucka killed a sweet old woman who never hurt nobody," he fumed. "The asshole needs to pay for that."

"And when his people come gunning for you? Where does it stop, Alejandro," Dugan countered. "When you're all dead or in Attica? Let the system deal with finding and punishing him."

Alejandro snorted and barked a short, bitter laugh. "The system? Who? The police? The DA? Where the fuck were they when she was trying to get home? Eating doughnuts? Sipping a martini with some other lawyers? She deserved their protection. But has anybody been arrested? No? I didn't think so. They could give a shit about what happens uptown, unless there's an election, or some white dude from midtown cruisin' the ghetto for crack or whores gets his ass shot. Then they're all over it."

Dugan conceded that the justice system had failed

Alejandro's community more often than it had succeeded. "But it is still our best hope," he said. "Without it, there is only anarchy and chaos. It's up to us to make the system accountable." The priest passed a hand over his brow. I'm so damned tired. He patted the boy on the knee. "God loves you, Alejandro. Your grandmother loves you. I love you. We want you to live and make something of yourself."

The boy drew his knees up and buried his face. "I shoulda been there," he cried quietly. "I was the only family she had, but she had to die alone and scared 'cause I was here."

It hurt Dugan's heart to hear the depth of the grief in Alejandro's voice. The priest wanted to take the grieving boy in his arms, tell him it was all right, that it wasn't his fault. But he knew that there were times for hard lessons that meant something and this was one of them. So he hardened his heart and his voice. "Yes, Alejandro, you should have been there," he said. "Life is all about choices. Some good. Some bad. You made a bad one, and so you weren't there when your grandma needed you."

Dugan let the words sink in. "But you have another choice now," he said at last, more gently. "In a month, you walk back out that gate a free man. You can return to the streets, back to the gangbanging, in which case I'll be visiting you someday in a real prison or at your grave.

"Or you can honor your grandmother and become the man she hoped you would be. You can take your gift and make a difference; you can be a poet and tell the people the truth so that they learn and maybe, just maybe, something will change for the better. Your choice, Alejandro. Good or bad, but it's your choice."

● ● ●

The day came for Alejandro's release, and the priest was waiting for him in the parking lot in his car. "Figured you might need a ride," he said. "It's a long trip on a bus."

Alejandro smiled and got in the car but was quiet for most of the ride back to Manhattan. Once back to the island, the boy spoke without looking at his friend and mentor. "I've been thinking 'bout what you said, you know, choices, and what my grandma would have wanted," he said. "Some things I can't change. I am still Boom, and I am still a Blood. I won't turn my back on the only family who ever cared about me 'cept my grandma. I don't trust your justice system—it wasn't there for me when I needed it, and it hasn't done nothing for my grandmother.

"But I'm done bangin' . . . no more guns, no more crimes." He turned to Dugan and gave him the smile that had charmed the counselor the first time he saw it on the face of a spiritually wounded eight-year-old boy. "Besides, I ain't got time for none of that shit anymore. I'm gonna be a rap star."

It was Dugan's turn to smile, but at the same moment he feared for the boy. Dropping out of the gang life wasn't like quitting a job. Alejandro would be a target for any gangbanger and wannabe who wanted to make a name for himself by gunning down the notorious Boom Garcia. He'd always have to watch his back—never knowing at a park, or a movie theater, or just walking down the sidewalk when the bullet might come. But Alejandro knew it better than he, so now was not the time to bring it up. "You going to get me a backstage pass when you play the Garden?" he asked.

"As many as you want," Alejandro said, and together they laughed. They'd driven the rest of the way to the rectory at Old St. Patrick's Church on Mulberry Street, where

Dugan lived and had arranged for his young friend to stay until he could get on his feet. The priest had also found him a job with a janitorial service company that, ironically, cleaned the New York Criminal Court Building at 100 Centre Street. Turning off the car, Dugan started to open his door, but Alejandro hesitated. "Father, I'm afraid. I ain't got nobody left."

Dugan swallowed hard. "I'm afraid, too," he said. "You've just got to take it one day at a time. We all do. And you got me, and folks you haven't even met yet."

Alejandro nodded and reached for the door handle. "Father," he said, "whatever happens, you know I love you, man."

Dugan tried to speak, couldn't, then tried again. "Yeah," he said, his voice grown husky. "I love you, too." He gave Alejandro a light punch on the shoulder, "Now, let's get out of here before we start crying like a couple of busters."

3

THAT WAS EIGHT MONTHS EARLIER, AND ALEJANDRO hoped that the big break he'd been wishing for was now on the stage in front of him in the form of ML Rex. He'd kept his nose clean, worked his job at the court-house—which started at 4:00 AM, two hours before even the early birds arrived—then went home in the afternoon to sleep a few hours before rising after sun-down to work on his lyrics. He'd established himself as one of the most promising young rappers in Manhattan, and the feeling at the Hip-Hop Nightclub was that fame and fortune were just around the corner.

Alejandro knew ML Rex's work. But while he could identify with the streets that created the anger and hatred, he looked at the gangsta rap scene like an old man looks back on the indiscretions of his youth—with a shake of the head and regrets for wasted time. He bore the other artist in front of him none of the animosity that had been displayed toward him at their meeting back-stage. But he also knew that the stare-down and postur-ing was part of the entertainment. After the "li'l bitch" comment, he'd jumped into the theatrics of the moment, and he and ML Rex were soon bristling at each other like a couple of junkyard dogs circling a bone—legs stiff, the hair on the back of their necks raised, teeth bared.

Playing it up, the MC stepped between them like a boxing referee breaking up a pair of prizefighters. Just in case, he took a quick look to make sure the massive bouncers the club employed—twin man-mountains named Joe and Jim—were ready to keep the peace. "Heh, heh, homes," he addressed the two rappers for the crowd's elucidation, "save it for the battle, save it for the battle." Once he had them separated, he turned back to the audience and shouted in the microphone. "Heh, heh, New York Citaaaay! Brothas and sistahs, have we got a special treat for y'all tonight!"

He waited for the cheers to subside, then continued with the boxing metaphor, "Presenting in one corner, Pentagram recording arteeest and Los Angeles homeboy, ML Rex!" A chorus of boos rang out at the mention of the West Coast metropolis, but they were drowned out by the applause from those in the crowd who were impressed that someone famous was on the stage in front of them. Best of all, they had not had to pay one extra cent for the show.

ML Rex ignored the reference to his former employer. They'll learn soon enough, he thought, when I make the announcement. Instead, he imitated a fighter, dancing and shadowboxing at Alejandro.

The loudest cheers erupted when the MC turned to the hometown hero. "And in this corner, a special welcome to NYC homeboy, Alejandro BOOOOOOOM! Garcia!"

The object of his introduction cracked a smile that threatened to split his face in two. Alejandro used the moment to steal a look behind him to the wings where two younger boys stood grinning back at him. They looked as out of place as a cat at a dog fight. For one thing, they were white, and there weren't many Caucasian faces in the crowd; and second, they were only eleven years old and weren't supposed to be in the nightclub at all.

In fact, if the MC had known their identities he might have gone into cardiac arrest, as Giancarlo and Isaac "Zak" Karp were the sons of the New York district attorney. However, the MC had nothing to fear as far as the boys saying anything. They were supposed to be at a friend's house studying for their bar mitzvahs.

Zak was the stockier of the two and dressed in the latest hip-hop fashion—swimming in a hooded sweatshirt three sizes too big with the waistband of his pants perched precariously on his butt. A New York Yankees ballcap was planted backward on his head and his feet sported a pair of Lugz ("For Thugs") boots—untied, of course. He was reveling in the tension of the moment, though he kept his face in a scowl that he thought made him appear older and tougher. Surrounded by so many rough-looking characters, he was glad of the comforting weight of the switchblade he kept strapped to his ankle and covered by his sock. If his father had known he was carrying again, Zak would have received the mother of all lectures about being "in felonious possession of a weapon" and probably been strip-searched before leaving the apartment for the rest of his natural life. But he felt an overriding obligation to be armed as the self-appointed bodyguard for his more delicate brother, Giancarlo.

Zak was a handsome boy, but Giancarlo was beautiful.

Drop-dead gorgeous women would stop on the sidewalks when he approached and gaze with envy at the porcelain skin, the rose-colored cupid lips, and curly black hair. But unlike his trendy brother, Giancarlo dressed like an old man from Little Italy in a button-down shirt and high-water slacks that showed several inches of white sock above his loafers. The dark glasses he wore were not for show either; he was blind—the result of a shotgun pellet from a would-be assassin's gun.

The attempted murder and subsequent blindness accounted for his brother's fierce protectiveness. But Giancarlo was oblivious to any perceived danger and turned his face this way and that like a radar antenna, beaming goodwill to all. In his hands, he clutched a bag carrying several harmonicas, which is how he and his brother came to be in the club in the first place.

A talented musician who played the harmonicas, as well as a button accordion, and was picking up guitar at dizzying speed for his age, Giancarlo was much sought after by older musicians in the Village, who considered him something of a child genius. He enjoyed all styles of music, but he'd wanted to expand his horizons by playing background harmonica with "turntable music" and rappers. One of the first to try out the hybrid sound was Alejandro Garcia, who had been introduced to the brothers through their mutual friend, Father Dugan.

The priest had explained that they were the sons of the woman who had placed him in charge of a multimillion dollar foundation to help the poor. Alejandro didn't know the full story, but apparently the woman, Marlene Ciampi, had made a fortune in the stock market and had essentially given a large portion of it to the priest to give to the poor. One of the many things Dugan had done with the money was pay for Alejandro's time at Xavier.

Alejandro had surprised himself by taking to the boys like an older brother. He figured it had something to do with having always wanted siblings. As a musician, he appreciated Giancarlo's talent. But he was also fond of Zak, who reminded him—rather disturbingly—of himself . . . a good heart but a dual nature that harbored the potential for violence and making wrong choices.

As for the rest of the decidedly strange family, he'd avoided meeting the father. He never said why to the boys—after all, the man was their dad—but as far as he was concerned, the New York District Attorney's Office was just another cog in a corrupt system. However, he'd met and liked the mother and the boys' older sister, Lucy.

The sister was an odd one, some sort of world-famous expert on languages even though she was only a few years older than Alejandro. The first time he saw her, he thought she was homely—a large nose set on too thin a face, made all the more severe in that she kept her dark hair cut short like a man's. In fact, he'd wondered if she was maybe a dyke, until he saw her once with her boyfriend, who seemed to think she was a cross between J. Lo and Britney Spears. The boyfriend's dedication made him take another good look at her, especially the curiously almond-shaped brown eyes that were so shot with flecks of gold as to be almost amber. He, of course, had heard of the term *inner beauty*, but seeing Lucy in a new light was the first time he understood what it meant.

She also possessed an unexpectedly wry and somewhat risqué wit. He even found himself flirting with her in Spanish, which she accepted good-naturedly and spoke better than he did. But it was with the understanding that the flirting was the end of the line, and it wasn't just because she was with someone else.

Lucy reminded him of some of the nuns he'd met at Catholic school—the nice ones who seemed at peace with themselves and with God. She was deeply religious, but he also sensed a wound that she bore with martyrlike stoicism. She'd built a wall around the pain so that only she would know it existed, but he could see it in her eyes, way down deep, like his secret. The boys hadn't told him what caused her such pain, other than to say "it was real bad."

The boys' mother, Marlene, was something else entirely. He thought she was pretty hot-looking for an "old lady," which to him was any woman in that forty-something category to which she belonged. Even the fact that she had a glass eye, or sometimes wore a patch, and had some small scars on her face, didn't detract from her overall classic Italian looks. But she was beautiful like a falcon was beautiful. There was a wariness about her, as the one good eye seemed to take in everything around her as though constantly assessing the potential for danger.

Watching her, Alejandro knew where Zak got his dual nature. She reminded him of some of the hard-core gangsters he'd known, which was surprising, because outwardly she was funny and charming. Still, he got the impression that the friendliness—while it may have once been a more dominant aspect of her personality—was now mostly a cover for her own dark secrets. He even suspected that it had to do with the attempt on Giancarlo's life. Once, he'd asked what had happened to the would-be assassins, but the boys had looked at each other and clammed up, except to say that their mother had "taken care of it."

"All right, all right, you know the rules," the MC announced to the crowd. "Each of our artists has one minute to lay his opponent low and then you, the folks that put the hip in Hip-Hop Nightclub, will decide the winner by making NOOOOOO-ISE fer yer favorite!" He turned to ML Rex and said, "As the guest, you have the privilege of going first." Then without waiting for a reply, he shouted, "Let's give a big Big Apple shout-out for the brother from LA!"

The DJ turned up the volume for the twin turntables he used to mix and match sounds and beats to a sixteen-count rhythm. ML Rex bobbed his head to get into the groove. The cocaine was fogging his brain, and his tongue felt suddenly heavy, but he figured it wouldn't take much to win this crowd over, especially as he planned to borrow liberally from "Ya Gonna Surrenda'," one of the tracks on his first CD.

Now I'm here ta tell y'all 'bout a sistah named Boom,
And the OG's rhymes that spelled his doom and gloom.
'Cause I'm the terminator, the instigator, the fine wine
of manipulators, ain't no one can match me,
'specially this masturbator.

Alejandro was disappointed. He'd recognized the song and had hoped for better competition. He was also embarrassed that the twins were listening to the crude language. Same old shit, he thought, as his opponent rapped and danced around using the cliché gestures of grabbing his groin or pointing his fingers at Alejandro as if his hand were a gun.

One way or ta-other buster's gonna be my bitch,
Sucking my dick or facedown in a ditch . . .
Ya punk, ya sistah, I'll take you down with my nine.
Ya gonna surrenda', it's jus' a matter a time.

ML Rex finished and stepped back from Alejandro, smiling with his arms akimbo in the universal body language for "Want a piece of this?" He felt pretty good about his effort—the hookers and his homie, Jones, seemed to think so, too. So he was surprised by the rather light round of polite applause he received. His opponent simply shrugged, smiled, and launched into his own rap at a signal from the MC.

Thas what you got? Thas all you can do?
Dis women as hos, and your brothas as fools?
There's babies crying 'cause their mothers on crack
Their daddies in prison, and you can only talk smack,
    Jack?
But thas a fact, can't take it back, you're way off track.

Alejandro mounted his attack like a chess player deliberately taking apart his opponent's defenses, and the crowd picked up on what he was saying and cheered at the end of every line. In the meantime, Giancarlo had pulled one of the harmonicas out of the bag and was lightly filling in.

You coulda spoke for them, you ought to be ashamed
You ain't got nothing to say, buster's got no game.

Go make your millions, wear your chains of gold
But it ain't music you're selling, it's your soul you've
  sold.

ML Rex scowled and unconsciously stepped back. He was used to the posturing and the disparaging remarks, but he'd never really given much thought to what he was saying. If asked, he would have probably shrugged and said he didn't care either. Music was a means to an end—his ticket out—not a soapbox for social commentary. But the kid was shaming him and the crowd was behind him.

It's over, way over, but you don't even know it yet . . .
We're through with gangsta shit and misery it gets
So go home to Mickey, Donald, and Goofy
We ain't got time for cartoons, and you're just plain
  spooky.
And while you're at it take your nursery rhymes
'Cause it ain't a matter of time . . .

Alejandro paused a couple of beats as he tapped his head with two fingers and concluded, ". . . *it's a matter of mind.*"

With that Alejandro turned to the crowd with his trademark grin. There was certainly no need for a vote as the crowd erupted and starting shouting, "BOOM! BOOM! BOOM!" The MC grabbed one of Alejandro's hands and raised it to signify the victor. "Let's hear it for the homeboy," he shouted.

Still smiling broadly, Alejandro reached in front of the MC to shake ML Rex's hand, but the other rapper turned his back on him and stormed from the stage. Alejandro shrugged but happily pocketed the two-hundred-dollar prize and bounded over to where the twins waited.

"Yo, li'l homies," he said and lightly touched clenched fists with Zak and Giancarlo, who never ceased to amaze him because the boy seemed so aware of his surroundings despite his lack of sight. It had been explained to him that Giancarlo's eyes had not been damaged by the shotgun blast. It had more to do with the message from his eyes to his brain being short-circuited by the pellet lodged there—that in fact, his sight occasionally snapped back like a signal from outer space, before it was lost again. "Okay, bros, time for you to get your butts home before your old man misses you and sends my ass to Rikers for contributing to your delinquency."

Alejandro escorted the boys to the back entrance of the club so that he could walk them to the street to catch a cab home. However, that meant they had to pass by where ML Rex was accepting the commiseration of the hookers and his business manager outside the dressing room. The rap star had his back turned to them, but as Alejandro and the twins approached, the business manager tapped his client on the shoulder and nodded toward them.

ML Rex turned and smiled when he saw the trio, but his eyes were hard. "Well, well, ain't it the li'l sistah," he said then, looking down at the twins, added, "and I see you found a couple more midget bitches. They sure grow 'em short in New York Citaaay." The hookers and the business manager laughed.

Alejandro tensed. Some times were harder than others to remember he'd sworn off violence. But even as he clenched his fists, he heard Dugan's voice in his head,

"Words are never worth killing or dying over, Alejandro. Walk away." Instead, he addressed the girls in Spanish, which wiped the smiles off their faces.

"What the li'l muthafucka say?" ML Rex demanded.

"Yeah," Jones repeated. "What the li'l muthfucka say?"

"He ask why we disgrace ourselfs," one of the women replied quietly. Her eyes were downcast and even the rouge on her cheeks could not hide her shame. But then her sister added, "He call you a scumbag and sez we should not be wit choo." She spat at Alejandro's feet. "He ees a fine one to talk. He use to be a beeg man. Boom, da beeg gangster . . . but he ees nothin' no more. Jes a li'l *niño* who loss hees *cojones* in jail."

Ever the peacemaker, Giancarlo felt the escalating tensions and tried to step between Alejandro and the two LA gangsters. At the same moment, ML Rex stepped forward to confront Alejandro and accidentally sent the blind boy sprawling.

Things immediately went from bad to really bad. Jones inserted his hand in his jacket as if reaching for a gun. At the same moment, Zak bent over to fetch his knife from its strap, but he never got any farther. Suddenly, he felt the back of his sweatshirt gathered in the grip of a huge hand that lifted him off his feet and transported him behind its owner, the bouncer Jim, who was surging forward with his brother, Joe.

Jones was not a small man, but he was dwarfed by either of the twin bouncers, much less both. "You pull anythang out of your jacket 'cept yo hand, punk, and I'll tear your fuckin' arm off and beat you wit it," the giants said in tandem. They both smiled, revealing a gold incisor with a diamond inlaid in each enormous mouth.

While his brother kept an eye on Jones, who slowly pulled his hand out of his jacket to show he wasn't holding anything, Joe leaned over and gently picked Giancarlo up off the floor. "They you is li'l man," he said gently; then looking at ML Rex like he was considering eating him for dinner, softly added, "I think maybe you owes my liddle brotha Giancarlo an apology."

For all his bluster, the rapper certainly knew when to fold his cards. "Didn' mean no harm . . . an accident, homie," ML Rex said, and acted as if he were brushing some imaginary dirt off Giancarlo's shoulders. "They you is, li'l massa. All cleaned up."

Jim leaned forward menacingly until his massive face was an inch from ML Rex's. "You ain't my homeboy, punk," he snarled. "I sugges' you keep your LA ass in LA. . . . This ain't no fuckin' Hollywood movie."

The rapper backed away and then mustered as much dignity as he could and headed for the door. "Move your big ass, bitch," he yelled at one of the hookers as they were leaving. In the open doorway, Jones turned back and shouted at the bouncers. "Fuckin' niggahs, I'll be back wit da Bloods ta shove a fuckin' barrel up yer asses and blow your shit away."

Not to be outdone in front of the women, ML Rex pointed at Alejandro and yelled, "And I'll catch up to you sooner than later. Watch your back, muthafucka, 'cause I'll be all over you." Then for good measure, he added, "But I'll make you watch what I do to the li'l white bitches first."

"Touch these kids, and I'll put a fuckin' cap in the hole where your brain is 'sposed to be," Alejandro shouted back. As soon as he said it, he felt stupid, like he'd stooped to schoolyard taunting. But before he could think of something more intelligent to say or do, Jim and Joe took two quick steps toward the door and the ML Rex entourage disappeared.

Zak laughed. "That was cool!" he said, mimicking the gangsta swagger that had come naturally to Alejandro. "I'll put a fuckin' cap—"

Alejandro whirled and cut him off. "Listen to me, Zak, that wasn't cool," he said. "I let him get me down to his level. . . . I been on that road before, and there ain't nothin' but misery at the end. Okay, hombre?"

A sobered Zak nodded, as did his brother. Looking at the pair of chagrined faces, Alejandro's brown eyes softened again and his smile returned. "Come on, bros," he said. "Let's get you a cab."

Alejandro and the boys stepped out into the New York City night just in time to see ML Rex's limousine pull away. A brown hand was extended from a window in back.

"Hey, he flipped us off!" Zak exclaimed He returned the salute.

"Let it go, dog." Alejandro laughed, slapping him on the back. He ended up having to walk the twins to Ninth Avenue before they could find a cab willing to pull over. "Crosby and Grand," he told the cabbie when the boys got inside, "no detours." He handed over a twenty from his recent winnings—an exorbitant tip, no doubt, but insurance to get the boys home safely.

Before he closed the door, Alejandro leaned in and recited his part of the ritual he'd begun with the Karp twins not long after they met. "Remember, do the right thing . . . ," he started.

". . . 'cause it's the right thing to do," they finished.

Alejandro nodded. "Peace, bros" he said and shut the

door. When the cab was out of sight, he thought about what had transpired between him and ML Rex and scowled. Shaking his head, he stalked off into the night. He had more important things to think about and wanted to see Dugan.

4

AFTER THE RUN-IN AT THE HIP-HOP NIGHTCLUB,
Vincent Paglia dropped ML Rex and his entourage off at
the Waldorf-Astoria. "Say, Vinnie, since you is shit for a
bodyguard," the rapper said from outside the limo, looking back at the hookers to make sure they noticed how
he'd regained control of the situation, "do you think you
can get here by ten o'clock tomorrow morning? I gots an
important, executive-type meeting at eleven."

Vinnie nodded and got back in the car. The rapper and
his group disappeared into the hotel, but the chauffeur
didn't drive off right away. He picked up the car telephone and dialed a number scrawled on the back of a
business card. When the man on the other end of the line
answered, he told him everything he could think of about
the night's events. He then listened for a moment, gave
an affirmative grunt, put the phone back in its cradle, and
drove home to his wife and little girl.

The next morning, he was back to drive ML Rex and his
business manager, Zig-Zag Jones, to their "executive-type
meeting." When they got back in the car, he noted that the
transaction must have gone well. The rapper was in great

spirits when they returned to the hotel to pick up the two sleepy hookers, who were scandalizing the dowagers in the lobby with skirts that didn't quite cover their assets. Making sure the girls saw the big spender in action, the rapper handed him a hundred dollar bill with a flourish as Vinnie held the car door open.

The group snorted, smoked, and drank the rest of the afternoon away as they hopped from one radio station to the next. Vinnie noticed that ML Rex greeted each of the DJs and show producers like they were long-lost brothers, engaged in the protracted hand jive on the way out the door, and then bad-mouthed them as soon as he was back in the limousine.

When he was through with the tour, ML Rex was ready to get down to even more serious "par-tay-yang" and instructed Vinnie to take him, Jones, "and the bitches" to the best restaurant in New York. Personally, the chauffeur thought that Salvatore's in Little Italy was the best in town, but he figured the wiseguys wouldn't appreciate him bringing a couple of niggers and their whores into a respectable family restaurant. So he'd taken them to Le Cirque on Fiftieth and Madison Avenue, across the street from St. Patrick's Cathedral. Then he smiled inwardly when the group was turned away at the door by the maître d' because "the young misses are not appropriately attired."

ML Rex put on a show standing outside the door, yelling and gesturing at the maître d'—"Racist mutha-fucka!"—until the man threatened to call the police. Paglia finally guided the rapper back into the limo with the promise that he'd thought of a better place. "There won't be any problems."

After suffering through a berating for being a "stupid

ass, muthafuckin' East Coast cracker," Vinnie had taken them to the Tribeca Grill—a see-and-be-seen spot with hipster pretensions, but not particularly discriminating about dress codes. "You'll like this place," he assured his charges. "It's Bob De Niro's joint . . . you know, the movie star."

Just to make sure there were no problems, he slipped the hostess the hundred dollar bill he'd been given earlier to seat the foursome right away, and figured the C-note was well spent. He'd been told by his new boss to make sure the rap star was kept "happy and high" until the appointed hour. Several times since he'd first picked up the niggers at La Guardia, he'd placed calls to a mobile number of some kid in Harlem, who'd shown up a half hour later in a black SUV to deliver cocaine wrapped in foil pouches. "Good shit," his charges told him, not that they'd offered him so much as a snort.

After dinner, Vinnie deposited the group outside the Studio 54 discothèque. ML Rex's mood took a quick upward swing when the bouncer recognized his face from the *Some Desperate S°°t Fer Ya* album cover and motioned him and his companions to the front of the line. "It ain't LA," he told the impressed hookers, "no palm trees or nuthin', ya'll understand, but New York ain't all bad, I guess."

A few minutes before midnight, Vinnie got a call from Jones, the manager, to pick them up in front of the nightclub. On the way, he punched in the telephone number on the back of the business card. He'd been told not to write the number down and clean it out of his phone's memory bank after each call, but his own powers of recall weren't very good so he'd cheated and kept the card. When the call was answered, he identified himself, then listened carefully. "Yes," was all he said before hanging up.

Pulling up in front of the nightclub, Vinnie was pleased to see that his party was in a good mood and drunk. In the limo, the rapper popped the cork off a bottle of champagne and ordered him to drive back to the hotel where they were going to kick the party into full gear.

Vinnie put the car in drive and eased into traffic. He got on Third Avenue heading north, but instead of turning at Fiftieth Street for the Waldorf, he continued on up past 110th and the northern border of Central Park, until he hung a right and drove into the heart of East Harlem.

Vinnie had no idea whom he was working for and had only met the man on the end of the telephone line once, who'd explained that he was not "the boss, just his messenger." Nor did he know, or want to know, what the strange instructions the messenger had given him might mean to the people in the back of the limo.

Despite his size and "don't fuck with me" look, he wasn't really a bodyguard, just a part-time chauffeur. Violence frightened him. In fact, the only reason he'd agreed to drive the obnoxious nigger and his pals around, and play the role of hired muscle, was because he owed certain disreputable folks about ten big—as in ten thousand dollars—in gambling debts.

Although there had rarely been any hard evidence to demonstrate it, Vinnie considered himself a gambling genius. During March Madness, he thought he'd perfected a system for hitting the over-under on the college games and placed a series of wagers with his bookie. Unfortunately, he didn't have the cash to make good as each game dug him into a deeper hole. He was considering whether to take the wife and kid and go on a long vacation to someplace, say Venezuela, but then two bad men had come to see him where he worked at the fish market beneath the Brooklyn Bridge. He'd been told in no uncertain terms that the people he owed needed a job done and that he'd been selected to do it.

A simple job, really, said the man in the cliché black suit who did the talking. All he had to do was chauffeur some asshole rap star around, act tough, and follow instructions given to him by another man at the other end of the telephone number he was supposed to memorize. Follow instructions and all his debts would be forgiven. Fuck up and he'd find out what it felt like to fall from the Brooklyn Bridge, but not before other bad men did terrible things to his wife and little girl. "And by the way, Vinnie, an equatorial climate wouldn't be good for your complexion, so stick aroun' and do what you're told."

Most of the instructions he'd received after that had been as easy to follow as he'd been told. The hardest part was parting with a thousand bucks for the chauffeur who'd been scheduled to drive Mr. Rex. After that, all he had to do was drive, look bad, and do whatever the nigger said . . . so long as it didn't mess up the plan. Oh, *and report any and all activities of ML Rex to the boss.* He did what he was supposed to and could tell that the man on the telephone had taken a special interest in the previous night's encounter with the little spic, Alley-Handro Garcia, or whatever his name was. What it had to do with where he was heading now he wasn't sure, but something gnawing deep in his gut told him it wasn't good.

As he drove into East Harlem, Vinnie sweated until his white shirt was soaking and dark spots were showing through his black chauffeur's jacket. This is no place for a white boy, he thought. He promised God that if he could just get through this ordeal, he would never bet on basketball games again. Now, football, there was a sport a man with a system could make some money at. . . .

Vinnie had counted on it taking some time before his party would realize that they were nowhere near their hotel. Two of them were from out of town, and the women were too busy with a crack pipe and their professional responsibilities to care. He glanced in the rearview mirror and could see the two men, but only one of the hookers; however, by the contented look on ML Rex's face, he could guess where the other woman's face was planted.

When the rapper finally did notice that instead of the Waldorf, Vinnie was pulling over to a curb in a dark and apparently abandoned neighborhood, the chauffeur had a story ready. "Thought you might want to score again before we headed back to the hotel," he said.

"Well, all right, dog," ML Rex said without the hooker missing a beat. "Now you thinkin'. For a moment there, I thought maybe you was takin' us to yer momma's house." This brought guffaws from Jones and the other woman, as well as a muffled chortle from his own girl. "Shee-it, my man," he added, looking out the window, "this place is more fucked up than my old 'hood." The rapper was staring at a wasteland of boarded-up buildings covered with mysterious gang hieroglyphics; some of the windows were missing boards, the empty spaces staring back at him like mouth and eye sockets in a skull.

At least in Watts there were homes with patches of grass and the occasional palm tree. This section of East Harlem near the river was wall-to-wall cement, asphalt, and brick. The only things growing were weeds that had found some crack in the fractured sidewalks and abandoned lots to exploit, and the rats. Rats the size of Jack Russell terriers scurried down the sidewalks and along the gutters; larger creatures seemed to be lurking farther into the shadows, avoiding even the weak illumination of distant streetlights and the three-quarters-full moon.

"Dis is East Hahlum," Jones's hooker said nervously. "We shouldn't ought to be heah."

"Relax, bitch," ML Rex said, annoyed because his girl had stopped her efforts when her sister started talking. "We got Vinnie here to protect us. Ain't that right, Vin?" The chauffeur grunted in the affirmative as the rapper consoled the hookers. "And we need a li'l more of dat nose candy and maybe a rock fer yer pipe. Now I suggest you get back to workin' it whilst we wait for the man."

All in all, ML Rex felt that the trip to New York had been a success. The humiliation at the rap club the night before had wounded his pride, and he'd spent the rest of that evening into the early morning hours roughing up the hookers and devising ways to get even. Maybe he'd fly some of the homeboys from the 'hood to town and spray that little muthafuckin' spic down. Then he'd buy the Hip-Hop Nightclub and pay some vagrant to burn it to the ground—with those big, dumb, ignorant niggahs inside, and maybe the little white punks, too. Just thinking about it made him feel better . . . well, that and the cries of pain he elicited from the prostitutes.

The day was better. The meeting with the distribution company for his next CD went exactly as he'd planned. He was on his way to the top, and there was nothing to stop him. Now, if they could just connect for a little more blow and get back to the hotel, all would be well.

• • •

Vinnie was waiting, but not for the coke dealer from Harlem. When he saw the dark sedan pull up behind the limo with its headlights out, he took a quick look in the rearview mirror and stepped once on the brake pedal. The half-dressed hookers were now sitting on the men's laps and bouncing up and down in tandem with their backs to him. He pressed the button to lower the windows in the limousine, then opened his door, got out, and waddled away from the car as fast as his tree-trunk legs could carry him. Behind him, he heard the rapper angrily exclaim, "What da fuck," and then, frightened, "Oh shee-it!"

Two figures in dark clothes with black ski masks pulled over their faces had emerged from the sedan, each walking up to either side of the limo. ML Rex's exclamation was in response to seeing the man outside his window raise his arm and point a semiautomatic handgun at him.

The rapper was fast enough to shove the hooker, who was concentrating on her task and oblivious to the sudden change in circumstances, into the line of fire. The first bullet caught her in the back of the head, spattering gouts of brain, blood, and bone chips over her customer, blinding him. ML Rex started to scream, as did the woman and the man next to him, but the next bullet cut him off as it entered his mouth. The hollow-point .45 caliber slug demolished his brain stem and blew a hole out the back of his skull the size of an orange. He was effectively dead at that moment, but the shooter emptied the remaining bullets into his head, except one last round he sent crashing into the skull of the dead prostitute. It was over in just a few seconds.

Meanwhile, Kwasama "Zig-Zag" Jones kept screaming, though more from shock than fear. After all, he was the one who'd tipped off the executives at Pentagram Records about his employer's impending betrayal. He'd been told to make sure that ML Rex was happy and distracted—and that they leave the bar before midnight. "The rest will be taken care of." He figured that would mean something bad would happen to the boy he'd first known in kindergarten as Marty, and now that the moment had arrived, he felt a small pang of remorse. But it quickly passed like a bit of indigestion. The way he saw it, the world was made up of losers and winners. ML Rex had been a winner until he made the stupid decision to strike out on his own and jeopardize Jones's meal ticket. That made him a loser.

Besides, Jones thought that it was high time he got the star treatment and had been working on his own rap lyrics. When snitching on his friend, he'd mentioned that to the record executives. They didn't say no, he'd thought when the limo driver pulled over to the curb. But shee-it, I didn't think they was gonna blow the fool's head off while he was bangin' the ho next to me. Thas cold. He was about to get out of the car and clean the blood and gore off his face when his self-assurance took a nosedive. The black-clad figure on his side of the car was pointing what, in his professional gangster's opinion, looked like an AK-47 assault rifle.

"No, no," he shrieked as he tried to shrink beneath the hooker who was scrambling to get off him and out of harm's way. "I ain't 'sposed ta die! I'm gonna be a star. . . ." His pleadings and the screams of the prostitute were drowned out by the roar of the rifle.

The shooter emptied the clip and replaced it with another. This time he aimed more carefully and made sure that each small burst caught each of his two victims in what remained of their heads. There would be no miracle recoveries for these potential witnesses. His task complete, the shooter with the assault rifle walked back to the sedan, where he placed the gun in the trunk of the car and covered it with a blanket before getting into the front passenger seat.

His partner on the other side of the limo stood for a moment watching the bodies twitch. Involuntary muscle spasms, he thought. Satisfied, he nonchalantly let the .45 fall from his gloved hand. It clattered onto the pavement, and he kicked it beneath the limo and returned to his car.

A block away, Vincent Paglia was still moving despite the pounding of his heart and rivers of sweat that followed the contours of his body. When the gunfire stopped, he pulled his cell phone out of his pocket and dialed 911. Trying to make his voice sound black, he said, "I wanna report a shootin.'" He gave the street address and hung up.

At last he reached Third Avenue, where he found a cabbie willing to take him to his home in the Bronx.

"Vinnie, is that you?" his wife called out when he clicked the front door shut.

"Yeah, baby."

"You have a good night?"

"Yeah, Katie. A great night, just great."

"Come to bed, Vinnie, it's late."

"In a bit, baby," he said. "I'm gonna unwind with a little ESPN." There was no response, so he went to the refrigerator and grabbed a beer. Twisting the top off, he walked as softly back to Annie's room as he could, where he stood sipping and looking down at the sleeping child. Please, God, get me through this . . . , he thought and began to cry silently.

5

DETECTIVE SERGEANT MICHAEL FLANAGAN OF THE
New York City Police Department homicide division and
his junior partner, Detective Robert Leary, were sitting in
their unmarked sedan just inside Central Park when the
radio crackled. "Shots fired, vicinity of 121st and the East
River, officers responding."

Flanagan calmly finished the meat potato pie his wife
had baked and placed in his brown paper lunch bag and
carefully took another sip of the coffee he'd picked up at
McDonald's. Next to him, Leary wolfed down the last of
two Double Quarter-Pounders with Cheese and two
extra-large french fries, and then set the whole mess
awash in his stomach by gulping the last half of the super-
size Diet Coke.

"Why in the name of the Saint Joseph do you bother
gettin' Diet Coke," Flanagan asked his partner when they
ordered. "That other stuff has barrels of bad unsaturated
fats, 'nough to plug the heart of an elephant."

Flanagan considered himself something of an expert
on diet and fitness. At forty years old, half of that as a
cop, he still had a full head of copper-colored hair and

was hard as a rock from a daily regimen of two hundred push-ups and two hundred sit-ups—all done in cadence with repeated Hail Marys and Our Fathers. The way he figured it, he was years ahead of any sins he'd committed, all the while adding years to his life by keeping the temple of his soul in shape. He'd even instructed his wife to make the meat pies with virgin olive oil, instead of butter, and "use whole wheat flour, not white."

Lena was a good girl, twenty-five years old and "right off the boat," as they say, from Ireland, he'd told Leary. She'd been introduced to him by an aunt on his mother's side after his first whore of a wife left for southern California with the kike doctor who'd done the ten-thousand-dollar boob job he'd paid for by working overtime. By comparison, Lena was skinny, flat-chested, and unappreciative of his attentions in bed—in fact, she pretty much lay there reciting Psalm 23, "I will fear no evil," like a wooden statue. But at least she made no demands that he try to satisfy her—like the first slut—when all he wanted was to finish, then roll over and go to sleep. He considered himself a good Catholic, better than most, and believed that a husband had a right to his wife's body without a whole lot of hoopla.

"I ain't kiddin' ya, Bobby, that stuff's gonna kill ya," Flanagan continued as he turned up the radio. He was genuinely concerned about his partner, as he liked having a good Irish Catholic boy in the car with him.

"I ain't prejudiced or nuttin'," he told Leary on their first day together, but he didn't like the way the black police officers smelled "kind of spicy," or that they talked "like they was gangbangers themselves. . . . No disrespect or nothin,' but I believe that we ought a be able to ride with our own kind." He just felt that when his ass was on the line, he could trust a good Irish Catholic cop, especially those like himself and Leary whose fathers had also been part of the thin blue line of the NYPD that had always stood between civilization on Manhattan and those who would destroy it.

So he didn't want Leary to eat himself to death. When the kid first joined the force some five years earlier, he'd been a twenty-three-year-old, six-foot-four block of ripped muscle, a former Navy SEAL who could really kick some ass when a perp tried to resist or needed a little persuasion. But in the years since—three in patrol and two as a detective— the fast food, proverbial doughnuts, and soft drinks had added a roll around the gut and the beginnings of a jowl. He was still a guy not to be trifled with, but Flanagan knew that he'd have to stay on him about his weight or he'd turn into a big tub of goo and have a coronary right there in the car.

Leary shrugged. "I don't have a wife like you, Mikey," he complained. "I'm livin' wit my mom and she don't cook, even when she's not hittin' the bottle."

The younger detective liked working with Flanagan, who was practically a legend in the department for his ability to crack the tough cases, not to mention that he'd been decorated for bravery after rushing into the World Trade Center on that terrible day to save people. He was a stand-up guy, too, who didn't chastise him when he shyly admitted that he was "a little prejudiced" in that he hated "niggers, spics and towel-heads, faggots, Jews, Chinks, liberals, and people from France. . . . Other than that I get along wit most everybody."

Leary's only complaint with his partner was that Flanagan sometimes mothered him, like with this weight thing. Well, that and his partner was also real religious and wouldn't tolerate any cursing in the car and was always on him about being more regular at Mass. Otherwise, he idolized the older detective and would have rather confessed his sins directly into the ear of God and been tossed into the fiery pit than see the look of disapproval in Mike Flanagan's green eyes.

"Well, I've offered before to fix you up with my wife's sister," Flanagan suggested. "She ain't much to look at, sort of like my ol' lady, if ya know what I mean. But them's the kind ya won't catch in bed wit some Jew doctor, which would only tempt you to put a hot one in her head."

Leary smiled and mumbled, "Maybe so." But he'd seen a photograph of Lena's sister and thought he'd rather continue taking his chances of getting AIDS from the hookers on Forty-second Street than marry *that*.

After wiping his face with a napkin from his bag, dabbing daintily at the corners of his mouth, Flanagan started the car and began to drive toward East Harlem. Almost on cue, a breathless patrol officer reported from the scene. "Got a homicide here . . . multiple victims."

Picking up the car radio mike, Flanagan responded. "This is Flanagan in homicide. I'm four blocks away and en route. Stand by." Even before the dispatcher could acknowledge the call, the detective had placed the red bubble on top of the car and punched the gas pedal. Before some uniform screws it up, he thought.

Flanagan saw the blue and red police lights bouncing off the buildings before rounding the corner and arriving at the scene of the crime. He was pleased to see that the responding patrol officers had already cordoned off a black limousine with wide bands of yellow crime-scene tape. He told them so when they rushed up to his car.

Excited and nauseated at the same time, the patrol officers, who were both young and at their first homicide scene, said they'd checked the victims—"two African-American males, two females"—for vital signs. Finding none, they'd set up the tape and backed off to await the arrival of detectives. Having given their report, they looked like golden retrievers waiting to be praised for retrieving tennis balls.

"Great job, boyos," Flanagan said, which brought smiles and jaunty finger salutes to the brims of their hats. They, of course, knew who Flanagan was and counted themselves lucky that he was the one who'd responded. "One of the truly great cops," they'd tell the other guys in the precinct later. "A class act all the way."

"Any witnesses?" Flanagan asked.

"Yes, sir," said one. "Well, sort of, sir. He ain't much of a witness. Sort of a looney, if you ask me, sir."

Flanagan furrowed his brow. "Where is he?"

"We got him sittin' in the patrol car," the officer said, pointing to where the detectives could see a dark figure rocking back and forth in the rear seat. "He was just sort of standin' in the shadows of that building across the street when we got here. He was shoutin' this crazy biblical shit. . . ."

"Careful with your mouth there," Flanagan warned. "No need to use foul language, especially in conjunction with the Good Book."

"Sorry, sir," the crestfallen officer apologized. "Anyway, he won't say nothin' that makes any sense. He was going to walk off so we detained him."

Flanagan nodded and patted the officer on the shoulder to let him know he was forgiven. He and Leary then walked over to the patrol car and opened the back door. The smell that billowed out nearly gagged him. Apparently, the witness did not believe in bathing regularly.

"Jaysus," Leary exclaimed. "Somethin' crawled up inside of this guy and died."

They held their breath and looked in. An older man, one of the thousands of New York street people, sat moving as though he were in a rocking chair as he looked out the windshield ahead of him. His long, frizzy hair was gray, greasy, and impossibly tangled; the jaundiced skin of his face supported only patches of a beard, and his eyes bugged out of his head like two eggs with blue dots on the ends. He wore an old army field jacket over a food-stained tie-dyed T-shirt that proclaimed Grateful Dead World Tour 1976, as well as baggy khaki pants held up by a rope belt and sandals kept together by duct tape.

"Hey, old-timer," Flanagan said and tried to smile despite the stench. "You see what happened here?"

The man kept staring ahead without reacting except that every once in a while his eyes widened as if he saw something frightening coming at him, only to have it pass him by. He was breathing hard through cracked and bloody lips as though he'd been running.

"Hey, my partner was talkin' to you," Leary said, giving him a poke in the shoulder with a big finger. "We got some murders here. And these officers say you was standin' across the street. Now you want to tell us what you saw? Or do we need to run you downtown on a vagrancy?"

At first the man remained silent and unresponsive. Then slowly, as though some unseen hand was turning his head, he looked at Flanagan. The blue-dot eyes cleared as if sanity had returned for a brief appearance.

"And I looked, and behold, a white horse," he said softly, his yellowed and broken teeth gleaming dully in the light one of the patrol officers was shining on his face. Then in the next instant, his voice boomed and spittle flew from his mouth so that the officers and detectives jumped back startled. "AND HE WHO SAT ON IT HAD A BOW; AND A CROWN WAS GIVEN TO HIM, AND HE WENT OUT CONQUERING AND TO CONQUER!"

As suddenly as he'd started bellowing, the man went silent again. He turned his head back to stare out the windshield, the eyes again focusing on something the other men could not see.

"Jaysus, Mary, and Joseph," Leary whispered. "What in the hell was that?"

"Revelations 6:2," Flanagan said dryly. "You should study your Bible more, Bobby." He turned on his heel walked back past the patrol officers, one of whom asked what they should do with the witness.

"He doesn't know anything. Let him go and fumigate your car," Flanagan suggested as he ducked under the crime-scene tape and looked in the limo. In the spotlight of the police cruiser, he could see the 10-78 tattoo on one of the victims, which he found ironic. Now who needs assistance? he thought.

He looked at the front seat, then turned around. "The chauffeur wasn't one of the victims?" he asked the patrol officers. "Where's the chauffeur?"

"We figured maybe he was one of the guys in the back."

"Dressed like a gangbanger?" Flanagan asked incredulously and rolled his eyes.

Flanagan stooped and looked under the limousine. "What have we here?" he announced, to ensure there would be witnesses to the chain of evidence. He took out a pen from his overcoat and reached beneath the limo. Withdrawing his arm, he produced a .45 caliber handgun, which he held with his pen in the barrel to preserve any fingerprints.

"We might have lucked out, Bobby," he said to his partner, who hustled over with a plastic evidence bag he grabbed from one of the patrol officers. "Our killers appear to have been a little clumsy or in a hurry. I'll bet you a dozen Our Fathers we got one of the murder weapons right here."

Leary started to smile but his face froze when a loud voice roiled over them from across the street. It was the vagrant standing half in and half out of the shadows with his arms upraised.

"AND ANOTHER HORSE, FIERY RED, WENT OUT. AND IT WAS GRANTED TO THE ONE WHO SAT ON IT TO TAKE PEACE FROM THE EARTH, AND THAT THE PEOPLE SHOULD KILL ONE ANOTHER, AND THERE WAS GIVEN TO HIM A GREAT SWORD!" Finished, the man stepped back until he disappeared into the shadows.

"Friggin' nutcase," Leary swore.

"Watch how you talk, Bobby," Flanagan replied. "There's enough cursin' in this world without you addin' to it."

6

EVEN AS ML REX WAS BEING CHAUFFEURED PAST the Waldorf to his rendezvous with a bullet, Andrew Kane rose up on the tiptoes of his Guccis and strained to hear the opening notes of a chamber orchestra playing in the ballroom of the hotel. The exact movement was difficult to make out at first over the murmur of the elegantly dressed crowd as he stood on the dais, but he quickly identified the composer.

Mozart, he thought, how passé. A few more notes and he knew the piece. . . . Salzburg Symphony No. 2 . . . Divertimento in B-flat Major.

Kane knew that when most people listened to Amadeus Mozart, they heard God-inspired genius. However, while he could appreciate the technical perfection of the boy composer, he couldn't help but reflect that all that talent had been wasted on such a pathetic little fool. He had no sympathy for weak people, and that Mozart had managed to die penniless and almost unnoticed at an early age had earned him Kane's contempt. Sometimes, he thought, the man upstairs has a wicked sense of irony.

Kane preferred Beethoven. Now there was honest passion—Allegro ma non troppo . . . from the Ninth—brooding, powerful, sensual. A composer who was willing to recognize the beauty in some of man's baser instincts. Mozart was dainty, mincing through his movements like a SoHo queer . . . pretty like an orchid, but just as fragile and unsubstantive. Beethoven was a man's composer with real meat to his work. The German's music was just as beautiful, but in a different way. Like the ocean in its fury. Or the way that two boxers punching the crap out of each other could be a thing of beauty. A Queen Anne rose rather than an orchid—lovely to behold but with wicked thorns poised to draw blood.

Settling back onto his soles, he shrugged his shoulders to resettle his tuxedo. A little tight, he thought, going to have to lay off the hors d'oeuvres at these soirées. Political campaigns can be hell on a boyish figure. He cast a quick sideways glance toward one of the full-length mirrors on the wall as if to catch himself in the act of slouching. Still, not bad, old boy, not bad at all for a man in his fifties . . . or even one in his thirties for that matter.

A short man, Kane needed the elevation of the dais to look over the crowd, all of them dressed in black and white like so many penguins, only these birds were adorned with all sorts of flashy jewelry. A perfect, toothy smile never faded from his face as he turned his head from side to side surveying the room, nor did the warm, welcoming light of his Aqua Velva–blue eyes. He radiated the impression that he was enjoying himself immensely and that, if only time allowed, he would have wanted to speak to each and every person in the room.

The truth was it made his skin crawl just to look at them. Yet, most people came away after meeting him thinking that they'd liked Kane the moment they laid eyes on him, a great asset for a man campaigning to become the next mayor of New York City. With every blond hair carefully combed into place above his tanned, square-jawed face, his public persona was so polished that he imagined people could almost see themselves in his reflection.

It was an image so complete that few people ever knew that there were really two Andrew Kanes. The one most people met was the glib, white-shoe lawyer—the only remaining partner of Plucker, Bucknell and Kane, a big Wall Street firm that mainly represented institutions and wealthy individuals for exorbitant fees. Anyone who could read a newspaper knew that the lucrative law practice, phenomenal timing in the stock market, and an astute sense for real estate development in Manhattan had made him one of the wealthiest men in a city of wealthy men.

Still, what was wealth without power? he mused as he looked down on the crowd. It was power that truly appealed to him, which had prompted his decision to finally seek public office after being a behind-the-scenes kingmaker for so many years.

Of course, the Fifth Avenue public relations firm orchestrating his campaign couched it as "giving back to the city that had given so much to Andrew Kane." But he saw the office of mayor as only a stepping-stone to greater things. Next would come governor or senator. And who knew, if he played his cards right, it was easy to imagine himself sitting at the big desk in the Oval Office. *The most powerful man in the world; the man with the finger on the button.* Just the thought of so much technological testosterone sent a shiver of pleasure from his head to his groin. *Lesser men have certainly done it . . . take Clinton for instance . . .*

Even this, the public Andrew Kane, the one he thought of as the faux Kane, was something of a chameleon. He could be a man of the people, appearing in Harlem or Inwood wearing a suit straight off the rack from Sears, properly crumpled and pilled around the collar as though to imply long days, and a man who, while rich, was at heart just plain folks.

Kane worked those audiences like a traveling revivalist. In blue collar, white neighborhoods, they leaped to their feet and shouted his name—led by shills hired to pump up the crowd—when he promised more union jobs on city contracts.

"Amen!" they yelled in black neighborhoods when he spoke out in favor of affirmative action quotas "to right the wrongs of the past." And when he promised the Puerto Ricans, Dominicans, Mexicans, and assorted other Latinos that his administration would back "fair and equi-table" immigration reform, he was lauded with "Viva Senor Kane!"

In a way, the media was even easier to manipulate than the people. A case in point was the hastily arranged "com-munity meeting" that afternoon by his press information office after a gang shooting in Harlem the night before.

"As mayor," he solemnly promised the array of televi-sion cameras alerted to the photo-op by his press secre-tary, "I will declare a War on Gangs and accept nothing but their unconditional surrender until our neighbor-hoods are safe for law-abiding citizens."

The pronouncements brought only polite applause from the live audience—they'd heard similar promises ad infinitum with little ever actually done to fulfill them. Their applause, however, was more enthusiastic when he added that he would make sure that the officers of the

New York City Police Department understood that it was their job "to protect and serve the public, including people of color."

Meanwhile, in the wealthy, mostly white enclaves of Manhattan, they listened to the same messages on their televisions and believed that they were hearing a promise to keep the blacks, Hispanics, and Asians in their own areas of the city. There, as far as they were concerned, the undesirables were free to kill each other. The police were, of course, expected to work for the people who actually paid taxes.

Kane was savvy enough to know that the public would turn off too much negative news. So he mixed in a little lighter pap that was near and dear to the heart of any New Yorker by vowing to have a personal talk with "my good friend" George Steinbrenner, the owner of the Yankees, as well as the owners of the New York Jets, Mets, and Knickerbockers, to see what could be done about the high price of tickets for sporting events.

"It's getting so a hardworking American family can't afford to go to a game, buy a coupla' hot dogs for the kids, and maybe (wink wink) a cold, frosty one for Dad. . . . After all, attending a baseball game is practically an American birthright and more important than ever since that terrible day of September 11, 2001." He'd found that mixing in a little 9/11 sentimentality with baseball, mom, and apple pie brought them to their feet every time.

Surprising to some in light of his wealth and social status, Kane enjoyed the support of many of the Harlem ministers, who pronounced him a "strong voice for the African-American community." Indeed, he brought tears to the eyes of many black matrons when asked to speak at their church services, where he'd recount his now-famous story of how he'd been abandoned by his mother in a Dumpster. "I don't bear her any ill will," he'd say, his voice cracking dramatically. "I'm sure it was the desperate act of some poor, troubled, unwed teenager. It was only by the grace of God, to whom we are giving praise today, that I was fortunate to have been adopted by such a loving couple, Michael and Elizabeth Kane." Who, he thought with a smile, just happened to live in Mount Vernon, the wealthy enclave north of Manhattan.

The story would lead into a popular "Kane sermon" that always struck a chord in the black churches—the importance of having both a mother and a father in the home. Then afterward, as he stood at the door and the congregation filed out, he would squeeze their hands and his eyes would brim with tears. "Thank you, brother. Thank you, sister. Remember me in November, and I'll remember you at City Hall."

The chameleon's color changed, however, when back among the people he normally socialized with in midtown Manhattan. Swimming through the cocktail parties and charity events like a shark through a school of mackerel, he preferred silk Armani suits that cost more than some of the just plain folks earned in six months. And he made sure the power brokers of the city understood that all that courting of the great, unwashed masses was just politics and the price to be paid to keep one of their own in charge of the city.

Teased by his wealthy acquaintances about his comments in the *Times* and *Post* about cheaper sporting events, Kane would smile and shrug, "Simple minds, simple pleasures." Then he'd look back over his shoulders as though watching out for eavesdroppers and add, "The Romans kept them happy with bread and circuses; we have beer and baseball."

He was always up for a good "nigger joke" at private dinner parties when the women retired to another room and the men turned to Cuban cigars and snifters of brandy. Unless, of course, some of the few blacks occasionally allowed into the circle were present—and usually trying so hard to fit in that the others laughed at them behind their backs and referred to them as "Michael Jackson wannabes." If some of the blacks were in hearing range, then the off-color humor might be directed at the Puerto Ricans or the "boat people" from Asia. Usually, the blacks would chuckle along with the rest, secretly ashamed not to object but telling themselves that they could do more good later "changing the system from within."

The press loved Kane. He could be counted on for a great quote, as well as picking up the tab at restaurants and bars. Moreover, he moved in the same social circles as the editors, station managers, and publishers, as well as the media stockholders. As such, attempts to portray him in anything but a good light were generally spiked by editors, who insisted that reporters make greater efforts to be "fair" in their copy. Because most of those reporters were generally too lazy, inept, or unwilling to really dig and take on someone like Kane, the hard-nosed stories usually died a slow death in some computer file. Or, they were turned into powder-puff pieces focusing on Kane's contributions to the arts and his open wallet for every charity that came knocking.

What few negative reports surfaced seemed to slide off his back like grease on a hot skillet. Then his press secretary would go on the attack, labeling the accounts as scurrilous slander by some unscrupulous member of the press "who is just trying to make a name for himself."

Kane glanced at his diamond-encrusted Bulova. Nearly

midnight. He was growing restless, flexing and unflexing the muscles of his well-knit body, and needed something to release the tensions of having to maintain the faux Kane for such a long period.

Still, he remained on the dais making small talk with the man at his side, Cardinal Timothy Fey, the archbishop of New York. The fund-raiser was to pay for Fey's pet project: a new cathedral—grander and more magnificent than St. Patrick's—to be located next to Ground Zero where the World Trade Center had stood.

A beefy, florid septuagenarian, Fey had been raised as a child on the violent streets of Belfast. He still spoke with an accent and retained something of the old parish priest that endeared him to New York's large Irish-American community. Despite the trappings of his office and the fact that he was one of the most powerful men in New York, he was generally viewed as a simple, pious shepherd of his flock.

The cardinal looked tired but was determined to greet the flock of men and women in tuxedos and thousand-dollar designer dresses who approached. And as Plucker, Bucknell and Kane was the church's law firm, its senior partner thought he ought to remain as a show of support.

Kane looked at his watch again and scowled. He leaned back slightly to see the man on the other side of the arch-bishop.

Father Riley O'Callahan was a rather nondescript spec-imen—average height, weight, curly but thinning blond hair, and a Vandyke beard—except he had a lazy eye that tended to drift off on its own when he was engaged in con-versation. Catching his attention, Kane raised his eyebrows and O'Callahan answered with a shrug.

As if that was a cue, O'Callahan looked down and

reached for the cellular telephone clipped to his belt. The priest stepped back and answered, listening carefully, then flipped the phone closed. He looked up at Kane and smiled. "Wrong number."

Kane smiled and turned back to the partygoers, nodding to those who caught his eye like a benevolent king looking out upon his adoring subjects. A moment later, his face drained of color and he felt as though he might faint.

The archbishop saw the change and reached for one of Kane's arms as though to steady him. "Andy, are you all right?" he asked.

When Kane said nothing, Fey and O'Callahan both turned to follow his gaze. He was staring across the room at three people, two men and a woman. One of the men was about O'Callahan's height, thin and well groomed in a sort of turn-of-the-century banker's way, complete with pocket watch and fob. His facial features were sharp though softened somewhat behind round, steel-rimmed glasses, and he had an efficient but essentially harmless look about him.

The woman, on the other hand, was rather large and, especially in view of all the black coats, ties, and dresses, garish as a Las Vegas casino in a low-cut red dress that exposed great expanses of her cantaloupe-size breasts, with matching red stiletto heels that looked capable of piercing tires. She was as out of place as a liberal Democrat at a National Rifle Association convention, but she gave the impression that most of the people in attendance were beneath her.

Yet, it wasn't the woman or the efficient man who had caused the reaction in Kane. That distinction went to the third in the party. He was tall—six foot five, by Kane's guess—with a rugged face that looked as though he'd gone a few rounds in a boxing ring . . . and lost. He walked with a noticeable stiffness in one leg, but there was nothing that suggested weakness in body or spirit.

While they'd never met, Kane knew from newspapers and television newscasts that he was looking at New York District Attorney Roger Karp. Seeing him across the ballroom, a single word had popped up in Kane's mind— *nemesis*—and he was reminded of the old saying about someone dancing on his grave. His stomach had knotted and he felt his heart pounding in his ears. For one of the few times in his life he was afraid.

Still, Andrew Kane would not have been who he was if he let any man's presence shake him for long. In fact, once he recovered from the initial shock, he welcomed the fear; it gave him a deliciously edgy felling. He pulled his arm away from Fey. "Yes, yes, I'm fine, thank you. Must be tired."

Kane wondered why he'd had such a strong reaction to Karp. It was simply remarkable that their paths had never crossed before. He made it a point to know who was who in the city. As the head of a large law firm for nearly thirty years, he knew of course that Karp had been the chief of the DA's homicide division and then the number two man in the office. He was also aware when Karp was appointed to fulfill the remaining years of the incumbent, Jack X. Keegan, who'd left that past winter for a federal judgeship.

Yet, Karp as a person had flown beneath Kane's radar, a nonentity . . . just another drone in a large, inefficient bureaucracy. Now, he found it disturbing that he knew so very little about what made the man tick.

According to his spies, the new DA was making an effort to reach out and recruit bright, young law students.

Meanwhile, the old guard who'd been killing time in the office since the days of manual typewriters were getting the message that they were either going to start pulling their share of the load again, or they were going to be passed up for promotions and the best assignments. The laziest among them might even find their asses out on the street. "He calls it a 'return to meritocracy,' " one of Kane's spies, who happened to be a member of the old guard, sniffed. "The lousy bastard."

Hardly anything to be alarmed at . . . every new politician and bureaucrat came to office promising reform, promises that were quickly forgotten. Like all men, Karp would prove to be another mere mortal with weaknesses to exploit. And I'm just the man to find them, he told himself.

With that reassuring thought, the color returned to Kane's face. He decided that the best defense was to attack. He stepped off the dais and headed for Karp with the surprised Fey and O'Callahan scuttling after him like baby ducks.

"Butch Karp, I presume," Kane said in a loud bon-homie voice, using the big man's well-known nickname. He extended his hand and did his best to bathe the DA in the glow of his warmest smile. "Andrew Kane. I don't believe I've had the honor, but I think you know his eminence, Archbishop Fey."

Karp smiled in return, though it looked as if he might have strained a muscle in his face to do so, and extended a hand. "Mr. Kane," he said without any real enthusiasm before turning to shake Fey's hand somewhat more warmly.

As the other two men exchanged pleasantries, Kane had the opportunity to study Karp. The DA was obviously not a man who spent a lot of time with a tailor, maybe just long enough to take down the hems and sleeves of whatever suit he could find at a tall and big man's store. Probably spends most of his free hours in sweats, he thought.

However, what struck him about Karp was the intensity of his eyes whether he was speaking to Fey or had turned to look at someone in the crowd. The eyes were gray and sprinkled with flecks of gold and gave Kane the mildly unsettling impression that their owner was trying to see beneath the surface of whatever he was looking at.

The examination was interrupted when the rest of Karp's party was introduced. The short man was his "special assistant," Gilbert Murrow. The woman, Ariadne Stupenagel, a journalist who was apparently writing a story for the *Village Voice* on Karp.

As they made small talk, a photographer from the *New York Times* seized the moment to snap a photograph of Karp and Kane, who placed a hand on the big man's shoulder as if they were best buddies. Beneath the smile, Kane detested Karp and was infuriated by the way the district attorney shrugged off his hand after the photo was snapped. But he was a firm believer in the old Chinese proverb: *Keep your friends close and your enemies closer*. So when he got a moment, he steered Karp aside "for a little private chat."

Away from the others, he launched into his spiel about "declaring war on gangs" and bringing law and order back to the streets of Manhattan. "But I can't do it alone," he said, allowing his face to melt into a mask of absolute sincerity. "I'd like your support and in return, you could count on mine. . . . You know it costs a lot of money to mount a campaign these days, and my sources tell me that the Republicans think they have a good shot at the office.

But I hear nothing but good things about you, and I'd like to have you on my team when I'm mayor."

Kane pulled out a business card from a small leather holder he kept in his breast pocket and extended it to Karp. "This is my private number," he said, "give me a call and let's do lunch next week." He'd said it with such charm that he was stunned when Karp looked at him as if he'd crapped in his pants.

"First of all," Karp said icily, "the New York District Attorney's Office is not a part of the mayor's office, so I would not be on your team. I have my own team, and we work for the people of the city and county of New York. Second, I don't *do* lunch, unless you call grabbing a potato knish and an Orange Crush soda between 12:11 and 12:13 Monday through Friday doing lunch. Third, I thought there had to be an election before one got to call himself mayor. Now if you'll excuse me, I need to get back to my friends."

Kane stood staring at Karp's back with his mouth open and the card still extended in his hand. He couldn't believe that he'd just been dismissed in front of a room full of people, each and every one of whom—he was certain, even without looking—had just seen and heard his humiliation and were now tittering behind his back. He felt the eggshell of the faux Andrew Kane cracking and was afraid that he was about to start screaming.

Fortunately, Murrow suddenly appeared and snatched the business card out of his hand. "Sorry," the DA's assistant apologized as his boss walked away, "it's been a long day, and we're getting a little cranky. We'll give you a call and maybe we can do . . ." he stopped and shrugged, ". . . I don't know, maybe dinner?"

With an effort, Kane pulled the smile back on his face.

"Sure, sure I understand, rigors of the campaign trail and all," he said as calmly as he could manage, but he really wanted to reach out and strangle the man.

Kane wanted to leave but thought that if he did, people would notice and think it was due to Karp's slight. He forced himself to remain, and in spite of himself, stole the occasional glance at the district attorney. So he noticed when the large black man, whom he'd assumed to be Karp's police bodyguard and chauffeur, left and then returned with a worried look on his face. The black man and Karp stepped away from the others and spoke briefly.

Then Karp raised his head. There were a couple of hundred people in the room and yet his eyes had immediately locked on Kane's. A shiver ran up Kane's spine, and there was that word again. *Nemesis*.

7

"JEEZ, BOSS, WHAT WAS THAT ABOUT?" MURROW
asked when he caught back up to Karp. "It wouldn't hurt
to have Andrew Kane's machine and money behind you
when you run, and you pretty much told him to kiss your
big Jewish ass."

"If I run," Karp reminded his special assistant, whose
main functions were to operate as his troubleshooter,
keep an ear to the ground for what was going on in the
office, and be the official keeper of his life. "And what
does the ethnicity of my derriere have to do with it? He
rubbed me the wrong way."

"What?" Murrow said, scrambling to keep up with his
boss's long-legged gait. "The nicest rich guy in all of
Manhattan, beloved by everybody from Donald Trump to
the Reverand Al Sharpton, plus assorted drag queens, taxi
drivers, and Broadway producers, the New York Rangers,
Yankees, *and* Mets en masse, as well as black anarchists,
Greenwich Village poets, and the art gallery crowd—"
Murrow took a breath—"rubbed *you,* Saint-I-Don't-Do-
Lunch-I-Do-Criminals Karp, the wrong way?"

"Can it Murrow," Karp growled. "It's late, I want to say

hello to whoever you say I have to and go home to bed. . . . It's been a long day, and I just didn't feel like being schmoozed by Mr. Schtick."

Karp was grumbling in part because he didn't really know what had set him off about Kane. True, he didn't like politicians in general, or white-shoe lawyers in particular. He didn't move in the same social circles as Kane and couldn't imagine spending any quality time with him. But if that was all it took to get on his shit list, most of Manhattan's population would have qualified.

As he moved toward the door and the possibility of a quick escape, Karp wondered briefly if he was guilty of reverse snobbery and weighed the evidence. Kane had lots of money, while he, as a public servant, made a merely comfortable middle-class living. Kane had lots of friends; he had only a few close ones, and even they thought he was a bastard a lot of the time. Kane seemed to move through life like a fish in water; he seemed destined to ram his head into brick walls. On the other hand, they were both successful in their chosen fields, which therefore meant that Kane was not worthy of licking his black oxfords.

Satisfied that he'd examined the issue objectively, Karp announced as much to himself as Murrow, "I don't know why, but I smell a rat whenever I see that guy. And *IF* I run, I don't want to have sold my soul to Andrew Kane."

The large, colorful woman trotting alongside the two men—rather precariously in her heels—snorted and grinned. "Don't let him kid you, Murry baby. He's running. He might not be willing to admit it to himself yet, but he's on the campaign trail. . . . And what a juicy way to start. I can see the headline now: DA Karp Slams Next Mayor of New York. Says 'Kane's a Weasel!' "

Karp scowled, an intimidating feature on a man of his

height and countenance. "That was off the record, Stupenagel. And besides, I called him a rat, not a weasel," he snarled under his breath so that the other partygoers would not hear.

Ariadne Stupenagel smiled even more broadly, the bright red lipstick she wore to match her dress leaving a ruby ring on her prodigious set of teeth. "Now, Butch, you know how it works," she teased. "If you want something off the record, you have to ask me *reeeal* nice *before* you go spouting off. . . . And 'weasel' is sexier."

Karp pulled up short and turned on the female journalist. He leaned forward until his face was only inches from hers. It irritated him that she continued to smirk when most men would have blanched at his expression; not only that, he thought that there was also a mocking look in her eyes, which made him even angrier.

Most women would have described Karp's face as rugged and, except when he was scowling, not unattractive. His close-cropped, tea-colored hair sported a distinguished dusting of gray at the temples, even if there were fewer trees in the forest on top. Further examination would have revealed that the body was still reasonably trim from a daily regimen of sit-ups, repetitions on an old rowing machine, and a short, but brisk, walk to work. Despite the damaged knee, there was a certain economy of motion when he moved that identified him as an athlete however long he might have been removed from his glory days.

"Then the deal's off," he said with as much venom as he could muster. "Go find some other *putz* to follow around. And if that *off the record* comment appears in print, I'll get Fulton . . . ," he nodded toward an even larger black man standing some ten feet away and surveying the crowd around Karp like a hawk watches a field for mice, "to follow you around until he catches you doing something illegal, which he will; then I'll throw the friggin' book at ya."

Murrow, who was four inches shorter than Stupenagel and seven shorter than Karp, jumped between the two like a little boy trying to break up a fight between his parents. "Come on, come on," he begged looking up from one face to the other. "We're all friends here, right? Hey, am I right?"

The tension passed when Stupenagel laughed and tousled Murrow's hair. "Murry, you sweet little hunk of man meat, one of these days I'm going to throw you on my grill and have you for dinner," she said. "You are so damned cute when you're trying to keep the peace. But don't worry, baby, Mommy and Daddy were just about to kiss and make up. Right, Butch?"

Murrow's jaw dropped nearly to his bow tie as his mind tried to imagine what she meant by her "grill" and whether he would survive such a roasting. He'd met the woman six months earlier and still couldn't believe the stuff that came out of her mouth, most of it sexual in one way or another.

The image of being slowly rotisseried by Stupenagel popped like a soap bubble, however, when his boss wagged a long, cigar-size finger at her. "Uh-uh, Murrow. Lesson number one: never ever believe that anyone in the press is a friend. They'd crucify their own mothers on page one if they smelled a Pulitzer, or even a free drink. Think of it as being the circus trainer in the lion's cage—as long as you have a whip, a gun, and are looking them square in the eyes, you're probably safe. But never turn your back on the sons (and daughters) of bitches, or they'll eat you for lunch."

"Ooooh, Butch, you know how it turns me on when

you start talking about whips and eating people,"
Stupenagel retorted, waving her breasts back and forth as
if offering a sample.

"In your dreams, Stupe," Karp groused but to Murrow's relief his boss was clearly trying not to smile at the
reporter.

"Believe me, big boy, you've starred in a few of my
dreams," she purred, giving what she thought was a pretty
fair Mae West imitation. "Now whatdya say we put our little boy to bed, and then I'll give you somethin' to dream
about. Oooh. Oooh. Oooh."

Karp rolled his eyes, but he felt the irritation that Kane
had somehow inspired drain away as if someone had
pulled a plug in his pool of anger. Stupenagel had been his
wife's roommate in college. As journalists went, she wasn't
a complete liar and malingering scumbag—which for
Karp was about as complimentary as he got of the press.
She'd been halfheartedly trying to get into his pants for
years, but they both knew that the banter wasn't serious
and that she'd also leave his comment about Kane out of
her story. However, it did remind him to wring Murrow's
neck on Monday morning for ever talking him into climbing in bed with the press—figuratively speaking—political
aspirations be damned.

Only six months earlier, Karp had been content to be the
chief assistant district attorney for the county of New
York, responsible for the day-to-day operations of the six
hundred–plus lawyers who prosecuted crimes committed
on the island of Manhattan. But then he'd been appointed
by the governor to fulfill the remaining term of DA Jack
Keegan, who had happily skipped off to a seat on a federal

bench. The term would expire at the end of the next year, and between then and now—about eighteen months—he had to make a decision whether to run for the office.

Karp's distaste for journalists was matched by his distaste for politics, especially the phony glad-handing that went with it, like attending this fund-raiser for a new cathedral.

Privately, he thought New York needed a new cathedral like it needed more terrorists in airplanes. There was a black-and-white drawing of the proposed cathedral on an easel next to where the musicians launched into a new piece (he had no idea what they were playing, but it was pleasant enough and sounded vaguely familiar). The drawing was divided by lines indicating how many millions had been raised so far. Fifty million *only* thirty million to go. He wondered how many of the homeless people who camped out at night in the doorways and alcoves of the city's churches and cathedrals could be sheltered and how many children might not have to go to bed hungry if all that money were going for good works instead of cement and stained glass.

However, as Murrow pointed out, if Karp wanted to be in a position two years hence to actually make a difference in people's lives, including the lives of the homeless and hungry, then he had to make nice with people who had money and influenced public opinion. So Karp had found himself nodding in at least tacit agreement with the well-heeled patrons at the fund-raiser when they chattered on about how the new cathedral would "help heal" the city from the pain of September 11, 2001. He was used to speaking his mind—what others thought be damned—but now he held his tongue and worried that he was already losing his soul on the altar of politics.

The mere thought of it made him grumpy. Back in the seventies, when he'd started out as a young, idealistic prosecutor, Karp had the privilege of working for Francis P. Garrahy. Incorruptible as granite and nearly as impervious to the storms that regularly regaled the office, Garrahy had been the district attorney so long that entire generations of New Yorkers believed he'd been appointed for life, despite seeing his name on the ballot every four years.

Under Garrahy's watch, the office had been run with integrity and a religious fervor for the rule of law. The secret to fighting fair and winning, he told his prosecutors, was preparation and attention to detail. "We only get one crack at 'em," he'd reminded them on a regular basis. "Take your time, do your homework, cross your *t*'s and dot your *i*'s. Go after them only when you know the answer to every question *before* you ask it."

Garrahy treated his staff with the same sense of fair play. Promotions and rewards were based on merit, not longevity or political connections. As a result, he'd created and nurtured one of the best-trained, best-prepared, and most highly motivated prosecutorial staffs in the country. The convictions rates followed as a matter of course.

The golden era of Garrahy had lost some of its shine by the time Karp joined the office. The old man was in his seventies by then and slowing down, while the size of his staff had grown exponentially along with a burgeoning caseload. It was too much for him to oversee as he once had. Worn out by the good fight, he'd left the door open for the efficiency experts, who appeared on the scene with their charts and graphs and "quality assurance" meetings with the staff. They tossed around catchphrases like "case management," which boiled down to trials being an inefficient way of dealing with rising crime rates and their insistence on more plea bargains and deals to clear up the caseloads.

Under Garrahy, the efficiency experts were more of a nuisance than a real problem. They were barely tolerated and often ignored by those who actually tried to make felons pay for their crimes like Karp and his colleagues like Roland Hrcany, V.T. Newbury, Ray Guma, and the woman who would become his wife, Marlene Ciampi. But then Garrahy died in office and his job was handed over to Sanford Bloom, a political appointee who had no business being out of prison, much less the New York district attorney.

During Bloom's reign, the efficiency experts became a real power. They decided that the attorneys needed to meet certain quotas in dealing with their caseloads, quotas that could only be reached by avoiding trials and making bargain basement deals. Felons who actually got any prison time at all were in and out before they had a chance to catch their breath and prepare for the next robbery or rape or murder.

Karp and those like him found themselves on the defensive, having to pick their fights and find ways around the experts to retain some semblance of a justice system that hadn't completely collapsed. Fortunately, when all seemed lost, Bloom turned out to be as crooked as the people he was charged with putting in prison and, thanks to Karp, soon joined them behind the walls.

Bloom was replaced by Keegan, who had headed the homicide bureau during Karp's early years and was Bloom's chief assistant district attorney through no fault of his own. Keegan was actually a decent sort—certainly on the opposite end of the moral spectrum from Bloom and one hell of a trial attorney himself. Unfortunately, he'd spent his ten years as DA mostly biding his time as he awaited an appointment to the bench. But at least he'd been smart enough to put Karp in charge of the details of actually prosecuting criminals while he handled the two-martini luncheons and highbrow dinner parties.

Keegan's time in office had stopped the downward spiral of the office initiated by Bloom, but had not reversed the process. That was Karp's dream. The lure of returning the New York District Attorney's Office to the respect it had enjoyed under the old man—with a few twists of his own—was the main reason he was now seriously considering putting up with the politics and compromises necessary to run for the office. Not, as he seemed to constantly have to remind everybody, that he had committed to the decision to run . . . yet.

Of course, deciding at this hour against seeking office would have just about killed Murrow, who splashed around in the muck of politics like a pig in mud. Armed with an eccentric taste in fashion—he preferred bow ties and vests, tweed coats, and pocket watches that he thought made him look dangerously intellectual—and an acerbic wit, Murrow also had a taste for intrigue that would have served him well in the court of Czar Nicholas. He was certainly in his element as Karp's de facto campaign manager and always hatching new plots to garner publicity.

One of Murrow's schemes Karp had reluctantly okayed was to allow Stupenagel to profile his personal and professional life for a series of stories she was calling "A Summer in the Life of the Big Apple's DA." She'd sold the *Village Voice* on the freelance piece, but had known better than to come straight to him with her request. Instead, she'd schmoozed Murrow—sometimes Karp wondered if that included a romp in the hay—who had then pitched it to him as the perfect opportunity to reach a segment of the population he might not otherwise. As Murrow mournfully pointed out, Roger "Butch" Karp was not exactly "in" with the young crowd.

The *Village Voice* was what Murrow and Stupenagel called an "alternative" newspaper, supposedly offering a different viewpoint from the big dailies and television stations. The few times he'd looked at it, the stories seemed to feature eccentrics, whistle-blowing city bureaucrats who'd lost their jobs probably because they actually were incompetent, and anyone with an "alternative lifestyle"—all of it sandwiched between advertisements for breast enlargements, banks, laser hair removal, phone sex, restaurants, escort services, and personal want ads. But Murrow had assured him that the newspaper enjoyed a strong readership with twenty-five- to forty-five-year-old professionals in Manhattan who cared about politics and actually voted.

Murrow had also pushed for Stupenagel's request that she be allowed to report how his professional life intersected with his personal life. "It will illustrate your warm, cuddly man of the people side, and show the people that they have a friend in the justice system," his special assistant pleaded when he balked.

"What if I don't have a warm, cuddly side?" Karp groused.

"You don't," Murrow responded, "but the voters don't have to know that until after the election."

Karp thought it over. If he was going to let any journalist close enough to do a personality profile that included some of his private life, it had to be Stupenagel. For all the bad judgment she'd exercised when picking a career, she had proved herself to be a loyal friend to his wife, Marlene Ciampi. He figured she would be the last journalist to screw him over, though it was still not outside the realm of possibility.

The deal was that she could sit in on the myriad of meetings that ate into his work schedule and, on rare occasion, any court appearances he might make. Such access came with the understanding that he could designate some closed-door conversations, investigations, and trial strategies off limits because they were too sensitive or inappropriate for publication. But she also got to pick and choose which public appearances outside the office that she would get to cover.

Of course, Stupe (as he happily referred to her at every opportunity) chose the summer months to play fly on the wall because she knew that violent crimes, especially murder, would skyrocket when the heat soared and tempers in the naked city were twisted tighter than a rusted nut. Nothing like a rash of homicides flooding the DA's office to fill a reporter's notebook, he'd thought when she'd explained her idea, especially if I would do something sensational, like crack under the pressure and beat a suspect senseless while she takes notes.

Originally, Stupenagel proposed writing three or four long pieces. "Depending on how bored I get sitting in your office, watching you shuffle papers and yell at slavish assistant district attorneys all day long," she complained one afternoon as he shuffled some of those papers. "Don't you ever actually *do* anything? You know, single-handedly capture a serial killer after a gun battle and then personally persuade a jury to send him to death row like they do on TV. Maybe even throw the switch yourself?"

"Nope," he shook his head and grinned. "Oh, I do spend a certain amount of time every day thinking of ways to bore people to death."

"Well, you've succeeded there," Stupenagel grumped. "No wonder Marlene had to leave." The moment the comment left her lips, she regretted it. "Sorry."

For a long moment, he had given her the famous Karp Stare—his gray-gold eyes narrowing into a disconcerting "You want to fuck with me?" look that had intimidated many a would-be perjurer on the witness stand into telling the truth. But then the look softened and he shrugged. "Don't worry about it. There's probably more truth to that than I care to admit."

8

SURROUNDED BY A FEW HUNDRED PEOPLE HE DIDN'T
know or want to know in a ballroom at the Waldorf-
Astoria, Karp recalled the conversation with the reporter
and thought of his wife with longing. But Marlene was a
thousand miles to the southwest at an art school in Taos,
New Mexico. It was half a continent in terms of distance,
but at least she was closer in other ways than she had been
a year ago when she'd sequestered herself on a Long
Island farm, away from their kids, away from him, away
from her previous life.

Sometimes it was hard to believe they'd both been
young, gung-ho prosecutors for Garrahy when they began
a torrid love affair that had grown into something much
deeper. She had long ago quit the district attorney's office
and moved through a variety of other professions, including owning a VIP security firm that made her millions
when bought by a larger firm that then went public with its
stock.

The move to Long Island she had explained as necessary to her subsequent career choice as the owner of a
company that raised and trained dogs for security uses

from protection to bomb-detection. But they both knew that the self-exile had little to do with dogs and everything to do with their marriage.

Lying at the heart of their rift was a profound difference in philosophy regarding the application of the law. He believed in—or more accurately had pledged his life, fortune, and sacred honor to—upholding the U.S. Constitution and especially the laws of the state of New York. A writ of habeas corpus was art to him; he reveled in the challenge of proving a case beyond a reasonable doubt, and believed in the sanctity of the jury system even with all of its problems. He felt deeply that adherence to the spirit, as well as the letter, of the law was all that stood between a free and open society and the twin evils of a police state on one side, or the Huns at the gate on the other.

Marlene, however, had no more patience for what she saw as the inherent weaknesses of a system that had been convoluted and bastardized until the courts were more about protecting the rights of the guilty than meting out justice for the victims. The tangible result of her dissatisfaction had been a willingness to take the law, as well as a gun, into her own hands.

Inwardly, Karp cringed away from thinking about that aspect of his wife's past. Otherwise, he would have had to admit that she was an unindicted felon, probably a murderer. While it was true that those she'd killed were men who arguably deserved it, including serial rapists and murderers, vigilante justice went against everything he believed in.

The episode that had sent her into exile at the dog farm was her response to the attempted murder of one of their twin sons, Giancarlo. Seeking revenge, she'd called upon an old friend—Tran Do Vinh, a former Vietnamese schoolteacher and Vietcong guerrilla chief—who ran an organized crime syndicate in the homeland of his former enemies. Despite his former and current professions, Tran was absolutely loyal to Karp's wife and daughter. At the former's request, he and his band had wiped out the population of a remote town in the hills of West Virginia—a murderous nest of vipers, to be sure, but still they'd been tried, convicted, and executed without the benefit of due process, and some of the casualties had been women and children caught in the crossfire.

Karp skirted the need to turn in his own wife because, so far as he knew, Marlene had not violated the laws of New York. In weaker moments, such as when she was playing black widow and happily trying to devour her mate, he'd admitted to himself that without her, his life would have been as colorful as a volume of the New York Criminal Code. She was yin to his yang, as she once explained to him, except that at the time she was naked and talking dirty and used the expression to elaborate on how their anatomical differences were so well suited to one another.

Still, his rationale had not prevented a philosophical cancer from growing between them. Marlene might have continued to move farther away from the family until she was lost to them forever—like a moon slowly escaping the gravitational pull of its planet—but in an ironic twist, she was brought back into orbit by the lethal abilities that caused the problem in the first place. That past winter, she had once again used her skills, only that time it was to stop Islamic terrorists from blowing up 100 Centre Street.

In one way, it would have been no great loss. The

building was a stark and artless gray monolith built during the Depression and designed as though the architect felt no need to consider beauty as an important asset for an edifice that would house the city courts, the district attorney's office, and the Tombs. However, on that day, the governor, the district attorney, her husband, and maybe a couple thousand other people, including a hundred or so children in the day care center, were inside.

Marlene and her daughter had figured out the terrorists' plan, and his wife had shown up in time to send them to Allah slightly ahead of schedule. But even then her efforts were almost too late and the bomb had partly detonated and destroyed part of the building, killing a dozen innocent people and injuring several dozen more.

With more blood on her hands, the demons that tormented Marlene had threatened to carry her over the mental edge into accepting the fact that for better or worse, she was destined to be a killer. But Karp had reminded her that this time, her actions had saved hundreds, if not thousands, of lives. Nor were they motivated by revenge or to mete out vigilante justice.

"Any citizen would have been obligated to act in that situation," he told her, "but not many would have been as successful. Maybe instead of tallying up another sin, you should see it as a shot at redemption. . . . No pun intended." He didn't know how much of his little speech she bought into, but instead of running back to her dog farm on Long Island after he was sworn in as district attorney, she'd remained in New York with her family.

Marlene insisted that they all view her return to the family fold as a one-day-at-a-time arrangement, and they knew not to push her beyond that commitment. But one day had turned into one week and then one month, then four more. Despite efforts at emotional self-preservation, he knew that the kids had begun to hope that the change was permanent. As a matter of fact, so had he.

Still, it was not as if a light switch had been flipped and she was suddenly exorcised of the ghosts and self-doubt. She had been falling down a deep, dark hole for a long time and, as she told him one night, she saw herself as desperately hanging on to the last rung of the ladder more than climbing back up.

Karp would wake some nights, suddenly conscious that she was not in the bed next to him. He'd get up and find her staring out a window or looking at her reflection, he couldn't tell which. If she didn't see him, he remained in the shadows so that he could watch without disturbing her. Sometimes he thought she looked like a wild animal trying to determine which way the forest lay over the constant hum of the city, others like a little girl lost, her cheeks wet with tears.

One night he found her sitting at the kitchen table with one hand around the neck of a bottle of Hennessey and the other around her Glock 9mm. She claimed to have heard a noise that roused her from her sleep. "I got up to see if we had a burglar, then stopped off for a nightcap." He smiled and joked that burglars weren't eligible for the death penalty in New York, but he'd never forget the longing way she'd looked down at the gun.

Marlene Ciampi . . . former Catholic schoolgirl from Queens, alumna of Sacred Heart, Smith College, and the Yale School of Law . . . crusading assistant district attorney . . . vigilante . . . self-made millionaire . . . was a deeply scarred woman. Deeper than the wounds she'd suffered back when they first started going out and she'd opened a letter bomb intended for him. She'd lost her left eye in the explosion and the injuries to her face had never completely disappeared, but it was the wounds he couldn't see that worried him.

She'd looked up from her gun that night with her one beautiful brown eye and he saw the death wish and wanted to break down and cry. Instead, he'd gently pried the bottle and the gun out of her hands and then picked her up as one would a child and carried her back to their bed. He'd held her tight for the rest of the night while she sobbed, as though he could surround her with his love and keep the bad things out. The next morning she was back to being the sassy Sicilian-American doll he'd fallen hopelessly in love with, acting as though the whiskey and tears had finally purged her demons. But he knew that as high as she was at that moment, she would eventually head down the other side of the hill, and he might not be able to stop the plunge.

Butch Karp, the man who daily made difficult decisions that profoundly affected the lives of hundreds of people and did it without blinking, didn't know what to do to help his wife. With the clarity of an ice pick in the head, the dilemma brought back to him the horrible days long ago when he was a teenager and his mother got sick with cancer. There had been nothing he could do then either, except stick her with a hypodermic full of morphine to ease the pain. He had tried to forget the worst of those times, but he would always remember wondering how he'd cope in a world without her.

What he was experiencing with Marlene was similar, except that he was afraid of losing her to guilt, not cancer, and this time there was no psychological morphine to offer. Any suggestions he made that she seek counseling were either laughed off during her up periods as unnecessary, or angrily thrown back in his face when she was down as an attempt to get rid of her. "It's all pseudo-science, mumbo-jumbo anyway," she argued. "They don't have any answers. They can't even agree among themselves."

Then to his surprise, one afternoon when he came home from work, she announced that she was going away for four months to an art school in Taos, New Mexico. She had never mentioned New Mexico or been interested in anything more than looking at art before, but he soon learned that it wasn't just an art school. When the twins, weren't around, she'd confided that the school was run by psychiatrists and was designed for women who were suffering from post-traumatic stress disorder. The painting and sculpting was actually part of the therapy. After the initial surprise in which a tiny male voice in his groin area expressed dismay at the thought of her leaving for four months, he'd reacted positively.

"Don't get your hopes up," she'd warned him. "I'm not sure I buy any of this 'healing through art' crap. Sounds like just another School of Quackery. But Taos is supposed to be beautiful, and I feel like I'm running to something instead of away."

Marlene had shown him a brochure from the Taos Institute of Art Healing. He thought that it looked alien. The buildings on the small campus were square, rose-colored structures that looked like the homes in *The Flintstones* cartoons. The landscape pictured in some of the photographs seemed even more foreign to him—a dry and barren wasteland made up of thorny bushes, dry grass, gnarled trees, and rocks, lots of rocks.

On one hand, he was a little jealous. As a child, his hero had been John Wayne. A Saturday just wasn't a Saturday without a twenty-five-cent double feature of the Duke riding across just such landscapes. He'd been mesmerized by Wayne's traditional characters—the rugged individualist, willing to sacrifice himself to stop grave injustices and rid the community of evil. Incorruptible. Indefatigable. Every year, he'd begged his parents to "go out West" for their family vacations. And even as an adult, Karp knew part of him was still trying to emulate his hero. But he also worried that the wide-open spaces of New Mexico looked like a place where things got lost, not found, and wondered what that would mean for his wife.

Marlene left at the end of April. Gonna be a long, lonely summer, he thought, as he watched her truck disappear down Crosby headed for the Holland Tunnel and parts west.

She'd been gone for a month, and there had not been a lot of correspondence or phone calls. She did write to tell him not to take it personally, but the counselors had urged her to learn to live with herself before she moved on to her relationships with other people. "For a while they want me to just paint and let my issues percolate to the top where I can deal with them one at a time."

Karp happily noted that she signed her letter, "I love you more than ever," but he got most of his New Mexico news from his twenty-year-old daughter, Lucy, who had gone with Marlene. She'd said it was "to keep an eye on my nefarious mother for her own good, as well as everyone else's." But he knew that Lucy's reasons were more complex than that.

All he had to do to gain perspective if he ever started feeling sorry for himself was think of his daughter. His entire family seemed to attract danger as picnics did ants. Lucy had been abducted and shot at before she was sweet sixteen. Then that past fall, she'd been kidnapped again, this time by the serial killer Felix Tighe. It turned out that he had been planting a series of car bombs for the terrorists leading up to their attack on the courthouse, but he had his own reasons. He intended to kill Karp, who had put him in prison, but not before he'd destroyed his family, starting with the rape, torture, and murder of Lucy.

Tighe had taken Lucy to the basement of an abandoned building and begun his torments when a former Catholic tertiary, a sort of lay order of aid workers, named David Grale, arrived in the proverbial nick of time to save her. A deranged killer himself, who lived in the city's underground tunnels hunting "demons" that he thought inhabited humans, Grale and his army of "mole people" had spirited Tighe away. The killer had never been seen alive again, but a rat-gnawed skull had been left at a church and later identified as Tighe's through dental records.

Lucy was probably the best, most moral person that Karp had ever known. Deeply religious and committed to the Catholic faith of her mother's side of the family, she claimed to have a direct line to the martyred Saint Teresa of Avila. According to his daughter, the saint appeared to her in times of need to offer advice and as a sort of spiritual sounding board. He didn't really know what to make of Lucy's visions, but there was no denying that she had an unusual strength and seemed to have come through her ordeal with Tighe in astoundingly good shape.

The "art school thing" was her mother's thing, Lucy said when she informed Karp that she, too, would be going to New Mexico. She planned to dedicate herself to missionary work, helping out with a Catholic youth cen-

ter that worked with Indian teenagers from the Taos
Pueblo. Lucy, who was a savant with languages and
spoke more than forty by his last count, said she was also
excited at the prospect of studying one of the oldest and
most unique languages in the world. She called the language Tiwa and said that only the Taos Pueblo Indians
spoke it.

Karp wondered how the mother-daughter bonding was
going as he moved through the crowd at the fund-raiser
shaking hands and graciously thanking those who
endorsed his candidacy. "But I haven't decided whether
to run yet," he heard himself repeating over and over
again until he wondered why he bothered.

Finally, he felt he'd pressed as many palms as he could
stand and gave Fulton a high sign as he started moving
toward the exit. Thinking about his own wife and daughter made Karp want to go home and see his boys, Zak and
Giancarlo. He'd been so busy between work and march-
ing to Murrow's calendar that he'd seen little enough of
them for the past month.

The previous night he'd been looking forward to a rare
evening with no engagements and suggested that they
take in a Yankee game, but the boys begged off, saying
they needed to go to a friend's house to study for their
bar mitzvahs. They got home late and popped their heads
into his room where he was propped up on the bed reading a book, *John Adams*, by David McCullough. He
invited them in for a chat, but they'd made a big show of
stifling yawns and headed off to sleep.

They were still sleeping that morning when he got up
and left the apartment for the office. He wanted to spend

a couple of hours going over old case files, looking for clues to what he suspected was a new serial killer in town.

Two days earlier, the *Times* had come out with a story, in the Metro Section, about three Catholic priests who had been reported missing in the past four months from the area encompassed by the Five Boroughs, including one from Manhattan. There'd been no word from them since and, despite the lack of any evidence, foul play was feared. It was still just a police missing persons investigation, and he wasn't even sure why it troubled him so much. But he thought he'd take a look in the archives and see if any killers with a thing for priests had been released from prison in the recent past. Nothing stood out during his cursory examination of the files. The potential suspects who had come to his mind were still locked up or, in one case, had been stabbed in the heart while taking a shower in his cell block.

When he got back to the apartment that afternoon, the boys were involved in different pursuits, each according to his personality. Zak was playing one of his violent video games with plenty of gunfire, explosions, bloodcurdling screams, and death rattles. Giancarlo was off in his room picking out a tune on an old guitar Marlene had picked up for him before she left.

"So how did studying go last night?" he asked.

Marlene and Lucy weren't the only ones in his family who seemed to be feeling the tug of spirituality. Not long after the women of the household headed west, he had been invited (with Murrow's fingerprints all over the offer) to speak at the synagogue about law and order in the city of New York, such as it was.

Although Murrow had insisted that he needed to curry the Jewish vote, Karp had been uncomfortable with the invitation. He wasn't much of a regular at services. Ever since his mother's illness and death, he and God had been on the outs. He thought that the Talmud was a wonderful set of rules to live by, but he felt like an imposter when he placed the yarmulke on his head to enter the synagogue with his sons, who'd asked to go.

Still, he'd delivered what he felt was a fairly germane lecture pointing out that the principles of the Judeo-Christian ethic were the foundation of western civilization, and in particular the U.S. system of justice. Civilized people could not steal, murder, lie, cheat, or covet what was not theirs to covet without the decay of their society. But he'd avoided talking about God's role, preferring to leave such things to the rabbi and those who believed that God gave a fig about the day-to-day lives of human beings.

The next day, he didn't think much about it when the twins spent part of the morning locked away in one of their private conferences, which were closed to all outsiders. So he was surprised when they emerged and announced that they had come to an important decision: they wanted to go through a bar mitzvah.

Considering that to accomplish this they would have to take Hebrew and religion classes, neither of which they'd shown any inclination for in the past, Karp thought he smelled a rat. He gave them a sideways look and asked, "Okay, so what's the *real* reason?"

The boys were always up to some moneymaking scheme, such as Giancarlo panhandling on the sidewalk in front of the apartment building playing his accordion behind a sign painted by Zak that read: Blind Musician.

Please Help. "You two con men hear about the take?" he asked, referring to the gifts of cash traditionally doled out by relatives and friends at a boy's bar mitzvah party.

The twins' faces had contorted into expressions of aggrieved innocence as they replied indignantly to his assault on their integrity. Giancarlo noted that he had always shown an interest in the Catholic side of his ancestry, "and now I'd like to know the other half." Zak said he simply thought it was a good idea to know what he was fighting for when he punched kids at school who called him a "dirty Jew. . . . Besides, the Old Testament has all that cool stuff with battles and lopping people's heads off and begetting."

An irregular at the synagogue, Karp wasn't sure how to go about getting the boys signed up for the bar mitzvah classes they needed to take to pass the rabbi's examination. So he called a young rabbi he'd met at the talk who mentioned that he worked with the synagogue's youth. Karp admitted to the man that he had some reservations about entrusting his sons' moral upbringing to a stranger. He figured there had been enough bad things done in the name of religion that he wanted to make sure there was a balance.

"Maybe you should consider teaching some of our classes," the rabbi said.

"What?" Karp responded. "Sorry, rabbi, but you've got the wrong guy. My Hebrew is largely forgotten. And to be honest, I'm not sure where I stand with God these days."

The rabbi just brushed it off. "I would not have suggested it, except that your reputation precedes you," he said. "I'm told there is not a more honest and forthright man in this city than Roger Karp."

Karp found himself blushing at the compliment. "Well,

your sources should know that I've bent plenty of rules and wandered a few steps off the path of righteousness," he said. For some reason, he thought of his folks at that moment, and added, "I was fortunate enough to have been raised by moral parents who provided great role models."

"And that's all we're asking you to provide these boys and girls," the rabbi replied. "They need role models. Even those who come from good families can use the reinforcement. We are trying to teach them how to live in today's world as honorable individuals. Surely, you consider yourself an honorable man, Mr. Karp?"

"I try." Karp shrugged.

"Then you would be perfect as one of our teachers," the rabbi said. He went on to explain that the synagogue was "progressive" and tried to relate historical Judaism to the modern world by introducing its bar mitzvah candidates to the sorts of Jewish men they could model themselves after. And, he further emphasized, he'd be a good model for the girls who were studying for their bat mitzvah.

"But what about the Hebrew and the religious stuff?" Karp asked.

"Well, if you can work in the occasional story from the Talmud, that would be good," the rabbi laughed. "But otherwise, we have other people for the language and 'religious stuff.' "

So Roger "Butch" Karp, the district attorney for New York County, found himself agreeing to several appearances in front of a class of eleven-year-old boys, two of them his sons, as well as three girls studying for the female equivalent, bat mitzvah. On one hand, he found the idea more intimidating than arguing a tough case in front of a judge and jury; on the other, it was a chance to spend more time with his sons and a chance to impart some of his own values.

In that light, he chose "doing the right thing" for the subject of his first talk. Walking into the classroom after Giancarlo and Zak, who wanted to distance themselves from the teacher, Karp introduced himself and asked if there were any questions.

A wiry, wafer-thin little girl with waves of nearly black hair framing her rose-colored cheeks, upon which a pair of big, round tortoiseshell glasses was perched, raised her hand.

"Yes," Karp said with a smile meant to put her at ease. "And your name is?"

"Rachel," she said primly. "I was named after the wife of the prophet Abraham, who as I'm sure you're aware is the father of Judaism, Christianity, and Islam."

The boys in the class groaned and rolled their eyes. But Karp ignored them and kept a smile glued to his face. "That's right, Rachel," he said. "And your question?"

"My mother is a lawyer and she says you have a lawsuit against the Lord," Rachel said.

Bursts of laughter filled the room. Rather pointedly, Karp responded, "Was that a statement or a question, Rachel?" He laughed. The serious look on the girl's face didn't change so he went on. "Please assure your mom that no official papers have been filed but the statute of limitations has not yet run out."

Sensing another question rising to the surface of Rachel's tongue, he quickly announced that it was time to move on to the day's lesson, for which he'd chosen a story from the Book of Daniel. "It's the story of Shadrach, Meshach, and Abed-Nego," he said.

Blank stares, except from Rachel. Giancarlo beamed happily behind his dark glasses. Zak kept his head down, stealing glances to the side to see how his classmates were buying the old man's spiel.

Better jazz it up, Karp thought, or I'm gonna lose the jury. "It might interest you to know that this story happened in what is today called Iraq," he said. A little more interest, but not much. "And Nebuchadnezzar was a lot like Saddam Hussein. He killed people he didn't like . . . without a trial." Better. Nothing like a little bloodshed to attract the average prepubescent eleven-year-old boy. "Lopped their heads off, dragged them around behind chariots . . . that sort of thing." Got 'em right where I want 'em. Even Zak is paying attention.

"Anyway, the Jews were slaves and most of them had to do a lot of hard work," Karp went on, presenting his case in chief. "But a few of the bright, good-looking guys, like these three fine fellows and their friend Daniel, worked in the palace as scribes and scholars. They were good at their jobs and worked hard, advancing on merit, which made the other court workers, who were lazy and incompetent, jealous.

"So their enemies tried to think of something else that would get the Jews in trouble with the king. These troublemakers went to the king and said that he should build a golden idol and that all the people should be forced to bow down and worship it. . . . Sort of like that statue Saddam Hussein had built for himself for the Iraqis to worship that we all saw pulled down on television. . . . Anyway, they got the king to agree that anyone who refused to worship the idol would be thrown into a furnace."

The idea of people tossed into a furnace made the

boys sit up a little. He was pretty sure that it was Zak who said, "Cool." He went on. "The people who didn't like the Jews knew that they wouldn't worship a golden idol. Of course, some did because they didn't want to die. But Shadrach, Meshach, and Abed-Nego refused.

"When the king told them that the only other option was to be tossed into the furnace, they said that they believed that God would save them. BUT . . . ," Karp said the word loud enough to wake up the sleepier among them and raised what he thought was a prophetical finger, "and this is important, they said that even if God decided not to save them, they still weren't going to bow down and worship a golden idol. They said they would rather DIE a horrible, painful death with their bodies bursting along the seams like ballpark hot dogs, and their hair catching fire, and their eyeballs popping like balloons from the heat, than do something they knew was wrong, just to save their lives. So the king had them dragged to the furnace and tossed in."

Karp's descriptions of the horrors of the furnace had the class hook, line, and sinker. Zak now had his head up and was proudly basking in the reflected glory of his father's grisly dramatics.

As he'd done so many times in the past with juries after reaching the high point of a closing argument, Karp now lowered his voice to deliver the coup de grâce. "You know what the king and his men saw when they looked into the furnace?" he said. The boys wagged their heads no in unison, while Rachel bounced up and down in her seat with her hand raised. Karp nodded affirmatively toward her. "They saw the three young men sitting among the flames, not afraid," Rachel stated. Karp smiled approvingly and continued. "They could have been playing pinochle. And you know what else?" More wagging heads. "There was a fourth man in the furnace because God had sent an angel to make sure they were okay.

"Well, the king told the three young men to come out of the furnace. When they emerged, there wasn't a mark on them. They didn't even smell like fire. The king was so impressed that he declared that the God of the Jews was the one true God."

Seeing the look of disappointment at the lack of fiery deaths, Karp quickly added. "The king then had his soldiers grab the men who had been conspiring against the Jews and had them all tossed in the furnace where they burst into flames like Roman candles and melted like wax while their screams went on and on." He had no idea if that last part was true, but it sure brought the jurors back . . . they were ready to convict. "So what do you think the moral of the story was?" he asked.

"Don't fuck with Jews or your ass will get burned," Zak piped up. He was pleased with his classmates' reaction until he saw the scowl on his father's face and looked back down at the floor.

"Anybody else?" Karp asked.

"Do the right thing, even if it means you might get hurt," Giancarlo said.

"Yeah, but they believed that God was going to save them, so it was no big deal to them," Zak sulked.

"They *thought* he would, but they didn't know it for sure," Rachel said, jumping into the debate and raising a few giggles from the boys, who whispered about Giancarlo's *new girlfriend*.

Nevertheless, the mortified Giancarlo finished his—and her—point. "Remember, they said that even if God didn't save them, they still weren't going to do something they knew was wrong."

At that moment, Karp could not have been prouder of his second son (by thirty seconds). Meanwhile, his older grumbled that it would have been a better story if God had fried Nebuchadnezzar with a bolt of lightning or cast him and all his friends into hell.

"Jews don't believe in hell," Rachel informed him. "That's a Christian invention."

"Well, they should," Zak said turning so his father wouldn't see the face he made at her. "Why else would anybody want to do the right thing ALL the time, like some little Goody Two-shoes brother I know."

Giancarlo stuck his tongue out at Zak, who nearly died of frustration when he realized that Giancarlo couldn't see him retaliate. The class was threatening to disintegrate into a tongue-and-giggle fest, when Karp cleared his throat. "I think what the story says to me is that there are times in all of our lives where it would be easier, and maybe safer, to give in rather than to stick by our principles. It's not about whether we get thrown into a burning furnace or are cast into the depths of hell if we don't, but whether we will be able to live with ourselves. I think it's about being able to get up in the morning, look in the mirror, and be proud of who you see standing there."

More blank stares. "And, of course, if you mess with Jews, your ass will get burned." Good to leave 'em laughing.

It had been only two weeks since that first class, but Karp was impressed with how seriously the boys were taking their studies. He had to respect turning down his offer of a Yankee game that Friday so that they could keep their

study date. The next day before heading off to the archbishop's fund-raiser, he thought he should encourage
them by showing that he was interested in their spiritual
pursuits. "So how did studying go last night?" he asked.

"What?" Zak stuttered, looking quickly at his brother,
who smiled beneath his dark glasses and bobbed his head
like Stevie Wonder but offered no reply.

"I asked, 'How was studying for your bar mitzvah?' "
Karp repeated.

"Oh, fine." "Great." "Learned a lot." The boys double-
teamed him with rapid-fire superlatives. Something
nagged at him about their reaction, but before he could
question them further, Fulton buzzed the apartment from
the ground level and said that Murrow and Stupenagel
had arrived.

Thinking about his boys put him in a good mood on the
way to the fund-raiser, so he didn't object when Stupenagel
dragged out her tape recorder and said she needed to ask
him a few questions for her story. "Why do you want to be
district attorney?" she asked.

"Who says I want to be district attorney?" he said.

Stupenagel gave him a pained look. "Okay, just suppose that you decide to run for office," she said, "why
would you want to be district attorney?"

Karp shrugged. "I could tell you the truth, but you cynical bastards in the press would just snort and think it was all
bullshit," he said.

"One, in case your sight is going with your hair into old
age, I'm a cynical bitch," she retorted. "Two, try me."

"Okay, then," Karp said, "how about I was raised with
the notion that we should try to accomplish something

worthwhile during our time on this rock. And I happen to believe that protecting the citizens of Manhattan from criminals is worthwhile. It also happens to be something that I am good at."

"Fair enough," the reporter said. "But considering everything your family has been through—the abductions, the assassination attempts, the Felix Tighes of this world—why would you put them even more in the spotlight?"

There's the real question, Karp thought. Good technique, would work in any courtroom—set them up with the soft pitch, then throw something hard and fast right down the pipe. "This is what I do," he said. "Does that mean I'm not supposed to have a family? And what about the guy who would step into my place? Should someone else be expected to put his family in harm's way because I wouldn't?

"Some jobs are more hazardous than others. What about the firefighter's family? Every time he goes on a call, there's a decent chance he won't be back. Granted, he's the one who dies, but is his family unaffected? I know my family has been through a lot because of my job . . ." now there's the understatement of the century ". . . but we've talked it over, and they have all said they support whatever decision I make on this." Well, all but maybe one.

At the fund-raiser, Karp allowed Murrow to steer him around to the various important people "you have to meet." He had done his best to be sociable and politely answered their questions about truth, justice, and the American way until he noticed their eyes glazing over.

They don't really want to know, he thought. As long as we're coming down hard on the riffraff, keeping them out of sight, away from the tourists, away from their lofts and penthouses . . . locking them up and throwing away the key if that's what it takes . . . that's all these people want to know about the justice system.

Just before midnight, Karp was beginning to hope that Murrow had run out of fresh faces to lead him to like a dog on a leash. But then his assistant spotted the archbishop and Andrew Kane and began to steer him in their direction. But Kane saw them at the same time and glided over to introduce himself.

Karp had disliked the presumed next mayor of New York the moment the man opened his mouth. He was too slick, too friendly.

I wonder what he's really like when he turns the switch to off, Karp thought after Kane introduced himself. He'd seen the evening news before leaving for the fund-raiser and caught Kane's press conference in which he'd declared his war on gangs. It was exactly the sort of meaningless platitude that made Karp dislike politicians. And it had made his skin crawl when the little weasel, as Stupenagel insisted, put his hand on his shoulder for the photograph. I hope the paper doesn't use it, he thought. I know it will come back to bite me in the ass.

At his signal, Fulton went out to get the car from the valet. He was gone longer than Karp expected, and when he returned, his big tough face was frowning. He motioned Karp away from the others.

"I just heard something over the scanner about a shooting and called in to see what was up," Fulton said when they were out of earshot.

The old fire horse raring to go at the smell of smoke, Karp thought with amusement.

When he took over as DA, he'd asked Clay Fulton to head up the team of NYPD detectives assigned to the district attorney's office. He and Fulton had known each other for nearly three decades when the former was a wet-behind-the-ears assistant district attorney and the latter a snot-nosed detective in the New York Police Department. The job with the DA's office was a step down for Fulton, who'd worked his way up to inspector for the department, one of the bosses. But Karp knew that his friend had tired of the bureaucratic mess and mounds of paperwork at the top and was itching to be a cop again . . . *like now*. Shootings weren't exactly big news on the island of Manhattan. He knew Fulton wouldn't have mentioned it if there wasn't something unusual about this one.

"Multiple homicide, four victims in a limo," the detective went on.

Uh-oh, Karp thought. Here it comes.

"One of the victims has been tentatively identified as a pretty big-time rap artist who goes by—or I should say, went by—ML Rex, also known as Martin Johnson. Also, the chauffeur of the limo is missing."

Shit, Karp swore to himself. A celebrity, which means a lot of media coverage and pressure to come to a quick resolution. "Any suspects?" he asked.

"No one yet," Fulton responded. "But the detectives at the scene seem to think it may be gang-related; apparently these rap punks are always shooting each other."

In spite of himself, Karp sighed. Missing priests and missing chauffeurs, a wife and daughter in the middle of a desert, and a gang-related murder of a celebrity. It was going to be a long, hot summer. Stupenagel would be pleased.

At that moment, he looked up and found himself staring into the eyes of Andrew Kane across the expanse of the ballroom. He knew then that he'd made an enemy for life, but he didn't let it bother him. If he wants a piece of Butch Karp, he thought, he's going to have to take a number and wait his turn.

9

SOME FIFTEEN HUNDRED MILES WEST AND SOUTH of New York City, and in some ways a thousand years removed, John Jojola willed his tired feet to shuffle to the tempo of a dozen hide-covered drums. Sweat dripped into his eyes beneath the elaborate kachina mask of painted wood, leather, and feathers that he wore to represent one of the ancestral spirits of his people. The pounding of the drums reverberated off the rectangular, salmon-colored adobe homes of the Taos Pueblo and throughout his body. As he danced, he prayed to the spirits of his people while the drummers sang to these spirits, asking for their help, the repetitive chanting broken occasionally by a ululating cry.

The drummers and dancers had been at it since dawn. Now, sweat glistened on the bare parts of their bodies in the afternoon sun and ran in rivulets through the layer of dust that covered them from head to foot. Jojola and the other exhausted men moved trancelike as they willed the beating of their hearts to become one with that of the drums and carry their tired bodies on into the night.

At various times of the year, the Taos people danced and let tourists—who brought their money to the reservation to purchase arts and crafts, as well as to gamble at the reservation's casino—watch, although no photographs were allowed. The visitors were particularly appreciative of the graceful women dancers in their tall, white deerskin moccasins at traditional festivals such as the Green Corn Dance. But most of the tribe's rituals and ceremonies were conducted in secrecy.

Every winter, from the first bitter days of December through the warming of early spring, the entire reservation was closed to all but tribal members, who used the time to reconnect as a people and carry on traditions that sustained their culture. In the privacy of the sequestered village, the men performed the masked kachina dances to promote harmony and order in the universe. If the rituals were done properly, the ancestral spirits would ensure abundant game, enough water for the crops, and the health of the people.

Occasionally, unforeseen circumstances or catastrophes would push the world out of harmony, and the tribal council would close the pueblo so that the kachinas might be implored to intercede on behalf of the people. Now was such a time.

A great evil seemed to be stalking the people—three young boys had disappeared in as many months—and the authorities seemed unable to stop it. So, after much debate in one of the kivas—a large, covered, circular pit in the ground where the men gathered for ceremonies and important discussions—the tribal council decided to conduct a dance to cleanse the reservation and ask for help from the spirit world. Officers from the tiny Taos Pueblo Police Department, wearing the traditional black skirt over their uniform trousers, were stationed on the roads leading to the pueblo to politely, but firmly, turn away anyone who was not a member of the tribe. Then the tribe gathered at the ancient pueblo, the heart of their culture.

Jojola was short and thick, but not fat save for a little extra padding around his waist that he figured was his right at fifty-three years old. He wore his hair long and loose in the traditional way, with the ends reaching the middle of his back, and still black except for interwoven tendrils of gray that ran its length like veins of silver in a coal mine.

Beneath the kachina mask, his face was much like the land around the village—darkened by the sun, lined with ravines, but otherwise wide and flat except for the generous nose that protruded like Taos Mountain, the volcanic peak that dominated the landscape immediately east of the pueblo. Widely spaced above high cheekbones, his eyes were usually coffee brown and reflected his gentle nature and lively sense of humor; but when angered, they turned dark and hard like flint.

Jojola had been dancing since the ceremony began without water or food and was entering the phase when exhaustion, deprivation, and the mind-numbing thudding of the drums produced hallucinations. In fact, he was sure that the kachina dancer next to him was one such hallucination because the spirit man danced like his childhood friend, Charlie Many Horses.

When their eyes met through the masks, he was sure of it. But that could not be. Charlie had been killed in a Vietcong ambush back in 1968 when they were both soldiers in the U.S. Army. He wondered if any of the other dancers were ghosts, perhaps the restless shades of men he had killed in those years.

Jojola had lived on the reservation all of his life—never venturing farther than the city of Santa Fe, seventy miles to the south, and that only twice—until he and Charlie were drafted into the army in 1966. On the way to Vietnam after bootcamp, the young men had a brief layover in Los Angeles and went out to see the sights. They found the city to be intimidating—dirty and indifferent—and wondered how people could live there without losing their spirit. While their people had lived in multistoried complexes long before the first European showed up, they spent much of their lives outside in the high mesa desert to the west or up in the Sangre de Cristo Mountains that hemmed in the reservation on the north and east.

Jojola and Many Horses were much more comfortable after they arrived in Vietnam and were sent to a firebase in the central highlands. Even though the grasslands and forests were more lush than the arid country they came from, they quickly adapted.

Both had grown up together tracking wild game, learning patience and stealth from their elders so that they could move to within a few feet of their prey. The army recognized that the young men moved through the landscape of Southeast Asia as easily as shadows, making no sound as they approached or leaving any trace of their route when they left. They were soon given a special assignment: stalking Vietcong and North Vietnamese Army soldiers as they traveled along the paths.

As a LURP team—for Long Range Reconnaisance Patrol—they would disappear into the bush, sometimes transported by helicopters, for weeks at a time, living off the land, setting up ambushes, then fading back into the landscape. The enemy soon learned to fear the "ghosts" who could slip into a village or compound at night, kill silently, and be gone before anyone raised an alarm.

The men did not enjoy killing. But they'd been placed in a situation where they had no choice and did as they were told out of a sense of duty. But halfway through their first tour of duty, their attitudes were changed by an act of evil.

In their forays, Jojola and Many Horses had been befriended by the inhabitants of a Hmong village. The Hmong were simple farmers who would have preferred to carry on as they had for centuries. However, the North Vietnamese, and their Vietcong allies, considered the independent-minded Hmong antithetical to their socialist aspirations and at best treated them with contempt and at worst, brutally. So the Hmong were sympathetic to the American forces, though this particular village stayed out of the fighting. But one day, the two Indians arrived at the village to discover that the people had been massacred, and worse, their ears had been sliced off because, according to a few survivors, they'd listened to "imperialist propaganda."

From that moment on, Jojola and Many Horses had repaid the enemy in kind. The ghosts who crept into the lairs of their enemy—even into the tunnel systems beneath the jungle floor, hunting the VC like ferrets after prairie dogs—were no longer satisfied with just killing. They removed the ears of their victims, stringing them together on pieces of twine, then returning to the firebase where they flung their trophies onto the barbed wire of the perimeter as a warning and a threat.

Many died and were so mutilated, but there was one man they could not catch. The survivors from the slaughtered village had not been able to identify the leader giving orders that day. Jojola and Many Horses believed it had to have been one particular Vietcong, a former schoolteacher who had proved to be their most formidable foe. They did not know his real name but he was referred to by his comrades and enemies alike as Cop, which meant tiger. Wholesale slaughters and mutilation had not previously been part of his tactics, but they assumed it was him because he controlled most VC activity in the area. He was also known to be a hard man who dealt harshly with "traitors" who fraternized with Americans.

For the next year and a half that took them well into their second tour, Cop escaped every trap they set for him, showing an uncanny ability to stay one step ahead. They would get a report that he was camped in a certain area, but when they arrived he and his men would be gone.

Occasionally, they would catch the rear guard he left behind to ensnare his would-be assassins and more ears were added to the collection, but the ears they wanted most remained on the head of their owner. Then one day when Jojola was in Saigon for a little R & R, Charlie received a report that Cop was in a nearby village. He'd left on his own to catch the man who'd killed their friends, but instead, he'd fallen into a trap and died.

When Jojola later found his friend's body, Charlie's earless head had been cut from his body and set on a stake. Seeing that, Jojola removed the big bone-handled knife he'd carried from Taos and slashed the muscles of his chest in self-mortification and swore a blood oath that somehow, someday he would meet and kill Cop.

With so little time left on Jojola's tour, and worried about his mental health, the army had allowed him to accompany the remains of his friend back to the Taos Pueblo. After the services, he returned to the army only long enough to be formally discharged; he then went home to his people.

When he first returned, he'd been hailed by the local press as an American hero. But he was a troubled young man, haunted by the ghosts of men he'd killed and the one he couldn't save.

At first he'd gone into the mountains and lived as a recluse, hunting and fishing, hoping that the ghosts would tire of such a lonely existence and leave him alone. But he'd missed his people and returned to the pueblo, only to meet an enemy he could not defeat, alcohol, turning to booze to muffle the voices of the dead and hide their faces.

For the next fifteen years, he'd worked as a manual laborer—at least when he wasn't sleeping off a drinking binge. During a brief period of sobriety, he met and married a young Taos Indian woman, Maria Little Deer. Marriage outside the tribe was prohibited—the spouses of the few who ignored the rule were not allowed to live on the reservation—which limited the number of available women. So he felt himself fortunate to find someone so beautiful and innocent, untainted by the world outside the pueblo, and he thought at first she might save him. But he'd eventually returned to the bottle and dragged her down with him. Together they'd made quite a spectacle, begging from tourists and the affluent influx of new residents flocking to what was becoming a trendy art community. They slept as often in the county jail as they had their run-down double-wide trailer on the reservation.

Then a miracle happened. Maria got pregnant and gave birth to a son in their home, attended by one of the tribe's midwives. He held the child and was ashamed that his once-strong hands shook like aspen leaves in a breeze and that his eyes had trouble focusing on the infant's face. He didn't hold the baby for long though; there was something wrong—his son was not breathing properly. The midwife took the child and rushed him to the intensive care unit of the Taos medical center. When Jojola arrived in another car, a nurse informed him that the doctors were worried that his son was suffering from fetal alcohol syndrome and needed extra oxygen to prevent brain damage.

Standing outside the nursery, looking at his son struggling to breathe in an incubator, Jojola broke down and cried. He prayed to the kachinas to intercede with the Creator on behalf of his child so that the boy would not suffer for the parents' sins. He promised that if they helped his son, he would never drink again. The spirits answered, and a few days later, the doctor released the infant to the Jojolas' care saying the child, whom they named Charlie after his friend, appeared to have somehow escaped the ill effects of their boozing.

That was thirteen years earlier, and Jojola hadn't touched a drop of alcohol since and slowly turned his life around. When he had been sober for six months and thought he could handle it, he began attending Taos Community College and eventually got his associate's degree in criminal justice and joined the Taos Pueblo Police Department.

Maria, however, did not follow. It had been easy to pull her down into the depths of alcoholism, but he found it impossible to bring her back up. She tried immediately after their son was born and at various times in between, but the disease controlled her spirit. Then one day he came home early from work and found her in bed with another man. He left so that he would not be tempted to kill either. When he returned, she was gone, taking everything she might be able to sell, but leaving him little Charlie.

Jojola had grieved—for her, and what he'd contributed

to with the booze, for himself and lost love, and for his son, who had no mother. Taking his son, he'd retreated into the arms of his culture, moving out of the trailer and into the ancient pueblo.

As he taught his son, when the Spanish arrived in the area in the late 1500s, they discovered nineteen pueblos—their word for towns—dotted along the Rio Grande River Valley running south to north. The interlopers hoped that they'd found the fabled Seven Cities of Cibola, which were said to be made of gold. But instead they discovered multistoried block houses. They were made of adobe—a combination of mud and stone formed into bricks and laid in walls several feet thick, then plastered with thick layers of mud to smooth the surfaces inside and out. The roofs were supported by logs, called *vigas* by the Spanish, brought down from the mountains, which were covered with smaller poles, called *latillas,* laid crosswise on the *vigas*. Dirt was then packed into the roof structure and then that was covered by mud as well.

Some of the rectangular homes had been built on top of others as high as four stories and reached by the use of rough wooden ladders. The bottom structures lacked windows and doors and were accessible only through holes in the roofs, constructed that way as a defense against raiding parties of Comanche and Arapaho. The Spanish discovered that the thick walls also kept the interiors cool in the summer and warm when the winter winds howled down from the north.

While not so grand and rich as the conquered cities of the Aztec and Inca far to the south, the pueblo Indians had farmed and hunted from these established, well-ordered urban communities for five hundred, perhaps more, years. Five hundred more years later, the Taos Pueblo, the northernmost of the New Mexico sites, was the oldest continuously inhabited community in North America.

"And it still looks much the same as it did when the Spanish first came," Jojola told Charlie. "Except now our homes on the lower level have windows and doors." He laughed. "The Comanche and Arapaho finally got tired of raiding us."

By tribal law, no electricity or plumbing was allowed in the village. Water came from a clear stream that ran through the village from sacred Blue Lake high on the southern slope of Taos Mountain. Bread was baked outdoors in igloo-shaped adobe ovens, and the homes were heated by wood fires.

Most of the nineteen thousand members of the tribe no longer lived in the pueblo all year round. They stayed during the warm months in modest houses and trailers with modern conveniences on reservation land. However, the families kept their traditional homes in the village, where they lived during festivals, in winter, and in troubled times when the tribe's members pulled in tight to each other like a herd of buffalo does when threatened by wolves.

A couple of hundred people did live in the pueblo all year round, including John and Charlie, when they moved into their family's traditional home. For the nine years that followed, Jojola had done his best to raise his son in the traditions of their people. He taught him to fish and hunt, and thank the animals for the sacrifice that gave the people food to supplement the corn and beans they raised.

Charlie was taught to live in harmony with the physical and spiritual world. And that in pueblo society there were two types of clans—warrior clans, responsible for issues outside the tribe, and spiritual clans that dealt with internal issues. "We belong to a spiritual clan," Jojola said, "the Gray Coyote, although that does not mean we are not also warriors."

On spiritual guidance for his son, however, Jojola did not just look to the old ways. Ninety percent of the Taos Pueblo inhabitants were Catholic, including him and his son, but it was a version of the Church of Rome intermixed with the beliefs of their own culture. He did not believe that there was only one way for a man to be closer to the Creator and be in harmony with the world. And in his most important decisions, he turned more often to the spirits of his people, including how he'd eventually learned to live with the ghosts that haunted him.

When Charlie was about six, Jojola had gone to a medicine man and told him about the spirits who haunted him. The old man advised him to go to Blue Lake. "Bathe in the waters. Fast and pray. Sleep beneath the stars, and we shall see."

Leaving Charlie with an aunt, he'd done as advised but nothing much happened until the last night after he fell asleep beside the fire. The howling of a coyote woke him and when he rose, he saw the creature sitting on its haunches across the still-glowing embers, the red coals reflected in its eyes.

Jojola was cautious. The coyote was known in many tribes as the Trickster, an animal with powerful medicine who wandered the night and saw things that were not readily apparent to others, including much from the spirit world. They could fight savagely when cornered, but preferred to live by their wits. Although generally good-natured, and often helpful to humans—such as by eating rodents that would have otherwise destroyed crops and spread disease—they were also mischievous, a trait that sometimes inadvertently caused harm.

So, aware of the coyote's penchant for tricks, Jojola was careful as he addressed the animal. "Good evening, Brother Coyote," he said. "How is the hunting?"

"The hunting is good, thank you for asking," the coyote replied, not in so many words but rather as thoughts that came to Jojola's mind. "I appreciated the rabbit you left for me the last time you were in the desert, so I have come to help you. I have talked to the spirits of your old enemies and they are angry and refuse to be quiet because you try to deny that they ever existed."

"But I want to forget them," Jojola said, though he figured that he was dreaming because coyotes do not speak to humans. "I did not want to kill them—not most of them anyway—but it was kill or be killed."

The coyote grinned. "They understand that. They understand that there is a certain economy to the world. Some die so that others live, whether that is the rabbit who feeds me, or my death that will feed the vultures . . . or even the soldier who kills or else will die. Things are the way they are in the world for a purpose, including that you lived while others did not. However, you do not live in peace with the past by simply ignoring it. If you would quiet your old enemies, you must weave for them a place in the fabric of your life."

When he awoke the next morning, Jojola was sure he had been dreaming. But when he cleaned up his campsite, there on the other side of the fire were the unmistakable tracks of a coyote.

So returning to the pueblo, he no longer tried to shut the ghosts out of his mind. Instead, he invited them in and found that the shades of men were content to be just memories and not ghosts. Charlie Many Horses was another story.

For more than thirty years he'd lived with the guilt of not being able to save or avenge his friend. Often he talked to Charlie when he went on walks in the desert at night when the veil that separated this world from the spirit world was thin. *I am sorry my brother,* he would think.

"There is no reason," Charlie always answered. "It was my time to die. This is your time to live, make the most of it."

"But if I had been there."

"We would have both died, and it would have rippled into the future like the waves made by a stone thrown into a calm pool. Your son, Charlie, would not have been born. Whatever you were intended to accomplish in the future would have died, too."

Jojola was thinking of the conversation as he danced.

"Let it go," the kachina said.

I cannot, Jojola thought; his hand strayed to his chest where he could still feel hard thin scars he'd made with his knife. *I swore a blood oath.*

The other dancer swooped past him like an eagle soaring on a thermal updraft. "I do not need blood shed for me, my brother. I would rather you remembered me as the boy who hunted deer and fished for trout in Blue Lake with you."

"I cannot."

"You must. An evil stalks our children, yet here you are thinking of an enemy from long ago who no longer matters. You cannot change the past, my brother, but you can change the future by focusing on the present."

"You're speaking in riddles, Charlie."

"I'm a ghost, John," Charlie's spirit said with his recognizable humor. "I'm supposed to speak in riddles. But I'm also telling you the truth."

Many Horses was, of course, right, Jojola realized. And now is not the time to argue with a ghost over philosophy. Three young boys, only slightly younger than his son, Charlie, had disappeared without a trace. Foul play was suspected and it was more than his spiritual duty to stop it—John Jojola was the chief of the pueblo's police department.

10

THE TWO YOUNGER MEN ROSE TO THEIR FEET AS the archbishop stood to leave the meeting. "You coming, Riley?" Fey asked. "Perhaps a game of chess before noon prayers?"

"In a minute, your eminence," Father O'Callahan said. "Go on without me, I have a few small matters to discuss with Mr. Kane." He paused and smirked at the old man's back before adding in a sarcastic tone, "Matters having to do with . . . St. Ignatius?"

"Oh well, that, yes, well, best leave all of that to you," Fey stammered without looking back and picked up speed for the exit. "Whatever you think is right."

"Yes, your eminence," O'Callahan said and smiled. "Whatever is right for the Holy Church."

Fey stopped for a moment at the doorway as if to say something; then he was gone and the door to the large meeting room at the archdiocese clicked shut. Kane leaned back in his chair and put his feet up on the long wooden conference table. He studied the stained-glass renditions of a half-dozen saints that ringed the skylight in the ceiling, wondering absently why anyone would become a martyr. Why get shot full of arrows, or stoned, or burned, or pulled apart by wild horses for a God that doesn't give a damn? Hell, better to die at least trying to be *someone* or make a buck like ML Rex—he could respect that—than giving it up for some silly notion like a Holy Ghost. Still, martyrs could be dangerous people; they were so damn self-righteous.

"Perhaps, it's best that you not challenge Fey like that," he said on further reflection. "His conscience might goad him into doing something . . . irrational."

O'Callahan snorted. "The old geezer wouldn't dare. It could bring down his precious church, and there'd certainly be no Saint Timothy's Cathedral."

Kane sat forward and fixed the priest with a chilly blue glare. "Perhaps it's best not to challenge him," he said again, his voice grown tight and dangerous.

O'Callahan blanched and nodded quickly. "Of course, you're right. No sense pushing any buttons."

Kane ignored the priest's groveling. He was used to getting his way, as he could be quite unpleasant if he didn't.

The truth of the matter was, the faux Kane, the one everyone loved, was no more than the eggshell of a personality that the real Kane had created around his true self. For all the media coverage he received, very little was known about his private life, and he paid millions to ensure that it stayed that way.

His biggest secret was that he wasn't really an orphan. The whole story had been concocted by his father, Michael Kane, a prominent Manhattan lawyer who had knocked up his own daughter, Kane's mother, Kathleen, when she was sixteen. The girl had been sent away to "school" in Switzerland until the child was born.

Most men in Michael Kane's position would have forced their daughter to give the baby up for adoption. But he had always wanted a son, and his scrawny, blue-blooded bitch of a wife had been unable to give him one following the difficult birth of their daughter. So after the boy's birth, he arranged to have Kathleen and her infant spirited back home, where the boy was "found" in a Dumpster by a man who worked for him and taken to a Catholic adoption agency.

A lot of money exchanged hands, and the child was then handed over to Michael and Elizabeth Kane with no one the wiser. In fact, they were widely lauded in the Mount Vernon community for opening their home to the unfortunate little bastard. Only the incredibly insensitive visitor ever dared note the remarkable resemblance young Andy bore to his blond-haired, blue-eyed, square-jawed adoptive father.

Young Andrew had sometimes wondered why he seemed so "different" from other people. Nothing seemed quite right. Not in his mind, not in his house. He had been ten years old when he walked in from school one afternoon and saw his father, Michael, and sister, Kathleen, in her bedroom doing what he'd seen the family Labrador retrievers doing. A few days later, he'd tried the same thing with one of the little neighborhood girls. When she cried and threatened to tell her mother, he'd hit her on the leg with a stick and promised to "poke your eye out" if she ever told. Her silence in the matter taught him the value of backing up words with the fear of extreme violence.

Of course, there were psychological ramifications for

the boy, one of them incessant bed-wetting. His father and "mother," Elizabeth, tried to make him feel bad about it. "Big boys don't pee-pee on themselves," they'd lecture. But he rather enjoyed the feeling of warm urine running between his legs and seeping into the mattress beneath him. Then when it got cold and uncomfortable, he'd buzz for the nanny to clean him up and change the sheets. He even took pleasure in seeing how angry the nanny would get to be roused from her sleep in the middle of the night. If she was mean to him, he'd do it again an hour later. He went through a lot of nannies.

The bed-wetting might have alarmed a psychiatrist, if one had ever been consulted, especially if it had also come out that young Andrew enjoyed setting fires and torturing animals. Bed-wetting, fires, animal torture—the three-point checklist for the budding sociopath. Yet, the only time counseling had been considered was after he drowned a puppy he'd been given for his twelfth birthday in the backyard pool. He'd admitted that he'd used the pool cleaner's pole to keep the animal away from the edge "to see how long he could swim." But he was so contrite and tearful that his father decided it was a secret better kept among the Kanes.

Instead of seeking psychiatric help, Michael Kane sent Andrew to a military academy "to teach you to behave like a man." In the first month, the boy was repeatedly raped by one of the older cadets, until the night he brought a steak knife from the cafeteria back to the dormitory. When the older boy demanded oral sex, Andrew pretended to oblige but then sliced off his antagonist's penis neat as a surgeon. The whole incident was, of course, hushed up with lots more money, and from that moment forward, there were no more sexual assaults involving

Andrew Kane, except for those in which he was the perpetrator.

Still, he was no mere brute. Andrew preferred to have his personable alter ego win the hearts and minds of the people around him, no matter how much money, blackmail, or coercion it took. Usually he resorted to violence only "when necessary" or to set an example, although the urge for revenge sometimes got the better of his discretion. He considered that a weakness, but it was also such fun that he allowed himself the occasional indulgence.

When he was fifteen, Andrew was home for Christmas vacation when his "sister" Kathleen stumbled into his bedroom. She had a bottle of Chivas in one hand and was loaded to the gills on the prescription drugs she gobbled by the handful. She'd decided that it was time to tell him the sordid truth of his conception. When she was through, she asked if he had any questions.

"No," he replied honestly. "Should I?"

Kathleen burst into tears and fled the room. Two hours later, she was discovered floating facedown in the family Jacuzzi. The autopsy determined she'd swallowed a month's supply of Valium and drowned.

Andrew accepted the news of his paternity and Kathleen's death with an equal lack of emotion, unless it was a touch of elation because, at last, the world was making some sense. He had not cried at her funeral, but instead stared at the man he now realized was his biological father. He'd then gone back to school and thought about what he'd learned and what he should do about it.

It wasn't that he'd loved Kathleen—in fact, he had no real notion of what might constitute love. But he took great umbrage at his father and the Catholic Church. They had conspired to let him believe that he was the unwanted garbage of some teenage whore who'd left him in a Dumpster. It was their duplicity that really galled him.

Michael Kane was the same man who dragged him to Mass every week, then beat his bare ass with a riding crop until it bled if the priest didn't give him a high sign after visiting the confessional.

"Evil little sinner," the priest would say if he confessed what he'd truly been thinking.

"Evil little sinner," his old man would sputter as he laid into him afterward.

When Andrew returned home that summer after Kathleen's suicide, he confronted the old man, who was sitting at his big mahogany desk in the family library. The youth said he thought that the *New York Times* might be interested in a story about how one of the senior law partners of Plucker, Bucknell and Kane had impregnated his own daughter and then cooked up a lie about adopting a poor little orphan boy.

"There are really only two options, 'Dad,' " he said. "Either way, it's time to face the music. You could suffer through the looks from your country club pals, until they kick you out that is . . . and the comments from the women at church . . . and the damage to the firm's reputation or . . ." The teenager stopped talking and circled around to where his father sat trembling and sweating, his mouth opening and closing. Rather like a fish, thought his son, who pulled open the desk drawer where he knew the old man kept the .357 Smith and Wesson revolver. "I suppose there's always this possibility," the boy said.

Andrew Kane then stepped back and gave his father one of his warmest smiles. A moment later, however, his smile turned to a frown as he sniffed the air. "Oh come now, Dad, big boys don't pee-pee on themselves."

"Andy, I . . . ," the old man finally blurted. His son held up his hand to silence him.

"You might want to write a note about how depressed you've been since the death of your daughter, blah blah blah," Andrew said, smiled again, and left the room. He then went to fetch something cold to drink from the refrigerator and was enjoying a tall glass of milk when he heard a muffled report of the shot that blew his father's brains all over a prized bound edition of the Federalist Papers.

Andrew waited for the maid to find the old man and start screaming before he strolled into the library, pleased to see that his father had taken his suggestion about writing a note. He figured that their score was settled.

Nearly four decades later, everyone who knew the secret of his paternity was dead, except his "mother," Elizabeth. But she was in a Connecticut mental hospital for the immensely wealthy, knitting small, pink baby sweaters for her "lost" daughter and reciting nursery rhymes ad nauseam. He never visited, and paid the doctors well to see that she never regained her mental health.

That left only the Catholic Church to pay for the insult. But he was taking his time, enjoying the game he was playing to bring it down from the inside.

Andrew Kane was, in a word, a sociopath, a medically convenient term to describe what in the days before Freud and Jung would have simply been thought of as evil incarnate. As a young man shortly after his father's suicide, he had taken an interest in self-analysis and diagnosed himself as having a narcissistic personality disorder with antisocial tendencies.

Like some housewife looking up her horoscope in a magazine, he'd eagerly read a handbook of forensic psychiatry, *The Diagnostic and Statistical Manual of Mental Disorders*, which described his particular way of looking at the world as "having a grandiose sense of self-importance or uniqueness; preoccupation with fantasies of unlimited success; exhibitionistic need for constant attention and admiration; and characteristic disturbances in interpersonal relationships, such as feelings of entitlement, interpersonal exploitiveness, relationships that alternate between extremes of overidealization and devaluation, and lack of empathy.

"Fantasies involve achieving unlimited ability, power, wealth, brilliance, beauty, or ideal love. In response to criticism, defeat, or disappointment, there is either a cool indifference or marked feelings of rage, inferiority, shame, humiliation, or emptiness."

Kane had no problem with the descriptions. Like the housewife with her horoscope, he chose to ignore anything negative and focused on the positives—"achieving unlimited ability, power, wealth, brilliance, and beauty." He didn't give a fig about ideal love, but he'd dedicated his life to the rest.

After the military academy, Kane had gone on to college and then the Harvard School of Law. Graduating magna cum laude and passing the bar with flying colors, he'd announced that he was ready to assume his rightful place as a young, but full, partner in Plucker, Bucknell and Kane.

Partner Ernest Plucker complained at the time that young Mr. Kane hadn't paid his dues and at most should begin as a junior partner. The next day, Plucker received a large manila envelope in the office mail containing several photographs showing him inflagrante delicto with a pock-marked Forty-second Street prostitute. After that "Uncle Ernie" was mum on the subject of young Kane's quick rise to the top.

Shortly thereafter, partner Robert Bucknell, the law firm's bean counter, was confronted with proof that he had been embezzling from the firm for years. He and Plucker decided to retire a few weeks later. The two former partners had since died, and Kane had never seen a reason to take on any more. Instead, he kept a cadre of young, hand-picked associates whose reputation in the New York courts was that they'd push any ethical boundary in order to win at any cost. He paid them so well that the small matter of partnership was moot for most. Those who chose to leave to advance elsewhere were encouraged to do so in other states.

Cold and calculating in everything he did, he sometimes imagined this inner self as a serpent coiled up within the skin of a human being named Andrew Kane. In fact, when he was young, he had sometimes wondered if those around him could hear the dry rustling of its scales as it moved. But being a narcissistic sociopath did not mean he was insane, at least not in the legal sense. To be deemed insane in the eyes of the law—and therefore not responsible for a criminal act, such as murder—he would have been unable to distinguish between right and wrong. Kane knew the difference; he simply didn't care. His only real concern with the legal mores of society was that he not get caught as that would interfere with his plans and make his life uncomfortable.

Kane had no friends and didn't want any. There were people who worked for him and people he appeared to be friendly with—whether it was extending an invitation to dinner or a game of squash. He liked rough sex but that, and as adornments at social functions, was about the only use he had for women. He used them all, men and women, for only as long as it suited him and then cast them off like condoms, including his two wives.

No one was close to the real Andrew Kane, and only a very few ever learned that he was more than he appeared. Not even his closest associates knew how far the tentacles of his empire stretched, or the myriad types of enterprises they grasped.

Many of his business dealings were legitimate, if kept secret. His real estate holdings in the United States were not limited to Manhattan but extended west to Chicago and Hawaii, and southwest to Houston. He also owned hotels in Europe, sweatshops in Asia, diamond mines in Africa, and oil rigs in the Bering Sea.

Kane had invested in the entertainment industry as well with principal ownership in movie studios and record labels. His ego reveled in knowing he could count on Broadway and Hollywood actors, rock stars, ballerinas, and artists to show up at his parties, all of whom would be expected to support his political ambitions. With so many celebrities on the menu, an invitation to a Kane affair was the most sought after in Manhattan.

However, his legal empire represented only a fraction of the hundreds of millions of dollars he was actually worth. For every tentacle that was latched onto a legitimate enterprise, another was into insider trading, drugs, prostitution, pornography, gambling, money laundering, arms sales, and extortion. Where it served his purposes, he made alliances with other criminal organizations, such as the Mafia. He even paid for a network of spies among the terrorist organizations so that he could mitigate any potential harm to his foreign and domestic investments should they do something drastic, like crash airplanes into the World Trade Center, which he'd learned were likely, with barely enough time to sell his holdings in the buildings.

Legal or otherwise, Andrew Kane was far removed from the day-to-day running of most of his empire by layers of dummy corporations and offshore banks. The business drudgery was handled by CEOs and board members who had no idea whom they actually worked for, just the notion that there was a boss somewhere who paid them well, so long as they produced and kept their mouths shut.

As O'Callahan groveled, Kane reflected on how easy it was to manipulate human beings. It usually took so little to get them to compromise their values; they were always so willing to look the other way, or to blame someone else. They were great for talking about ethics—companies, including several of his own, were forever holding sensitivity-training seminars to address sexual harassment or racism in the workplace—and then the CEOs would turn around and screw their secretaries or tell nigger jokes at parties.

The crowning glory for him was the day the spinmeisters for the Clinton administration essentially told the American public that there was nothing wrong with the president of the United States getting blow jobs from chubby interns in the Oval Office and then lying about it under oath. Indeed, if the polls were correct, the American public had been convinced that integrity and honesty were not requisites for the nation's highest office. I should fit right in, he thought with a chuckle.

Even men with no obvious vices always had their

Achilles' heel. Take the archbishop. He supposed that Fey was what most people would consider a decent and moral man. Even Kane's network of spies had found no obvious chinks in Fey's moral armor. The archbishop had none of the sexual vices that had scandalized the church in recent years.

Perhaps he hit the sherry a bit too much, as evidenced by the veins in his rather large, red, and bulbous nose. Nor was he above accepting a few personal gifts from his friend and legal advisor, Andrew Kane, who donated lavishly to the archbishop's projects, as well as buying a helicopter for the archbishop's personal use. The helicopter had been a gift after Fey granted Kane an annulment from his first wife; a large check with lots of zeros for the cathedral had paid for the second. But generally the churchman lived a life without sin, except one—the sin of pride. He saw the new cathedral as his legacy, something he would be remembered for after he passed on to his reward.

Such a benign dream alone would not have left him open to the manipulations of Kane. But Fey did have another weakness: his love for the church. He would have done anything to keep the church from harm. So over the years when priests were accused of committing sexual indiscretions, Fey allowed the archdiocese's law office of Plucker, Bucknell and Kane to settle the cases out of the public limelight, not realizing he'd invited a serpent into the garden.

Early on, Kane had learned that any payments from the church bank account amounting to less than one million dollars did not have to be approved by the church council. Whenever a complaint arose because some priest molested a young woman, or violated a boy, one of his young, tough associates would negotiate a sum with the victim's family, who were promised that the offending priest would be sent away for sex offender treatment and never allowed to serve in a position of trust again. If that didn't mollify them, well, there were other, less pleasant, ways of reasoning with uncooperative people.

When families received their check from the church, they had to sign papers agreeing they would not seek criminal charges or any further recompense from the church. They were further counseled by priests carefully chosen by Kane and his associates, who noted that in accepting the offer, the victims and their families were protecting the church from a "few bad apples," and therefore acting in accordance with the wishes of God. The counselors went to great lengths to point out that the Christian faith was based on the premise of forgiveness—that Jesus on the cross had even forgiven murderers, as well as his tormentors. "How can we do any less for a few troubled priests?"

The careful application of money and guilt had kept the New York archdiocese out of the same sort of ongoing scandal that had rocked the church in Boston. As promised, Kane saw to it that the aberrant priests were sent to specialized sex offender treatment programs in rural areas where they would not attract much attention, such as a facility for the worst offenders near Taos, New Mexico, called the St. Ignatius Retreat. However, what he didn't tell the victims and their families—or the archbishop—was that many of the priests were brought back into the fold and assigned to new parishes, often in similar positions, their "cures" highly suspect.

Andrew Kane, who made millions in legal fees he charged the church, couldn't have cared less about protecting it, except as it fit into his plans for vengeance. In fact, he fantasized about the look of dismay on Fey's fat face when the press would find out about the accusations and payoffs and cover-ups through a carefully orchestrated release of the information. The New York church would be rocked to its foundation; then he'd top it all off with the final revelation that would bring down the house. His special little secret.

Of course, there would be some fallout on his firm. But he would clasp his hands together piously before the television cameras and note that Plucker, Bucknell and Kane was merely the church's legal counsel and obligated to represent their client's civil law interests in negotiations with the families. He would, of course, disavow any part in allowing the offending priests to return to their duties. "A horrible breach of trust, compounding previous errors," he imagined himself saying. "But Plucker, Bucknell and Kane was kept in the dark about these nefarious dealings or we would have severed our ties to the church." Any criminal charges, he'd add, were the responsibility of the NYPD and the New York District Attorney's Office, which had *obviously not done their jobs.*

Kane was kept informed of what Fey was thinking and doing by Father O'Callahan. As a young priest a dozen or so years earlier, O'Callahan had been in the habit of sexually assaulting young women who admitted to adultery in the confession booth. Instead of Hail Marys and Our Fathers, he'd demanded sex unless they wanted their husbands to learn of their sins.

The blackmail had come to Kane's attention when one of the young women told her husband and a complaint was lodged with the archbishop's office. Negotiations proved difficult. The young husband, already the cuckold, did not want to accept the church's money and threatened to go public. The problem required a special solution.

One afternoon a few months after reporting the assault, the young woman was in the laundry room of her apartment complex when she was paid a visit by a large man who spoke in thickly accented English. Her husband later discovered her locked in their dark bathroom, crying uncontrollably, and babbling about the "horrible things" that would be done to her if they didn't accept the church's offer. When her husband turned on the light, he saw that one of her eyes was swollen shut and surrounded by an immense, purple bruise.

The law office of Plucker, Bucknell and Kane was notified the next morning that the couple had reconsidered and would accept the $750,000 they'd been offered. Kane reduced the offer to $500,000—for the trouble they'd caused him—but they came into the office, signed the papers, collected the check, and then left the state, their car already packed.

Ever since then, O'Callahan had been utterly loyal to Kane, who'd liked the young priest's complete lack of morals and thought that with a little guidance, he might prove useful. The priest was bright, Machiavellian in his love for intrigue, and certainly not troubled by a conscience; he'd never seen the church as anything expect a place where he could exercise control over women to satisfy his sexual desires.

Kane had repaid O'Callahan's loyalty by suggesting to Fey that a certain bright young priest who had recently come to his attention might make a good personal secretary. The timing of the suggestion was perfect. Just a few weeks earlier, Fey's longtime secretary had suffered a most unfortunate accident when he was mugged on Second Avenue as he was walking to St. Patrick's for evening Mass. The old man had been given such a knock on the head that he was rendered an imbecile and sent to live the remainder of his days at a monastery in upstate New York. Fey gladly accepted Kane's suggestion and made O'Callahan his secretary.

O'Callahan had proved his worth several times over, none more important than his handling of Fey regarding the clergy sex offender cases. The payoffs had troubled Fey, but (with Kane's coaching) O'Callahan convinced the archbishop that the money was spent and the incidents kept secret for the greater good of protecting the Holy Church.

"Why should a few troubled priests ruin so much important work done on the behalf of so many others," O'Callahan counseled. "Millions of people count on the church for hope and comfort in these troubled times. These indiscretions by a few misguided and damaged men would shake the public's faith to the core. At the same time, shouldn't we forgive our troubled brothers and get them the help they need while removing them from temptation?"

Whenever Fey seemed to waver, O'Callahan would up the stakes by pointing out that the new cathedral he wanted to build would be in great jeopardy if New York's Catholics closed their wallets at the same time they lost their faith. "And losing *our* cathedral would be a tragedy," he'd coo, "for the faithful, for New York City . . . and for you, your eminence."

With his conscience lulled to sleep, Fey closed his eyes to the payoffs, preferring that O'Callahan and Kane sign off for him on the checks. When he suspected that he wasn't being told the worst of it, he decided that even those details were best left for people better equipped to deal with them.

Most of the time, a simple threat was enough to keep Kane's vassals in line. However, every once in a while he felt it necessary to revert to lessons learned in childhood and *poke someone in the eye with a stick*. The other night during the archbishop's fund-raiser he'd been waiting for a telephone call to hear that such a message had been delivered to ML Rex.

He did not allow anyone to take anything from him— not his women, not his possessions, not his money—and he dealt with thieves harshly. But there was one sin against his pride that would send him into a blind rage that even he recognized was unhealthy for his aspirations: the sin of betrayal. Nobody, but nobody, fucked over, or walked out on, Andrew Kane.

Among the fiefdoms of his kingdom was principal ownership of a major recording label that itself was comprised of a half-dozen affiliates, one of them being Pentagram Records. The company was a personal favorite of his; he'd created it, chosen the name, and dedicated it to the wonderfully violent gangsta rap. Music is dead, he thought, whenever he listened to what the studio produced. But still there was something that commanded his respect about so many illiterate assholes with so little talent making so much money by writing hardly comprehensible songs about shooting people, selling drugs, and abusing women. Now, that was the American dream.

The idea that one of these so-called musicians he'd created—a low-life gang member who owed every cent he'd made to Kane—had the temerity to walk out on his contract had infuriated him. That's the problem with niggers . . . they have no sense of loyalty. And the loyalty of his subordinates was paramount with Andrew Kane. Once they'd sold their souls to this devil there were no refunds and no returns.

While few knew that he owned Pentagram, his people would make sure that the lesson taught to ML Rex reached other artists with his labels who might consider looking for greener pastures. Yet, as satisfying as it was, the execution of ML Rex was only a move in a chess game with much larger ramifications than the death of one more foul-mouthed nigger. Someone had something that he wanted very badly—something that could ruin all of his plans, even make his life uncomfortable—but the usual forms of persuasion had not worked. In a way, ML Rex had died for someone else's sins against Kane.

Kane considered himself a "big idea" sort of guy who left the details of carrying out his plans to his underlings, especially O'Callahan. That's why he felt irritated when the priest mentioned the retreat in New Mexico. "So what was this about St. Ignatius?"

"Oh probably nothing," the priest replied, remembering the glare and not wanting to see it again today. "Just a call from Tobias about some Indian cop coming around and asking questions about missing kids."

"So why are you bothering me with this?" Kane said quietly as he studied his immaculate fingernails. "Didn't I ask you to make sure there were no problems at St. Ignatius?"

"Yes, sir," O'Callahan replied, feeling the sweat break out on his forehead. "I wouldn't have bothered you except for our 'friend' out there."

Kane lifted his gaze to lock into the priest's eyes. "But, of course, I'm sure it's nothing," O'Callahan went on, clearing his throat. "I'll handle it."

"Good, Riley, make sure you do," Kane said and went back to studying the saints on the ceiling.

11

"Chief Jojola! Chief Jojola!"

Charlie Many Horses called to him from the edge of his dreams. Except that the voice did not sound like his friend, nor had Charlie ever addressed him as chief.

In his dreams, Jojola was still dancing. He wet his parched lips with his tongue and kept his legs moving to the beat of the drums. At some point he knew that he would move beyond the hallucinations and into a dimension where he hoped the spirits would offer a clue to help him stop whatever was happening to the tribe's children.

"JOHN JOJOLA!"

The voice continued yelling, but Charlie had turned his back and walked into the dark. The others in his mind's village gave him disapproving looks; the dance was sacred and wasn't supposed to be interrupted with shouting. But the voice was insistent. "Chief Jojola. There's an emergency, sir!"

Jojola's feet gradually stopped moving like a windup toy running down. A wave of irritation passed over him; he thought that he had been on the verge of communication with the kachinas, but the feeling was gone with the dream. He opened his eyes and saw the worried face of Officer Larry Small Hands bending over him.

When Jojola recognized the young officer, his grip relaxed on the big bone-handled knife he kept beneath his pillow. Still, he was disturbed that for the first time he could remember since he was a child, someone had managed to walk up on him while he was sleeping. Must have been one hell of a deep dream, he thought, though the details had already faded by the time he sat up.

Meanwhile, Small Hands's face could hardly contain his excitement, and Jojola realized that whatever it was that caused the officer to enter his house uninvited—a cultural no-no in the close quarters of the pueblo—had to be important. The Taos Pueblo Police Department rarely dealt with major crimes. Felony investigations on Indian reservations were the purview of the FBI, an agency that put little manpower or resources into such investigations so very little ever got done. Anything off the reservation and not within the Taos city limits was handled by the Taos County sheriff.

Jojola and his men generally dealt with misdemeanors and traffic violations—most of their cases consisted of domestic violence incidents and drunk drivers. But he knew in his heart this was no wife-beating or DUI. Trying to sound official, the young officer said, "They found a body over by the gorge. It might be one of ours."

Jojola knew that Small Hands was talking about the missing boys. But which one?

The first to disappear had been an eleven-year-old whose alcoholic parents hadn't even bothered to report him missing back in March. When a schoolteacher finally called the police department to say that the boy hadn't attended school for several days, Jojola went to the parents' run-down trailer to look in on him. "Li'l shit took off 'gain," the father said. Even through the screen door, Jojola could smell alcohol on the man's breath. "Goo' riddance, goo' fer nuthin' li'l shit."

Jojola had insisted on looking around the trailer, but the boy was gone. Still, he wasn't unduly alarmed. He knew the boys' parents; both of them were rarely sober, and when they weren't hitting each other, they were hitting their kids. He didn't blame the child for running away and was determined that when he was found this time, he'd make sure the boy was placed in a foster care home with one of the tribe's stable families.

Most such runaways turned up in Albuquerque, the biggest city in New Mexico about 135 miles to the south, where a large population of street kids lived off handouts and petty crimes. He called the Albuquerque police and faxed them a photograph of the missing boy. He assumed that sooner or later the APD or Department of Social Services would come in contact with the boy and bring him home, as they had the first time he ran away.

When the boy still hadn't turned up after two weeks, Jojola drove down to the city. He cruised the places where the homeless kids gathered to skateboard, socialize, and smoke marijuana; one park in particular had a reputation as a hunting ground for pedophiles, who'd offer the kids money and/or drugs for sex. But there was no sign of the boy.

A month later in April, a second boy disappeared from the reservation. This time the red flag went up and stayed there. This child was only nine years old and came from a good home. Both of his parents were successful artisans—their paintings sold for thousands of dollars at the highbrow galleries in Santa Fe—and the child was active in his school and the Catholic church youth group. He also belonged to the young Taos dancers who were being trained to carry on the traditions. Now he was just gone.

It was now May and a third child had been missing for a week. A twelve-year-old altar boy had disappeared as he walked home after Sunday morning Mass. There'd been several possible sightings of him that afternoon, but nothing substantiated. The most promising had been that of a passing motorist who thought he saw a boy matching his description talking to "a really big, older guy" near the main reservation entrance. The pueblo kids sometimes gathered there because of the convenience store located just outside the boundary. "I haven't seen him before, but he just seemed to be asking for directions, 'cause the boy was pointing down the road. I figured the big guy for a priest, so I didn't think anything of it."

"A priest?" Jojola asked. "How did you know that?"

The witness looked at him like he was an idiot. But Jojola didn't think there was any such thing as a stupid question, unless it was the question that didn't get asked and turned out to be important later. "He had on the black shirt and pants, and I'm pretty sure I saw the collar," the witness said. Then he laughed and added, "Either that or he was Johnny Cash."

Desperate for any connection, Jojola had gone to see Father Eduardo, the priest who ministered to the Taos Pueblo. The Franciscan was a tiny, wizened old man of indeterminate age who seemed to have adapted to his desert surroundings by blending in. His face was as gray and rough as the mesas, his arthritic hands gnarled like the roots of the juniper trees, but he was the perfect man for the job of blending the Church of Rome with pueblo customs.

When the Spanish first settled in the area, they'd forced the Indians to work as slaves and to accept the Catholic faith while prohibiting the natives from practicing their religion on pain of death. In 1619, the conquerors built an adobe chapel dedicated to San Geronimo, or Saint Jerome, that became a symbol of their domination. But the Indians revolted in 1680, chased off the Spanish, and destroyed the church. The pueblos remained free of Spanish rule for twelve years and accepted their return only when the overlords promised to end forced labor, recognize the Indians' right to their ancestral lands, and to stop interfering in their internal affairs, especially their religion. The San Geronimo Chapel was rebuilt and from that point on, the priests looked the other way when the faithful also continued with their traditional practices. Father Eduardo even went one step further, blessing such "pagan" events as the Mudhead Kachina Dance, used to encourage rainfall, "as just another of the wonderful ways man has of relating to God and the world he created." He was much loved in the community.

Despite his age, the priest's grip was still strong when he greeted Jojola. The police chief knew that the old man was no simple rural priest, either, but a well-read man whose mind had lost none of its quickness or his hazel eyes their youth. He loved the children of the pueblo most of all and had personally badgered every businessman in Taos, and many in Santa Fe, to raise money for a youth center on the reservation. Those who did not contribute to renovate an old farmhouse were hit up for the money to buy Ping-Pong and pool tables, as well as subsidize a snack bar.

The disappearance of the boys distressed the old man considerably, but he shrugged helplessly at the description of the big priest. "Doesn't sound like anybody I know; you might check at the St. Ignatius Retreat," he suggested. "It's run by the New York archdiocese, but they have little to do with us here or even the archdiocese in Santa Fe. I don't know any of them well, plus most are apparently there on vacation and come and go."

Jojola was aware of St. Ignatius, located in the foothills just north of the reservation, but he had never been there himself. So he was surprised when he arrived because the retreat looked more like a prison to him than a vacation spot for priests. The buildings that constituted the main compound were surrounded by a twelve-foot-high wall, and he was stopped at the gated entrance by a guard, who made him wait while he went back inside his gatehouse to summon someone with the authority to meet with him.

A few minutes later, a thin, balding man in running sweats came out of one of the buildings and jogged over to the gate. He extended a hand—Jojola couldn't help but notice how limp and wet it was compared to Father Eduardo's. "Excuse the attire, Chief . . ."

"Jojola."

"Chief Jojola. I'm Dr. Tobias, the administrator for St. Ignatius. What can I do for you?"

"You're not a priest then?" Jojola asked.

Tobias chuckled—rather forced, Jojola thought—then answered. "Oh, I'm a priest all right, Brotherhood of Jesus," he said. "A Jesuit, but I'm also a psychiatrist."

"A psychiatrist?"

Tobias nodded. "Well, yes. Our object here is to provide a place where priests from the New York diocese can come to relax and unwind from the trials and tribulations of their service to man and God. For some that simply means time away to do nothing more than pray and, perhaps, read a good book.

"But others of our guests have deeper issues, including alcoholism and even drug abuse, so we offer professional counseling and rehabilitation to help them overcome these afflictions. Lay people often don't realize, but the awesome responsibility of being good shepherds can be a very stressful occupation. Priests, after all, are just men and subject to many of the same vices that trouble the rest of the modern world."

Dr. Tobias did not invite him into the compound so Jojola had to ask about the large priest while standing at the gatehouse. "He's not in any trouble," he said . . . yet . . . "but he may know something about a boy missing from the Taos Pueblo." As someone trained since childhood to note the minute behavior of animals he tracked, he thought he detected a reaction from the administrator—almost a flinch.

But Tobias shook his head. "No, doesn't sound like anyone here," he said. "We require our guests to remain on the property. They are, after all, here to get away from the outside world, especially those in rehab. I'm sure you understand."

Not really, Jojola thought, but said, "Sure. Makes sense to avoid outside temptations." Again, he thought he noticed some fleeting troubled expression pass over Tobias's face and wondered, but the psychiatrist then smiled.

"Well, sorry I couldn't be of more help," he said. "Perhaps the man you seek is not a priest at all but someone in a black shirt and maybe a white undershirt that looked like a collar. Happens all the time. Black seems to be 'in' nowadays."

"Yeah, could be," Jojola replied. At the same time, his mind was jumping ahead. All he'd told Tobias was that he was looking for a tall, heavyset priest. He'd not said anything about what the man was or wasn't wearing, especially not a collar, which was becoming more rare. Father Eduardo was usually in a T-shirt and jeans except when he was actually performing church services. Slow down, Jojola, he thought, he might have just assumed it. Still, there was something about Tobias and the whole walled "retreat" that troubled him.

With a third child having disappeared, the tribe was in an uproar. Except for the possible sighting of the last child, there'd been no other sign or word of the boys. Jojola was feeling the pressure from his people, but he wasn't getting much help from the outside. The FBI agent in charge of the Santa Fe office said he'd look into it, but there'd been nothing from him since. Neither had the Taos County sheriff done much other than offer a bored deputy who took the missing-persons reports. "But otherwise, Sheriff Asher told me to tell you that there's no evidence that a crime occurred off reservation property. He says you need to talk to the feds."

Ever since the disappearance of the second child, Jojola had made almost daily calls to the Albuquerque police, who were more cooperative but had no better answers. He then began driving down on weekend nights, when the street kids tended to be more active. He'd stopped at the city morgue, but the only decedent of the approximate right age was a white youth who, high on methamphetamine, had stepped in front of a long-haul truck on its way to Truth or Consequences, New Mexico.

"We have no idea who he is, and probably never will,"

the deputy coroner said. "He was pretty messed up by the collision. We couldn't even get a good likeness from your artist to send out to police agencies around the country." The man shook his head sadly. "He'll be buried in the county cemetery. No headstone, no services. His parents will never know what happened to him. The sad thing is there are thousands like him every year around the country who disappear and no one knows whether they were murdered or died accidentally . . . or are living the good life beneath some bridge."

Jojola left for home more troubled than ever. He wondered if one of the missing boys was lying on some cold steel table in another city with a John Doe toe tag, or was already buried in a pauper's grave. His people believed that the souls of the Taos Pueblo's dead could only rest if buried in the land of their ancestors. He needed to find the children and bring them back home, one way or the other.

As Jojola awakened to the news that one of the boys might have been found, he also felt a tinge of desperation. He'd noticed one constant about this mystery: each boy had disappeared on the day of a full moon. There was something particularly chilling about that—especially because in a little more than two weeks, the moon would be full again.

If Officer Small Hands got it right—he'd overheard a sketchy radio dispatch on the county sheriff's frequency— a grave had been discovered out in the desert west of the reservation. He hopped in his police truck and, leaving the reservation, ten minutes later reached Highway 64 and headed west as questions raced through his mind.

If the child was buried, that meant he'd been murdered. But what manner of man, or monster, could walk among the people, kidnap three boys, and not be noticed? And did all three boys suffer the same fate, or was there still hope?

He believed he knew the answer to the last question, although he did not want to accept it yet as fact. The ugliness of these thoughts contrasted with the beauty around him. It was a diverse land. The mountains were covered with pine forests and aspen trees. Lively streams raced down from the heights. Where the mountains stopped, the land grew flat, much of it irrigated for farms and ranches. Coarse old cottonwood trees stood shoulder to shoulder along the streambeds, and the blossoming wild plum trees colored the roadsides with purples and pinks.

However, just a few miles west of the pueblo, the land turned into high desert. In the far distant past, it had been subject to repeated coatings of molten lava from the volcanic peaks and rifts in the earth's surface. Ten thousand years after the last eruption, the land appeared flat to an observer on the ground, but from the air a viewer would see that it was crisscrossed with deep ravines, etched into the hard ground by flash floods. The terrain wasn't what most people pictured when they thought of a desert. There were no great expanses of sand. *Hard scrabble* was the best description—a land of rock and arid soil to which tough survivor plants like the silver-green sagebrush, stunted junipers, prickly pear cactus, and hardy grasses clung desperately.

The afternoon sky was blue as turquoise, empty except for a few fluffy clouds that wandered across the great expanse like lost sheep. As he looked west, Jojola noted a sort of shadow running north to south, hovering above the land and dividing the desert in two. The Rio Grande Gorge.

Ten miles west of the pueblo, Jojola reached the Taos Gorge Bridge, the longest and perhaps most beautiful single-span steel bridge in the world. As always, when he began to cross, he got the impression that the earth had opened its mouth and was about to swallow him.

Unlike most canyons in the American West—such as the Grand Canyon, which had been carved by the Colorado River—the Rio Grande Gorge had not been created primarily by the forces of water. A river, the Rio Grande, ran through it and certainly contributed to the continued erosion, but the geological anomaly of the gorge was that it was technically a rift, or tear, in the earth's surface. It was as though giant hands had grabbed the planet's fabric and pulled it a quarter-mile apart along a nearly straight line that ran from the Colorado border for several hundred miles through New Mexico. The giant had plunged his fingers in deep, too; the sheer red and gray cliffs plunged nearly eight hundred feet to the green river below.

Some of the Taos reservation land bordered the gorge on its eastern side, but Jojola was headed to the west end, where he was out of his jurisdiction and into that of the county sheriff, with whom there was no love lost. But if Small Hands had heard correctly, the body belonged to one of his community's children and he felt he had a moral right to be present when it was removed from its clandestine grave.

Reaching the western side of the bridge, he turned right on the first dirt road he came to and headed north and parallel to the gorge. About two miles up the rutted and seldom-used road, he saw a collection of vehicles and two groups of people. The largest group seemed to mostly be made up of members of the press, including newspaper reporters with their notepads, and the television crews with their cameras, boom mikes. Three TV satellite trucks were parked nearby—one from Santa Fe and two from Albuquerque, which irritated him as it was more than a two-hour drive and no one had bothered to contact his office in all that time.

Of course, it was no surprise that Sheriff Douglas James Asher, known to his few friends as DJ, of Taos County, had thought to contact the media first. He was constantly courting the press and running for an office he'd held for more than twenty years. Nor was it a surprise that he wasn't particularly worried about garnering the Indian vote. The Anglo and conservative Hispanic electorate had swept him into office every four years on his law and order ticket.

Jojola was just as glad to see that Asher was doing what he did best as a lawman and that was appear before television cameras looking concerned and diligent, neither of which described him well. But the distraction allowed Jojola to slip unnoticed over toward the second group of people some thirty yards away.

Stepping over yellow crime-scene tape laid on the ground, Jojola brightened to see the woman who was obviously in charge of whatever was going on at the site. Her name was Charlotte Gates, a forensic anthropologist from the University of New Mexico in Albuquerque.

Anthropologists as a whole were not always the most popular scientists with American Indians. For more than a hundred years, they'd unearthed and collected the remains of native peoples for the purpose of studying the bones of the earliest inhabitants of the continent. These scientists did not seem to understand that to the descendants of the dead, this was no different from a French anthropologist coming to New York and exhuming the remains from a cemetery there. What would they have thought of their grandmother Edna's skull and pelvis ending up on display in a Paris museum?

Laws had been passed in recent years requiring that the remains of American Indians be repatriated with their descendants for reburial. Unfortunately, by accident or otherwise, many of the remains stolen over the years had simply ended up in boxes or display shelves with no identification or even an indication of their origin.

Char Gates was different. Her area of anthropology had to do with forensics, or the use of anthropology as it applied to the law. He knew she was considered to be one of the best in the country, a frequent lecturer at the finest state of the art crime labs including the FBI facility at Quantico, Virginia. Most of her work in the field revolved around locating and excavating human remains for the purpose of identifying their owner and assisting law enforcement in determining if the cause of death was accidental or suspicious.

As she had once explained to Jojola, she read bones the way other people read books. "They tell me stories," she said. "By reading the bones I can tell if that person had lived a good life or a poor one, was well fed or was plagued by disease and malnourished.

"I look for scars from breaks or old wounds and compare them to medical charts to help identify the owners. We can attempt to match the teeth in a skull to dental records. I can tell the sex of the individual, and if female, whether or not she ever gave birth. And to a reasonable degree, the bones can tell me the deceased's height, weight, and age."

Jojola had once visited Gates at her Human Identification Laboratory on the University of New Mexico campus. He found her hard at work applying clay to a skull of an unidentified person that had been found in the mountains. Several hours later, he'd shivered as he looked upon an uncannily lifelike bust of a woman.

Gates had a morbid sense of humor about her work that he suspected helped her cope with a grisly business. But she also treated the bones with respect. "After all, they once belonged to a living human being who loved and was loved, laughed and cried."

Jojola was pleased that Asher had the sense to bring Gates to the scene, though he suspected it had more to do with her ability to attract the television crews looking for a good story than because the sheriff actually cared about the job she did. He sauntered over to where she was kneeling with her back to him. "Whatcha got, Char?" he asked.

Gates turned and squinted. Her face was deeply tanned from twenty-some-odd years of trekking about in the deserts of the Southwest. She was not a vain woman about her looks, though the clarity of her green eyes set against the mahogany of her face was striking. Deep lines radiated from the corners of her eyes, but he knew a lot of them could be attributed to her smile, and she smiled when she recognized him.

Gates liked the Indian police chief, too. He was smart, spiritual, good-looking, and she found him entertaining to watch. Just seeing his bow-legged stroll was enough to make her giggle, although she knew he could cover more ground on foot than any other human she'd ever met. She nearly laughed out loud seeing him standing there now with the toes of his cowboy boots pointed in nearly opposite directions. She looked back at where several of her current graduate students were working on their hands and knees around a hole they'd been digging.

"Young male, buried in a shallow grave approximately eighty centimeters deep, partly mummified due to desiccation, including what appears to be significant loss of blood prior to death," she said. "Judging by the decomposition, I'd say he's probably been here for at least two months."

Gates paused with a slightly puzzled look on her tan face. He asked what was troubling her.

"Well, I'm just surprised none of the local critters dug him up," she said. "A bear or badger, either one will scavenge a cadaver . . . even one of the local ranch dogs. And there's plenty of sign that your clan cousin—*el coyote*—has been here. But nothin' tried to get to him."

"Is he one of my boys?" Jojola asked.

Gates shrugged. "I don't deal with conjecture. We'll try the usual methods of identification—dental records, medical records. We may even try to hydrate the skin on his fingers by soaking them in brine and see if we can get a print. . . ." The scientist would have droned on but she saw the pained expression on his face and stopped. "Sorry, John, sometimes I have to play the role of scientist or the horror of these things would drive me into the looney bin. But if I was a betting woman, and I'm not, I'd say this is probably one of your boys. We're not finished exhuming the body, but the hair and bone structure of the face are consistent with an early pubescent American Indian."

Jojola nodded. "Cause of death?" he asked.

"I don't do cause of death, either," she replied. "That's the coroner's job. I just read the bones and tell him what's written there." Again she got the look. "Okay, okay . . . I happened to notice that the skin and musculature at the anterior of the neck has been cut—approximately twenty centimeters from beginning to end—by a *very* sharp instrument . . . a razor or, perhaps, a very well-honed knife. The wound is deep . . . the bastard who did this nearly severed the head. We've had to take extra precautions to brace the skull and neck vertebrae so that they don't separate from the body when we get him out of there. I will be very surprised if there's not some sort of mark on the neck vertebrae from the blade of whatever did this."

As she finished her dissertation, Gates walked over to the grave, and Jojola followed. The area around the hole had been marked off into a gridwork of squares with stakes and string. The graduate students, all responsible for their own grid, were carefully removing dirt and debris. They placed the material in plastic buckets, which were marked with a number corresponding to the grid the material came from. The buckets were then carried to another work station where one at a time the buckets were dumped onto a screen. Another graduate student sifted the material on the screen with the fine dirt passing through, leaving any larger objects behind. Anything that could not be attributed to the natural surroundings— rocks, plants—was taken to another table that had been set up where two more graduate students carefully logged a description of the items, as well as the grid number, in a notebook.

Jojola noticed how careful the students were when removing dirt caked around what was clearly the body of a small human being. They were using small whisk brooms and wooden picks to remove the last bits of dirt because, Gates explained, metal instruments might nick a bone and create false evidence. The anthropologists had worked their way down, centimeter by centimeter, until three-fourths of the body was exposed, revealing that the dead Indian boy—Jojola didn't need to wait for the coroner's official report—was lying on his stomach with his arms behind his back and tied at the wrists. Long strands of jet-black hair protruded from the dirt caked on his head.

"Where are his clothes?" Jojola asked.

Gates shrugged again. "They may be under the body, but I doubt it. We won't know until we can get him out, which may be another couple of hours. But he was nude when buried. We haven't found much other than the body, except for one rather curious item you might be interested in."

Jojola smiled despite the circumstances. Gates could talk all she wanted about her scientific objectivity, but at heart she loved playing Sherlock Holmes. The anthropologist led him over to the evidence table. As she'd noted, they hadn't found much. A couple of pieces of brown and green glass. A rusted beer bottle cap. Using a forceps, the scientist held up the largest item on the table—a set of amber-colored beads on which a gold medallion hung. "We found this lying on top of the body . . . obviously thrown in by the killer after the victim."

"Rosary beads?" Jojola asked. "What is so curious about that . . . most of my people are Catholic, including all three of our missing boys." He knew that something was wrong about the beads, but his legs hurt and his mind was tired; he wanted Gates to lead him by the hand on this one.

"Yeah, but how many pueblo children are walking around with a set like this," she said. "Wood maybe, but I'd bet these cost a pretty penny. The medallion doesn't feel heavy enough to be solid gold, but it's at least gold plated. You tell me how many of your boys would have a set like these."

None, he thought.

"As a scientist, I don't try to solve crimes. I merely report on the evidence that's within my field of expertise," Gates went on before smiling wryly. "But here's my two cents of deductive logic. First of all, the boy wasn't killed somewhere else and brought here to be buried. My guess is that darker ground you see beneath the neck and chest will test positive for blood, and lots of it . . . it's soaked in there pretty deep.

"Second, I don't think this grave was just a random spot chosen to hide a body. In fact, it's not particularly good for that purpose. It's near a road with some—if not a lot—of foot traffic from hikers. If I have the story straight, a couple was out here walking their dog when it took off after a coyote, then stopped here and started digging. The dog got as far as uncovering the fingers before the couple realized what they were.

"So the killer chose this spot for some other reason, perhaps one that only makes sense to him. Which leads to my next point and that is that there are ritual aspects to this. In other words, the murder wasn't committed to silence a potential witness, or in a fit of anger. The knot binding the wrists is fairly intricate—not your standard

Boy Scout half hitch or some haphazard wrap—it took time and thought to accomplish. Another thing . . . there is a rope around the victim's neck, and my guess is the victim was led here like a lamb to the slaughter."

Gates saw the sudden revulsion on Jojola's face. "Sorry. That was insensitive."

Jojola shook his head and swallowed hard. But he kept his mouth shut, afraid that the anger he was feeling might boil up out of his gut as he pictured the boy—naked, cold, bound, afraid—being hauled across the desert by a leash. He tried, unsuccessfully, to put the image out of his mind as Gates continued.

"Judging by the position of the body with the feet barely in the grave, I'd say the victim was on his knees when the killer cut his throat from behind, then shoved him in the grave. The bastard then tossed the rosary beads in, like some sort of calling card or message."

Jojola frowned. "You think he was brought here and . . . and . . . and what? A human sacrifice?"

Gates nodded. "Yes," she said, her voice grown husky with emotion. "And I think he came here . . . to the Gorge . . . for a reason. It meant something to him to kill the boy here. The burial was almost an afterthought. And I bet we find the other two boys somewhere along the rim."

A chill ran down Jojola's spine. "So we're dealing with a serial killer." It was a statement, not a question.

The anthropologist looked back at the grave before she replied. "You're missing three boys, all of the same approximate age. You might check with the police in Taos and Santa Fe to see if there are any similar reports of missing Anglo or Hispanic kids, but my guess is he has a thing for Indian children. These guys are addicted to patterns of behavior. There's one other thing we'll have to wait on the coroner to determine. Something that might help you nail his ass in court when you catch him."

"What's that?"

"Most serial killers have a sexual component to their murders. If the boy was sexually assaulted, the coroner may be able to find enough trace evidence that was the killer's semen for DNA tests. Catch him, test his blood, and voilà, killer on a silver platter."

"What makes you think the killer's a he," Jojola asked.

"Well, number one is I can name the number of female serial killers in the past twenty years on one hand," she said. "You men seem to have cornered the market. The other is, the neck wound was a single stroke. Even with a very sharp blade, it took a strong person to do that."

Gates held the rosary beads up in front of his face. "Something else that might help. Look closely at the medallion."

Jojola did as he was instructed. The back was blank, but the front side had the stamped image of what looked like a church, or more accurately, a cathedral. The building seemed vaguely familiar, but he couldn't place it. He was about to ask if she recognized it when there was an angry shout.

"What the hell is *he* doing here?" A burly man in a snow-white, straw cowboy hat, green uniform shirt, and sunglasses was stomping across the desert toward them. He was somewhat hindered in his movements by the too-tight blue jeans he was wearing, which made his more-than-ample beer belly hang over a salad plate–size silver belt buckle like spilled jelly from a tabletop. His body looked as if it belonged to two different men—the top half was disproportionately large compared to the tiny hips and legs that looked ridiculously inadequate for supporting the bulk above them.

"Evening, sheriff," Jojola said politely when the man drew close. "We heard that a citizen might have found one of our missing boys. I came over to render whatever assistance to your people I can." As he spoke, Gates sidled out of the line of fire toward where her graduate students had stopped working and were watching the action. She motioned for them to continue their efforts.

"Don' give me no evenin', sheriff bullshit, Jojola," Asher roared. His jowly face was beet red and he was wheezing like an old bellows from his effort to cross the thirty yards of desert, but he still managed to bellow, "Yer out a yer friggin' jurisdiction. Even if you weren't, the feds would handle anything more serious than another damn drunk Indian passed out in the gutter."

Asher was several inches taller than Jojola and outweighed him by fifty pounds. A Colt revolver hung Old West-style from the gunbelt around his hips. But he still remained at a safe distance from the Indian police chief as he ranted.

"That's true, sheriff," Jojola conceded mildly. "But seeing as how the deceased was kidnapped from the reservation, I'd think the media . . ." he nodded to where the members of the press, who were beginning to wander over to see what all the shouting was about ". . . might be interested in a show of interagency cooperation. And since the feds, as usual, are nowhere to be seen, I'm all you got."

Asher stopped at the mention of the media and looked behind him. In his opinion, the press was a bunch of smarmy liberal bastards, no matter how many beers he bought them on the county tab. They'd love a story for the evening news about how the conservative white Republican sheriff berated the poor noble savage. He lowered his voice to a menacing hiss. "Bullshit! Now, get the hell out a my crime scene 'fore I have you arrested fer interfering with an investigation . . . *chief.*" The way he said *chief* made it clear he was not referring to Jojola's official position, but as a sarcastic slur.

"No problem, sheriff," Jojola replied, his voice grown flat and his eyes flinty. "I was just leavin'." He took a step toward the sheriff and said in a low tone. "But if you ever disrespect me or my people like that again, I'll cut your tongue out of your fat face and feed it to my dog."

The smirk disappeared from Asher's face and was replaced by fear as he stumbled two steps back. His hand drifted to his revolver but another look at Jojola's face told him it was safer to draw a handkerchief from his back pocket and use it to mop up the beads of sweat that had popped out on his forehead.

Intended as an insult, Jojola turned his back on the sheriff, exposing himself to a coward's attack. He walked past two sheriff's deputies who also had wandered over to see what their boss was yelling about.

"If he shows up here again, arrest him, ya hear?" Asher snarled to the deputies as he stormed past them and headed to his car.

"Yes, sir," they replied, but it was clear from the look on their faces that they did not relish even the idea of trying to apprehend Jojola. They'd heard rumors that back in his drinking days, he'd sent four of their predecessors to the hospital when they tried to rough him up as he was staggering back to the reservation. And that was just with his fists, feet, teeth, knees, dirt, and rocks. Now, they could see the bone handle of his big knife jutting out from behind his back where he kept it in its sheath.

Jojola chuckled as he walked away. Sometimes having a reputation as a dirty fighter wasn't a bad thing, he thought.

12

As He trudged back to his truck, Jojola caught a sudden movement out of the corner of his eye and turned just fast enough to see a bushy gray tail disappear into a clump of low-lying junipers. "Well, brother," he said, "I see you are up to being helpful today. Thank you for leading us to one of our missing sons." One of the junipers trembled slightly, as if something had brushed past it.

John moved closer to the trees to see if he could get a better look at the coyote. He wondered if it was the same animal that had crossed his path on the highway. But as he moved around the clump, he came across the tracks made by two humans headed in the direction of the grave. One was made by small bare feet. The boy. The others by a very large man. Two hundred eighty pounds at least, he judged from the depths of the tracks in the sand, which also revealed that the man was wearing sandals and walked with a limp.

Jojola turned back to the stand of junipers. "Thank you again, my brother. There will be a bone for you outside my door tonight."

The beauty of the day was now lost to Jojola as he

drove back toward the reservation. He couldn't get the image of a huge dark shadow of a man limping across the desert pulling a crying child on a leash. He picked up his cell phone and called the Taos Police Department, asking for Detective Jorge Avila, a friend of his.

After the usual exchange of pleasantries and insults, Avila asked, "What's up?" He liked Jojola but knew the Indian wouldn't have called during business hours just to chat.

Jojola told him about the grave by the gorge, but not the suspicions about a serial killer being on the loose. "You have any reports of missing children, or hear of anything from the guys over in Santa Fe, particularly boys between the ages of say eight and thirteen?" he asked.

Avila hesitated long enough to let Jojola know that he was aware that he wasn't being told the whole story before answering. "There's always some kid running away," he said. "They usually turn up at a friend's house or Albuquerque, but you know that as well as I do. Nothing out of the ordinary though. Why?"

"Just workin' a hunch, Jorge," Jojola replied. "I'll fill you in later if it pans out. Thanks."

"Sure, John, you tight-lipped son of a turkey buzzard," Avila said with a laugh. "*Vaya con dios, amigo.*"

Jojola laughed back. "You go with God, too, my friend." He hung up just as he pulled into the parking lot of Father Eduardo's youth center to pick up his son, Charlie, who was standing and laughing with three adults, two of whom he recognized. One was the priest. The other was a young white girl he knew only as Lucy. Outwardly, she was not terribly attractive, even for an Anglo. He estimated her to be in her early twenties with a nose that rivaled his own and short, mousy brown hair. He'd originally taken her for a young man, as she had few curves to suggest otherwise.

He knew that she worked as a volunteer at the youth center and had at first figured her to be another guilt-ridden liberal out to right the wrongs of the past. They showed up, hugged a few poor Indian children, and left after a few weeks feeling better about themselves.

However, this girl was different. Jojola was a spiritual man and never stopped trying to grow in that regard. And yet, there were times since he had met the girl a month earlier that he felt in awe at the depth he perceived in her. It wasn't like she was trying to come off as some sort of saint. She possessed a healthy sense of humor that included a lot of sexual reference that made Jojola, who was a bit old-fashioned around women, blush. But there was something old about her eyes—green like Gates's but with flecks of gold—that gave him the impression that she had a soul older than his own.

Lucy was young and so he thought that it was possible that she didn't fully recognize her own depths. He wondered if she could speak to the spirits like some of the tribe's elders. But for all her spirituality, she was also warm and genuine, which was particularly evident with the kids at the youth center, all of whom, including Charlie, took to her like bees to honey. "She knows more than forty languages," his son told him one day. "She can speak Swahili and a bunch of Chinese. She's also learning Tiwa."

Jojola had taken his son's statement as an exaggeration. He figured she might know a couple of languages and had picked up a few words in several others, but forty? And the idea of her learning Tiwa was a joke. The language was unique to the Taos Pueblo and not taught to outsiders, even nice ones like Lucy.

Still, he had to wonder one day when he dropped Charlie off at the youth center and she'd greeted his son in the traditional manner. "Good morning, little brother." He was surprised, not just because she knew the words—which he figured she might have picked up by listening to others—but her inflection was as perfect as someone born to the pueblo. He'd later heard some grumblings among a few of the elders that the "strange" white girl might be a *bruja,* a witch, because she seemed to be learning Tiwa by magic. But they were in the minority. While many were not sure what to make of her gift for language, they recognized that she had a good heart and were not overly concerned. A few even suggested that if the spirits moved her to learn Tiwa as easily as some people drank water, then there had to be a reason for it.

Jojola didn't recognize the third person standing with his son. She had her back to him and he noticed the soft curls of black hair that covered her head and fell to her shoulders—too curly for Indian, but he thought she might be Hispanic. Only when she turned to face him did he realize she was none of the above but more likely Italian or Greek. She was a petite woman, one of those who were fortunate to keep their looks, making her age difficult to pinpoint, but he guessed somewhere between midthirties and early fifties. Whatever her age, she'd kept herself in shape and had nice curves in all the right places.

Jojola smiled as he got out of the truck and walked up to the trio. "Okay, Father, what did he do this time?" he said, indicating his son.

Charlie frowned until he realized that his father was joking.

• • •

It was not so funny a month earlier when Jojola got a call from the police chief of Taos, an old friend who'd been in the same class at the police academy. "I got your boy here, John," Bob Simmons said. "Sorry to have to tell you this, but they caught him shoplifting at the Taos department store. He was trying to wear a brand-new pair of Air Jordans out of the store but they had him on the surveillance camera. I talked to the store manager and told him that Charlie was a good kid—just made a mistake. He agreed not to press charges, but thought you ought to know."

Jojola sighed. He'd done his best to raise his son in the traditions of their people, which held honesty and respect for others above all virtues. Yet, it was one thing to raise a child in the ancient ways, and then have him grow up in a modern world. A bow and arrow was pretty boring compared to a Nintendo game. How could a homemade pair of moccasins compare to the latest basketball shoes sold by star athletes.

When it came to being able to afford the material goods of the white world, Taos was a poor pueblo. Those who had a talent for art that the white world had taken a fancy to over the past thirty years or so did all right. Some moved into Taos or even Santa Fe, where they were much sought after to attend fancy parties thrown by wealthy Anglos and Hispanics. Some of them hardly seemed to remember where they came from and only bothered to show up for the big festivals.

The diaspora of the young was one of the major issues facing the pueblo. Far too often, the pueblo's best and brightest went off to college, got a taste of a wider world, and didn't return, or again, only for family occasions and visits. There wasn't much work on the reservation—a few jobs in the casino, and some managed to start businesses, most of them catering to the seasonal tourist industry.

Meanwhile, alcoholism and drug abuse were epidemic on all the pueblos throughout the Southwest. One of the smaller communities down south had once reported that 100 percent of its adult population had either drug or alcohol addictions.

It was tough on the kids from the pueblo when all they had to do was walk a few miles into town and see what the Anglo and Hispanic kids owned. As his friend the Taos police chief had told the store manager, Charlie was a good boy but that had not kept him from trouble, mostly getting into fights with the town boys and playing hooky until the latest call.

Jojola drove to Taos and picked up his son at the police station. The first five minutes of the drive home, he held his temper and said nothing, hoping the boy would initiate the conversation. But Charlie sat quietly with his hands on his lap and his head down.

Finally, Jojola couldn't wait any longer. "Why did you do it, son?"

Charlie shrugged, and they drove on in silence for another minute. Then he blurted out, "I wanted new basketball shoes like the town kids got."

The answer angered Jojola. Even during his desperate affair with alcohol, he'd never resorted to stealing. "You shamed me, Charlie," he said. "And worse, you shamed yourself."

"You don't know what it's like," his son responded, tears streaming down his cheeks. "You think just because we live at the pueblo with no electricity and no television that I don't know what I'm missing. The rest of the world doesn't live like we do, and I'm tired of it. You know what some of the town kids call me? Fred Flintstone, because I live in a house from out of the Stone Age."

Jojola was stunned. He realized that while he was searching for his own peace of mind, he had brushed over what such a simple life might mean to his son. He would have to give it more thought, but at the same time, he could not excuse the theft of the shoes. "What do you think should happen now, Charlie?"

Charlie burst into tears. "Are you going to kick me out of the house?"

Jojola pulled over to the side of the road and put his arm around his son. "No, Charlie," he said. "There is nothing you could ever do that will make me stop loving you. I will always be your friend, and our home—the home of our ancestors—is as much yours as it is mine. I just want you to think of the ramifications of your actions. It's not just that you might get caught and punished. But say you got away with stealing those shoes, and say every boy who wanted new shoes just took them. The store would go out of business, and the people who make those shoes, their plants would close. All those people would be out of work; their moms and dads would be ashamed not to be able to put food on the table. I know this sounds like an exaggeration and maybe it is a little, but the point I'm trying to make is that sometimes our actions have consequences far beyond what we imagine. Do you understand?"

Charlie stopped sniffling and nodded his head. "Is there something I can do to make it right?"

Jojola thought about it for a moment, then turned the car around and headed for the department store. With an apprehensive but willing Charlie in tow, he went in and asked to speak to the manager. When he appeared, Jojola said, "My son would like to know if there's something he can do to make up for his mistake."

The manager considered the request. "Well, I don't need any help in the store," he said. "But I suppose he could ask Father Eduardo if there is some community service he could do. That would satisfy me."

So father and son had continued on their journey and gone to the youth center to find Father Eduardo. The priest said he had a job he thought that Charlie could do. He'd been contacted by the administrator for the St. Ignatius Retreat, who'd asked for cheap labor to help clean the retreat offices and meeting rooms once a week. "They are apparently short-staffed," he said. "I have one man, Lloyd Bear, who is trying to work off a guilty conscience and make a little money. He says he could use a boy's help and is willing to pay five dollars a night. It's kind of a late night, but Lloyd could drive Charlie to the retreat on Fridays after supper and then bring him home."

Jojola did not know Lloyd Bear very well. He was one of those who had gone off to college and not returned for many years until just recently. Still, he seemed nice enough when he took Charlie to meet him. "I will keep a good eye on him," Bear promised. "And it's just for the summer."

The job had gone well, and Charlie was excited by the money he was making. "I'll go into that store and buy those shoes by the end of the summer," he announced.

Now that Jojola had met Tobias, he had second thoughts about allowing Charlie to work at the retreat. But Father Eduardo didn't seem to have any problems with it, and it wasn't a good lesson for Charlie if he backed out of the agreement now because some psychiatrist gave him the creeps. He was proud of how his son had accepted his "work-release" program. He hadn't told Charlie yet, but he'd gone back to the store and purchased the Air Jordans as his son's "parole" gift.

Charlie had scowled when his father asked the priest in front of the women if he was in trouble again. But when he realized it was just teasing, he'd laughed along with the others when the priest answered, "Saint Charlie the Much Aggrieved? In trouble? Why nothing except that he inherited his father's habit of paying attention to pretty women such as these two here. I take it you've met Lucy Karp, who works with me, and her mother, Marlene Ciampi?"

Jojola nodded to Lucy. "I know Lucy but have not had the pleasure of meeting her mother." With the words out of his mouth, he felt like he'd made a complete fool of himself. Not had the pleasure? Where in the hell did that come from? He tried to recover by looking into the eyes of the woman, only to find out that one of hers was glass. Not knowing what else to do, he'd dropped his gaze only to find that he was now staring at her breasts. He'd quickly looked up to see her mouth adopt a strange little smirk. Come on, Jojola, get a grip, you're blushing like a schoolboy.

Generally, Jojola steered well clear of white women. He'd found they either wanted to rescue him or get him into bed, sometimes both. Years ago when he first got back from 'Nam, he'd gone along for the ride, so to speak, only to regret it in the morning. The worst were the lost women who thought that they wanted to be Indians. Some claimed that they'd discovered that they had one-tenth of a percent of Cherokee blood in them; others just knew that in some past life they'd been an Indian princess and were desperate to get back to their roots. Those saw him as their ticket into the tribe until he carefully explained that the people of the Taos Pueblo did not intermarry with other people. That got him labeled as a "reverse racist" on more than one occasion, until he finally decided that steering clear was the best course.

Marlene Ciampi extended her hand and said, "The pleasure's all mine." She gave him the knowing smile that women get when they've got a man flustered and on the run. But it was a friendly smile, full of humor at the situation.

Jojola smiled back, but he felt a jolt when their hands touched. It wasn't some man-woman chemistry he felt; more like sticking his finger into a spiritual light socket. Apparently, the waters ran deep in the women of this family. Only with Marlene Ciampi he sensed a battle going on beneath that surface between the light and the dark. He recognized it because he'd been there.

When their hands touched, the smile had disappeared briefly from the woman's face, too. But she'd recovered quickly.

Searching for an escape route out of the strange situation, Jojola looked at what she was holding in her left hand and got another shock. She was holding a string of rosary beads on which hung a gold medallion. He'd seen the twin of those beads not much more than a half hour earlier.

The woman followed his gaze and handed the beads to her daughter. "These are Lucy's," she said. "I'm afraid I'm something of a fallen Catholic myself. Father Eduardo and I are locked in a debate about whether I am too far gone to be saved."

The priest chuckled and patted her on the shoulder. "So long as you have the breath to ask for forgiveness, it is never too late, my child," he said.

Marlene Ciampi laughed, too, but Jojola noticed the change in her one good eye. The humor was tinged with sadness. He pointed to the beads in Lucy's hand and asked, "Can I ask where you got that?"

Lucy looked puzzled and held the beads up so that the setting sun struck the medallion. "These? A friend in New York City, Father Michael Dugan, gave them to me before I left," she said. "He runs a foundation my mother created with some ill-gotten wages made off the blood, sweat, and tears of the proletariat. These are a little showy for my tastes, but he was determined to give them to me."

"Can I ask what church that is," he said pointing to the engraving on the medallion.

Lucy looked where he was pointing. "You don't get out much do you?" she said. "It's St. Patrick's Cathedral."

"They're really nice. You wouldn't happen to know where your friend purchased the beads?" Jojola asked.

Lucy shrugged. She noticed the tension in his voice though he was trying to disguise it as friendly chatter. But she saw no reason to prevaricate. "I don't know for sure, but there are a number of little shops around the cathedral that cater to tourists and sell all sorts of gaudy holy junk."

The girl's mother broke in. "Are you some sort of collector of rosary beads, Mr. Jojola? Or can I ask why the third degree?"

Jojola looked at Marlene and realized that like his friend, Detective Avila, she was letting him know that she was aware that he wasn't asking idle questions. He admired her intuition, but he hesitated as he tried to think of how to respond.

The thought had quickly passed through his mind that given the circumstances, there could be a connection between the rosary beads found at the gravesite and these women. He was too good a cop to ignore such coincidence, if that was indeed what it was. But then he remembered that Lucy and her mother had not arrived in Taos until April, a month after the first boy disappeared and several days after the second. He also realized that Marlene would know if he tried to lie. "I'm working on a case in which an identical set of rosary beads is part of the evidence," he said.

Marlene and Lucy exchanged a look as if they'd expected him to say something of the sort. The mother was the first to speak. "Why don't you, Charlie, and Father Eduardo join us for dinner? Lucy and I are on a quest to find the best Mexican restaurant in northern New Mexico and you look like a man who knows his chilies."

The priest begged off saying that he had to close up the center in an hour. But Charlie had looked at his father with puppy dog eyes and Jojola nodded. "I know just the place, El Taoseno Restaurant," he said. "Best green chili in the world."

"Good, we'll buy the first round," Marlene promised.

"You're on," he said, "but I'm a cheap date—nothing stronger than Coca-Cola. Nobody loves a drunk Indian, you know."

The mother laughed. "Wasn't that the name of a movie starring Anthony Quinn?"

Jojola smiled in return. "Yeah, typical Hollywood. Get a Greek to play an Indian."

"Well, okay, then," Ciampi said. "Coca-Cola it is for you, though I'm personally hoping they have great margaritas. Did I tell you I am also searching for the perfect margarita? You won't mind if I toss back a pitcher or two? Lucy's my designated driver."

That's the polite sort of question you ask an alcoholic, he thought. More of that intuition; bet nothing much gets past this woman.

When he got in his truck, his son looked at him sideways and grinned. "A cheap date? What was that about? You know she's married, don't you?"

"Hell, yeah," he answered. Hell no, he thought. Somehow the probability that a good-looking, middle-aged Anglo woman with a daughter would be married seemed to have slipped my mind. "I was just being friendly."

"Yeah, right," Charlie said with a wink. A moment later, he was laughing and howling at the same time as his father grabbed the ticklish part of his knee and squeezed.

I love to hear him laugh, Jojola thought as he led the way out of the parking lot. It reminds me of his mother . . . she had a laugh like that. It had been a long time since he'd thought of Maria but, he discovered, it still cut like a knife.

13

"WHAT WAS THAT ALL ABOUT?" LUCY ASKED HER
mother as they followed the Jojolas to the restaurant.

"What was what all about?" Marlene replied.

"Oh come on," her daughter exclaimed, rolling her
eyes. "The deep looks, the pregnant pauses ... THE
FLIRTING!"

"I was not flirting," Marlene protested. "As you know, I
am a happily married woman—to your father, I might
add. I just wondered what he found so interesting about
your rosary beads. I'm sure you picked up on the fact that
he wasn't just asking idle questions."

Lucy nodded. "Yeah, I noticed it when he saw you
holding them. It was like someone turned on the cop
lightbulb. Whatever this case is that he's working on, it's
important to him personally as well as professionally. But
don't change the subject. You were flirting, or at least he
was and you absorbed it like a sponge."

Marlene turned her face to her daughter and gave her
a wet and loud Bronx cheer. "You're misinterpreting
friendly repartee between two *mature* grown-ups. Not
everyone is governed by hormones, no matter what that

twenty-year-old body is telling you. Now quit with the aspersions on my moral character," she said. "Or do I need to send a note to Dan Heeney about a certain young cowboy who seems to have his eye on a little filly named Lucy?"

"I have no idea what you're talking about. And you wouldn't dare," Lucy said blushing. Both women laughed, a sound that had been sparse in their relationship for the past couple of years but seemed to be making a comeback as of late.

As the giggles subsided, Marlene admitted to herself that John Jojola was indeed an attractive man. Not so much his looks, which were more exotic than handsome, though he had a nice smile that showed well against the bronze skin of his face, nor his physique—muscular, but shaped like a barrel. It was more the way he carried himself as though his body was simply the outward expression of some inner quality that made him seem taller than he actually was and self-assured. He's a lot like this land, she thought, steady, strong . . . harsh in a way but with a beauty that grows on you.

She also found his boyish shyness around women to be charming. Like most people, he'd had a difficult time trying to decide if he should focus on her one real eye or pretend that he didn't notice and look her in the eyes. Then, in his confusion, he'd dropped his gaze to her tits. She laughed out loud recalling the moment he realized what he was doing—and that he'd been caught—and blushed like a virgin at a strip show.

"What are you laughing about?" Lucy asked, an eyebrow raised suspiciously.

"Nothing, just a moment of silliness," Marlene answered. You have to admit he regained his composure quickly, she thought, and his eyes were laughing at his own discomfiture. She also liked that when he did look back at her face, it was without pity for the lost eye. In fact, his gaze was the sort most women enjoyed, polite admiration. But she had no illusions of the attraction going any further.

During her darkest days of hiding out on the dog farm on Long Island, when her nights were drowned in booze and self-loathing, she'd barely resisted the advances of Billy, the handsome young dog handler who'd made it known that he would come running if she whistled. The thought of trying to exorcise her demons on his tan, well-sculpted body had crossed her mind on a number of occasions when the loneliness threatened to strangle her and she felt she couldn't sink much lower anyway. But in the final analysis, she was still the Catholic schoolgirl who'd never been the sort to sleep around, even when she was single. The bottom line was she loved the man she'd married, and there was no one else she was willing to share her body with.

Just thinking about Butch, as well as the other two main men in her life—her sons, Giancarlo and Zak—made her homesick. Still, she was glad she had come to this big spiritual land and felt some of the power that seemed to mold the people who lived here like John Jojola. Nor was she ready to leave it yet . . . if ever.

Just before she fled New York City in April, Marlene felt like an overripe tomato about to burst in the sun. She knew that her family took her continued presence in the home after stopping the attempt to bomb the courthouse as a sign that she was returning to normal, whatever that was. But the truth was that every day she had to combat the urge to run away, back to the solitude and unquestioning loyalty of her dogs. There were too many dark memories, too many ghosts in New York City.

Leaving the loft on Crosby and Grand, she and Lucy headed north on Broadway until turning west into the Holland Tunnel. As they emerged on the other side of the Hudson River, they'd cheered as though they'd thrown off the shackles of city life and were embarking on some grand adventure. The high continued as they hit Interstate 80 and headed away from the rising sun.

The happy talk lasted most of the way across Pennsylvania, as they made a big show of mother-daughter bonding. But it couldn't last. By the time they hit Indiana, Marlene was beginning to regret encouraging Lucy when her daughter said she wanted to come on the trip.

It had seemed like a good idea, a way to recapture the closeness they'd once shared. They'd planned the route together, lying side by side on the living room floor as they poured over maps and tourist guidebooks. Their favorite was a photography book on New Mexico called *Land of Enchantment*, ooohing and aaaahing their way through page after page of exotic scenery.

They talked about what they were going to do when they arrived. And how, while they would be together, they would have their own projects "so we won't be getting into each other's hair." Marlene was going to learn to paint and sculpt. She avoided talking about the therapy side of the art center and Lucy let it be. Lucy was excited about the opportunity to assimilate a new language. "Tiwa—it's one of the oldest, most unique languages in the world; only the Taos Pueblo Indians speak it." She, too, skirted the deeper issues.

Through their friend Father Dugan, Lucy found a job

working at the youth center on the Taos reservation. It wasn't going to pay much, but enough to give her a little spending money while her mom paid for their rooms at a historic hotel called the Sagebrush Inn. "They even have fireplaces in the room," Lucy reported, after finding the inn on the Internet.

They'd agreed that as they drove they should take their time, get off the interstates as much as possible, and travel along the smaller "blue" highways that would give them a chance to explore small towns and see the real America. They'd tried their best to hold onto the original plan and the camaraderie—even taking a quick automobile tour of several of Indiana's famous covered bridges and agreeing that Clint Eastwood was far too old and wrinkled to be playing the leading man in romantic films anymore.

Yet the laughter was becoming strained and the conversations labored. Small talk and road games only went so far when there were deeper issues—internal, as well as between the two of them—waiting to break through to the surface. Gradually they fell silent, lost in their own thoughts as great expanses of the Midwest passed with only enough verbiage to arrange a restroom stop or something to eat. It began to seem like the monotonous fields of newly sprouted corn would never end; each town with its water tower and neat, tree-lined yards with American flags began to look like the one they'd just passed. At the beginning of their trip, they'd eaten at whatever they thought qualified as a quaint small-town café, thumbing their noses at the poor souls on the interstates who had no choice but to suffer through McDonald's and Taco Bell. But by the Nebraska-Iowa border they were tired of overfriendly or overgrumpy waitresses in stained aprons, and the way big sweaty men in John Deere hats and overalls stopped talking when Marlene and Lucy entered and stared at them as if they had come from another world.

The women decided to hop back on Interstate 80 so they could get there quicker, convinced that the miasma that had taken over the trip would evaporate when they crossed into the Land of Enchantment, as if it were the Land of Oz. They stopped only for gas, the restroom, and food—joining the poor souls who ordered their meals at the drive-thru, and kept going.

It was an unhealthy silence that built up inside of them like the thunderstorms that rose above the prairie every afternoon. The driver kept her eyes on the horizon, trying not to let the white lines passing under the hood hypnotize her into falling asleep at the wheel. Meanwhile, the passenger pretended to read a book—going over and over the same page when she'd lose focus—or simply stared out the window at the succession of isolated farmhouses and insectlike irrigation machines that spit and crawled across the fields.

By the time they reached the town of North Platte, three-fourths of the way across Nebraska, the politeness was gone, replaced by a testiness that had them both on edge and looking for a reason to fight. They got their chance when Lucy was pulled over doing ninety-five miles per hour.

"Going a little fast back there, ma'am," the trooper noted as he looked at her driver's license.

"I told her to slow down, officer, but you know kids, they never listen," Marlene said with a smile, leaning over from the passenger seat. She was hoping to sweet-talk her daughter out of a ticket, but Lucy took it differently.

"Don't treat me like a child," she snapped. "You were driving just as fast an hour ago."

"Oh, please," Marlene laughed. The trooper was peering in the window and although she couldn't see his eyes behind the sunglasses, his mouth was turned down in a frown. "I guess I should be driving, if you're going to act like a child."

"Fine!" Lucy exploded and opened the door, nearly hitting the trooper. She popped out of the car like a jack-in-the-box and stormed around the back of the car, as Marlene flung open her door and met her partway. "You want to drive, you drive," Lucy yelled, "but don't act like you haven't broken every law in the book and a few they haven't even thought of yet."

"Lucy that's enough," Marlene said. It was her turn to be angry. "You're such a saint. Breaking a rule or two might get you to stop walking around like you have a Bible stuck up your butt."

"At least I didn't run out on my family and shack up with Billy the Dog-boy of Long Island," Lucy sneered.

Marlene's hand responded without her thinking about it and slapped her daughter soundly across the cheek. More surprising, Lucy slapped her back. Suddenly the women were grappling, scratching, and shrieking. The alarmed trooper moved to break it up, but he wasn't fast enough, and the two wildcats tumbled off the shoulder of the road and down into an irrigation ditch filled with knee-high water. Mud, water, and curses flew every which way.

The young trooper was still trying to figure out how his day had turned into something out of the movie *Thelma and Louise,* and how he was going to get the women out of the ditch, when they suddenly sat down on their butts and started laughing. They were quite the sight—their clothing soaked and covered with a film of gravy-colored mud, as was their hair and the uncovered parts of their bodies.

"You look ridiculous," Marlene said between guffaws.

"Well, you're not exactly dressed for the opera," Lucy chortled.

The whole incident seemed impossibly funny, and they laughed until they were gasping for breath. Only then did it occur to them to look up at the trooper, who was standing on the edge of the ditch scratching his head. "You ladies aren't from around here are you?" he said.

Marlene and Lucy looked at each other and burst into laughter again. "Nope, we're from New York," they said in unison.

"Well, I guess that explains it," the trooper replied to additional gales. "Now, if you'd kindly stand up and give me your hands, I'll help you out of that ditch."

Once they were standing on the road, Marlene insisted on being allowed to change their clothes right then and there. "You're not getting in my baby like that," she warned Lucy.

Nebraska State Trooper Henry "Hank" Hudson was thinking that the boys back at the shop were never going to believe this one, when Marlene asked if he was going to watch them disrobe. He stammered and turned as red as the flashing light on top of his car. "I, uh, I'll just, um, stand over here," he said, fully aware now that neither woman was wearing a bra beneath her wet shirt. He turned and bumped into the rear of the truck, causing the women to laugh again.

Marlene produced a towel and a bottle of water with which they cleaned up as best they could before jumping into new shorts and shirts. "You may turn around now, officer," she said. "And do your duty to my poor child." But Trooper Hudson had been through quite enough with those two and let Lucy off with a warning. He even smiled when he said he hoped they'd wait until they reached Colorado before they decided to go for another swim. "Public nudity is illegal in Nebraska."

"The Mother of All Irrigation Ditch Battles," as the incident would forever be known in the family, proved to be the best thing that could have happened. The tension that had been building up for the past five hundred miles had been released, the way rain seemed to drain thunderstorms of their spite.

"I'm sorry, Luce," Marlene said as she pulled back on the highway, "for everything. I haven't been much of a mom."

Lucy shook her head. "You've got nothing to be sorry for. God seems to have some crazy plans for this family; you're just playing out the role given to you. Besides, I think that whole mom thing is vastly overrated. Look at all the messed-up kids raised by perfectly normal, nonfelonious mothers."

Marlene knew forgiveness wasn't as easy as all that and there would be tougher discussions. But at least it seemed that there would be time to delve into them, and for now it was enough that they could joke about it. "Well, you certainly turned out well, in spite of me," she said.

"Yeah, Saint Lucy the Virgin," her daughter replied.

"Yin to my yang," Marlene added, and they both laughed.

Reliving each moment of their battle and the consternation of "that cute" trooper Hudson, they drove across the border into Colorado, headed for the distant purple shadow on the horizon they figured was the Rocky Mountains. Humor had returned to the car, but there was something else that had been missing until the fight: the ability to really communicate on a level that would have been impossible until Trooper Hudson had pulled them over.

Marlene talked a little about the fears and guilt that drove her to seek asylum at the tail end of Long Island. "I'm not quite ready to go into this real deep," she said. "But I want you to know that it had nothing to do with any of you, except maybe—rightly or wrongly—this idea that I was somehow protecting you all from me."

Changing the subject to something lighter, Marlene even brought up her passing infatuation with Billy the Dog-boy of Long Island. But she had a motive that went beyond girls talking about guys.

Lucy had never told her parents much about her ordeal with the monstrous Felix Tighe. She said she couldn't remember everything, but Marlene believed that she recalled more than she let on and was trying to spare them the horrific details. The doctors at the emergency room where Lucy had been taken said she'd been sexually assaulted, though the lack of any semen or other bodily fluids indicated that the penetration was with an object other than his penis. So technically, Lucy was still a virgin, something she'd insisted she would maintain until marriage. But, especially after talking to Lucy's boyfriend, Dan Heeney, who told her that Lucy no longer wanted to fool around, Marlene was concerned that her daughter's interest in men had been crushed.

However, she wasn't quite ready for Lucy's response when Marlene noted that Billy had one fine set of buns.

"You fuck him?" Lucy asked.

"God, Luce," Marlene chuckled to cover her surprise at the question, "for a saint, your mouth would do a sailor proud."

"I learned at the knee of my dear mother," Lucy said. "So did you engage in sexual intercourse with Billy the Dog-boy? Maybe a little doggie-style?"

Marlene looked at her daughter, who was smiling but with anxiety written all over her face. Daddy's little girl wants to know if Mommy's been cheating on her hero, she thought, and was glad she could honestly answer, "No. But there were a few times when I wanted to."

The answer seemed to relieve Lucy, though she disguised it with humor. "Good, I'd hate to have a litter of puppies for siblings," she said. "Though to be honest, they might be easier to house-train than the two I've got."

Marlene smiled and thought maybe the moment had come to probe a little. "So have you given any more thought to when you're going to finally let Dan into the Promised Land?"

The smile disappeared from Lucy's face. "I don't know, Mom. Maybe never. It used to be I couldn't wait to get married just so we could do it. But sex just doesn't seem to hold any appeal for me right now."

Marlene nodded and bit her lip to keep from crying. She didn't care what her husband thought regarding even a Tighe's right to be considered innocent until proven guilty. If someone, probably David Grale, hadn't killed the asshole, she would have put a bullet through his black heart and happily accepted the consequences.

Before the mud-wrestling incident, the ensuing silence after Lucy's admission would have destroyed whatever chemistry they'd been experiencing. But while it was clear that Lucy didn't want to talk about sex or Tighe anymore, they now shifted into other subjects without missing a beat.

That evening they checked into the Brown Palace, a

famous hotel in downtown Denver from the days when cattle barons ran that part of the country and insisted on luxury when they came to town on business. After showers to remove the remaining traces of Nebraska, the women retired to the bar, where they downed pitchers of margaritas until the bartender said he had to close. They then staggered back to their room, where they fell asleep on the same bed, curled up together like a couple of kittens.

They woke up the next morning with an unkind troll banging drums and cymbals in their heads and a taste in their mouths not unlike a muddy Nebraska irrigation ditch. But they accepted their hangovers as a reasonable price for the change that had come over their relationship. As they climbed back in the truck to continue their journey, they were more than just mother and daughter. They were friends who'd finally gotten past the bullshit and could truly start on that grand adventure they had sought when crossing the Hudson into Jersey via the Holland Tunnel.

Rather than take Interstate 25 south to northeastern New Mexico, the women decided to first head west on Highway 285 out of Denver and into the looming mountains. For the first time in her life, Marlene, who took the first driving shift, was intimidated by a road. Normally fearless and lead-footed, she now crawled around curves that seemed designed to launch unsuspecting motorists off precipices or into forests.

After a harrowing climb up a narrow valley, they reached the top of Kenosha Pass. There the world seemed to open like a book as they looked with awe over hundreds of miles of flat plain ringed on all sides by snowcapped mountains. Even the sky seemed bigger than it did back east. Limitless. "Closer to heaven," Lucy whispered.

Driving down the other side of the pass, Marlene experienced something akin to vertigo. The thought crossed her mind that if she wasn't in her truck, she might have just dissipated into the immensity of her surroundings, like water sizzling off a hot skillet. The feeling continued for Marlene as they crossed the high-mountain plain called South Park. Only she began to imagine that the clean, crisp mountain air was stripping away the defenses she'd erected around her psyche, or soul, peeling each layer like sunburned skin. She wondered if there would be anything left by the time they reached New Mexico. *At least anything worth saving.*

Feeling vulnerable and shaken, she turned her thoughts to her husband, whom she considered the most stable force in the universe. When they met almost thirty years earlier, he was just recovering from the blow of his first wife leaving him for a woman. Most men she knew would have let that batter their egos into a simpering shell of manhood, or an angry misogynist. But he'd accepted his first wife's departure as simply a sad ending to an important chapter in his life, one he blamed on his own preoccupation with his job and failure to be a good husband, rather than her betrayal.

Marlene believed that her husband's lack of recrimination was connected to his mother's death from cancer when he was in high school. She knew the loss had shaken him to his core, but it was one of the few areas in their relationship where he allowed no trespass. He explained that it wasn't something he liked to talk about, and that he'd put it all behind him. "Part of life," he'd say before immediately changing the subject.

As a result, Marlene knew only the easy-to-talk-about aspects of his younger years. He'd always described himself as fortunate to have come from a family situation in which he had the support and unconditional love of both parents. He'd thought of his home, he said, as a refuge where he always felt safe and secure. When Lucy was born, it was something he told her he wanted for their children. Lot of good it did him, she thought as she passed through the shadow of fourteen-thousand-foot Mount Princeton, having made the mistake of choosing Marlene Ciampi to plant his seed in.

Whatever their role, Butch was as good and decent a man as any Marlene had ever known. In fact, better than all but a very few, and most of those were priests or monks. He wasn't religious in the sense that Lucy was religious. He didn't go to the synagogue or celebrate the holy days. But he lived by a code of personal conduct that drew a line in the sand between right and wrong with very little no-man's-land in between. While other men, even basically good men, would find ways to justify bending the rules or looking the other way for personal gain or to avoid problems, Butch stuck to his principles, even if it cost him professionally, financially, or personally.

However, such values weren't always easy to live with, especially because she was no angel. There were times when she thought him impossibly rigid and wished that he could lighten up, be more human, or at least accept that not everyone, including his wife, saw the truth through the same prism.

When they talked about it, she'd pointed out that the world ran on compromises and that no one knew what was right for everyone else *all* the time. He'd shrugged and said, "I can only say what's right for me. I do happen to believe that rules are the cornerstone of civilization and that compromises, while necessary in personal relationships, when used by the government to simply make things run smoother or for the greater good erodes the foundation. It's like most of the people who keep the district attorney's office in business. The first time they commit a crime, it's usually out of desperation or stupidity; they may even feel remorse. But once the line is crossed, the next time becomes easier, the voice of their conscience quieter, until it is silenced altogether. The same for us when we start fudging on the rules, or look the other way. It becomes easier until the little voice that tells us something isn't right becomes mute. The government wants access to private information, or maybe relaxed search-and-seizure laws, and because we're afraid of the next terrorist attack or the criminals, we go along with it. We tell ourselves that when the threat is gone, we'll go back to the way it was . . . but will we? Can we?"

It made her angry that she could think of no better argument than that she believed there were times when the ends did justify the means. Take the Iraq War, for instance. As far as she was concerned, Saddam Hussein was just another murdering piece of shit who needed to be cast from the circle of humanity. The world didn't need an excuse to take him out, any more than most of those same bleeding hearts who protested the war wouldn't have shed a tear if a homegrown mass murderer were gunned down in their neighborhood by the police. Except that then they would understand the threat because it was right outside their door. Yet she knew that her husband would have insisted that Satan himself be given his Sixth Amendment right to a fair trial.

It was because Butch was who he was that she didn't want him to go into politics. She thought that for all his real-world experience with the worst of human nature, her husband could be incredibly naive. He had this dream of returning the office to the days of old man Garrahy. But as much as she loved him and admired his principles—most of the time—she also felt that he was kidding himself to think that one man could make a difference. The district attorney's office had changed, turned into a monster of a bureaucracy. Its mission was no longer the dispensation of justice, but giving the appearance that something was actually being done to rein in the criminals. She worried that his refusal to bend would leave him broken and dispirited when he finally had to accept the futility of his quest.

Marlene would have preferred, if he insisted on remaining with the DA, that he stay in the second spot—let someone else deal with the bureaucratic headaches, the press, and the politics. Better yet, she thought he should go into private practice. "You've done your share, more than your share," she told him one night as she was lying in his arms resting between amorous bouts. "Let someone else pick up the gauntlet. You could choose among the biggest law firms, all of which would kill to have Butch Karp come on as a partner. Exercise that fine mind in front of the Supreme Court, become a justice yourself. Or, if you like, hang a shingle out of the Village and defend NYU students' right to smoke pot." He didn't say anything, but she felt his body grow tense, and it had taken her very special attentions to get him to relax again. She'd stopped talking about it that night and instead fell asleep and dreamed of running away with him to some distant island where the population had no concept of legal briefs.

When he'd called a family meeting some weeks later and asked their opinion of his running for office, she'd declined to give hers. "I haven't been around enough lately that I feel I have a right to say," she insisted. But one of the reasons she'd left for New Mexico was she didn't want to be a wet blanket on her husband's aspirations.

However, it was not the main reason. That was far more personal, dark, and deep than whether Butch ran for office. After her son was shot, she had no qualms about asking her friend, Tran Do Vinh, the Vietnamese gangster, to seek retribution. She felt she had all the prima facie evidence necessary to live with her decision. A family she had befriended had been brutally murdered and her son blinded by the men she wanted Tran and his men to kill. The law had stumbled when it was supposed to protect the innocent, and then acted as though it was powerless to deal with the murderers. So she had taken it upon herself to set justice back on its feet.

It wasn't as though she didn't feel any guilt for arranging what was essentially the execution of other human beings, some of them "collateral damage," otherwise known as women and children. They'd joined the other unquiet ghosts whose deaths she'd had a hand in; but their voices and faces, the nightmares and personal sacrifices, were a price she'd thought she could live with.

She wasn't, however, as prepared for the look in the eyes of her husband, even if he loved her too much to say what he was thinking. *Felon. Murderer?* He mostly chose to ignore it, but she knew that it put him in conflict with his principles. She hated being the one—probably the only one besides his children, and they never would have done it—who could make Butch Karp look the other way. She wondered if she was any better in the final analysis than the people she'd killed or had killed. Yes, they had been vicious men who preyed on the innocent people who had no one else willing to step up, including the law. But that same law—the law Butch, and at one time she, had sworn to uphold—held that murder was murder, even when it was evil men who died.

Haunted by a guilty conscience, hurt by her husband's unspoken censure, worried about her influence on her family, she'd moved to the dog farm in part to get away from the constant reminders and from there, perhaps, fade away until no one remembered Marlene Ciampi. But her family wouldn't let her go quite so easily.

Butch had gone to great lengths to point out that her latest fatal outburst—the run-in with the terrorist bombers—had not only saved many innocents lives, "and mine," it had not been motivated by revenge or vigilante justice. When she looked in his eyes, she saw that he was speaking the truth about how he felt and that made a difference. The mayor of New York had even given her a commendation for bravery that further reinforced the notion that maybe she wasn't a completely lost cause. It was enough that for the first time in a year she'd felt comfortable sleeping in her own bed with her beloved husband snoring beside her. But the issues didn't just go away.

As she'd told Lucy following their mud-wrestling exhibition, there was also the belief that she needed to protect her family from Marlene Ciampi. She considered herself a magnet for violence. She knew that a good percentage of the danger her family had experienced over the years had more to do with her husband's career than her penchant for trouble. Even the letter bomb that took her eye and scarred her face was intended for him. But that was in the line of hazards associated with his job. She, on the other hand, gravitated toward danger—not always consciously— like heroin addicts drifted toward Times Square looking for a fix. Nor did she always weigh the unintended consequences of her actions. Case in point, Giancarlo had been placed in harm's way because she took on the role of avenging angel for the murdered family.

What was the old saying? Live by the sword, die by the sword. Marlene had been convinced for years that sooner or later, she would be the one who got careless or moved a split second too late, and wouldn't survive. She didn't want her family near when the sword fell, especially if it came down on their heads as well.

Again, her family had refused to let her wallow in that mire of self-indulgence. Giancarlo wouldn't even let her apologize for what happened to him. Sometimes she wondered where he came from, as it was hard to believe that such an angel was actually a child of her womb. He was such an old soul that he often made her feel spiritually immature. For the most part, Giancarlo had accepted his affliction as just part of his growth as a human being, like puberty. Instead of feeling sorry for himself, he'd focused on music and the inner person. It was as if he were exploring the phenomenon of being blind in a sighted world like a spelunker who drops his flashlight in a cave. A new challenge, but nothing to panic about. He said he did feel sorry for those who had been blind since birth. "At least I have home movies I can play up here," he told her, tapping his head. Still, there'd been a number of times that she'd noticed a fleeting sad look on his face when his brother, Zak, left to play a sport or got involved in a project that required sight. Only then did she understand that some of his good cheer was just him being brave.

Lucy and Giancarlo were much alike, almost too good to be true. As she and her daughter drove south through the San Luis Valley of Colorado, Lucy had returned to the subject of Felix Tighe. But it was only to point out that what happened with Tighe wasn't Marlene's fault; he was out to destroy their entire family because Butch had destroyed his and put him in prison.

Of all her family, Marlene worried the most about her influence on Zak. There was no doubt that he was her son. He wasn't a bad kid—he had a big, generous heart and was loyal and brave to a fault. But he'd shown early on that he was willing to cut corners to achieve his ends and lied like Pinocchio if it was easier than telling the truth. He was like her, too, in that he didn't hesitate to resort to violence if he felt that he or someone he loved, particularly his brother, was threatened. It wasn't only school bullies who had to worry, either. When the terrorists attempted to kidnap Giancarlo, one had ended up with Zak's knife planted firmly in his thigh and their plans thwarted.

Zak actually admired her for the traits that troubled her husband and worried her other two children. If she'd been willing, he would have happily had her recount every bloody incident like a boy listening to his father's war stories. She wasn't willing but that didn't stop her from worrying that the longer she was around him, the more her personality would rub off on him.

Marlene was not at all sure why she chose New Mexico for her escape. She'd been talking to Father Dugan one afternoon after meeting with the board of the charitable foundation she'd financed and he ran, when he asked how she was doing. He was aware of her self-exile, probably from Lucy, and had an inkling of what troubled her.

Maybe it was her Catholic upbringing, but Dugan was the one man she felt she could confess to without his judging her. So she'd talked about the demons of guilt that rode her back and her concern that she was a danger to her family. "Sometimes I feel like I'm just going insane, and soon I'll end up pushing a shopping cart full of all my earthly possessions up and down the Avenue of the Americas," she said. She said it with a half smile, but even that disappeared when she whispered, "And to tell you the truth, there have been times when I've doubted whether I want to live at all."

Dugan had not brushed off the suicidal ideation, nor had he given her the standard Catholic priest spiel about it being a mortal sin. Instead, he'd reached inside his desk and pulled out the brochure for the Taos Institute of Art Healing. She'd looked at it briefly, then smiled and slid it back across the desk at him.

"Therapy?" she asked. "Been there, done that. Most of the psychologists I've met need as much help as I do, maybe more. I've had it with lying on a couch talking my ass off—excuse the French—while some guy who couldn't make it in a real science sits there saying, 'I see. I see,' when really they don't see any more than any street-corner philosopher. And I'm not the sort to sit in a circle with ten other loonies to compare war stories so that we'll feel better because the others are even more messed up than you are. Or maybe practice falling backward into each other's arms so we can learn to trust."

Dugan slid the brochure back. "You need to talk to

somebody, Marlene, who can speak to you objectively," he said. "You know I'm always here for you. But I don't think you need a priest as much as you need someone who can tell you where you're full of merde—excuse the English—and where you're not. I think you need to get away from New York City, and I don't mean digging a hole out in Long Island and jumping in. But somewhere you might actually enjoy being. Forget the therapy crap if you want, and just look at that beautiful country. I know these people and have sent other troubled souls to them with great results. I have an old friend who is a priest in Taos working with the Indians, and he recommends them highly as well, based on some of the work they've done with victims of domestic violence on the reservation. . . . And who knows, maybe you're the next Georgia O'Keeffe—she lived and worked in Taos, you know. Sell your paintings and make enough money so you can start another foundation to help the poor and assuage your feelings of guilt because you sent a few miscreants back to hell where they belong. Pardon the blasphemy; we Catholic priests, of course, believe that every life is sacred. Some are just more sacred than others in my book."

Dugan paused and reached across the desk to take her hands in his big rough ones. She thought his eyes looked tired and sad as he quietly added, "Or you can do nothing and wait until the demons win and you're no longer around for the family who loves and needs you. We all need you, Marlene. There is more good in your soul than you know, and I have a feeling that before the end that will matter to many people."

Marlene smiled and squeezed his hands. Then more to humor her friend than a real interest, she took the brochure with her and said she'd think about it.

When she got home she put the pamphlet on the night-stand and there it sat for a week before she went to bed one night and with nothing else to read, picked it up. She had to admit that there was something about the photograph on the front page of Taos Mountain, a pointed cone blanketed with snow and pine trees rising from what looked like a desert, that intrigued her. Maybe it was the nothing-to-hide honesty of landscape; it was just there. She opened the brochure to read what it had to say about its art programs and how they were tailored to help women who were "suffering from post-traumatic stress disorder associated with violence in their lives." She thought that the writer of the brochure was probably talking more about women who were victims of violence, rather than perpetrators, but she called the center the next morning anyway.

The administrator who took the call assured her, after Marlene gave her a brief synopsis of her background, that the center's clients did not fit a single mold. "We don't use the word *victim*," she said. "Not because it's not accurate, but because the word is debilitating; it allows us to sit around felling sorry for ourselves, or engage in self-destructive behavior, instead of taking responsibility for our own recovery. We, of course, have women who have been raped or beaten or shot, often by people who are supposed to love them. But we also have women who have done the beating or shooting, though granted for some it was in self-defense. You may be unique in your circumstances, but you are not alone in being unique."

"So how long will it take for you to screw my head back on straight?" Marlene asked as a test. She figured that anyone who was offering a cure through finger painting was either a quack, a con, or kidding themselves and her.

"That's up to you," the administrator said. "We offer classes in different forms of self-expression through art, with the idea that it might lead to asking yourself the right questions for the answers that are already there. I know that sounds like a lot of gobbledygook, but you might eventually understand what I mean. But there's no responsibility to perform here. No requirements, other than you follow a few basic rules mostly having to do with respecting the rights and privacy of the other clients. If you want to talk to one of the counselors, gain a little insight from an outsider's perspective, you talk. If you just want to splash paint around or pound on clay, well, we believe in a form of therapy where the best answers are the ones you can discover within yourself if given space and time, which is what most people don't have in our world. . . . By the way, do you like Mexican food, or I should say, New Mexican cuisine?"

The tangential question caught Marlene off guard. "Yes," she said, "such as it is here in Manhattan."

"Then even if you come to Taos and decide we're full of bullshit, you won't be wasting your time," the administrator said with a laugh. "You haven't lived until you've set your mouth on fire with our Hatch chilies or gorged on a blue corn enchilada smothered in homemade green pork chili. And did I mention, Taos is one of the most beautiful places in the world."

Marlene liked the administrator and the low-key approach appealed to her. What the hell, she thought, I could use a vacation, and I've always wanted to be an artist . . . at least as of five minutes ago. "Okay, you've convinced me. How do I sign up?" she asked. "And are there any rules against margaritas?"

The family had taken her sudden announcement well.

At first the boys had looked dismayed at the thought that she was leaving them again, only this time she was going farther. But after she explained she was enrolling in an art school, their faces brightened at what they thought was really a further sign that she was again interested in normal mom things instead of shooting people.

Marlene hoped so, too, but she couldn't completely break from old habits. Despite assuring Lucy that she was heading west unarmed, she'd secreted her Glock 9mm beneath the driver's seat of the truck. It was cheating, but she meant it only as a security blanket; she was as lost without a gun nearby as other women were without their purses.

14

AFTER CROSSING INTO NEW MEXICO, THE TWO
women stopped at a hot springs resort in the mountains
called Ojo Caliente. Lucy, who was a walking, talking
tourist brochure, said that since ancient times the Indians
had thought that the mineral baths had healing properties. The two women didn't know about that but the out-
door pools—with varying degrees of temperature from
bathtub warm to just shy of scalding—certainly took care
of a number of aches and muscle knots that had formed
while they were driving across half the continent.

As she settled back in a pool that night, Marlene was
amazed by the stars overhead. When she was talking to
the Taos center's art director, the woman told her that
one of the reasons the Santa Fe–Taos area was considered such a painter's paradise was its clear light. She said
scientists had actually ascertained that the skies over
northern New Mexico were the clearest in the United
States. "Consequently, our sunrises and sunsets, the way
the light strikes cloud formations and the landscape, is
unique," the woman said. "I hate to use the word,
because it means different things to different people, but

what always comes to my mind is *pure*. Sometimes it's like seeing, really seeing, something or someone for the first time."

The night sky Marlene was marveling at could also be attributed to the clarity. At an elevation of about eight thousand feet above sea level, there was less atmosphere to block the fainter stars and, removed from any major town or city, less light pollution to compete with the starlight. In one region of the sky, there seemed to be more stars than there was space between them, a veritable roadway of twinkling lights of various sizes, brightness, and even color—incandescent white, yellow, red, even an icy blue.

"The Milky Way," Lucy said, following her gaze.

Intellectually, Marlene knew that the night sky was not a flat surface through which the stars as pinpricks of light shone through. Astronomy had been required at Sacred Heart Catholic High School, and she'd been on the usual field trips to the planetarium. But only now could she fully comprehend that the universe had depth and form. Only now did she really understand what an insignificant piece of rock she and the rest of mankind were floating around on, and how even smaller that made her.

Only a couple of days earlier, Marlene might have recoiled at the thought. She'd been stripped of her shell by the purity of nature, humbled before its age and grandeur. But now, aided by a bottle of red wine, she felt that perhaps the cleansing had a reason. Instead of approaching this phase of her life as a glass so full that there was no room for anything new, she had been emptied and was ready to learn again. With that thought came the overwhelming feeling that there were forces in motion that in her current state she could not understand, at least not yet, but that in some way she had a role to play in some drama as Lucy and Dugan had each noted. She hoped that it would be as a hero and not a villain. But for the moment she was content to soak in the beauty of the night as a chorus of yipping and howling suddenly rang down from the hills around Ojo Caliente as the coyotes greeted the rising of the full moon.

The Land of Enchantment proved to be as exotic during the day as at night, when the women left the resort in the morning to complete their journey to Taos. Coming from the East where the undergrowth and hardwood forests occupied every inch of ground not kept clear by man, this land was almost barren, the vegetation sparse and built for survival in an arid climate. There was something almost alien about the rust-red and white rock formations and hills—mesas, according to Lucy—so flat on top that they looked as if some giant had scraped them off with a trowel. It was a land full of surprises. They would be driving along what appeared to be a flat stretch, unbroken for fifty miles, and suddenly the land on either side of the road would plunge off into deep ravines that would cause either driver to hit the brakes and crawl along as though the space might suck them over the edge.

New Mexico was beautiful, they agreed, more vivid than their photography book had been able to portray. But it was in a way they struggled to define. Not the awe-inspiring grandeur of the Colorado mountains. More subtle. As if the land was patient enough to wait for its qualities to ensnare the viewer over a long period of time.

As they continued south, the women noticed that the highway was a death trap for a variety of animals. Deer, raccoons, skunks, rabbits, snakes, and indistinguishable lumps of bloody fur littered the blacktop and shoulders. These attracted the carrion eaters, including the large black bird standing in the middle of the road next to the remains of a badger when they stopped the car to take a photograph of Taos Mountain, which had appeared in the distance.

Marlene thought the bird was a crow, but Lucy informed her that it was a raven. "In many Native myths, the raven is often a thief—sometimes good, in that he takes things back that someone else has stolen and gives them to the owners, but there is also an evil version who is greedy and steals for his own purposes."

Marlene had turned to look at her daughter for the discourse on Indian mythology. When she looked back, the raven was staring at her with a piece of bloody meat dangling from its shiny beak. It cocked its head to the side and fixed her with an eye so black that it would have looked empty except for a glint. With a casual motion, it threw its head back and tossed the meat down its gullet. The bird then gave her another look and opened its beak to caw. She got the distinct impression that the creature was laughing at her and shivered involuntarily.

Get ahold of yourself, Ciampi, she thought, it's a big black bird. They don't laugh, especially not at people. She decided that Lucy's Indian mysticism talk and the alien landscape had gotten to her. The bird, which had taken a couple of steps toward her, had injured its leg at some point in the past and walked with a limp. Good, maybe that'll slow you down and somebody will run your ass over, she thought. Then maybe the badger's cousin will come along and pick at your bones. The bird gave an angry retort and flew away.

"Guess he didn't like us disturbing his lunch," Lucy said.

"Yeah," Marlene agreed, "guess not. Fuck him."

• • •

The women drove into Taos and were instantly charmed by the adobe buildings and narrow streets. A wedding of a young Hispanic couple had just taken place with the newlyweds, their family, and friends driving around the old town square honking their horns as shopkeepers came out of their stores to wave along with the locals and tourists.

The romance of the place did not fade when they pulled into the parking lot of the Sagebrush Inn south of town. As Lucy had noted from the inn's Web site, the Sagebrush had been built in 1929 as a way station for travelers on their way to Arizona and points west. It had also served as a magnet for artists and writers. The painter Georgia O'Keeffe had lived and worked there for a time, as had the novelist D. H. Lawrence.

The original building was now the cantina and lobby. The rooms were plastered with the ubiquitous adobe and featured ceiling beams of polished logs and were furnished with heavy Spanish-style furniture covered in geometrical Southwest designs. The bathrooms were works of art with tiled floors and sinks. As promised, their adjoining rooms each contained its own small fireplace, and they were delighted that the evenings were cool enough to light a fire and sit side by side watching the flames and holding hands.

Marlene was just as delighted that she only had to leave her room and cross the courtyard to reach the cantina. It featured a big wooden bar of the sort seen in cowboy movies. The walls were decorated with Navajo blankets, the namesakes of longhorn cattle, and various styles and qualities of Western art including, the bartender told her, several originals by the famous Indian painter R. C. Gorman.

At night, the cantina was packed with customers there to dance to a country-and-western band. Many of the patrons looked like they'd also stepped out of one of those movies. The men wore cowboy hats and pointy-toed boots, and the women full-length fringed skirts or jeans with belt buckles the size of chastity belts. Granted, some of the men were what natives referred to as "California cowboys," in that their western finery was all for show, and they'd never been closer to a horse than a carnival carousel. Their hands were soft, having never known a day's hard labor, much less a lifetime of it.

Of course, there were real cowboys, too. Men who worked on the ranches outside of town. When they shook her hand, it felt like she was gripping a piece of wood or rough leather; they were the hands of men who worked with rope and barbed wire and horses. But as hot and dusty as their work could be, she never saw them slumming when they came into the bar. They always dressed up in new blue jeans so tight—to the sighs of the women from New York City—that it seemed it would be impossible for them to do anything except stand up straight. Along with the jeans, the men wore fancy western shirts with Southwest patterns and mother-of-pearl snap buttons, and well-shined dress-up boots. They sported the big silver belt buckles, too, only theirs had engravings on them like 1999 Taos Bull-Riding Champion.

The Anglos, as the women learned whites were referred to, weren't the only race represented in the bar. Half the crowd was comprised of Hispanic men, who wore their own versions of western finery, handsome with their trim moustaches and dark, piercing eyes. The Latinas were their physical matches with their shining black hair and dazzling white smiles. Some of these vaqueros and senoritas, according to the bartender, were from families who had lived in the area since the sixteenth century. "They actually consider Mexicans who cross the border to work in this country to be outsiders," he said. "More so than the Anglos."

Of course, he noted, the Indians had been in the region much longer than any of them, but only their men were represented at the Sagebrush cantina. Some wore big black hats with round crowns and flat brims with lots of silver encircling their wrists. Others simply wore their dark hair loose so that it fell about their shoulders.

Anglo, Hispanic, or Indian, they all seemed to be accomplished western dancers. After a margarita or two, Marlene and Lucy allowed themselves to be taken out onto the dance floor and swirled, spun, and dipped. Sometimes their partners moved at such breakneck speed that it might have been alarming except that there was also the feeling that their partners were in complete control and so they learned to relax and just go with it.

The men were unfailingly courteous, tipping their hats, opening doors, and rising from their seats if a woman stood or approached their table. They also addressed women as "ma'am," and in such a way that it didn't sound like an age thing but a gallantry that was all but lost in New York City, even in polite company.

A couple of young cowboys took an immediate fancy to Lucy. After a couple of weeks, one in particular, Ned Blanchet, had persisted enough in staking his claim that Marlene began teasing her daughter about her "new boyfriend."

Ned was a ranch hand—"We don't call ourselves cowboys," he'd politely informed them—who worked on a spread east of town and had a nighttime job as a watchman at a Catholic retreat in the foothills north of the city. It was apparent that he didn't have much formal education; in fact, he proudly announced soon after they met that he'd quit high school and started working at age fifteen. He wasn't much to look at—his thin features a bit too irregular, his teeth never having been introduced to an orthodontist, and his ears stood out like satellite dishes. But Marlene thought that there was something about the Southwest sun and weather that gave even a homely face a rugged quality that made up for some of the niceties; not to mention he had a lean, lithe body "to die for . . . not that I noticed."

Lucy confided to her mother that her "friend, not boyfriend," Ned, wasn't the pushy sort. In fact, he'd never ever tried to kiss her (a remark tinged with just a hint of disappointment, to Marlene's delight). He was the perfect romantic cavalier.

Once as they were leaving the dance floor, a tall, bodybuilder type, who'd been leaning on the bar and drinking heavily most of the night, made a remark about Lucy's breasts, or lack thereof, as she and Ned passed. Ned had immediately spun on his boot heels, but Lucy, the eternal pacifist, insisted that he let it go. But the other man, who was obviously one of the aforementioned California cowboys in an ill-fitting straw ten-gallon hat and brand-new boots that had never seen the inside of a stirrup, did not.

"Looked like a couple of boys dancing out there," the man announced in a booming voice. He was apparently impressed with his own size, bank account, and the fact that he came from Los Angeles. "I guess that's what you locals would call coyote ugly."

This time Lucy wasn't able to stop Ned when he turned and walked back to where the loudmouth smiled as he approached and struck a karate pose. A second later the stranger was on his back, laid out by a single punch to the nose from a man he outweighed by forty pounds.

"Apologize to the lady," Ned said evenly.

"Ned, it's not necessary . . . ," Lucy began.

Ned looked her in the eye and then back at his stunned opponent who had raised himself on his elbows as blood poured out of his nose, ruining his expensive new shirt. "Sorry, Lucy, but this is a matter of principle. Now," he spoke again to the man on the floor, "apologize unless you want me to put the toe of my boot where the sun don't shine . . . pardon the expression, Lucy."

The man looked once at Ned's boots, then his balled fists, and then the steel-gray eyes. The band had stopped playing and the crowd was quietly watching the drama, hoping for more action. But the man swallowed his pride and tried to make amends despite his broken nose. "Thorry. Nhidn't nean it."

"That's better," Ned replied. "Now I'm going to turn my back and escort the lady to her seat. When I turn around, I think it'd be best if you had skedaddled on out of here. I don't know much 'bout Los Angeles, but out here, we still treat women with respect." The man did as told and was last seen spinning the wheels of his Porsche in the gravel parking lot and heading for friendlier territory.

At her seat, Lucy acted mortified that violence had been done on her behalf. She spent several minutes lecturing Ned that "words aren't worth fighting for," and that she would have preferred if he had simply "ignored the asshole." The young cowboy took the tongue-lashing with his head bowed, hat and hands on his lap. "Yes, ma'am. Sorry, Lucy, won't happen again. Yes, ma'am. No, ma'am."

When Lucy decided Ned had suffered enough, she bestowed a smile on him like a queen showing mercy on an erring, but much-loved, subject. "Well, aren't you going to ask me to dance, my Galahad?"

Ned's head popped up and he broke into a gap-toothed smile. He had no idea what a Galahad was, but it sure sounded fine coming from Lucy's pink and promising lips. He scooted back his chair and stood in one fluid motion. Extending his hand, he said in his best knight errant, "I'd be mighty pleased, Lucy, if you'd do me the courtesy of a dance."

Under other circumstances, another city perhaps, Lucy would have laughed at the exaggerated chivalry. But here in the American Southwest, gallantry was as natural as the yipping of the coyotes she could hear coming from the desert late at night as she stood on the balcony outside her room. She smiled demurely and gave up her hand. A minute later, she was laughing wildly and Ned was beaming as they whirled to the frantic pace of the "Orange Blossom Special."

At her seat, Marlene wondered where the cowboys— or ranch hands—were when the world needed them. She liked Dan Heeney, a sweet, intellectual boy, but he was not the sort to make a frightened young woman feel secure in the arms of a man again. She didn't see Lucy, a scholar and language savant, settling down with a barely literate ranch hand, either. But for the moment she was happy that Lucy was discovering that a man could be both hard and soft. And for once, you horny slut, you don't mean that sexually, she thought as she left the young couple dancing slowly, chest to chest, to the band's rendition of Willie Nelson's "Blue Eyes Crying in the Rain."

Marlene went back to her room, undressed, and,

breaking one of the rules of the center, called her husband, who, once he'd established that there was no emergency, reminded her that there was a two-hour time difference. "It's 1:00 AM in Manhattan, you know," he said yawning in her ear.

"Well," Marlene purred, "I just thought you might want to know that I'm lying naked on my big king-size bed, with a fire going, which made me feel all . . . ummmm, how should I put this . . . ummmm, all warm and fuzzy . . . if you know what I mean." She paused. "But I guess you want to go back to sleep. . . ." She paused again but didn't have to wait long for the response.

"No, that's okay . . . I really wasn't tired." Butch sounded suddenly wide awake. "Uh . . . what was that you were saying about being naked?"

Two weeks later, as she pulled into the parking lot of El Taoseno and alongside the Jojolas, Marlene recalled how the rest of that conversation had gone and laughed again.

"Now what?" her daughter asked with mock exasperation.

"Nothing," Marlene said sweetly. "I was just thinking of something your father said a couple of weeks ago."

"Oh good. Glad you remembered him," Lucy teased. "Father's Day will be coming up soon."

Marlene smiled. Daddy's little girl had always been beautiful in spirit even if she was no supermodel. However, she seemed to be blossoming, thanks, perhaps, to the desert air, Southwest sun, and the devoted attentions of a nice young man. In New York, she'd been too pale and thin. But her mother noted how good a tan looked on her daughter's face and the rosy glow of her cheeks. She was even putting on a little weight in the right places through her newfound love for burritos, black beans, and fried sopapillas drenched in honey for dessert.

Marlene didn't kid herself that Taos had effected some sort of miracle cure for Lucy's deeper issues, any more than it had for her. They left the door open at nights between their adjoining rooms, and there were many times she'd been awakened by Lucy crying out in her sleep. Troubled, it seemed, by dreams of demons and betrayal, but in the morning, Lucy, looking haggard, would say she couldn't remember the nightmares.

During the days she was a happy, active young woman. There'd been some initial frustrations out at the pueblo. Apparently, the Taos Indians were a secretive bunch when it came to sharing their culture and language. She'd explained to her mother that unlike almost all the other American Indian tribes who had been moved onto reservations that were not their traditional lands, the Taos Pueblo was the ancestral home of its people. Thus, they'd never lost continuity with their past or their language. She understood that they were protecting their culture from outside influences, and she'd respected their wishes. But she was gradually picking up the language by listening carefully to conversations between members of the tribe. Her gift for acquiring languages had impressed some of the natives—as it had language experts and brain researchers around the globe—and she reported that they were starting to open up a little with her.

The Jojola boy in particular seemed to have developed something of a crush on her daughter. He engaged her in conversation every chance he got, which was how Lucy, then Marlene, knew that his father was the police chief for the pueblo. The boy had noted with pride that his dad was a decorated war hero from the Vietnam War and, sadly, that his mother had died when he was a young boy.

Inside the restaurant, Lucy suggested that she and Charlie eat at a separate table "so that you two can talk business." When they were seated and had ordered drinks—a Coke and a margarita—Marlene smiled at Jojola. She dreaded the question that came to her tongue, but knew that whatever role she was to play made it necessary. "So, John," she said, "tell me why you're so interested in Lucy's beads."

15

ON THE SUNDAY MORNING A WEEK AFTER THE archbishop's fund-raiser, Butch Karp found himself in another uncomfortable situation arranged for him by Murrow. There he was, a tall, white Jewish district attorney standing at the pulpit of a black Baptist church in the middle of Harlem. Not that he minded being there; on the contrary, one of the things he loved best about New York City was the diversity of culture. But he felt as though he was intruding in a time set aside for something more important than politics.

"I'd like to thank you for giving me this opportunity to speak to you this morning," he said. "I know this is a time for family . . . and for worship. You don't really need some guy to stand up here and tell you that you deserve better from the district attorney's office of the county of New York; you already know it. So while I appreciate the invitation extended to me by the Reverand Jacobs"—he indicated a round man with a face the color of roasted coffee seated off to his side, who nodded solemnly back—"I realize that this is not the reason you are here today."

Murrow had been the one to accept Jacobs's invitation,

seeing yet another opportunity to make political hay. "Give a little speech after the sermon," he'd said, "then join the congregation for a potluck afterward. Shake a few hands, hang around, and answer a couple of questions, eat and make loud comments about the deviled eggs being the best ever and that the chocolate cake is absolutely sinful. In and out, two hours max."

Karp was not entirely comfortable with Murrow's cynical view of politicking. But he also knew he could not blame his assistant for doing what it took to get elected in the twenty-first century. He'd gone along with it, knowing that it was part of the warm-up drills in preparation for a campaign, just like the glad-handing at the fund-raiser.

Still, if only it was as easy as Murrow had tried to make it sound. He looked out on the congregation and saw attitudes as varied as their faces and the hues of their Sunday finery. Some wore conservative suits and dresses of brown and navy blue. But others were proud as peacocks and nearly as gaudy in royal purples, shocking pinks, canary yellows, and fire-engine reds. Most indicated that they were at least going to show him the courtesy of listening to what he had to say, even if they sat with their faces blank and their hands on their laps. But others leaned back in the pews with their arms crossed and eyes bright with wariness, if not outright hostility. He was, after all, *the man*.

Some of the hostility he understood. He represented a system that had sent too many of their sons, brothers, fathers, cousins, and uncles to prison. While he made no apologies for prosecuting criminals who deserved it, he also knew that the law was hardly color blind.

He was well aware that to many officers of the New York Police Department, DWB—driving while black—

was a felony. And that north of 110th Street, constitutional protections against illegal search and seizure were often suspended during routine traffic stops.

Nor had the district attorney's office been much better at ensuring equal protection—and prosecution—under the law. He knew the statistics as well as the criminal justice professors who cited them for the media. A black was much more likely to be prosecuted for the same crime as a white; the charges were apt to be higher and plea bargains less appealing. But the discrimination was spread throughout the system like a cancer that had metastasized.

Frightened by a fear-mongering and exploitative media that sold newspapers and advertising minutes by playing up violent crime committed by poor urban blacks, which was actually down from a decade earlier, jurors were much more apt to convict a black man based on the same evidence. Then judges handed down stiffer sentences and were much less likely to grant probation.

Small wonder, Karp thought, that they see us as the enemy, not an ally. But an even greater sin in his mind was the lousy job the criminal justice system was doing of protecting the law-abiding citizens of the black community from predators in their midst.

Most of the distrust and hostility he knew was generalized. But he was also aware that some of it was directed at him personally. Old accusations that he was a racist had cropped up again, ironically due to his efforts to reintroduce integrity to government.

One of the first things he had done when he took over for Keegan was to beef up the Rackets Bureau, which was responsible for pursuing allegations of official corruption and malfeasance. Corruption investigations were not something his two predecessors had taken very seriously—Bloom because it was a threat to himself and his cronies, Keegan because he did not want to rock any political boats that might upset his dream of becoming a federal judge.

In the past, the bureau had been the dumping ground for the bottom tier of assistant district attorneys who were too lazy or too incompetent to be entrusted with actually trying felony cases. They weren't any better at special investigations. From the bureau chief in charge on down to the lowliest ADA on the totem pole, most exhibited an extreme reluctance to go after anyone with more political juice than a cop on the take (and even then only if he or she lacked friends on the force) or some building inspector willing to take a blow job from the slumlord to look the other way on health code violations.

They could not have imagined actually pursuing cases against anyone at the higher levels of government—such as a judge taking a bribe to throw a case involving a Colombian drug cartel, or city council members accepting illegal gifts in exchange for special favors. Adding to the bureau's miasma, its investigators, who were supposed to do the legwork to gather evidence needed to bring charges, were retired cops who got the job because someone was owed a favor or knew someone who knew someone. They saw no reason to work any harder than the attorneys, so very little actually got done.

Within a month of taking over as DA, Karp had cleaned out the bureau as if he were beating the dust out of an old rug. He'd lured his old friend and colleague V.T. Newbury away from the U.S. Treasury Department and placed him in charge. Newbury was the blue-blood scion of a named senior partner of a prestigious Madison Avenue law firm. His family could trace its ancestry to the first boatload of immigrants to bump into Plymouth Rock. He was so wealthy that he had no real concept of money. But for reasons of his own, Newbury had gone into public service—first at the New York DA's office and then for the U.S. Treasury Department—rather than a comfortable, if hardly challenging, partnership in his father's firm "defending plastic surgeons from middle-aged women unhappy with their boob jobs." Affable and charming, he was as sharp as one of his monogrammed tie tacks, and nearly impossible to faze. He was especially accomplished at investigating and prosecuting white collar crimes, the more complex and technologically challenging the better he liked them.

Together, they'd offered the worst of the bureau's attorneys early retirement, if they were eligible for it, or their walking papers if they weren't. Those they felt could be "rehabilitated," as V.T. put it, were kept on with the warning that their next stop if they didn't shape up would be the wide sidewalk in front of 100 Centre Street. The vacated positions they filled with young, aggressive assistant DAs, some of them right out of law school, and all of whom were led to understand that an outstanding performance in the Rackets Bureau was a quick way to ascend to the lofty heights of the felony trial bureaus.

After Clay Fulton had his DA's police squad together and running smoothly, Karp asked him to take a look at the former cops working in special investigations. "Weed out the ones who don't belong there, and find me someone who does," he said.

Heads had soon rolled. The vacancies were filled with a cadre of some of the NYPD's former finest who'd tired of fishing for stripers off the coast or playing bridge with their wives and jumped at the chance to get back into the business. Fulton allowed them flexible hours, and somehow Karp found small pockets of money to bolster the wages so that it was a nice addition to their pensions.

With the new attorneys and investigators in place, Karp left Newbury alone with a simple directive for the bureau: "Root out corruption, prosecute the guilty, convict them, and send them to prison for as long as the law allows. And another thing, where appropriate accept no lesser pleas." He intended to make examples of those who betrayed the public's trust, convinced that citizens would continue to lose confidence in the justice system until they could see that it was administered fairly and equitably. As long as he was in office, no man was above the law—whether he ate his dinners in Gracie Mansion or sold crack on the corner of 125th Street and Adam Clayton Powell Boulevard in Harlem.

Karp knew that an amped-up Rackets Bureau was going to bring a lot of heat back in his direction as important people started getting their feathers ruffled. It was simply unfortunate timing that the target of one of Newbury's first investigations were several black city council members who were reportedly taking bribes to keep the police away from a certain Harlem nightclub suspected of fronting for a drug-dealing operation. That's when the old accusations of racism began to resurface.

Word of the investigation was leaked to the press, probably by those with reasons to shift the focus to a white district attorney who might have an ulterior motive. "He's only pursuing this because it's Harlem," one unnamed source complained to the *New York Post*. "Everybody knows that it's little rich white boys and girls who finance the cocaine trade, but it's always poor black boys and black businessmen, who can't always control everything that goes on in their establishments, who go to prison."

Fulton, who knew Karp as well as anyone outside his family, had angrily reported to his boss that the old nickname KKKarp was being bandied about. The name had originally been pinned on him because he'd failed to convict a rich white teenager who had a habit of killing elderly black women. Karp had done his best in that case, the only one he ever lost, but the defense attorney just beat him. His efforts didn't stop the rabble-rousers in the black community from complaining that he'd thrown the case because the killer and his parents were wealthy and white.

A lot of the former criticism had died down that past fall after Karp stepped in partway through the trial of two white police officers accused of gunning down a black immigrant. The black assistant DA prosecuting the case had been injured by a car bomb, so he'd had to take over. The defendants' lawyer, Roland Hrcany, an old friend and former assistant DA, had argued the shooting was in self-defense and appeared to have the jury sold on his story. But in the eleventh hour, Karp had proved that the cops' version of the shooting could not have happened the way they said it did. The officers were convicted and the agitators in the black community had no ammunition.

However, if the current allegations being investigated by Newbury and his staff were true, there were a number of prominent members of the black community who had reason to play the race card. They had to hope that the DA's office might back off when Karp realized the racist accusations might cost him the black vote and the race for district attorney. He didn't care. If winning the election meant looking the other way, he didn't want the job. Over the years, real-world cynicism had made inroads into the ideals of the young attorney who'd emerged from the University of California-Berkeley law school all bright and shiny and ready to take on evildoers, but it had not yet submerged them beneath the oily waters of political expediency.

When the Rev. Jacobs extended the invitation to speak to his congregation, Murrow had suggested that Karp talk a little about his days as a basketball player. He'd been a prep All-American in high school, and one of the most sought-after recruits in the nation before signing with Cal-Berkeley. Some pro scouts even thought he might be the next Bill Bradley, until a very large man landed on his knee during a game in his sophomore year and turned the ligaments into something resembling chopped spaghetti. Finished as a pro prospect, he'd turned that same competitive fire into pursuing his law degree, and kept it burning until he was one of the best trial lawyers in the country.

Karp raised an eyebrow at Murrow's suggestion. "Wouldn't that be stereotyping to assume that just because they're black they'd be interested in old basketball stories?"

"I prefer to think of it as finding something that would interest any audience, an icebreaker to make everyone more comfortable," Murrow sniffed. Even though he reveled in the dirty game of politics, he hated that anyone would think it had corrupted his liberal values.

"It's okay, Murrow, I know you're just trying to help," Karp said. "But if I can't find something more important to talk about than basketball with these people, then I shouldn't be wasting their time."

While the whole world—beginning with his assistant

and Stupenagel—seemed to assume that he would run, Karp had not yet committed himself fully. So it caught him a little off guard when, after the sermon, Jacobs introduced him as "a candidate for district attorney, who's here to talk to us a little bit about what can be done to make sure our kids are safe and decent people who can walk the streets of their neighborhoods without fear."

Karp rose from his seat in the front row and climbed the three steps to the pulpit where he began with his apology for interrupting their service. "I appreciate the Reverand Jacobs's announcement, but I should say that I haven't decided whether to run or not," he continued. "However, I did want to talk to you a little bit today about what you have a right to expect from whoever is in that office. Then at least you'll have something by which to judge the job I do or whoever replaces me."

The faces in the audience remained as they had been. About the only time they ever saw an official white face from midtown or lower was when they were being wooed for their votes. He knew it; they knew he knew it. "I wanted to begin by reminding you that you have all been given two promissory notes from your government," he began. "They're known as the Declaration of Independence and the Constitution. Yet, your government, including the entity that I represent, has too often failed to make good on those notes in your community. Here today many of you and your loved ones have been victims, not only of violent, senseless crime, but also of a system that failed to live up to its promises. We have only to look at the statistics."

Karp paused. He knew the numbers he wanted to cite. He knew them by heart, but thirty years in the theater of the courtroom had taught him that half of the battle was delivery and style, including the well-timed pause to let the jury know that the real goods were coming. "The leading cause of death in this country among young black males is homicide. Not car accidents. Not heart attacks or lung cancer. But murder.

"And one out of every three black men between the ages of twenty-one and forty-five is in a penitentiary. But that isn't where the ramifications stop. For every death or incarceration of a young black man, there may be a young black woman trying to raise their children on her own. An entire generation of black children in America is being raised with no permanent male role model in the home."

As he climbed into his speech, Karp noticed that some of the heads in the audience were beginning to nod in agreement and voices added the occasional "That's right," and "Oh, you know that's true." But he was only warming up, thankful that he believed in the message he was trying to impart.

"Your schools are battle zones," he said. "Teachers and children are afraid to walk the hallways—afraid they may be assaulted or robbed or raped in the one place outside of their homes where they should be safest."

"Amen," shouted an old woman in a lavender pantsuit sitting in the front pew.

"Your neighborhoods are overrun with drug dealers and violence. The question is why?" Karp continued. "On the drive over here, I didn't see any cocaine bushes or gun factories. But drugs and guns are tearing apart the fabric of your community, stealing your young men's lives, and destroying others with crime."

An angry voice shouted from the back of the room. "So what you gonna do 'bout it? We vote for you and you wave a hand over Harlem, and it will be all better, right? Shit, we done heard all that crap 'fore and nuthin' ever changes."

Some of the congregation stuck up for Karp. "Let the man speak, Bernard," a man yelled back at the antagonist. But Karp held up his hand. "He's right. You've heard it all before and nothing changes. And I'm not going to stand up here and tell you that if I do run and I am elected to a full term as district attorney that I can fix all the wrongs."

The congregation was paying more attention. "It would be great if I could tell you that I'd put a police officer on every corner and in every hallway of your schools. But that would be a lie. The district attorney doesn't tell the chief of police where to assign his officers. But I will tell you what the district attorney can do and what I promise to do as long as I am in office."

Karp paused again to look at the faces in the congregation as he'd been trained to do with jurors. "I think it's time that we pursue a policy of no tolerance for violent crimes in the schools, whether they're committed against teachers or students. We will prosecute any crime committed on school ground to the full extent of the law. No deals. No second, third, or fourth chances. Do the crime and you're going to do the time.

"I'm not going to promise a war on gangs," he said, aware that Andrew Kane had been campaigning hard in Harlem on that platform. He cringed, remembering how the photograph of him and Kane standing together, the mayoral candidate's hand still on his shoulder—like we were best buddies—had appeared in the *Times* the next day under the headline Gotham's New Batman and Robin.

"That's just a slogan and doesn't mean anything. There's already a war going on in your neighborhoods. We don't win that war by arresting or prosecuting our way out of the mess we've created. What we need is a way to broker a peace . . . and we begin to do that by bringing credibility back to the system and ensuring that justice is as blind to race and social status as she is portrayed."

A few minutes later when he'd wrapped up his speech, Karp looked over the congregation. Although some were still sitting with their arms folded, he thought the looks were more contemplative than hostile; more than a few were even smiling at him. He smiled back.

"Now, from what I understand, comes the real reason you were willing to sit through my spiel, the food, and to be honest"—he looked at Murrow, who was sitting in the second pew with Stupenagel, and gave them a quick wink—"I'm kind of hoping for a piece of chocolate cake." A few laughs and a smattering of applause greeted his closing. He was ready for the jury to head off to deliberate the merits of his case.

A half hour later, he was balancing a plate of food in the basement of the church and trying to conduct several conversations at the same time when the man who'd yelled from the back of the church pushed his way through the people around him. Fulton intercepted the man, who scowled up at him and said, "So the brotha would side with his white massa against another brotha?"

Fulton smiled, though Karp thought it looked more like the beginning of a snarl. "That's right. Now can I help you?"

"It's okay, Clay, thanks," Karp said and stepped from around his bodyguard.

The angry man looked sideways at Fulton but turned his attention back to Karp. "I wanted to show you sumpin'," he said opening his wallet and flipping to a photograph of a good-looking teenage boy. He was posing with a basketball in one of those player cards, wearing the uniform of Harlem High.

"This is my son, Jumain," the man said with pride. "He was a damn fine hoops player. Was gonna be the next Michael Jordan . . . least that's what he always tol' his momma and me. He was a good boy. He never did no drugs. Didn't run with no gangs. Got good grades and practiced hard so that he could get a basketball scholarship and move the hell out a this shit hole."

With a sinking feeling, Karp noted that the man was referring to his son in the past tense. "That picture was taken twelve years ago," the man went on, only now tears were creeping into his eyes and he struggled to get the words out, "not too long 'fore he was walkin' home from practice one night when a liquor store was robbed round the corner from our apartment.

"It was a cold night . . . snowing and the wind blowin' so Jumain was bundled up in his Chicago Bulls warm-up jacket that his momma had saved all year for from her job doin' nails at Tina's Boutique." The man shook his head at the memory. "That boy loved that coat, almost as much as he loved playing hoops.

"Anyways, a woman looking out the window of her apartment saw the whole thing even though it was night 'cause of the streetlights. She tol' the investigators from the DA's office that Jumain was runnin' . . . that boy ran everywhere to stay in shape and he probably wanted to get home and out a the cold. But a dark sedan pulled over to the curb and out jumped a man with his gun pointed at my boy's back. He may have yelled somethin'—the woman didn't know 'cause her window was closed and the wind was howlin'—but she said Jumain nevah turned his head, he jist kept runnin' . . . runnin' home to his momma and me. But he nevah got there."

As the man spoke, Karp racked his brain. The name Jumain rang a bell, but he'd heard thousands of names over the years and couldn't say why this one was familiar though he had the sinking feeling that he should and would soon.

"The woman told the investigators from the DA's office she heard a pop, pop, pop . . . jist like that, three pops . . . and sees my boy fall to the sidewalk and lie there with the snow turnin' red. The man who shot him ran up with his gun still pointed at my boy, then used his foot to roll him over. Then she saw another man in a suit who had been drivin' the car standin' on the street and lookin' up at her, so she got scairt and went back to watchin' TV until she heared the sirens. When she looked out again, they was puttin' my boy in the ambulance. And she sees the men in the suits giving orders to the po-lice officers . . . that's when she realized that they was the po-lice, too."

The man drew in a trembling breath and wiped at his eyes and nose with the sleeve of his frayed blue blazer. "Jumain was dead 'fore they even got him to the hospital. I never got to say good-bye. He was jist gone."

Karp began to offer his condolences, but the man angrily brushed him off. "You want to know what the worst of it was, Mr. DA man . . . the worst of it was they lied," he hissed, the hatred in his eyes burning so near the edge that Fulton moved closer. "Them detectives says they found a gun on my boy and that he had threatened them wit it 'fore he turned an' ran. They says maybe he was the one who robbed the liquor store and shot that man. Too bad for them a witnesss saw the man who robbed the liquor store and he was five inches shorter than Jumain and wearing a blue sweatshirt with a hood pulled down, which don' look nothin' like a red Bulls jacket.

"Of course, any niggah runnin' in Harlem after dark is up to no good and deserves to get shot, ain't that right, Mr. DA? But they lied through they teeth. My boy ain't nevah carried a gun. He hated guns, had friends who died 'cause of guns, wanted out of Harlem 'cause of guns.

"There was an investigation for what good it done. Some fancy lawyer who worked for the po-lice department reviewed the evidence and said that even if Jumain wasn't the robber, he was armed and the po-lice was protectin' themselves. And the DA agreed.

"Oh they tried to pay his momma and me to sign some papers sayin' we wouldn't sue y'all. But we wouldn't take it, uh-uh, they can keep their blood money. And when we wouldn't sign them papers, they sent some jive ass big white muthafucka who tol' us it was in our best interests to realize that Jumain was gone and they wasn't nothin' gonna bring him back. 'Take the money and forget your son,' he says. Sounded like some sort a foreign dude, too. But you don' send no white boy to Harlem to 'timidate the niggahs. Me and a couple of my friends showed him the business end of a Louisville Slugger and sent him on his way a hurtin' muthafucka . . . if he didn' already have a limp, he would have after we fucked him up."

A sort of wild light had come into the man's eyes when he talked about what had been his only opportunity to hit back for his boy, but they softened again as he closed his wallet and placed it back in his pants. "That's what we got for a justice system uptown, Mr. DA, a baseball bat and each other. So don' come aroun' here tellin' me 'bout no promise notes. 'Cause it's lies and bullshit, Mr. DA, it's a muthafuckin' ferocious disregard for the truth."

There was little Karp could say. He remembered the case now. Jumain Little. The shooting took place back in the days of Bloom. He'd thought it was fishy then—three bullets in the back. But Bloom and his experts said the police department Internal Affairs report had called it a justifiable shooting. They'd spent all of two minutes on it at the weekly meeting of bureau chiefs, and then it was lost in the floodtide of a million other cases.

Karp made a mental note to try to find the case file though he doubted there would be enough evidence to reopen the case, especially with the eyewitness missing. For now, all he could do was commiserate. "I'm sorry, Mr. Little," he said. "I remember watching your son play in the state championship that winter. He was the best I'd seen in a long time—"

"Sorry don' cut it," Bernard Little interrupted. "I 'spose you tellin' me that you wasn't in charge and so it wasn't you who covered up my son's murder." The man's tears were falling freely, but he made no more attempts to wipe them away.

"No," Karp said. "I wasn't in charge, but I was still part of the system. If there was a cover-up, then yes, the system I worked for failed you and it failed Jumain. All I can say is I'll try to do better. I agree, sorry doesn't bring your son back, but I still believe what I said about those promissory notes."

"Bullshit," Little spat back. Fulton tensed, but the expletive seemed to take the final ounce of venom out of the man. "You won't get my vote, but don' worry none," he said. "No one else will neither. I don' vote no more, though before my son was murdered by the po-lice I never missed. But I don' want no part of puttin' some other fuckup in power so that they can do some other boy like they did Jumain."

With that, Bernard Little turned and walked off, his head up and shoulders back. The Rev. Jacobs, who'd been at Karp's side during the exchange, watched him go and shook his head. "I'm sorry he lit into you like that," he said. "It's been nearly twelve years, and he's still hurtin' like it was yesterday. He and his wife lived for that boy. She ain't never been the same neither—used to sing in the church choir, a lovely woman, but ever since just sits in her pew rockin' and not sayin' nothin' to nobody."

The minister paused and sighed. "Can't say I blame her or him. Jumain was a fine young man. Just seems we lose our best and brightest, the ones we need to point to and tell the youngsters, 'Grow up to be like Jumain Little and you'll be something someday.' But he's gone, and there ain't no one around here who believes it was anything but murder."

Karp swallowed hard and shook his head. "Nothing to apologize for," he said. "Mr. Little is telling the truth as he knows it, and if he's right, it's me and my predecessors who should be apologizing. I had a college professor in law school once tell me: There is no statute of limitations on murder, nor is there a statute of limitations on grief."

16

KARP LEFT THE CHURCH THAT AFTERNOON AND waited on the sidewalk with Murrow and Stupenagel for Fulton to get the car. He felt drained and just wanted to be home with his sons. Like Bernard Little wants to be home with his, he thought.

"Loved that about no statute of limitations on grief," Stupenagel said, writing furiously in her notebook.

"Yeah, boss, you were great," Murrow chimed in. "Didn't know you were such a philosopher. I could practically hear the fife and drums in the background when you were talking about the Constitution. I was about to—"

"Murrow, Stupe, shut the fuck up," Karp said. He didn't yell or snarl, but there was no mistaking that he meant exactly what he said.

"Sorry, boss, I . . . ," Murrow started to apologize, but his voice trailed off, and he looked as if he might weep.

Stupenagel patted Murrow on the shoulder. "It's all right, Murrow. You just happen to be witnessing a rare thing: the price of being an honest man in a dishonest world. Sometimes it makes them forget who their friends are."

"Stupe . . . ," Karp began to growl, but she held up her hand.

"Save it, Butch. Didn't you just get done reminding everybody about the Constitution, which just so happens to contain one very important amendment; in fact it's the very First Amendment . . . and includes something about free speech. Or was that just for the voters?"

Karp's mouth snapped open to reply, but he shut it as Fulton pulled the Lincoln town car up to the curb. He allowed Stupenagel to get in first, followed by Murrow. As they headed back downtown on Central Park West before cutting over to Broadway, he kept his face turned to the window. Maybe it is hopeless, he thought, and maybe I don't need the grief. Let someone else fail the next Jumain Little. But his wallowing in self-doubt was interrupted by a woman's voice from a long time ago. "You may never be the big fish in the big pond—"

Another female voice interrupted his recollection. "Since you're feeling all nice and chatty," Stupenagel said, "I'd like to ask you a few questions."

Karp sighed. "Fire away."

"That speech back at the church sounded an awful lot like a man who has made a decision to run for office," she said.

"There you go," he said, sounding a little more irritated than he intended, "the press jumping to conclusions as usual. If I decide to run, you'll be one of the first to know. But I haven't decided anything."

"Man, lighten up, Karp," Stupenagel said. "Here," she said as she began digging around in the garbage bag–size purse she carried. A box of condoms ("ribbed for her pleasure"), three lipsticks of varying shades of pink, and a large cigar fell out before she located what she was looking for—a pint of Don Pedro brandy. "Medicinal purposes," she said as she twisted off the top and took a swig before passing it to Murrow, who dutifully took a sip and handed it to Karp.

An infrequent and unenthusiastic drinker, Karp nevertheless took a large gulp and made a bitter face. He started to pass the bottle back to Stupenagel, but she nodded to hand it back to Murrow, who declined.

"What's the matter, Murry baby, afraid I'm going to get you drunk and sit on your face until one of us cries uncle?" she asked.

Murrow turned red but tried for the snappy comeback. "Can I use a snorkel?"

Stupenagel smiled and leaned over to stage-whisper in his ear. "You can use any toy you want, big boy. And if you run out of gadgets, I have a whole closet full."

"Better load up on batteries, Murrow," Karp said. "The woman once took on the entire New York Jets team to get a story about Joe Namath." Ever since he'd known Stupenagel they'd batted the sexual banter back and forth like a hormonal tennis ball. When he told Marlene about Stupenagel's lighthearted come-ons, she'd simply shrugged and said the journalist had acted the same way toward Marlene's boyfriends in college. "I don't expect her to behave," Marlene had said. "However, I'd cut your balls off with a dull knife."

"Unfair," Stupenagel laughed. "It was only the offensive line. Besides, I don't think Murrow needs any help. Once he loosens up the bow tie and the sock garters, I'll bet he's the Energizer Bunny. Takes a lickin' and keeps on ticking."

"That's a Timex, Stupe," Karp laughed. "You're mixing your advertising metaphors. I just hope you'll give him back to me in one piece."

"Would you two quit discussing my impending deflow-erment in front of my face," Murrow protested. "I am quite satisfied with my current love life, thank you very much."

Karp and Stupenagel laughed. But the journalist reverted back to her professional demeanor and resumed her questions.

"Why put up with it?" Stupenagel asked.

"Put up with what?" Karp replied.

Stupenagel rolled her eyes. "All the crap. All the baby-kissing and pleasant exchanges of meaningless platitudes, which I know you hate. And all the cynicism, diatribes, and criticism. The guys like Bernard Little who can't sep-arate you from Bloom," she said. "The accusations about you being a racist. The spotlight that will fall on your fam-ily, especially Marlene. And what if, after all that, the vot-ers turn you out? Or worse, say you win and then four years down the line you are spent and broken and noth-ing has changed? What if the inertia of the system is impervious to the will of Roger 'Butch' Karp? That's what I meant when I asked you a simple question: Why put up with it?"

Good question, he thought. Same things that Marlene worried about before she left. But again, he heard the voice of his mother. "Let me tell you a story," he said.

"Oooh, I love stories," Stupenagel said. "Is there a sex scene?"

Karp fixed her with *the stare*. "You going to shut up for a moment or would you rather ask and answer your own questions?" Stupenagel took another sip of the brandy, gave it to Murrow, and made a motion as though she was zipping her lips.

"The summer before I entered high school, I went

away to this basketball camp run by Claire Bee, who you may not remember, but he was legend as the coach of Long Island University when LIU was a real power in the forties and fifties. Adolph Rupp, the coach at Kentucky, was there, and Frank McGuire, whose North Carolina team had just beat Kansas and Wilt Chamberlain in triple overtime to win the NCAA championship.

"Anyway, I was a star in the junior high league. The newspapers wrote up my games, and my head grew as big as a basketball. Granted, I worked at it. I was a real preparation freak and competitive—actually at everything I did, including school. My attitude at school was there was no reason not to get an A. I was the same way when I played ball; it wasn't enough for me just to go out there and have fun, I wanted to win every game.

"So I was going to go to this camp and show everyone—all these big names—what I was made of . . . and they were going to be in awe . . . probably offer me a dozen college scholarships and maybe a pro contract on the spot. But for the first two weeks, I couldn't get a shot off. I had the ball slapped back into my face so many times, Spaulding was imprinted on my forehead. I was down and unhappy . . . ready to give up.

"So I called my parents and said I wanted to come home. They asked why and I told them a bunch of kids' excuses. 'The food's no good . . . I'm bored . . . I miss my friends . . . I'm not learning anything.' So they said, 'Well, okay, we'll come up and get you.'"

Karp paused as he thought back. The foot traffic on the sidewalks was light, a Sunday, which made it actually easier to see the individuals and wonder what their childhoods had been like. His had been wonderful.

• • •

Ruth and Jules Karp were first-generation Americans whose parents had come from Poland and Russia and spoke mostly Yiddish. The new immigrants had established the Karp tradition of success through hard work, respect for others, a love for their adopted country, and the importance of family.

His paternal grandparents had arranged to send all four of their children to college, two of them to law school. Every Friday night, Butch and his family would go over to his maternal grandmother's Brooklyn home for Sabbath dinner, which his grandmother always made from scratch—rolling the noodles by hand, turning the fresh pike into gefilte fish, and baking fresh bread to go with the boiled chicken and sponge cake. The next night, the family would take the subway into Manhattan to have dinner with his father's parents. However, that grandmother was ill so they always went out to eat.

Jules Karp was a lawyer who never practiced law. He'd graduated and passed the bar during the Depression at a time when lawyers were making about five dollars a week. But he had a family to support, starting with his wife and Butch's older brother, so he'd gone into business selling women's beauty care products. However, his father's friends were lawyers and the Karp family home was a meeting place where the great legal questions of the time were debated over scotch and cigars. It was where as a child sitting next to his father's chair, listening quietly to the conversation, he learned to love the law. And when he first heard the name Francis P. Garrahy spoken with respect, even by the famous defense attorneys who dropped by the Karp home.

Ruth Karp had paid her own way through Hunter College by working at Macy's, where the attractive brunette had been named Miss Macy's. Even working full-time and taking as many hours at a time as the administration would allow at the school, she'd graduated Phi Beta Kappa. She'd become a schoolteacher, though that was because teaching was one of the few occupations open to women at the time. She never said it in so many words, but he always knew that she would have preferred to be something more . . . a doctor, maybe even a lawyer.

In her own quiet way, Ruth Karp was ahead of her time. She spoke eloquently about equality for women and Negroes, and involved herself in politics. He remembered how he canvassed the blocks with her as she stumped for Adlai Stevenson; theirs was one of the few precincts nationwide he carried. She had such empathy for other people's troubles, once pointing out the gold stars in the windows of homes in the neighborhood. "Oh," she cried, her hand to her mouth. "Those are for the neighborhood boys who died in the war." He, of course, knew that—those older kids, the ones Karp and his pals had looked up to, wanted to be like when they grew up, had gone away and not come back. They were just heroic memories, but not to his mom, who had sons and understood those other moms' unbearable sorrow.

"Ahem," Stupenagel cleared her throat, bringing him back to the present. "Anyway," he said, "my parents drove up, and I got in the backseat of the station wagon, but they didn't leave right away." He could see the scene clearly: his tall, handsome father in the driver's seat, his beautiful mother on the passenger side. They'd asked him why he was so unhappy and he'd repeated the lame excuses. "Okay," his father had said. "If it's that bad, we'll take you home."

All the time he was talking to his dad, his mother sat quietly listening. She wasn't much of a sports fan, not until high school did she attend his games, and couldn't have cared less if he kept playing basketball. In fact, it was their inside joke that his schoolteacher mother, who worked the *New York Times* crossword puzzles with a pen, at least pretended not to know a damn thing about the very essence of life for a boy growing up in Brooklyn during the fifties and sixties.

"Who's the Mick?" she'd asked innocently.

"Geez, Mom, everyone knows that's Mickey Mantle."

"Well, then who's the Big Dipper?"

"Ma, are you kiddin' me or what! It's Wilt 'the Stilt' Chamberlain."

She would smile and say, "Oh, of course, I forgot." And he would understand that it was her way of telling him that sports were for fun and not really important in the grand scheme of things, notwithstanding the *NYT* crossword puzzle. The only thing she ever said about his athletic endeavors was that she expected him to approach them as he did all the challenges of his life: that he prepare himself as completely as possible, and that he do the best he could. But now as his father got ready to drive her son back home to Brooklyn, she spoke.

"Let me ask you a question."

Forty years later, he remembered how silent the moments were between when she said that and when he asked what was on her mind. He saw the headlights of the truth coming at him in those moments and knew he would not be able to avoid the collision.

"Is the reason you don't like it here because you're not the star? Is that what's going on?"

More silence, but he knew he'd been caught like a

cockroach in the middle of the kitchen floor when the light goes on. There was nowhere to hide. She had always been able to see right through him.

"Yes," he said quietly.

Ruth Karp nodded and spoke again. There was no anger in her voice, no remonstration, just the quietly stated truth. "You're only fourteen. I know you thought you were ready for Madison Square Garden. But you're just a boy and still learning. I think you should stay and watch the guys who are better than you, see what they do, compete with them. If you do, I think you'll learn and you'll have fun.

"If you still want to go home, we'll take you. And you can be the big fish in a small pond. But I don't think you'll be happy. You may never be the big fish in the big pond, but you'll never know if you don't try."

Of course, he'd stayed, and he had blossomed. The coaches changed his shot and soon he was all but unstoppable. When he returned to Brooklyn and entered high school, he was years beyond where he would have been and one of only three players to ever start for the varsity as a freshman. He'd gone on to have a stellar high school career, and the scholarship offers had poured in . . . thanks to a woman who insisted on the truth.

"There are many valuable lessons I learned from my parents," Karp said, finishing his story. "But I think the greatest gift I ever got from my mother was that lesson sitting in the backseat of their car: Always be honest with yourself. If you're going to give up, give up, but don't make excuses. She detested phoniness and that's a trait I inherited from her."

Karp was silent for a moment, his eyes still on the sidewalks. Then he smiled, recalling how some lessons bore repeating. When he was still a young assistant district attorney, he'd tried several men for the murder of two NYPD cops. After a long, grueling court battle, the jury hung. Despondent, he'd gone back to his office where he sat making all sorts of excuses to himself why he shouldn't try the case again. The next time he might lose, and he hated to lose. But he'd thought then, too, of that afternoon at the basketball camp and started to laugh. You're just making the same excuses, he'd told himself, only on a different type of court. He then thought about the victims' families who'd attended every day of the trial and were counting on him to bring justice. Back in the game, he got busy, prepared better, tried the case again, and won it. A slam dunk.

"There'd been one other thing I got from that afternoon in the car," he told Stupenagel. "As I was getting out, my mom slipped me an envelope and told me to read what was in it when I had a moment alone." He would never forget her eyes and the smile on her face.

"Why would I put up with it?" he repeated Stupenagel's question. "Believe me, I've asked myself that a thousand times, and until just now I didn't remember that the answer has always been contained in the words someone else wrote that my mother passed on to me in that envelope." He closed his eyes and saw the words again written in his mother's strong, flowing cursive.

"It is not the critic who counts, nor the man who points out where the strong man stumbled, nor where the doer of deeds could have done them better.

"On the contrary, the credit belongs to the man who is actually in the arena—whose vision is marred by the dust and sweat and blood; who strives valiantly; who errs and comes up again and again; who knows the great devotions, the great enthusiasms; who at best knows in the end the triumph of his achievement.

"However, if he fails, if he falls, at least he fails while daring greatly so that his place shall never be with those cold and timid souls who know neither victory nor defeat."

The car stopped at a light, and Karp paused to take in the scene, a snapshot of a New York sidewalk on a Sunday afternoon. A young man in an expensive suit, probably putting in the extra hours to climb to the top of his chosen profession—one hand holding a cell phone to an ear, the other waving an umbrella before him like a sword. Past a tiny elderly woman, her face like a sun-dried prune, her body swaddled in a colorful floral dress and scarf of some Slavic origin, shuffling along with her thin brown hand outstretched, hoping for one of those tourist dollars the mayors were always talking about bringing in . . . and ignored by the pretty blond woman, her young breasts bouncing like rubber balls beneath a tight T-shirt, who could have never imagined that she would ever be as aged or destitute as she moved around. Two Hispanic kids—boyfriend and girlfriend—strolling slowly with their arms around each other, oblivious to anything but young love . . . including the Hasidic Jew in the wide-brimmed black hat and sideburn curls who patted the young black bike messenger on the back and sent him pedaling like a fury into traffic. Karp knew that if he rolled down the window and listened closely, he would hear accents and languages to rival the Tower of Babel. But they were all his people, and they were counting on him to show up for the game.

"Why put up with it? For them," he said, gesturing

toward the sidewalk. "But most of all, for her." He looked at Stupenagel. "Does that answer your question?"

The reporter nodded without looking up from her notepad. He was surprised to see a tear fall and create a blue puddle where it contacted the ink. She glanced sideways at Murrow, who was sitting with his mouth agape looking at his boss, and said in a husky voice, "Murry, honey, you better close your mouth before I stick my tongue in there."

Murrow ignored the innuendo. "What was that?" he asked quietly as the car pulled up to the curb at Grand and Crosby. "Did your mother write that? Oh my God, the voters will eat it up."

Karp said nothing. He was lost again in memories as he got out of the car. But Stupenagel shook her head. "They might eat it up, but that was Teddy Roosevelt."

Later that evening, Karp took the twins to the synagogue, where he was scheduled to teach another bar mitzvah class. "We all know the story of David, right? Remember, he killed Goliath with a rock," he began once the class got settled, figuring that a little bloodshed right off the bat would get their attention.

"Yeah, he used a slingshot," Zak said admiringly.

"A sling, Zak," Giancarlo corrected him. "You put a rock in it and swing it around and at the right moment you let it go and the rock flies out."

"I hardly think that is the point of this story," Rachel said imperiously.

"Whatever," Zak replied to both.

"As I was saying, young ladies and young gentlemen," Karp said. "This is a story about David, only now he's the

king of Israel. He's got everything he could want ...
palaces, gold, jewels, and people to do all his work for
him ... a couple dozen wives."

"Cool," the boys intoned.

"Chauvinists," Rachel sniffed.

"But there came a time when he sent his army out to
conquer some other folks, but he didn't go with them—
which was unusual in those days because kings usually
went to battle with their troops. Instead, David stayed
home and one night he saw this real hottie named
Bathsheba bathing."

"A Peeping Tom," Zak piped up to the general amusement of his classmates.

"Yeah, maybe." Karp laughed, too. "In violation of
Penal Law Section Blah Blah. Anyway, his servants told
him she was the wife of one of his captains, a guy named
Uriah, who by the way was an Arab though they called
them Hittites in those days. But Uriah was away at the
war, so David sent for Bathsheba and when she arrived,
he made love to her."

"Sexed her up," Zak whispered, to giggles all around.

"What was that, Zak?" his father asked.

"Nothin'."

"He said, 'Sexed her up,' Mr. Karp," Rachel said help-
fully despite Zak's murderous glare.

"Thank you, Rachel, I thought that might have been
what he said. Now, Bathsheba got pregnant and when she
told David, he worried that people would talk, so he sent
for Uriah and told him to go have sex with his wife." Karp
shot a look at Zak that preempted the crude comment
that was on its way from his brain to his tongue. "But
Uriah said he wouldn't while other men were fighting and
dying, so David sent him back to the battle. Only he also

sent a letter to his general, Joab, and told him to put Uriah in the front of the fight so that he'd get killed. Sure enough, Uriah got waxed."

"That stinks," Zak said. "I thought David was supposed to be a good guy."

"Yes, yes, it did stink," Karp acknowledged. "And I guess it goes to show you that no one is all good, but that's not my point. . . . With Uriah out of the way, David married Bathsheba and she gave birth to their son.

"Now, David figured he got away with one. But one day, the prophet Nathan showed up and told David a story about a rich man who had all sorts of sheep and a poor man who only had one. A visitor came to see the rich man, Nathan said, who directed his servants to go kill the poor man's only lamb for a feast."

"That stinks, too," Zak muttered.

"Would you please be quiet," Rachel said, "or you'll miss the point."

"David was pretty upset himself, Zak," Karp said. "He said that the rich man should be killed for such a thing. But Nathan told him, 'You are the rich man. God gave you everything, including many wives, but you just had to have Uriah's, too. And to top it off, you are guilty of conspiracy to commit murder.'" Well, maybe that's not exactly how it went down, he thought, but it doesn't hurt to toss in something they've heard on the television cop shows.

"Well, David knew that he had done wrong and he apologized to God. But God decided to punish him anyway and caused the baby to get sick and die."

"But that's not fair," Zak protested, with the rest of the class murmuring in agreement. "The baby didn't do anything. Why didn't God kill David instead?"

Karp scratched his head. "Well, I have to admit that I

don't always understand the celestial justice system. And sometimes the God that's in the Torah seems a little unfair or harsh—like when he sent the bear to tear up all those children just because they were teasing Job." Uh-oh, he thought, rampaging, bloodthirsty bear has distracted them from the point of all this. "But if you look at this story from the point of view that it's trying to teach us something, what would you say that might be?"

The class collectively knit their eyebrows and pursed their lips in concentration. Again, Rachel bobbed up and down in her seat, waving her hand, while Karp purposefully made sure he looked the other way.

"Well, it's about what can happen if we're greedy," Giancarlo finally ventured.

"Yes," Karp said. "I think that's right. But I'm looking for something else." After a full minute of more facial contortions from the class, he sighed and called on Rachel.

"I think it is a lesson that God is stronger than we are and if we don't do as he commands, horrible things may happen," Rachel informed the others. For once, they didn't roll their eyes—the possibility of hearing about these horrible things had caught their attention, even if they had to hear them from a girl.

Karp thought about it for a moment and shrugged. "I suppose that's another way of looking at it, though I don't like to think that God does things to innocent babies just to force us to obey his commands. However, I think it does remind us that the decisions we make have consequences. And that those consequences may be entirely unintended or something we couldn't foresee."

"Yeah, but," Zak said, "the only ones who paid for David's decision to bone Bathsheba were Uriah and the baby."

Karp made a mental note to talk to Zak about his vocabulary. "Well, let me make two points. One, is that yes, the baby died, but I can tell you that as a parent, there is no greater pain in the world than to lose a child. Even the possibility"—he stopped and looked at Giancarlo, seeing him as he'd lain in that hospital bed clinging to life—"is worse than anything you can imagine.

"But there's one other point I'd like you to consider because I think it's important in today's world. Sometimes people make bad decisions saying, 'Even if something goes wrong, or it's against the law, I'm the only one who gets hurt by it.' Then they have too much to drink and get in a car and kill somebody on the highway. Or they use drugs and say it's nobody's business, but they don't think about all the crimes committed, including murder, because of the drug trade.

"The point is that David did something he knew was wrong, and then thought he got away with it because Uriah was dead. But those things have a way of coming back to haunt us. We can't always know how the choices we make will affect us, or the people we love, on down the line."

Karp looked at the class. "Anything you'd like to add?"

Zak scowled. "I still think it was lousy for God to kill the baby and not David and Bathsheba."

Rachel sighed melodramatically. "My mother says it's not up to us to question the will of God."

Karp sighed. His mother and father, who like him were not observant religious types, had never agreed with the literalists who interpreted everything as the will of God. His mother in particular despised the sort of thinking that could conclude that something like the Holocaust was part of God's preordained plan or a punishment for the sins of the Jewish people. He himself confessed to "felonious bafflement" at the ridiculousness of such reasoning.

"Well, in this case I have to concur with you, Zak," he said. "The baby suffered for his parents' sins. Unfortunately, it happens all too often in today's world, too. Every day children suffer because their parents are drug addicts or make the decision to commit criminal acts. They're neglected, or born addicted to crack, or they're physically abused."

"But why does God punish the children instead of the parents?" Zak asked.

Karp was stumped. He'd asked himself that question in various forms for decades and never reached a conclusion he was comfortable with. "I'm sorry, Zak," he said. "I don't have a good answer for you. Maybe it's not a question of God allowing bad things to happen, or God punishing us. It's sort of the easy way out to blame God for poor or evil choices people make, or to blame God for something that just happens by accident or because of bad luck. Maybe it's sort of a test. We have free will and can choose the right way or we can choose the wrong way. Each of us has to make those decisions throughout our lives. And how we choose affects not only us, but sometimes other people, as David and Bathsheba learned."

"Still, doesn't make it right," Zak groused.

Karp nodded. "No, no, it doesn't." But he was thinking about how much this son reminded him of his wife.

Three days later, on one of those lovely early June evenings in New York City when the new leaves on the trees were still lime green, and the salt air was blowing in from the harbor fresh and warm as a cup of espresso at the Ferrara café on Grand Street, Karp was standing with his sons in front of their loft building when Clay Fulton pulled up.

With the twins sent inside to work on their homework, the big detective explained that there'd been an arrest in a quadruple homicide. And "it seems that the twins, Zak and Giancarlo, were also present during the altercation. In fact, they may have been in the middle of it."

"WHAT!" Karp exploded. The head of every pedestrian within fifty feet of the loft building turned to look at a big man turning red as he swore. "GODDAMMIT, YOU'VE GOT TO BE FUCKING KIDDING ME!"

"Sorry, man," Fulton said, flipping open a notepad to read. "The detectives were checking out the club. They weren't getting a very friendly reception—this Garcia is apparently well liked. One of the bouncers, one Jim Mitchell, was trying to provide a character reference for the suspect when he noted that Garcia was friends with, and I quote, 'Them two little kids whose daddy is the district attorney.'"

Fulton closed the notebook. "Um, the detectives are going to want to get a statement from the twins, but I told them it could wait till after school tomorrow."

Karp hardly heard the rest. He punched the security code for the building door and stormed up the five flights of stairs to the loft without waiting for the notoriously slow elevator. He burst into the apartment like Job's bear looking to tear into a couple of children. "ZAK! GIANCARLO! Get your little butts out here, now!"

The twins shuffled out to the living room in their pajamas. Their faces were masks of angelic innocence, or those of puppies who know by the sound of the master's voice that they're going to get a rolled newspaper on their snouts but aren't exactly sure for which transgression.

"Wah?" mumbled Zak, trying to look sleepy and therefore less culpable.

"What's the matter, Dad? Are you okay?" Giancarlo asked, going for the concerned son approach.

"Want to tell me where you were a week ago Friday night?" Karp asked.

"Studying . . . we were going over our Hebrew lessons . . . ," Zak began but his brother elbowed him in the ribs.

"Don't bother, Zak," Giancarlo said. "He's onto us. We weren't studying. We went down to the Hip-Hop Nightclub to catch the act of one of our friends."

"Why'd you lie to me?"

"Would you have let us go if we'd told the truth?" Zak replied.

"Hell no," Karp exclaimed. "You don't belong in a nightclub. It's against the law, and in case you haven't figured it out yet, it's my job to enforce the law. Isn't it enough that one member of this family regularly tosses jurisprudence into the wastebasket? But that's not even the point. The point is you lied and betrayed my trust. So this whole bar mitzvah thing is a scam for getting out of the house and bar hopping? And I'm a schmuck for teaching these classes while you're planning your next caper?"

The boys protested. They were sorry. They really were interested in going through with their bar mitzvah. It just happened that on that particular Friday night, a famous rap star was going to be at the club and their friend was going to battle rhyme with him.

"The guy who got wasted," Zak volunteered. "ML Rex."

"Yeah, and what about the fight you were apparently in the middle of?" Karp asked.

"Nothing happened," Zak explained. "I wasn't really going to stab anybody."

Giancarlo slapped a hand to his forehead, "God, Zak, you are such an idiot."

"You . . . you . . . you weren't going to stab anybody?" Karp sputtered. "What in the hell were you doing carrying a knife? That's felonious possession of a weapon. Are you so frightened that you feel you need to carry a knife everywhere you go? Or are you just hoping to get a chance to assault someone?"

Zak rarely knew when to keep his mouth closed, nor did he now. "It wasn't such a bad idea when those terrorist guys tried to grab him," he muttered pointing to his brother.

Karp had to think quickly. The truth of the matter was that if Zak hadn't been armed and ready to rumble that day, the whole event likely would have turned out much worse. But he couldn't let Zak get away with that sort of reasoning or he'd turn into another Marlene.

"Just because it worked out that time, doesn't make it right. What is it about you and your mother that you feel you can just do whatever in the hell you want? What if everybody just started carrying weapons and used them when they decided that it was justified?" He paused to catch his breath then added, "Go get me the knife."

As Zak stomped off to his bedroom, Giancarlo tried to defend his brother. "Dad, I know it was wrong to go to the club. And I know it's wrong for Zak to carry a weapon. But ever since this happened"—he passed a hand over his eyes—"he's been terrified that something worse is going to happen to me."

"I know that," Karp said. "But we can't just run on possibilities and potential. Someone's going to get hurt, and eventually it will catch up to Zak."

The object of their conversation appeared and handed

over the switchblade with the same reluctance as a gun-fighter giving up his six-shooter to the town sheriff. "How'd you find out anyway?" he asked sullenly.

Karp shook his head. "That doesn't matter. What matters is your role in all of this. Remember the conversation we had on Sunday about how sometimes the choices we make have consequences we can't foresee or that we don't intend?" The twins nodded their heads and waited for the shoe to fall.

"Well, it appears that you are now material witnesses in a homicide investigation," he said as the boys' jaws dropped simultaneously. "Tomorrow, you're to come home right after school; then we'll be taking a little trip down to police headquarters to tell them what you know about your pal Alejandro Garcia."

17

KARP ARRIVED AT THE TOMBS, WHERE FULTON introduced him to Michael Flanagan, the lead detective on the ML Rex homicide, who in turn introduced them to his partner, Robert Leary.

"I recognize the name," Karp said, shaking Flanagan's hand. "You're one of our heroes from the World Trade Center."

Flanagan flushed and said, "There was a lot of bravery that day, Mr. Karp. The real heroes died trying to save people. I was just doing my job."

Karp nodded. That was the common response since 9/11 from the firefighters and police officers who'd laid it all on the line. Just doing their jobs, as if running into a towering inferno that was coming down on their heads was no different from rescuing someone's pet cat from a tree or writing a traffic ticket. He supposed in a way it wasn't much different from what firefighters faced every time the alarm went off or police officers when trying to apprehend an armed suspect. But it didn't change his respect for the special kind of courage they'd exhibited that day.

The detectives led them to a small room adjacent to

one of the interview rooms, where, looking through one-way glass, Karp could see a short, good-looking Hispanic youth in an orange jail jumpsuit. He was sitting quietly at the table with his hands clasped in front of him, but Karp couldn't tell if he was praying or simply waiting.

"He didn't do it," the twins had shouted as soon as they recovered from their initial shock. Giancarlo had explained, "Alejandro used to be a gangbanger. He even shot a guy who threatened him. But he's against violence now. If you heard his rhymes you'd know. Ask Lucy, she'd heard him. He's a friend of Father Dugan's, too."

"Yeah, well, as the two of you know better than most, sometimes good people make bad decisions," he'd said. "It isn't just the threats at the bar. A witness—the chauffeur—puts him at the murder scene."

"The witness is lying," Zak said. "Or he's as blind as Giancarlo."

"Thanks, Zak," his twin replied dryly. "But he's right, Dad. Something is wrong with that witness."

Despite his anger with the boys, Karp assured them that there would be no railroading of their friend. "If he's innocent, it should come out in the wash."

"Yeah," Zak retorted sarcastically. "Innocent guys never go to prison."

The comment troubled Karp. Innocent guys did go to prison. It was one of the main reasons he was personally against the death penalty except in the most heinous cases. But all he could do for now was listen to what Detective Flanagan had to say and hope the police were doing their job. "So what have you got?" he asked the detective.

Flanagan cleared his throat and looked at his notepad. "As you know—and by the way, sorry about your boys getting mixed up in all this, my sister's got a passel of 'em and they'd try the patience of a saint. Anyway, the perp—or I guess I should say suspect—is one Alejandro Garcia, aka Boom—DOB 4/6/85. Spent eighteen months on a juvie for reckless endangerment—put a round in a rival gang member's butt. Last known residence before his incarceration was 106th Street, the James Madison tenements in Spanish Harlem. We picked him up outside of Old St. Patrick's on Mulberry Street where he'd apparently been visiting his priest—"

"Yeah, we figured he might be willing to confess to us, too," Leary interjected with a smile, but shut up at a stern look from Flanagan. "Confession is nothing to joke about, Bobby."

Karp held up his hand. "Just the facts, detectives. You'll get me confused with all the extras."

Flanagan gave him a funny look, as though he'd just been corrected for his grammar, but nodded and continued. "As I was saying, the suspect got into a beef with the two male vics with the female vics present. One of your kids was apparently pushed to the ground, things got dicey till the bouncer showed up, and Garcia was overheard threatening to kill the deceased."

Karp wondered why police officers always felt it necessary to go into cop speak—victims were vics, perpetrators were perps, and all the rest sounded like a Humphrey Bogart movie. But after the last look he got when he interrupted the detective, he decided to ignore it and asked a question. "Tell me about the witness, this chauffeur?"

"Yeah, him," Flanagan said, flipping to another page in his notepad. "One Vincent Paglia, works at the fish market under the Brooklyn Bridge by day, drives limos part-time by night. Not your most upstanding citizen—a few beefs for gambling, one for assault, and another for solicitin' an undercover policewoman—but nothin' that's gonna ruin him for a jury." He looked up quickly at Karp. "Sorry, that's your side of the business.... Uh, he's a big boy, three-hundred-pounder if he's an ounce. Says Mr. Rex or Johnson, what have you, was trying to locate an old friend and they got lost. My guess is they were looking to score—all the vics tested positive for cocaine. Anyway, he's parked at the curb when he sees these two guys coming, one of them carrying a rifle, and figures something bad is going down. He jumps out of the car and hightails it out of there like the hounds of hell is after him. He hears the shooting and keeps running. Makes his way over to Third Ave., catches a cab, goes home, and stays there. He says he figured it was a gang hit, and he didn't want to get involved . . . claims that his conscience was bothering him, and he was going to come forward but we found him first through the limousine service. After we heard about the altercation at the nightclub from a confidential informant and brought Garcia in for questioning, our boy Vinnie picked him out of the lineup. Went right to him, no hesitation—says he saw him at the club the night before and then got a good look at his face in the streetlight before he took off."

"Anything else tying Garcia to the murder scene?" Fulton asked.

Flanagan said he wasn't sure. "A .45 caliber Colt was found beneath the car that we believe will probably turn out to be one of the murder weapons. It's with the crime-scene guys now being tested for latents and ballistics. Who knows? Maybe we'll get lucky again."

"Anything useful from the limousine?" Fulton asked.

"We impounded the vehicle," Flanagan said, "but there's

no fingerprints we can't account for and nothing else that's a help."

Karp's eyebrows nearly met as he frowned. "So how does Garcia know where to find our victims in East Harlem at just the right time?"

Flanagan shrugged. "Vinnie ain't copping to it, but I figure they're scoring from some dealer in Spanish Harlem, who passes the word on to the Inca Boyz, Garcia's gang. He sees an opportunity to make good on his threat and shows up instead of the dealer. Maybe it's something more, too. There's some big money in the music business and these"—Flanagan looked at Fulton and seemed to change his mind—"gangsters are always shooting each other. Maybe this Garcia was trying to make his bones, get a rep to sell records." The detective nodded to Garcia through the one-way glass. "He hasn't said much to us other than the usual denials. Maybe you can do better."

Accompanied by Fulton, Karp walked into the interview room. The suspect leaned back in his chair with his hands behind his head, his face and eyes betraying no emotion—the typical insouciance of a stone-cold gangbanger.

"Hello, Mr. Garcia, my name is Roger Karp and I'm the district attorney for the county of New York," he said. "This is Detective Clay Fulton of the New York City Police Department currently assigned to my office."

"District attorney . . . so they bring in the Big Dog to fry my ass," Garcia noted.

"Actually, Mr. Garcia, I will not be the prosecutor who handles this case, if there is a case," Karp said. "However, it seems that you have some people who believe you're innocent, including my two boys, Zak and Giancarlo."

At the mention of the twins, Garcia brightened for a moment. "Nice kids," he said.

The warmth of the statement caught Karp a little off guard. "I think so, too," he said. "Unfortunately, they are now involved as witnesses in a murder investigation. So I thought I would see if there's anything you'd like to tell me before this goes any further. But first, I want to advise you of your rights."

"Flanagan and his pal already did," Garcia said.

"Well, indulge me then, because I want to make sure you understand them and the seriousness of the allegations," Karp said and proceeded with the Miranda warnings.

"Just to be clear, you understand you have the right to remain silent?" Karp repeated. "I can't force you to talk. This conversation is being recorded and anything you say to me can be used in any court proceedings against you. Understand?"

"Yo, chief, I *comprendo* okay?" Garcia was back to being a gangster.

Karp fixed the boy with his stare, but the suspect met his look without flinching. "I take that as a yes," he continued. "You also understand that you have the right to have a lawyer present—the taxpayers will even provide one free of charge. And at any time during this conversation, you have a right to stop and ask for a lawyer. *Comprende?*"

"*Sí,* homes," Garcia said, stifling a bored yawn. "I already tol' the detectives I understood, and now I got to repeat it to you. Yes, I understand everything you've said. And like I also tol' the detectives, I didn't kill nobody, but there's nothing much I can do about it. They want my ass at Attica, maybe a nice little cell on Death Row, and that's what they'll get."

"Who's 'they'?" Karp asked. He was puzzled. Garcia

sounded as if he had someone other than just the detectives in the next room in mind.

Garcia looked at him for a long moment as if weighing something, then shrugged. "Maybe you're 'they.' "

"Look, if you've got information," Karp said, "you're going to have to trust me and the justice system to follow up on it."

Alejandro snorted and laughed. "Trust you? Fuck that noise, homes. Hell, the fuckin' system is as corrupt as any gang, and you're part of the system. Now, if you're through, I'm ready to go back to my cell and wait to see what kind of justice they're serving tonight."

"But I'm not done asking questions," Karp said. "And while you're at it, drop the gangbanger circle jerk; the boys tell me you were an A student at Xavier."

"Well, then, Mr. District Attorney, with all due respect to your family, who I like, fuck off, I'm through answering." Garcia stood up and yelled. "Guard. We're finished in here."

After the guard escorted Garcia off to his cell, Karp met out in the hallway with Fulton. "What do you think?" he asked.

Fulton's brow furrowed. "To be honest, I was expecting more claims of innocence. These guys usually have all sorts of alibis to offer; of course, the alibis are almost impossible to verify or will stink to high heaven. As you know, Rikers and Attica are full of innocent men . . . at least if you believe their stories. I don't know what to make of this one though. Guess I'll ask around and see what the word is on the streets, now that we have a suspect. You want a ride back to the apartment?"

Karp shook his head. "No, I'll walk," he said. "I can use the exercise. Besides, our young friend here reminded me of something I thought of at the church the other morning but forgot about. Give the wife and kids a hug for me."

"Will do," Fulton said. "By the way, I liked that bit you said in the car on Sunday about the man in the arena. It reminded me of you."

"Thanks, Clay," Karp smiled. "I'll try to live up to the compliment."

"You already have, my man," the big detective said before turning to walk away.

Karp left the Tombs and walked the short distance to the courthouse building at 100 Centre Street. Normally, he could have gone through a tunnel from the jail but the partial detonation of the terrorist bomb had damaged the sub-street-level areas of the building, including the walkway. As he went up to the front entrance, he glanced to either side as he had for nearly thirty years, to read the inscriptions carved into the marble. One side read: "Every Place Is Safe to Him Who Lives in Justice. Be Just and Fear Not." And the other: "Why Should There Not Be a Patient Confidence in the Ultimate Justice of the People." There was nothing particularly awe-inspiring about the statements—no Jeffersonian eloquence to them—but a reminder that every time he entered the building, he had an obligation: that he was one of the bankers entrusted with the care of those promissory notes he'd mentioned in the Harlem church. It always made him stand just a little taller.

Since it was after-hours, there was not the usual line standing at the security gates. None of the sad or angry or terrified faces of humanity who regularly passed into the hungry mouth of the New York justice system. Just a young black guard, who looked surprised to see him.

"Evening, William," Karp said.

"Why, Mr. Karp what brings you to my home this evening? Trying to get a jump on tomorrow?" The guard liked the district attorney, who addressed him by his Christian name William, as opposed to Willy like everybody else.

"Justice never takes a day off, William," he called back as he headed for the elevators for the interminable ride to his office on the eighth floor.

After the explosion, concerns about the building's integrity had caused the DA's offices to be moved until the engineers could determine that the whole thing wouldn't come down in a high wind. Even then, the building maintenance people had decided that with the offices vacated, it would be a good time to add a new coat of the sort of putrid yellow paint to the walls. A lot of filing cabinets, desks, and other office equipment had been shuffled around, which he decided was why he couldn't find the Jumain Little file when he went looking for it. He left a note on Murrow's desk asking him to try to find it in the morning and was about to leave when his private telephone line rang. He figured it was the boys, as only a dozen or so people in the world—half of them his family—had the number.

"Yeah, what's cookin'?" he said into the receiver, expecting to hear Zak or Giancarlo.

Instead, the voice was that of an older man, but strangely muffled. "Garcia's not your killer."

Karp thought the caller was trying to disguise his voice. Which means he's worried I might recognize it. "Who is this?" he demanded. "How'd you get this number?"

"It's not important," the caller said. "What's important is that a killer is still on the streets. You have no idea what you're up against, but you will. Then we'll see whether those promissory notes are still good. But all you need to know right now is that Garcia didn't do it, and he's in danger, especially in the jail."

"And how do you know that?" Karp asked.

"Because he was at confession with his priest," the caller said. "It's up to you to take it from there. You won't believe me, but I'm warning you that you can't trust anyone outside your family and closest friends. Not the police. Not the government. Good-bye, Mr. Karp, for now."

"Wait," Karp said but the line went dead.

A half hour later, he was back at his loft. "You know who Garcia goes to for confession?" he asked the twins.

"Father Dugan," they said. "Ever since Alejandro was a kid."

Karp swore. He suddenly felt as if he were in a play in which he did not know his lines or what would happen in the next scene, much less how the story would end. Just that he had a role and was expected to wing it.

18

THE NEXT MORNING, MURROW FOUND KARP JUST AS
he was heading out of the office with Fulton. "We don't
have enough to do without digging up old cases like
Jumain Little?" his assistant asked with a raised eyebrow.

"Just do it," Karp snapped. Bernard Little's distraught
face had disturbed his dreams along with Alejandro
Garcia's scornful one. He was in no mood to be second-
guessed, especially after being lectured twice in one day
about the corruption of the system he loved.

"Hey, just asking," Murrow said, raising his hands in
mock surrender. "You told me to keep an eye on your
schedule. Where are you headed?"

"Yeah, sorry, Murrow." Karp sighed, wondering when
he was going to get over his latest churlish stage. *Maybe
when Marlene gets home.* "I just want to follow up on that
one, okay? And we're off to pay a visit to an old friend."

A half hour later, a toothless old bag lady, dressed in a
faded and threadbare floral print dress and sagging nylons
several sizes too large for her thin legs, showed them into
the office of Father Michael Dugan. She had on a cheap
blond wig set somewhat off-kilter on her head, which was

showing patches of netting where the hair had fallen out.
The makeup on her eyes appeared to be a half-inch thick,
and the ruby red lipstick on her wrinkled lips looked as if
it had been smeared on with a finger. She turned as if to
leave but stuck out her hand with a pleading look in her
eyes. "God bless you, sirs, how about a little something to
help me wet my whistle later?" she asked hopefully. She
leaned forward and leered, "Or maybe you'd like me to
earn it, eh sweeties?"

"Thank you, Leanore," Dugan said, rising from behind
his desk, which was an old door laid across a foundation of
milk crates. "Remember, you're not supposed to panhan-
dle from the people who come to see me. Or solicit
them."

The old woman looked to the priest and back to Karp
and Fulton. She sniffed and wiped her nose with the hand
she'd been offering. "I was just hoping for a tip," she said,
not bothering to hide her disappointment. As she passed
by, she whispered "cheap bastards" so that Dugan
couldn't hear.

When she was gone, Dugan smiled and shrugged.
"Sorry about that . . . my new receptionist is a little rough
around the edges. Apparently, she was really something to
look at back in the days of burlesque, but got into prostitution . . . *apparently is* still willing to practice the world's
oldest profession when it's dark and the johns are too
drunk to see the wrinkles. We're hoping a real job will
give her something to get through the winter without having to live down in the tunnels."

Karp's stomach had flip-flopped at the thought of
Leanore plying her trade, but he quickly recovered to
shake Dugan's hand, which was roughly akin to placing
even his big mitt in a blood pressure sleeve and pump-

ing. He noted that the priest looked as if he could still play for Notre Dame despite the more than forty years that had passed since he last pancaked a middle linebacker. His broad chest and well-defined shoulders filled out the black T-shirt he was wearing, and the muscles stood out on his forearms like thick snakes. There was certainly no sign of age in the crisp blue eyes.

"Hey, Butch. Hi, Clay," Dugan said. "It's been too long."

Fulton smiled and shook the priest's hand. "Top o' the mornin' to you, Father," he said in his best, but poor, Irish brogue.

"I see my favorite Black Irish is looking fit as ever," the priest smiled.

"Yeah? Well, looks like you've been hitting the weights yourself," Fulton replied.

"Just the weight of the world, my boy. The weight of the world keeps me in shape."

Karp, who figured that even he could carry the pigskin through holes created by the other two men, waited for the banter to subside. There was rarely any rushing Father Dugan, as calm and unhurried a man as he had ever known. Not that he was lazy or phlegmatic, far from it. He almost single-handedly managed the millions of dollars Marlene had used to create the charitable foundation he ran as her appointee and still found time to minister to his folk, many of whom would see no other priest. He was just efficient, methodical, and steady as the Hudson River.

Soon enough, Dugan turned to Karp, his expression having grown serious. "I'd like to believe that this is a social call," he said, "but I'm sure it has to do with the arrest of Alejandro Garcia."

Karp hesitated. What he was doing was a little irregular. This was still a police homicide investigation. He might even have to ask the governor to appoint a special prosecutor and remove his office from the case because of the involvement of the twins. But in thirty years of dealing with the worst aspects of human nature, he'd learned to trust his gut feelings, and his gut was telling him that this time it was okay to do a little nosing around first. There was something about this case that was troubling him, something he couldn't put his finger on. While he realized that most cases did not call for Sherlock Holmes and were as simple as they seemed, there were things swimming around beneath the surface of this one that he wanted to understand before letting it go.

Karp acknowledged that he was there about the arrest of Alejandro Garcia. He left out most of Flanagan's report—after all, the priest wasn't supposed to be privy to such things—but repeated what the caller told him. "So is it true?" he asked.

Dugan considered the question for a moment. "I am in a difficult position here, Butch," he said at last. "As you know, I am not at liberty to divulge what is said to me at confession. And I think there are those in my business who believe that I shouldn't even admit one way or the other who does or doesn't come to me. These things are between a man, his priest, and his God." He pursed his lips. "But God loves justice more than he loves the rules of the church, so I will tell you that Alejandro Garcia was with me until close to midnight."

"Close?" Karp asked.

"I'm not absolutely sure," Dugan replied. "After he left, I was . . . distracted by another matter. It was probably a quarter after midnight before I noticed a clock again."

Karp was doing the math in his head. The church on

Mulberry Street was probably twenty minutes by car from the murder scene if traffic cooperated. The 911 call of shots being fired came in about ten minutes after midnight. If Garcia left ten or fifteen minutes before midnight and had a car waiting for him, he could have made the drive to East Harlem and been waiting. So when did the limo driver make his call to the drug dealer, and how did Garcia find out in time? "Did Alejandro get or make any calls while he was with you?" he asked.

The priest thought about it for a minute. "No, but I have to confess that I wasn't around him the entire time he was here, so I couldn't swear to it," he said.

Karp smiled. It could be difficult keeping up with Dugan's choices of words, the wit coming through even what had to be an uncomfortable situation. He didn't know why he suddenly felt disappointed that the alibi didn't clear Garcia; it was easier if he was the shooter. Maybe it was because he didn't want the twins or Dugan disappointed. Or maybe he resented Garcia lumping him together with "they"—whoever they were—and he was going to prove that the system wasn't as corrupt as the boy thought by looking under every stone before he convicted his ass.

"I know you won't tell me, but I have to ask: Did he say anything at confession that would have a bearing on this case?" Such as that he was on his way to murder Martin Johnson and whoever else happened to be in the car, he thought. Make this easy. Get the press off my back.

"You know I can't reveal that," Dugan answered. "Only he can release me from my obligation, and he won't."

"Why not?"

The priest shrugged. "Loyalty, but that's all I can say about it."

"Why didn't you tell the police all this when Garcia was arrested?"

"He didn't want me to," Dugan said.

"Why? He has a decent, if not airtight, alibi. 'I was with my priest' goes over pretty well with most juries, too."

"Same answer, loyalty. There's more to it, but let's just say that part of it is also that he doesn't trust you, or more accurately, he doesn't trust the system you work for," Dugan said. "The jury is still out on you personally as far as Alejandro is concerned."

"He's testing me?" Karp frowned.

Dugan looked down at his ragged Chuck Taylor basketball shoes as if they might talk to him. "In a way. You'd have to understand where he's coming from; he has reason not to trust the system, but even that I'm not at liberty to talk about."

"You know this could turn into a death penalty case—multiple victims, lying in wait?" Karp warned, knowing it wouldn't do any good.

"I know, but that doesn't release me," Dugan said. "I'm sorry; I wish I could be of more help to you and to him."

Karp nodded and turned to leave, but the priest grabbed suddenly for his elbow. "I am telling you this as a friend who knows his heart, not as his priest, but Alejandro did not commit this crime," Dugan said.

"I understand, Father," Karp said. "But you have to understand that right now it doesn't look good for him. Even with the alibi."

Late that afternoon, Karp was back in his office talking to Murrow, who had been unable to locate the Jumain Little file. "It's probably in the building somewhere," his assistant said. "They're still finding furniture and filing cabinets in every nook and cranny. One of the judges complained that his special ergonomic chair was missing. It turned up in the ladies' restroom on the tenth floor. He sent it out for fumigating."

"Well, keep looking. I hate to think that our Stone Age filing system has been spread to the four corners of the courthouse because of a little bomb," Karp said as the twins came bounding in the door followed by Fulton. He'd been tied up in meetings, so the detective had volunteered to pick up the boys after school and bring them down to the Tombs for questioning.

"Here you go," Fulton said. "Pretty Boy Floyd and Baby Face Nelson are remanded to your custody."

"Who?" the boys asked in mid-bounce.

"Never mind," Karp replied, "just a couple of old-time gangsters from your grandfathers' era. Back when they robbed banks and didn't sing about it."

"Oh, yeah, coppers," Zak said, launching into his best James Cagney. *The Public Enemy* was a favorite old video in the Karp family collection. "You dirty rats, you'll never get me to talk."

"I hope you were a bit more serious when the detectives asked you questions," Karp said.

The boys' good humor screeched to a halt at the mention of their interviews. "They did fine," Fulton assured him. "Pretty much what we heard with a couple of nuances. Seems this guy, ML Rex, apparently didn't take kindly to being shown up on the stage by Garcia and picked a fight. Mostly words until Giancarlo here tried to make the peace and got knocked down. Sounded to me like our suspect was reacting to threats made toward the boys."

Karp gave Fulton a quizzical look. He wondered if the

detective believed Garcia's story. Earlier, the detective had come to him with the latest news from the streets. One of the more interesting bits was a call he'd received from an executive with a music distribution company. "He says that his company and Martin Johnson had worked out a deal in principle to distribute the next ML Rex CD. Apparently, the vic planned to walk out on his contract with Pentagram Records."

"So?" Karp asked. "The entertainment industry is notorious for a lack of loyalty and double crosses."

"Yeah, but this cat says that Pentagram has a reputation for defending its turf."

"So Pentagram killed him instead of taking him to court and forcing him to honor his contract, or buy his way out, like a zillion other disgruntled musicians?" Karp scoffed. He shook his head. "Wouldn't that be shooting the golden goose? If record companies ran around rubbing out every artist who reneged, we'd all be listening to Wayne Newton."

"A fate worse than death," Fulton acknowledged. "But I'm just telling you what the dude told me. The two main theories on the street are that one, Garcia did it to 'make his bones' as a bona fide East Coast rapper, like Flanagan says; or two, that Garcia was set up to take the fall for an unknown reason and wasn't there."

"Unknown reason?" Karp said. "Why would someone go through all the trouble? Hell . . ." He stopped and picked up a mug shot of Vincent Paglia taken from one of his prior arrests. "That means our witness is bad at eyewitness identification or he's lying. Pretty damn complex just to nail some Puerto Rican kid from the projects. And if someone wanted to kill Martin Johnson, why not just do it and leave it as a mystery instead of cluttering it all up with red herrings? Why take the chance that one of the pieces of the puzzle won't fit?"

Fulton started to shrug again but Karp held up a hand. "Yeah, yeah, I know. You're only telling me what the dudes told you. I appreciate the information, I really do. I was just thinking out loud."

The rest of the day had been taken up with the meeting, and there hadn't been much time to ruminate anymore. But the photograph of Vincent Paglia was still on his desk when the boys arrived from their meeting with Flanagan and Leary.

Giancarlo came around the desk to hop up on his father's knee. Karp put his arm around the boy and squeezed. There was another thing he had to worry about. Giancarlo's doctor had called after lunch with the news that he'd taken his son's MRI and CAT scan to some visiting Israeli brain surgeon at Beth Israel Hospital. "Maybe the best, most innovative guy in the world," Giancarlo's doctor said. "A real pioneer in microsurgery, with balls the size of my head . . . thinks he can fix anything, including Giancarlo's eyesight. No guarantees; like anything having to do with the brain, there are risks. But he's the best shot right now."

Karp begged off making a decision, saying he had to talk to Giancarlo and Marlene. "Of course, and that's fine," the doctor said. "I don't want you to rush, but I have to tell you that Dr. Zacham is an extremely busy man and is mostly doing this as a favor to me for setting up his stint at Beth Israel."

Karp thanked him and promised to get back as soon as he talked to his family members. He looked at his blind son now, nestled in his arms, and imagined what it would be like if something went wrong, cringing away from the blackness of the thought.

Zak, who believed himself to be too old and sophisticated to be climbing onto his father's lap—at least in public—fiddled about the office. After testing the springs on the couch until his father scowled, he wandered over to the desk where he nonchalantly picked up the booking photograph of Vincent Paglia. "Hey, the guy who was driving the limo," he said. "I saw his fat ass drive by when that guy, ML Rex, flipped us off at the Hip-Hop."

Karp rolled his eyes. "Zak, your mouth is—"

"Oh that reminds me," Fulton interrupted. "Just before I picked up the Wild Bunch here, my wife called. It's one of those small world things, but it turns out her cousin works as a chauffeur for the same company as our witness, Vinnie Paglia. In fact, he was supposed to be the driver for ML Rex et al while they were in town, but Paglia begged for the job . . . paid him a thousand bucks, said his little girl was a rap fan and he wanted the client's autograph, plus he figured there'd be a big tip . . . apparently some of these hotshots who blow into town drop a lot of cash on a good driver who knows how to keep them happy and high. . . ."

"Yeah, yeah," Karp said, circling his finger to speed it up, "and . . ."

"And, well, there are two things that were strange about that, according to Helen's cousin. Apparently it's common knowledge in that circle that our boy Vinnie seems to have racked up substantial gambling debts with some wrong people. Normally, he doesn't have a quarter to wave around much less a thousand bucks. Used to complain to the cousin that his wife gave him his lunch money every day like a little kid."

As Fulton spoke, Karp felt as if the tumblers inside his brain were clicking into alignment—not quite there yet, but close. "And the second strange thing?"

"Vinnie's kid is a three-year-old little white girl, whose daddy is an itinerant Eye-tie gambler with loose mob connections."

Karp looked puzzled by the comment. An exasperated Zak spelled it out for him. "How many three-year-old little white girls with a wiseguy for a daddy want a rap star's autograph; duh, I mean Dad?"

Shooting his son a look, Karp said, "Boys, excuse us for a minute."

"WHY?" they complained vociferously. "WE WANT TO STAY!"

"Because I said so, is why," Karp replied using the inarguable reasoning of fathers everywhere. At his signal, Murrow grabbed the boys and escorted them outside. "Let's go play Guess the Crime He Committed down in Judge Farkus's courtroom. He likes kids and is handling arraignments this afternoon."

As soon as the door closed, Karp looked at Fulton. "I want this guy found yesterday."

"A setup?"

Karp nodded. "Smells like it to me. He pays for the job because he's part of the hit."

"Makes sense," Fulton said. "He arranges to meet Garcia, who in turn sets up his alibi with who better than a priest. Garcia knows how much time he has so has a nice drive up to East Harlem, waits for Vinnie to clear the limo, and starts blasting. In the excitement, loses the gun but can't spend the time crawling around under the car in the dark looking for it."

"Yeah, maybe," Karp said but the frown deepened as he leaned back in his chair to stare at the ceiling.

"Still, pretty complicated for an eighteen-year-old gangbanger," Fulton mused. "The usual MO is a drive-by;

don't aim just shoot, then run. This was an execution—
calm, cool, collected, and no chance of survivors."

"Yeah, an execution."

"So why does Vinnie wait for the cops to find him? He
knows they will when they check with the limo company."
Karp wasn't talking so the detective answered his own
question. "To make his story about being the terrified
chauffeur work. But what's he get out of it?"

"Fifty thousand dollars," Karp said.

"What?"

"Fifty thousand dollars. Isn't that how much reward
money the victim's record company, Pentagram Records,
was offering for the arrest and conviction of the killers?
Maybe he got a down payment . . . enough to pay your
wife's cousin a thousand dollars to collect an autograph.
He figures nobody ever hears about that—your cousin's
not about to report it to the IRS as income. He does the
dirty deed, waits a few days to be found by the cops, then
picks Garcia out of a lineup."

"But why wouldn't he expect Garcia to now turn
around and finger him back?"

Karp was back to silent mode, so the detective filled
in the blank. "Who's going to believe a Puerto Rican
gangster nicknamed Boom with a record for shooting
people over a hardworking family man? Especially when
there's the incident at the Hip-Hop. But if this was too
complicated for Alejandro, it would have been rocket
science to Vinnie, who ain't the shiniest penny in the
fountain. So he's doing a favor for someone and gets to
collect the reward money, pay the mob, and live happily
ever after . . . or until next month when he's blown the
money on the horses. But who's pulling the strings?"

"Pentagram."

Fulton looked at Karp, who'd stopped looking at the ceiling and was looking at him. "Huh?"

"Pentagram. Remember the call you got about Pentagram defending its turf."

"Yeah, the one you thought was bullshit."

"So sue me, it's the first time I've ever been wrong. And the reason I was wrong is there's something else going on here that I don't understand yet that goes beyond some punk walking out on his contract. Let's proceed cautiously; nothing changes officially, but I want to talk to our Mr. Vincent Paglia as of yesterday."

"Already on it, boss," Fulton replied and left as the twins and Murrow stuck their heads in the door. "Nothing PG-11 rated," the special assistant said.

Karp picked up his telephone and waved them into the room as he dialed. "You're all on super double-secret probation if a word of this gets out." He turned his attention to the receiver as the line rang.

A cultured voice answered. "Newbury Gang. Corruption's our game."

"Is that the way you answer the phone these days? Sounds a little cavalier," Karp said.

"Saw it was you, boss," V.T. Newbury answered. "We trace every call that comes in, just so we can locate the anonymous tipsters if we have to and see if they have an ax to grind or any real information. We have all sorts of gadgets, real James Bond stuff. In fact, I have a little pen here that can pick up conversations within thirty feet and if you click it twice in rapid succession, it sends a little SOS signal to whoever might be listening in. Much better than wiring someone; harder to spot and best of all, you can actually write with the pen. No one ever knows the difference."

"That's all very exciting, V.T., but how about you use

some of your gadgetry—so long as it's legal—and find out everything you can about Pentagram Records."

"Isn't that the record company of our departed rap singer—and I use the term *singer* loosely," Newbury drawled. "Sinatra or Mel Torme, now those guys could sing, but . . ."

"V.T., please," Karp replied. "I want to know who owns it, and if they have any ties to our witness in the ML Rex murder investigation, Vincent Paglia, or to our suspect, Alejandro Garcia."

Newbury assured him that he'd have the information ASAP. Karp hung up knowing he could count on his old friend.

"Told ya . . . ," Zak began and Giancarlo finished, "the witness was lying."

"Okay, my two virtuous misters—'I Was Just Studying My Hebrew.' Remember, not a peep of this or you don't see your next birthday."

Karp studied his sons; almost twelve and they'd been involved in more kidnappings, shootings, and bombings than most police officers experienced in their careers. "Why does my family keep getting caught in the middle of these things?" he asked no one in particular. Once again, the idea that he was acting out a role in a drama jumped into his head. If so, he realized that the curtain had closed on Act I, and was about to open again, but he still didn't know his lines.

Meanwhile, at his desk several floors up, Fulton flipped through the cards on his Rolodex, found the one he was looking for, and punched in the number.

"Flanagan," said the voice on the other end.

"Yeah, hey Mike, Clay Fulton here. My boss would like to talk to the witness, Vincent Paglia, pronto."

The line was quiet for a moment. "What's up?" Flanagan asked.

"Don't know yet, but he may be more involved than he told you."

"Oh yeah? Like what? Care to let the lead detective working the case in on your little investigation?"

The implication was clear in the detective's sarcastic tone, but Fulton ignored it. He'd worry about turf some other time. "I'll fill you in later, in person, okay? This came to us sort of roundabout. Just see if you can find him real quick."

Flanagan's attitude changed quickly. "Sure, you bet," he said. "We know where he works at the fish market. Sean and I will scoot down and pick him up."

"Thanks, Mike," Fulton said and meant it. Man, it's nice when the team works together, he thought as he replaced the receiver.

19

THE LITTLE BLACK GIRL, HER HAIR DONE IN CORN-
rows laced with small pink ribbons, stared into the television camera as a single tear rolled slowly down her round,
brown cheek. She sniffled and looked up at the kindly
white man who knelt next to her on the sidewalk in front
of a building whose true color was difficult to discern
beneath years of graffiti.

"Please," she said in a trembling voice, "I want don't to
be afraid . . ."

"Cut!" the director filming the political ad for Andrew
Kane's campaign yelled. "The line is, 'Please, I don't want
to be afraid to go to school.' Take five."

"Shit," the child exclaimed. "Sorry, Mr. Kane, I flub-
bed it."

"That's okay, Phoebe, we'll get it the next time," Kane
said, standing up and patting her on the head. Stupid little
nigger, he thought.

The ad was intended mostly as a local insert on BET—
Black Entertainment Television—and a Harlem cable
channel, though his PR firm had lined up a test audience
of white guilt-ridden liberals to see how it would go over

with them. If they reacted well, the firm might find a spot during a break in one of those white, guilt-ridden liberal sitcoms like *Will & Grace*. No wealthy conservative he knew would be caught dead watching a show about gay men, so he wouldn't have to worry about one of his GOP friends taking exception to his "playing up to the Negroes" in the ad.

In the opening scene, he and the Rev. Billy Jacobs of the Harlem church would walk together down a sidewalk locked in deep conversation but occasionally stopping to talk to concerned-looking business owners. And as they strolled, Kane's voice-over talked about the escalating violence of gangs "creating a war zone where neither talented visiting musicians like ML Rex nor our own schoolchildren are safe." The camera would then shift to a scene of Kane escorting Phoebe through a gauntlet of rough-looking hoodlums—who, like Phoebe, were actors hired to play the part—to get to her graffiti-covered school.

The child was then supposed to look at him with a tear on her cheek, actually a drop of glycerin, and say, "Please, I don't want to be afraid to go to school." Then he would stand, look resolutely at the camera, and say, "As mayor, I'd declare war on the gangs. With your support, this is a battle I know how to win." The last being an obvious reference to the lingering difficulties for President Bush in Iraq.

The camera would then pan back to show the Rev. Jacobs gazing at Kane and Phoebe before turning to the lens himself to say, "I know who I'm voting for in November. A mayor who'll represent all the people . . . Andrew Kane."

Getting the reverend to participate had taken a bit of

arm-twisting. If Jacobs had his way, he wouldn't have anything to do with Kane. But a youthful indiscretion cost him his freedom of choice.

While Kane had a personal vendetta aimed at the Catholic Church, it wasn't his only target of religious opportunity. Whenever possible, he made his presence felt in Protestant churches, synagogues, Buddhist monasteries, and mosques. The best way to manipulate the masses, he believed, was through the institutions they trusted the most. There was the added side benefit of corrupting the duplicitous so-called men of God.

Often their support could be bought with gifts of money. Others required a touch of blackmail. Some had weaknesses for women, some for men, some for children—the Catholic Church wasn't the only hunting ground for pedophiles. Some were into drugs, or they secretly (so they thought) liked to dress up as females and haunt the drag queen bars in Soho.

In the case of Rev. Jacobs, the minister was terrified that his congregation would learn that he had been an FBI informant against the Black Panthers in the late 1960s. One word to the wrong people, one of Kane's associates had pointed out to him, and he knew he was as good as dead.

Unfortunately, Kane reflected, not every churchman was so easily reduced to servitude. This Father Dugan was proving to be a real nuisance and, in a sense, was responsible for the death of ML Rex.

The trouble had started in December when a certain filing cabinet disappeared from the New York District Attorney's Office after the terrorist bombing. There were two sets of files inside the cabinet that worried him greatly. They were the proverbial Achilles' heel.

One set were those arising from the sexual assault allegations made against the Catholic clergy. While the church council did not have to approve any settlement under a million dollars, there was a bylaw that the council's auditors had to be notified of the payoffs and that a report of the allegations had to be forwarded on to the DA's office for review. Before that happened, Kane or one of his associates would mark them No Prosecution, even though they were often provable cases.

The other set of files concerned allegations of malfeasance brought against one of the firm's other major clients, the New York City Police Department. The charges were investigated first by the department's Internal Affairs Division, but the investigators' findings were then passed on to Plucker, Bucknell and Kane, which had been retained by the department for two primary purposes.

One was to review the IA reports and then pursue a course to reduce the liability of the department and city from citizen lawsuits by settling cases out of court. Kane and his associates accomplished this in the same way they handled the sexual assault accusations made against the Catholic clergy. Victims of police misconduct—or in some cases, the families if the victim didn't survive the encounter—were quickly offered sums of money to forget any claims. In exchange for the money, they were required to sign papers stating that they were dropping all rights to sue or seek any other sort of redress against the officers, the NYPD, or the City of New York.

However, that did not cover the firm's responsibilities. A city statute required that in any instance of alleged police misconduct in which a monetary settlement was reached, the Internal Affairs report had to be reviewed for potential criminal charges by an independent law firm, which then passed them along with any recommendations to the DA's office.

Kane didn't try to save every cop who got in trouble. With most, he actually looked at the cases on their legal merits and, if warranted, passed them along with recommendations that the district attorney review the facts for the purpose of considering charges.

In fact, he saw some cases as an opportunity to hang certain types of officers out to dry. He especially delighted in recommending prosecution for otherwise upstanding officers who may have made an error in judgment or an honest mistake. There'd even been times when the people who worked for him arranged for false allegations—a prostitute claiming an officer raped her, or a drug dealer complaining of a shakedown—to be brought against officers who had interfered with one of his criminal enterprises or who represented a danger to someone under his protection.

There were some cases that couldn't be brushed under the rug. These needed to be handled more delicately—especially if the press or one of the community activists got wind of it early and made a simple case of police brutality the cause du jour.

Of the two, the press was usually the easiest to sidetrack. He might take the reporter or editor to lunch and point out that "not all the facts are known and you might want to approach this with a little caution. . . . And hey, now that we're through talking business, what are you doing next Saturday? I'm having a little get-together, and there are a couple of Hollywood types I'd like you to meet, in case you ever dust off that screenplay you were telling me about last month."

Usually, the community activists could be bought off with contributions to their causes and bank accounts to at least take a wait-and-see approach. If not, they were encouraged to take their activism elsewhere, like California.

Occasionally, Kane ran into someone with ethics, and courage, but they were few and far between. And of course, not every case could be dealt with as quietly and efficiently as he would have liked.

On rare occasions, the media or the activists bit into a case and held on no matter what strings he pulled, or the victims refused to be intimidated. He then had to call on his bulldog associates to win the court battles that could not be averted with money.

Such had been the circumstances that past winter when the district attorney's office charged two police officers with murder for the shooting of a black immigrant they—wrongly—thought was trying to sell them drugs. He'd assigned one of the newer additions to his staff of associates, a former assistant district attorney named Roland Hrcany, to represent the officers. The case was going well and looked like it would result in an acquittal—which would have further solidified his standing with the police officer's union—but then Karp had stepped in for the original prosecutor and the officers were convicted.

Over the years, Kane had built himself a loyal following within the NYPD by protecting certain officers and detectives from criminal charges. These officers tended to be rogues, already corrupt or well on the road, who proved useful sometimes when he needed the long arm of the law for his own purposes. He'd commanded their loyalty by overturning any IA recommendations to pursue criminal charges with a letter he included in their files, which were stamped, like the Catholic clergy cases, No Prosecution.

In all the years that his firm had worked for the police department and the Catholic Church, none of his recommendations had been overturned. In fact, he doubted the files had even been looked at because of the men who'd been in the office of district attorney during that time.

The first had been Sanford Bloom. Kane liked dealing with people like Bloom. They were so basic in their desires and the way they went about asking for what they wanted—no slow corruption of their moral fiber or gentle bending of their principles to look the other way. Bloom wanted money, cash, straight out. Not even for doing anything in particular, just an understanding that he would make special concessions for Kane's clients and never, ever question one of his recommendations. But Bloom was greedy and stupid and wound up in prison.

Bloom's successor, John X. Keegan, had been more of a challenge. Keegan, unlike Bloom, was an essentially honest public servant and not the sort to be swayed by anything as crass as money stuck in a brown envelope and left in his desk drawer on the first day of every month.

When Keegan first became DA, Kane briefly considered having the district attorney's office burgled to remove the No Prosecution files just in case Keegan got nosy. But Kane didn't know if Keegan, who'd been with the office for decades, was already aware of the files and would wonder why they were missing.

It was also a matter of how Kane viewed the world. He not only believed that every man had a weakness to be exploited, but that he was the one who could find and use that weakness. The existence of the files represented a real risk to him. Even a cursory examination of either set would have shown where he and his associates had ignored obvious criminal acts and recommended against prosecution. The very least he could expect would be disbarment, and his involvement might even rise to the level of criminal conspiracy. If not, the exposure would probably ruin him politically if the press ever found out. He had no doubt that his privileged relationship with those jackals would disappear in an instant for that big a story, especially if it could be backed up with paperwork proof. Without the files, even if allegations were made in specific instances, he could rely on the concept of "plausible deniability"—one of his favorite terms of the late twentieth century. In other words, he couldn't be expected to recall every case reviewed by a firm as large as his, and that in the final analysis it was up to the Manhattan district attorney to review the file and decide whether to accept his recommendation.

Allowing the files to remain in the DA's office after Bloom was exposed, Kane realized, was one of the pitfalls of having a narcissistic personality disorder. Logic dictated that he destroy the files; his ego made him think that he could get away with it. He could play with fire, which would make the business of corrupting Jack Keegan that much more exciting.

Kane had wined and dined the district attorney and made sure he was on the A-list for all the best social gatherings, as well as the famous parties in his penthouse on Seventy-ninth Street and Madison Avenue or at the hunting lodge in Vermont. He quickly learned that Keegan didn't have the usual chinks in his armor: He liked women but was deft at avoiding being compromised; he made no overtures about needing help with his campaign finances; nor was he a closet homosexual, a drunk, or a drug addict.

Kane was growing a little frustrated when, in an inspired moment over cognac with Keegan in the quiet of his study, he pretended to be somewhat tipsy and shared his dream of someday becoming mayor of New York City. And, "if the truth be told, and all modesty aside," he said with an embarrassed smile, "I dare aspire to even bigger dreams."

Inwardly, Kane was smiling to see Keegan looking thoughtful and rising to the bait like a fat trout. Emboldened by the brotherhood of 90-proof alcohol, the district attorney confided that unlike many of his law school classmates, his dream had not been to be the next Clarence Darrow or Francis Garrahy. No, it was his ambition to someday be appointed to the U.S. Supreme Court. "Where I feel I might make some small contribution to this great country," he'd slurred patriotically and, to Kane's thinking, pompously.

After that night, Kane made sure that his parties included the people whom Keegan would see as being helpful in achieving his dream, such as members of the House and Senate judiciary committees and their staffs, presidential advisers and attorneys, and important autocrats with the U.S. Department of Justice. He even managed the occasional appearance of one or two of the justices themselves, around whom Keegan fawned like a new puppy. With beautiful women, movie stars, and pro athletes thrown into the mix, Kane laughed as he watched his good friend fall into his web.

For his part, Keegan was a man who knew where his allegiance lay. Although he considered it simply professional courtesy toward a fine lawyer and good friend, he, too, neglected his duty to review the No Prosecution files and paid no more attention to them than had the felonious Sanford Bloom. The files had remained sealed and locked away in the filing cabinet.

However, when Keegan called him to announce that he'd been appointed to a federal judgeship—something Kane already knew as he'd practically drawn up the papers himself—he made the decision that the files needed to be retrieved. He had very little information on the man who would be replacing Keegan, a selection he had not participated in, which he chided himself as an oversight on his part.

All that his spies seemed to be able to tell him about Roger Karp was that he was a straight shooter. Keegan also informed him that Karp wasn't the sort to party or hobnob with society folks.

When Kane had asked Hrcany, who'd been hired because of his skill and experience but was unaware of the firm's more nefarious deeds, what he knew of his former colleague, he was told that Karp was virtually devoid of vices. "I think the only things he loves are his family and the law." Karp apparently lacked even Keegan's ambition and had mostly risen to his current position, according to Hrcany, "because he enjoys what he does, and he's the best trial lawyer in the state."

It was hard for Kane to imagine that anyone in today's world got anyplace on merit, but true believers, like martyrs, could be dangerous. So until he could figure out how to bring Karp into the fold, Kane decided that he would stop sending No Prosecution files to the DA's office, and claim it was an oversight if questioned later. In the meantime, the old files, which were kept in a cabinet just off the DA's main office, would be removed and destroyed.

Then the terrorists tried to blow up the courthouse and messed up everything. Fools, he thought. Amateurs. The whole scheme was poorly executed by bumbling idiots. The building had been damaged enough, however, that the DA's office had been abandoned for a period of time, the filing cabinets moved to other locations. Or at least that's what he thought after his burglars tried to find the No Prosecution filing cabinet and came back empty-handed.

Then he was stung by a nasty turn of events. It began with a worried telephone call from O'Callahan. A priest, Father Michael Dugan, had been in that morning requesting an audience with the archbishop. He wouldn't tell O'Callahan much other than it seemed that one of his former parishioners had come into possession of certain government files that indicated corruption within the police department and the church. Pressed for more, Dugan shook his head and said he wasn't personally in possession of the files. He told O'Callahan, "You'll just have to believe that these files could destroy the church in New York. I must talk with the archbishop alone." To stall until he could speak to Kane, O'Callahan said he would pass on the request to the archbishop.

The files could only be from the No Prosecution cabinet, and for one of the few times in his life, Kane felt fear grip his gut as if he had eaten too many green apples. He ordered O'Callahan to have their people watch Dugan around the clock and try to discover the whereabouts of the files. The task seemed nearly impossible. The priest ran a foundation and met with dozens of people every day. Therefore, it was a matter of luck that one of his spies was watching Dugan's office when he saw a Hispanic teenager leave the building. The spy knew he'd seen the young man's face before and so had followed him to his place of employment: the district attorney's office.

"His name is Alejandro Garcia," O'Callahan reported. "He works as a janitor in the courthouse at night. We checked the city employment records, and he was working during the time of the bombing and afterward. He could easily have removed the files as part of the cleanup crew. It's got to be him."

It wasn't conclusive, but Kane agreed. He considered whether to have Garcia and Dugan killed. But he had no idea where the files were or who else might know about them. Plus it was difficult for his men to follow Garcia into his neighborhood. The kid might have given up the life of crime, if his spies were correct, but he still had the fierce loyalty of his gang behind him, and efforts to find him in Spanish Harlem had been met with hostility by the locals.

Kane decided on a different tack. He had O'Callahan make overtures to Dugan and, through him, Garcia. A certain interested party would pay a great deal of money for the files, Dugan was told. The same party was also willing to see that Garcia was signed to a major recording contract. "As you noted yourself," O'Callahan had reasoned, "that information could be harmful to the church, as well as the police department, and think of the people who would suffer if either of those institutions was damaged by the contents of those files."

Surprisingly, Dugan and Garcia had turned out to be

more true believers. Instead of taking the money and recording contract, the priest had threatened to go to the district attorney if a meeting with Archbishop Fey wasn't arranged. That's when Kane came up with his grand plan. If he couldn't kill Garcia, at least not right away, he would frame him for murder. The teen could contemplate spending the rest of his life in prison, maybe even the death penalty, or he could turn over the files.

So the plan had been to make it look as if Garcia had murdered ML Rex as part of the East Coast–West Coast rap war. It had been almost too easy. They'd found a patsy, Vincent Paglia, through one of his mob connections, to take the victim to the nightclub where Garcia was known to be a regular at their open-microphone night. The MC had been paid by Pentagram Records to arrange a battle rhyming confrontation between the two, and then a miracle happened. Not only had the entire audience heard the two young men putting each other down, but afterward Garcia had actually threatened to kill the rap star in front of a half-dozen people. It was almost too rich that the DA's kids were two of those witnesses; it was just the sort of devilment that Kane loved.

It was an excellent plan. The cops tracked Paglia down, who'd fed them his story. Then an anonymous caller led the detectives to Garcia and the altercation at the Hip-Hop Nightclub. Garcia was picked up for questioning, and Paglia picked him out of a lineup.

With that accomplished, Kane had sent O'Callahan back to Dugan. "If he gives up the files now," one priest explained to the other, "the witness recants, says he made a mistake. Half the files before the witness goes to the cops, half after your boy is released."

"What if he gets out and we don't give up the second half of the files?"

O'Callahan pretended to look shocked. "What? You mean we could not rely on your word . . . *tsk, tsk*, what is this world coming to?" But then his expression hardened. "We either have all the files in our hands, or he doesn't walk out of jail alive. The Tombs can be a dangerous place."

"What if he decides to take his chances at trial and turns the files over to the DA?" Dugan asked.

O'Callahan had shrugged. "He won't live out the month and neither will his friends, including you."

Dugan had started to rise from his seat as if to attack O'Callahan. But the black-hearted priest wasn't stupid; he'd brought plenty of muscle with him to make his offer.

"Who is this 'we' you keep mentioning?" Dugan said, sitting back down. "Does the archbishop know about this?"

"You've seen the files . . . you tell me what you think the archbishop knows," O'Callahn sneered. "As far as 'we,' that's a need-to-know security clearance that I'm afraid you don't have. So, what's it going to be, Mike?"

"We'll think about it," Dugan snarled and stormed out of the room.

Both O'Callahan and Kane assumed that after the priest and Garcia had a chance to think, they'd come around. Then after Kane had the files, the pair would have an unfortunate, and fatal, accident. But they seemed to be taking their time thinking, and he was running out of patience.

Kane reached down as his cell phone suddenly began buzzing on his belt. He snapped it open and answered. "What is it?" he said sharply.

"We may have some trouble," O'Callahan said.

"Apparently, the district attorney wants to talk to their star witness."

"What about?"

"We're not sure. Karp's office wanted him picked up, but fortunately we got the word first and told him to leave work and lay low until we got to him."

"Kill him."

"What? Without Paglia we won't have an eyewitness putting Garcia at the scene."

Kane shrugged it off, telling O'Callahan that he was sure the police interview with Paglia had been video-taped. "Our friends at the district attorney's office will fight tooth and nail to see that it's admitted into evidence. In the meantime, I will make sure our public defender boy in the Legal Aid Society, who has been conveniently appointed to represent Mr. Garcia, does a poor job of opposing the prosecution's motion to admit the video-tape.

"And I believe the DA should be receiving that final bit of evidence putting Mr. Garcia at the scene any day now. There will be only one way—our way—for Mr. Garcia to avoid being convicted of murder and sentenced to spend the rest of his life in prison, or perhaps death by lethal injection if Mr. Karp is so inclined."

O'Callahan cautiously tried to point out that perhaps it was a little premature to kill Paglia. "Maybe the DA just wants to go over the facts with his star witness."

"I said kill him," Kane hissed. "Even if they don't suspect anything, he's dumb as a stick and might get tripped up. But first question him about whether he told anyone about this, like his bitch wife and their little brat. I haven't decided yet if they need to join him in the great beyond, too."

Kane could tell that O'Callahan still had reservations. Going to need to have a discussion about following orders without all the questions with that boy, he thought. However, he'd accepted the usual congratulations on the brilliance of his thinking. After all, he's just being accurate.

Kane flipped the cell phone closed and looked up to see Phoebe watching him. He flashed his warmest smile. "Come on, Phoebe," he said as he offered her his arm. "It's showtime."

20

THE FULL MOON WAS JUST RISING IN THE EAST
above Queens as Vincent Paglia heaved his vast bulk up
the stairs leading to the footbridge that crossed from
Spanish Harlem over the East River to Randall's Island.
He wasn't happy being in that part of town so late at night;
he didn't trust the spics, beaners, and Ricans, but he figured that at his size, most robbers would choose a less
threatening target.

When he arrived a few minutes earlier, he'd parked
behind the dark sedan of his handlers, as he thought of
the men who'd brought him into this nightmare. He
noticed that a twin of the sedan was pulled up at the corner and he could just make out the glow of the driver's
cigarette. He quickly turned his head, as he'd been told to
ignore the second car: "They're there for your protection." Not that I believe that crap-o-la, he thought, but I
got no choice.

Reaching the top of the stairs, Vincent paused to catch
his breath and looked toward the middle of the bridge,
where he saw two more dark figures in the moonlight. It
was Thursday night, and he wished that he were home

with his wife, Katie, a nice, big girl with plenty of meat on her, which, he joked to his friends "keeps my balls off the sheets." She'd probably be in bed, as would their three-year-old daughter, Annie. If Katie was sleeping and not in the mood for a tumble, he'd probably see if he could catch a little baseball on ESPN, maybe place a few lazy bets if he could talk some bookie into taking his action. But the man on the phone had insisted on this meeting. There'd been a call at work Wednesday—something his boss had not been too happy about, especially when he then made an excuse that he wasn't feeling so good and wanted to take the rest of the day off. He'd been told to go get a room at the American Hotel on Lexington and not to go to work the next day, either. He called Katie at the hotel and told her that he was going to go tie one on with his cousin in Jersey and sleep it off over at his place, hanging up rather than listen to the angry buzzing of her words.

Paglia sat in his room at the American watching sports on television until the guy called again, insisting that they meet at midnight on the footbridge. "Nothing to worry about," the man said. "We just want to go over your story before the cops or the district attorney talks to you again."

A midnight meeting on the bridge made him nervous. He didn't like heights and he couldn't swim, but more than that, he didn't trust these men. They were stone-cold killers and he wasn't. But as he waddled toward them, he tried to look at the bright side; if he played his cards right, not only would he be free and clear of the bookie who held his chits, there was a nice little payday at the end of the road from the record company. Minus the ten big he owed, he'd pocket forty thou . . . and a guy with his smarts and sports acumen could turn that into a couple million, easy.

After the murders, Paglia had been instructed to go home and wait for the cops to show up. To get Katie out of the house, he'd started an argument over sex, which always got her to pack up and head to her mom's place in Brooklyn with Annie until she cooled off. Then when the detectives arrived, he "broke down" and told them his story as it had been prepared for him by his handlers.

Just to be sure, his handlers had given him a photograph of the Garcia kid. Then a few days later, he'd been called to go downtown and pick him out of a lineup. . . . Which reminds me, I was supposed to burn the picture, better do that when I get home.

Now, he got to be the hero at the trial and collect the reward. He felt a little sorry for the kid, especially if they sent him to Death Row, but sometimes it just came down to every man for himself, and he had a wife and a little girl to consider.

As the men on the footbridge turned toward him, Vincent wished he'd insisted on a public meeting place. He'd suggested it, but they reminded him that they couldn't be seen together. "For everyone's safety." Now, with sweat breaking out on his brow and soaking his armpits, he reminded himself that these guys needed him to finger the Puerto Rican. They couldn't suddenly have their only witness disappear. Still, the weight of the gun he'd borrowed and never returned felt reassuring tucked into the waistband of the sweatpants he was wearing.

Vincent could see that the middle span of the footbridge had been raised so that there was a gap in the middle. It would remain that way until morning. He'd heard that it was because one of the loonies from the psychiatric hospital on the island had escaped one night and made her way to a subway platform, where she promptly pushed a businessman and father of four in front of a train. But there was something chilling about the gaping hole in the path, like it was waiting to swallow him. He recognized the men on the bridge as the two who'd first come down to the fish market and told him what was up. They were both about the same height; the subservient one was a little heavier than the leader, who held out his hand. "Hey, Vincent, thanks for coming," he said.

As if I had a choice, Vincent thought. "No problem," he said. "What can I do for you guys?"

The leader smiled, his teeth gleaming wolfishly in the moonlight. "We just wanted to go over a few things so that there's no mess-ups," the man said. "Sorry about dragging you out here at night, but you understand we have to be extra careful right now. We didn' even want to talk about it on the cell phone. You know, it's too easy for someone else to listen in."

"I didn' know that, but good thinkin'," Paglia said. "But there's nothin' to worry 'bout. I was drivin' the limo, looking for this address, when we got lost and pulled over to the curb. Then I see'd these two hoodlums walk up, one of them with a machine gun or sometin'. I take off running, but not before I get a good look at their mugs in the streetlight. They start blastin' and I don't stop movin' till I get to Third and catch a cab. I'm scared 'cause I figure it's a gang hit, and hide out until the cops come find me. Then I fingered the Puerto Rican kid." He shrugged. "Simple enough."

The leader smiled again. "Yeah, simple. Good job, ya got it down." He strolled over to the railing and looked over. The water passing beneath the bridge appeared calm and slow, but he knew that looks were deceptive. That little bit of the East River was known as Hell's Gate, so-called by sailors in the old days because of the powerful currents caused by the interplay of river and ocean tides. Those treacherous waters had carried many a ship onto the rocks, and drowned plenty who were unlucky enough to wind up in the waters.

"Nice view, eh, Vincent," the man said looking southwest at the skyline of Manhattan. He wasn't worried about any passersby seeing them. The two others Vincent had seen in the other car were now at the bottom of the stairs to prevent any sightseers from approaching. "Hey, look at Gracie Mansion all lit up," he said, pointing to the mayor's residence on the banks of the river. "They must be having some sort of shindig."

"Yeah, nice view," Vincent replied, though he'd never given such sights much thought before. He was a city boy, lights were lights, and he didn't like having to move closer to the edge of the bridge to hear the man. They were only fifty feet or so above the water, but to him it looked like two hundred.

"Now, Vincent, I need to ask you a question and you need to answer me honestly," the man said without taking his gaze from the skyline. "And I'll know if you're lyin'. You know that, don't ya?"

Vincent swallowed and nodded. He didn't like the way this was going.

The man turned to him and placed a hand on his shoulder. "You won't get in trouble so long as you tell me the truth, okay?" Vincent nodded again, so the man continued. "Have you left anything lying around like phone numbers or that photograph we gave you of the kid . . . just in case the police decided to look into your story? Not that they will, but we want to be safe. And please, Vincent, understand we're looking after your best interests, as well as ours. We just want to be sure there are no loose ends that could come back to haunt either of us."

Vincent doubted that the man had his best interests in mind, but the man probably had his own and he was sure that they still needed him. He resolved again to throw out the photograph when he got home. There was also a twinge of apprehension about the business card with the telephone number that he'd accidentally left in the limo. But no one had mentioned it, so he figured no one had noticed. "No," he said. "I did like you said and burned the photo and memorized everything else."

"Good. Good," the man said. "Now have you told anybody 'bout this? Like your wife? I mean that would be understandable if you did. A little pillow talk between romps in the hay, ya know what I mean? That I could understand. No problem, I just need to know, in case Mrs. Paglia needs to go on a nice, paid vacation until this is all settled. Nothin' worse than that, okay?"

Vincent shook his head. He'd thought about telling Katie. The killings weighed on his conscience. But she was a good girl, the sort who went to Mass several times a week. He'd promised her when the baby was born that he'd quit gambling. She'd warned him that she would leave him if she learned he was lying to her like her no-account father, who'd drank and gambled away every paycheck he'd ever received. She wouldn't understand how he could have racked up ten thousand dollars' worth of bad debt, and then had to go along with some murders to dig himself back out of the hole.

"Nah, I ain't told nobody, including her," he said. "She wouldn' put up wit it."

"That's good, Vincent, that's real good," the man said, flashing that predatory grin, "because it's better to be a widow than to be dead."

It took Vincent Paglia a moment to realize the significance of the statement. Too late, he began to reach for the gun at his waist. There was a heavy pressure on his neck and then *bada-bing*, it was as if he'd been struck by a bolt of lightning. His brain filled with a bright light and then the world went dark.

"Help me hold this pig up," said the leader, who'd grabbed Vincent and propped him against the railing the moment his partner pressed the stun gun against the fat man's neck.

The other man tossed the stun gun off the bridge and got a grip on his side of the twitching, unconscious body. Together they heaved Vincent Paglia up and over the rail and watched as he hit the water with an enormous splash and disappeared beneath the surface.

"No chance he'll wake up and swim to shore?" the second man asked.

The leader scanned the surface of the water but, as expected, no large man had surfaced to stroke his way to the beach. "Nah, Tarzan himself couldn't take a thousand volts and then swim in those waters," he said. "With the tide running out, he won't surface again, if at all, until they find him washed up on Long Island. An unfortunate suicide victim . . . all those gambling debts. Took the jump." The man looked up. "Full moon tonight—all the crazies will be out."

Three hours later, the moon was directly above and casting dense shadows among the trees in a part of Central Park known as the Rambles. Located just west of the Metropolitan Museum of Art, the area lived up to its name with rambling, thickly forested hills and gullies that the architects of the park intended to leave in its wild state.

A careful observer, had any dared be about in that part of the park at that time of night, would have noticed that many of the smaller shadows near the ground were moving in the same general direction. Flitting from one dark spot to the next, some slipped upright through the brush like wraiths, while others scurried on all fours, squeezing beneath the undergrowth. For the most part they were silent except for the wheezing of lungs that spent too much time in cold and damp places without much sunshine or fresh air.

The careful observer may have also noticed that the moving shadows were spread out in a rough circle around a tall, wiry man who walked in their midst, his features hidden in the hood of his robe. Pulling back the hood, David Grale stopped and sniffed the damp air as his army of "mole people" skittered and snuffled along the carpet of old leaves. His dark hair hung in wet, lank strands around his thin face, which was as pale as the moon above the treetops. Whether it was the lunar lighting or an internal energy source of their own, a faintly mad glimmer shone in his eyes as he peered ahead in the direction that his followers were scampering. He sniffed again, catching the scent of rotting vegetation and beneath that the sickly-sweet odor of a greater corruption.

An emaciated creature appeared at his side. It was clothed mostly in rags, which barely covered the gray skin stretched too tightly over protruding bones. There was something almost amphibian about the way it hopped about and squatted on its haunches like a frog. The luminous eyes seemed impossibly large and protruded from its skeletal head, as it used its long, yellow fingernails to comb over the patches of what might have once been blond hair on its head.

"What news, Roger?" Grale asked the creature. The creature once known as Roger Pack had been a mildly successful stockbroker on Wall Street, but his affair with the bottle had destroyed his career, ruined his marriage, and in a manner not unlike a leaf swirling down from a tree in autumn, eventually brought him into the tunnels where he did not have to face what had become of his life.

Roger smiled. The few remaining teeth in his mouth gleamed yellow in the moonlight. "This way, Father," he said. The words ending in *s* came out as a hiss. "Are you coming, Father. Thisss way. Thisss way." He looked around and nervously licked his thin lips. As with many who lived in the deepest labyrinth of tunnels and sewers beneath the city, even moonlight and the distant glow of the streetlights and hotels of Fifth Avenue frightened him.

"It is an evil night," Grale said. "But lead on, Roger. Let us see what mischief is afoot."

"Yes, Father, an evil night, Father," Roger replied. "But come, we are near. Can you smell them, Father?"

"Yes," Grale replied. He'd long ago given up trying to disabuse his followers from referring to him as Father. In another life, he'd been an unordained Catholic lay worker, but that was enough for the miserable mole people, at least those who were not aligned with the forces of evil, to accept him as their spiritual guide and bestow upon him the title of priest. With him as their inspiration, they'd committed to his cause of hunting demons who he believed possessed the bodies of men in the dark places beneath the city, and sometimes above the tunnels, too.

Roger scampered into a tangle of growth ahead. Grale pushed through more slowly until he reached a small clearing on the other side.

Tourists were sometimes surprised to learn that in a

city of eight million people, many of whom walked its paths on a daily basis, there were parts of Central Park so wild that it was almost primal forest. No one went to these places—at least no one of good intent, unless necessary such as now.

When Grale's eyes adjusted to the moonlight, he saw that a dozen mole people were gathered around two shallow holes that had been dug into the forest floor. It was from the holes that the smell of rotting flesh emanated. Walking up to them, he saw why. Lying in each hole was a human body—children by the size of them—though it was difficult to say for sure because of the amount of decay and the dirt that partly covered their naked corpses.

Even his mad mind shrank from the thought of what had possessed one of the mole people to come sniffing along here and then dig to get at what lay beneath the disturbed ground. They were forever hungry in the tunnels of the city, forever in search of something other than rat meat and the garbage they could scavenge from the Dumpsters late at night.

"Sheila found them, Father," Roger said, pointing to another wretched soul who hovered near the graves. Bent over at the waist in the shape of a C, Sheila was naked except for a loin cloth that loosely covered her genitalia; her breasts were little more than folds of skin that hung like pale bats from her chest.

"Give me my prizes, Roger," she whined. "Give me what is mine."

Grale looked askance at Roger, who shot Sheila a dirty look before producing the prizes from the dark folds of his rags. He held them up and the moon flashed on medallions of gold that dangled from . . . "rosary beads," Grale muttered. He'd expected Sheila's treasure—it was not the first time he'd been to graves such as these—and yet it was always with a new sense of doom and sadness.

Among the demons he hunted were a number who hid within the Catholic priesthood, preying on children for their sexual needs. Several in the past month had felt the blade of his knife as it laid open their throats; after which they'd been carried down into the depths and left for the rats. But there was one he sought more than all the others, one monster worse than the rest . . . the one who left the rosary beads with the gold medallions of St. Patrick's as his calling cards.

He was drawn to the man, whose name he did not know, like a comet to the sun, and like those celestial bodies, passing in the dark, close and yet so far. Keeping an ear open for reports of missing boys in the various non-white Catholic communities, he and his underground army would watch those streets and wild areas, hoping to catch him before his next sacrifice. Several times over the past decade, they nearly had him. That one night in the New Jersey marshlands, when they'd come upon the still-warm body of the Vietnamese boy and heard the monster rumbling off through the brush like some sort of insane bear. Running as fast as he could, his knife drawn, Grale arrived at the roadside only to see the disappearing taillights of the killer's vehicle.

It had been many months since Grale had last heard rumors of the demon—these two bodies appeared to have been killed a very long time ago—and he sensed that his quarry was far away. Maybe gone forever from New York, killing and defiling in some other community. But he felt the man's presence in the clearing as though he were watching from behind one of the ancient trees.

Walking to the edge of the graves, he dropped a set of

beads back into each grave. "I will pay you for your prizes, Sheila," he said in a voice that tolerated no objection. "But these must remain with the bodies for the police to find." He knelt at one grave, noted the horrible gash that had severed the throat, knew that the bodies had been sexually assaulted to satisfy the lust of a dark god that demanded blood and perversion.

Grale administered last rites, feeling that God would understand. When he finished, he chose one of the more respectable-looking and dependable of his group—one who merely looked like one of Manhattan's ordinary bums—to carry a message for him to the *Village Voice*.

"Ask to speak to Ariadne Stupenagel, tell them to say to her that Grale has a message for her," he said. "She will come. Then when you are sure she understands how to find this place, tell her to call the police."

Grale then appointed two more of his most trusted lieutenants to stand guard over the graves until the morning. "They are not to be disturbed," he warned, noting the faces that turned away looking guilty. "Or the transgressors will feel my blade as surely as the one who did this thing."

The last threat probably wasn't necessary. Except for a creature known as Spare Parts, who was the acknowledged king of the mole people, Grale's word was the closest thing there was to law in the tunnels, and he was regarded with superstitious awe. But it never hurt to capitalize on that, and he'd seen the hungry looks.

Grale was about to push back through the bushes around the clearing when a shadow passed between the moon and the earth. The mole people around him yammered and mewed in fear, and he had to catch himself as he staggered forward like a man struck by a blow.

"He has killed again," Grale whispered. "God, give me strength."

Fifteen hundred miles to the west, a great bear of a man limped across the sagebrush desert near the Rio Grande Gorge. Other than labored breathing through his broad, flat nose, he made no sound, nor did he respond to the frightened whimpers of the ten-year-old boy he pulled along behind him with a rope. The boy was naked, without even shoes to protect his feet from the sharp rocks and prickly pear cactus. But if the child tried to stop because of the pain, he was yanked forward so hard by the noose around his neck that he choked and gasped for air.

It had been easy enough to capture the boy, as well as those who'd preceded him. Indian children were taught to trust Catholic priests implicitly, and this one had willingly climbed in the truck when asked if he could help direct him to the grocery store. He'd taken the child to an abandoned shack on property owned by the St. Ignatius Retreat and left him hog-tied on a filthy mattress until he could return for him that night.

Father Hans Lichner stood more than six and a half feet tall and weighed in at close to three hundred pounds, most of it muscle from the hard labor he put his sixty-three-year-old body through, chopping wood and gardening. His face was nearly covered by a full beard, which was usually littered with bits of his last meal. Tonight he wore sandals and a brown monk's robe with nothing beneath it.

The limp was the result of the American bomb that had fallen through the roof of his family home in Berlin in

February 1944 when he was four. His shattered leg had been improperly set by a town veterinarian—the family's real doctor having long since died in the snows outside of Leningrad, as had Lichner's father. But the deformed leg was still better than what had been done to his mother and older sister a year later when the Russians arrived and made him watch as they gang-raped the screaming women and then slit their throats. He'd been bayoneted and left for dead. But American soldiers found him and took him to a hospital.

After his release from the hospital he was sent to an orphanage established by a Catholic relief organization, where the priest who ran the facility had taken a special interest in the sad little boy. He'd endured the nightly abuses from the sweating priest, who, when finished, would beat him and call him horrible names. "This is your fault, you filthy creature," he'd ranted.

Like the other orphans, he'd hoped that some nice American couple would adopt him and take him away from the nightmare of the orphanage, but no one wanted a lame little boy when there were so many healthy ones available. His hope had turned to anger by puberty, much of which he spent torturing animals; he'd been especially fond of playing the role of one of the ancient Jewish patriarchs and "sacrificing" his prey by slitting their throats in the basements of ruined buildings.

As a teenager, he'd discovered that the bloodletting aroused his sexual desires. However, he perceived girls as filthy creatures like his mother and sister, who he had come to believe had not screamed in agony but with pleasure during their rapes and deserved having their throats cut. Instead, he'd taken up where his former tormentor left off and begun raping younger boys at the orphanage.

Not just any boys, however, but the dark children of Cain, the offspring of the unnatural mating of German women and Negro servicemen. He made himself believe that by raping these evil children he was insulting Satan.

As it came time for him to leave the orphanage, he grew afraid. He knew no other life than the strict discipline of his Catholic overseers, nor did he want to leave the objects of his sexual desires for a world in which they might not be so plentiful. So he'd joined the Jesuit order and studied to be an elementary schoolteacher so that he would always be near his boys.

After his ordination, he'd applied to go to the United States, where he knew there were many more dark children. Once in America and assigned to the New York archdiocese, he discovered that his calling was more important than he'd at first believed. The filthy brown children were threatening to overrun the country, indeed the world, as the Führer had predicted; they all grew up to be criminals and drains on society, breeding like beasts. Godly white men needed to step up, and he had been chosen.

However, the final act that had pushed his warped mind over the edge occurred without having been planned. At a summer camp in the Catskill Mountains, he had fondled an Asian-American preteen who pushed him away and said he was going to tell the counselors. They'd struggled and the boy had fallen backward and struck his head, knocking him out. Afraid, Lichner had waited until he could spirit the comatose boy into the woods, where he dug a shallow grave. His plan was simply to bury his victim but the boy had moaned in pain.

Instead of pity, however, the boy's suffering aroused him. He'd raped the boy and then he was struck by an inspiration born from the images of his family's deaths and his sacrifices of the animals. He was Abraham and the child, Isaac. But this time God had not stayed his hand as he pulled back his victim's head and, using a pocketknife, hacked crudely at the neck until his arms were covered with blood and his victim was dead. When a search was later launched for the missing boy, he'd made sure he was assigned to the area where the grave was located and prevented its discovery.

That was many years ago, and he'd perfected his ritual, buying the curved Assyrian blade that enabled him to dispatch his sacrifices with a single slash. It was risky business. He knew others would try to stop him in a misguided belief that he was committing murder. How could the sacrifice of mere animals be considered murder? And indeed there were several close calls. Twelve years earlier, he'd nearly finished with that Puerto Rican child, but he'd allowed his lusts to overcome his good judgment and raped the boy in Central Park too near a footpath before he'd cut the child's throat. Unfortunately, a couple had come along and heard the boy's cries and chased him away. The child then reported him to his parents, who'd gone to the church with their complaint.

Fortunately, there were those who understood his mission; chief among them was Andrew Kane, whose law firm represented the church. Kane arranged the payment that bought the silence of the boy's parents, a couple of drug addicts who killed themselves with the money, and good riddance.

At the time, Kane knew only about his sexual preferences. But Lichner confessed the true nature of his work—believing that he'd found someone else who understood the necessity. A few days later, the lawyer called him into an office at the archdiocese where he told him that the archbishop himself understood that Lichner was performing an important service for God. Of course, Kane said, he should understand that the archbishop could not openly embrace his mission. The unbelievers would raise a stink and might even prevent Lichner from continuing. However, in exchange for the archbishop's secret protection, he was from time to time to make himself available to perform some service on behalf of the church.

Most of these services turned out to be as a sort of messenger sent to intimidate miscreants who dared threaten the church and its priests over a few sexual indiscretions, such as the slut who threatened his good friend, Father O'Callahan, who'd become his intermediary with Kane. Usually all he had to do was appear and let his size—and what he believed to be his God-inspired inner spirit—cow these people, then suggest that they accept the money the church was offering for their silence. Occasionally, he'd resorted to physical violence. Only once, shortly after the incident with the Puerto Rican boy, were the tables turned. He'd been sent to warn the parents of a young nigger who'd been shot by a police officer—a good, white Catholic detective whom the church had wanted to protect. But he'd narrowly escaped a beating himself; there was simply no reasoning with the inhuman members of that race, and there'd been too many to fight that night.

There was one troubling aspect to his mission when he was in New York. Several years earlier, he realized that he was being hunted. By whom and to what end, he didn't know, but several times he'd sensed his pursuer near and fled. It filled him with a sense of dread. One man he did not fear, but this one traveled with an army of disgusting subhuman creatures who appeared to have crawled from the bowels of the earth. So when the Vietnamese child escaped his vehicle six months earlier when the trunk did not close entirely and again he was accused of sexual assault by the parents, he had not objected when O'Callahan suggested that he needed to disappear for a time.

They sent him to New Mexico and told him to attend classes for sexual offenders. At first, he'd taken umbrage at the label. As if he was nothing more than a crass pedophile, rather than a German warrior sending a message—no, a challenge—to Satan. He complained in a telephone call to O'Callahan that the doctors at the retreat were forcing him to participate in group therapy. But his friend had urged him to "say what you know they want you to say. The sooner you make them happy, the sooner you can return to us."

That was enough to make Lichner start being an active, even amiable, participant at the retreat. It was more difficult to carry on his work in Taos; the population was smaller and it was not as easy to move about without being noticed. He prayed nightly to return to New York City, where he sensed that great events were unfolding in which he hoped to play a pivotal role. He'd known that ever since September 11, 2001, when the brown-skinned Hittites had crashed the airplanes into the World Trade Center. On that glorious day, he'd looked up and seen the demon's face in the smoke that billowed from the two towers and knew that the time of reckoning was drawing near.

However, for now he had to play the game with the psychiatrists. But he still kept his covenant with God. Every month during the full moon when Satan was at his most powerful, Lichner would sacrifice a new Isaac to remind Lucifer who was in charge: the God of Abraham, not some fallen angel.

Tonight was such a night. The blood of Isaac would again be spilled in the desert. As he trudged across the soft soil and washes filled with sand, his stride still purposeful despite the limp, he thought about what was to come and felt the old stirring in his groin. He had to remind himself that the act was not about his personal pleasure—that he felt any joy was just one of the rewards allowed to him by God. Still, anticipation made him want to hurry so he gave the lead rope a hard tug that caused the child to cry out. "Silence, Isaac," he snarled in German. "Soon enough you may complain in hell."

At last he came to the edge of the gorge and followed a thin path along its rim. He had to admit that the setting was even better than Central Park, where he'd buried many of his earlier sacrifices. It was unfortunate that the police had discovered the graves of the other Indian boys; he'd had to drive much farther this time to make sure he wasn't discovered. But it was still nearly perfect for his purposes. Earlier in the day, he'd prepared a shallow grave with one end facing the abyss where he imagined his victim's soul would find easy access to hell and deliver the message that a soldier of God stood between Satan and domination of the world.

He was in no hurry. He'd waited for the eleven o'clock bed check and then stuffed pillows and blankets beneath his sheets to make it appear that he was still there, on the small chance that someone would look in on him later. Then he left, knowing that he didn't have to be back until just before morning Mass. He'd made his way out of a little-used back gate on the retreat grounds and to the abandoned shed where he kept his victims and an old truck he'd purchased and secreted there. Fortunately, the moon had provided enough illumination that he'd been able to drive the gravel road along the gorge without using his headlights until he arrived at the spot where he and the boy would walk.

Arriving at the grave, he yanked the boy to his knees. *"TEUFEL!"* He bellowed the German word for *demon* toward the gorge. The idea was to challenge the demon to rise from the depth of the earth and force him to witness the demise of another of his servants.

Reaching into the folds of his robe with his right hand, Lichner produced his long curved knife. With his left hand he grabbed the child's dark hair and pulled the head back until the boy was forced to blink up at the brilliant moon.

"Ich schicke Ihren dinener zu Hoelle!" he cried. (I send your servant to hell.) With a swift motion, he drew the blade across the child's throat. Blood gouted from the wound as the priest stood back and used his foot to shove the dying boy face first into the grave.

Stooping, Lichner wiped the blade in the sand. He would clean it better later, but now he had three final tasks to perform as he lifted his robe and knelt behind the convulsing body. When he was finished with the first he removed the rosary beads from the pocket of his robe.

The gold medallion gleamed dully in the moonlight. He'd seen the box of beads while attending a seminar at the archdiocese—intended he supposed for special parishioners, but he'd thought they would add a nice touch to his own rituals. He tossed the beads in on top of the corpse and picked up the shovel to finish the job.

A thousand miles to the east, David Grale looked up at the same moon as he recovered from the invisible blow that told him of the murder of another child. "The time of reckoning draws near," he croaked in a strangled voice as his followers looked at him with fear and scurried for their underground homes.

21

"GO AHEAD, MY SON," FATHER EDUARDO SAID AS HE placed his arm around Charlie Jojola, who stood with his head down in front of his father, Marlene Ciampi, and Lucy Karp.

"You tell them," the boy implored.

The priest shook his head. "It is not right for me to say something that was revealed in confession," he said. "In fact, I cannot make you do this at all. But I think you know that you should."

The boy nodded. He scuffed his feet in the sand of the recreation center courtyard, but wouldn't look up or speak.

With his heart sinking, John Jojola thought this must be some new trouble his son was mixed up in. But he tried not to let the disappointment show in his voice. "Come on, Charlie, spit it out."

Charlie frowned. "You'll get pissed, and I won't get my new shoes."

"How did you know about the . . . ," Jojola began to say, then thought, Heck, teach a kid since childhood how to cover his tracks, he ought to be able to disguise that he'd been snooping in the old army chest I keep under the bed. "Doesn't matter. Yeah, I may get angry if you've done something wrong, but a man takes responsibility for his actions whatever the consequences."

Jojola stopped himself. He didn't have the energy for this on Saturday morning after a long, sad week. Two days earlier, on Thursday, another boy had been reported missing from the reservation and was presumed dead. And a few days before that Char Gates had called to tell him that another grave had been found along the rim of the gorge about two miles south of the first one. "Same MO," she'd said. "Throat slit. Rosary beads."

Now, this fourth abduction had the reservation as stirred up as a nest of hornets. The hotheads were forming vigilante posses to roam the desert at night, and he was worried that they'd end up shooting each other or some tourist out for a moonlit hike. Angry words were also flying around about the lack of effective police work; never in front of his face, but he knew it when knots of men would stop talking as he approached. An agent from the Santa Fe office of the FBI had finally shown up on Friday, took a few notes, said he would talk to the sheriff about forming a multiagency task force, and left.

After the agent was gone, the pueblo's council decided to close the reservation to all but tribal members. Jojola approved of the decision. It would be very hard for an outsider not to be noticed now, and the chances of some tourist getting shot for asking a child for directions would be greatly reduced. But the tribe counted on tourism dollars, and the decision was not an entirely popular one, especially at the height of the season; more accusations had flown about responsible parenting being a better alternative. Nor did closing the reservation mean the children were safe; with permission or without, leaving the reservation to hit the candy and toy stores was too much of a temptation, especially for the boys most at risk.

Trying to protect these children was foremost in his mind. Still, he was the father of a son who was in need of some of that responsible parenting. He knelt in front of Charlie so that he could look in his eyes. "No matter what, you're still my son. I love you and we'll deal with it."

Charlie looked at him and then up at the priest, who nodded, "I looked at some photographs of naked women doing stuff with some guys," the boy muttered, his voice barely audible.

Marlene and Lucy both almost choked on the laughter that jumped into their throats. Jojola also had to suppress a smile as he asked, "That's it?"

"No, that's not it," Father Eduardo said. "That's what he thinks he's in trouble for, but it's more important than that. Start from the beginning, Charlie."

Charlie scuffed his feet around a bit more then began to speak.

The night before, he'd gone out to the St. Ignatius Retreat to perform his community service obligation of taking out the trash, sweeping, and vacuuming. Because the priests did not finish their meetings and classes until ten, Charlie and the man he worked with, Lloyd Bear, could not start until then and often didn't finish until after midnight, which meant the boy got home late and tired. This time, however, he was looking forward to his duties.

The previous week, he'd been emptying the wastebasket in the office of the administrator, Dr. Jonathan Tobias, when he noticed the middle drawer of the desk was open and he glimpsed the cover of a magazine. No one was around, so he'd carefully pulled the drawer open until he got a good view of the cover photograph depicting a nearly nude woman with huge breasts, bound and spread-eagled on a bed and looking up in apparent fright at a large black man clad only in a loin cloth who was standing above her with a whip in his hand. The main headline of *REAL SLUTS* magazine promised photographs of Virgins Gang-banged with Enormous Cocks! and Country Girls on the Farm with the Animals They Love. He knew it was wrong but he was about to open the magazine for a peek inside when he heard Lloyd walking down the hall. Reluctantly, he'd replaced the magazine and slid the drawer closed just in time.

Then last night, he'd gone back into the office, relieved to find that only the small reading lamp on the desk was on and no one was around. He opened the drawer and was happy to see the magazine still in its place. He pulled it out and was soon engrossed in the photographs—he'd heard about such things from some of the older boys but . . . He almost didn't notice until too late the voices coming down the hall. Panicking, he'd quickly returned the magazine to the drawer but, feeling guilty, decided he couldn't face whoever was approaching and instead stepped behind the heavy curtain in a dark corner of the room.

The voices stopped outside the office and then, to his horror, he heard the door open and two men entered. One of the voices he recognized as belonging to Tobias. He'd been introduced to the doctor the first night he arrived on the job. Tobias had told him in no uncertain terms that he was not to go near the priests at the retreat. "They are here to meditate and relax, not be bothered by children." Nor was he to go anywhere or do anything except the jobs assigned to him.

Charlie thought the admonition was overkill, as Lloyd Bear had also warned him on the drive over never to go anywhere except on his instruction. "You are not to speak to any person there, unless you've cleared it with me. Understand?" the man said. Charlie nodded. He did not know Lloyd well, but he seemed a little overly zealous about protecting the privacy of the priests at the retreat. Charlie had noticed that he was never far from where he was working.

Quivering with fear behind the curtain, Charlie wished he'd followed the man's instructions. He had not recognized the voice of the second man, who was obviously angry at Tobias. "Goddammit, you're supposed to be keeping an eye on your people, especially him," the man said.

"There's no proof he's involved in any of these . . . um . . . disappearances," Tobias protested. "He was in his bed at eleven, as are all of our clients, and attended Mass in the morning."

"With only eight hours in between when y'all were asleep at the wheel," the angry man said sarcastically. "He could have just about driven to Denver and back. In the meantime, there's two fuckin' dead Injun kids buried out on the gorge with their fuckin' heads about cut off. Another missin' for two months, and now a fourth has disappeared. I could give a shit about them little red niggers, but that fucker Jojola is nosing around, and he ain't stupid. So you git yer ass on the fuckin' phone to New York and tell 'em to take their problem child back or the lid may come off this pack of fuckin' perverts."

Again, Tobias tried to protest. "I do wish you'd watch

your language, I am a priest. We're not a prison; we're a treatment center for men of the cloth who are troubled by society's ills, such as alcohol and drug abuse as well as . . ."

"As well as poking little boys in the behind," the angry man finished. "Save the bullshit, we're knee deep in it already, and I'll speak however the fuck I want. You were told that he was a special case and needed to be watched 24/7. Fuck, he's big as a goddam buffalo; how the hell can you lose him?"

"As I said, we're not a prison, and there's no proof we lost him." Tobias sniffed in an attempt to show some spine. "How would he accomplish these unfortunate actions? We have guards at the gates, and no one could borrow a retreat vehicle without my knowledge."

"I don't know how," the angry man sputtered. "But if it ain't him—and New York warned you that he might have a little bit more of a problem than one of your run-of-the-mill butt bangers—then what's with the fuckin' beads in the graves. Whoever it is, he's practically pointing his finger at this place, saying 'Come find me.' "

Tobias sighed. "I know. I know. I'm not saying it's him, but he thinks he's fooling us with his participation in our therapy sessions. Says the right things, and is eager to please. But the doctors here agree with me, he's a dangerous man who belongs in a psychiatric hospital. But what am I to do? For some reason, New York is determined to protect him."

"Yeah," the angry man agreed. "He seems to have 'em by the short hairs, all right. But you need to lock him in his room and not let him out until we get New York to take him off our hands. Much more of this, and even the feds are going to get off their asses and be all over this place."

The two men walked back out of the office still bickering. With his knees shaking and an urgent need to urinate, Charlie remained behind the curtain a few minutes until he thought the men wouldn't return. Stepping from his cover, he picked up his trash bag and had just left the office when a large hand grabbed his shoulder from behind.

"Vat are you doing in here, *Mein Kind*," said a heavily accented voice. The hand spun him around like he was a toy, and Charlie found himself staring up at the face of the largest man he had ever seen. The giant was wearing a priest's black shirt and collar and black pants, but it seemed that darkness filled all the space around him, too. His voice was gentle, but his red-rimmed eyes burned.

Charlie thought he might faint from the foul odor of the man's breath as he struggled against the man's grip. "I was just taking out the trash," he cried.

"Let the boy go!" The voice of Tobias came from somewhere behind the giant.

"I caught him sneaking out of your office, Herr Doctor," the priest said but released his grip.

"I was emptying the trash," Charlie said, holding up his bag as proof.

Tobias's eyes narrowed. "How long were you in there?" he said.

Charlie thought quickly. "I just went in and came right out."

The psychiatrist seemed to consider that for a moment. "All right, thank you," he said. "You may go. I'm sure the father did not mean to frighten you."

Charlie dared not look up at the priest. The giant's eyes softened; he looked almost kindly, but that only reminded the boy of a science fiction movie he had seen in which the space alien could make its features conform to appear human. "Ja, that's right, little one," he said with a smile, mussing Charlie's hair with a huge paw. "I vas just making sure you vas not doing anything naughty. I did not mean to frighten a nice boy."

"That's okay, I wasn't scared," Charlie lied. He'd turned and walked down the hall as calmly as he could. He turned the corner and received another fright. Lloyd Bear was standing there as if he'd been listening. He grabbed Charlie by the arm and escorted him quickly down the hall. "I told you not to go anywhere or talk to anyone without checking with me," he hissed.

Charlie thought the man looked frightened, as well as angry. He decided not to tell him the truth, either. He held up his bag again, "I was just getting the trash."

"That's all," Charlie told his father and the others. "I'm sorry I looked at the magazine and sorry that I spied on people."

John Jojola smiled grimly. It was obvious that the time had come for him and Charlie to have "the talk" about sex. And culturally, eavesdropping was considered extremely rude for a people who lived in such close proximity as those in the pueblo; they were trained from early childhood to tune out other conversations. But in this case, I'm glad he did.

"It's okay, son. Heck, me and Charlie Many Horses found a *Playboy* once that we hid in the woods and looked at until the pages fell apart," he said. He looked quickly at Eduardo. "Of course that doesn't make it right, and we'll need to talk about some of what you saw. But right now I'm more interested in what Tobias and the other man were saying. Are you sure about what you heard?"

"Yes," Charlie said very much relieved that apparently not only was he not in any major trouble, but he was helping his dad almost like a detective.

Jojola nodded. He wondered about the priest who'd accosted Charlie. The tracks he'd found near the first grave had been made by a big man. One strong enough, as Gates had noted, to nearly decapitate a human being with a single slash, which he knew from personal experience in Vietnam was harder than the movies made it out to be. The single witness they had to one of the abductions had said he'd seen a large man dressed in black talking to the child.

I wonder who the second man talking to Tobias was? Obviously someone paid by whoever it is in New York who wants the doings at St. Ignatius kept under wraps.

"Was there anything else?" he asked his son.

Charlie thought for a moment. "I think I saw the big priest once before. He was walking across the courtyard."

"Yeah?" his father said.

"Yeah. I remember because he walked with a limp."

Jojola turned and asked Father Eduardo if he could take Charlie into the center for a soda pop. He wanted to talk to Marlene Ciampi, who'd listened to Charlie's tale with a frown on her face but without comment. Eduardo gave him an appraising look, but said nothing as he beckoned the boy to follow.

"And oh, Charlie," Jojola called to his son.

"Yeah, Dad?" the boy said, half worried that the lecture or grounding or whatever he'd expected was now about to manifest itself.

"You done good. You were scared, but you held yourself together like a man. I think if you can still find them, those shoes are yours."

The sun on the southwestern desert did not shine more

brightly than Charlie Jojola's smile at that moment. It was only with extreme reluctance that he followed the priest into the rec center instead of bolting for home and the army chest under the bed.

"You done good, too, John," said a female voice behind him. He turned to find Marlene Ciampi smiling at him.

At dinner the evening they first met, he'd asked about the rosary beads and was surprised to find out that Marlene was no ordinary tourist, or even the art student she claimed to be. She was the wife of the district attorney of New York City for one thing. But more than that, she was a woman of surprising depth, and powerful currents ran beneath the friendly surface.

Never in a million years would he have imagined striking up a real friendship with a white woman. Yet, in the month since they'd met, he felt as though he'd discovered a kindred spirit that he'd known with only a few men of his tribe. One reason, he believed, was that she seemed as haunted by the past as he had been.

He'd even invited her to Blue Lake, one of the holiest places of his people, and outsiders saw it only by invitation of a tribal member. The trip began in an offhand manner when she'd remarked on the photographs of former president Richard Nixon that seemed to adorn many of the walls in the pueblo homes, including his own.

She'd asked about them with a quizzical look and the comment, "He's not exactly the most popular president . . . outside of New Mexico, anyway . . . though in his dotage he managed to salvage some of his reputation because of his diplomacy with China. But a lot of people still resent him for the breach of trust and the lies."

"Yes, Watergate, the missing minutes on the tape," Jojola acknowledged. "But you have to understand, that was all outside world stuff to us. We are a sovereign nation, you know, surrounded by and bound by most of the laws of the United States. Many of us, including myself, served in the U.S. military and consider ourselves to have dual citizenship. We are Taos, and we are Americans. Or as my uncle used to joke, 'We're the first Americans. We just needed better immigration laws.' What affects the United States, of course, affects us, but what we care most about is what happens here on our ancestral lands. Blue Lake provides us with our spiritual lifeblood, the stream that flows through the heart of the community, the ancient pueblo. But for many years, the United States government did not recognize its own treaties that Blue Lake belonged to us, and instead considered it U.S. Forest Service land. For decades, we sent delegations to Washington, D.C., to ask that the treaty be honored and the lake returned to us. But we are not a pushy people and did not understand the white saying that the squeaky wheel gets greased—especially in the nation's capital. To us that concept is rude, and such a person would be less, not more, likely to be heard by the elders or tribal council. So our delegations would go and politely sit around, ignored until it was time to return home with empty hands. But in 1971, for reasons that are still unclear, President Nixon learned of our request and insisted that the treaty be honored and Blue Lake given back to us. Ever since, he's been a hero to the Taos Pueblo as we remember what was important to us, and it was not Watergate. I guess it's all about perspectives."

Jojola had described for her the beautiful crystal-clear waters of the lake nestled high up in the arms of the Taos

Mountain, surrounded by conifer and aspen forests. "It sounds lovely," Marlene had remarked, and before he thought about it, he invited her to see for herself. As they drove to the lake, he told her how his people believed that the waters had healing properties for both the body and soul and that if she wanted, she could immerse herself in the snow-fed waters.

"Why, John Jojola," she replied, "are you trying to sneak a peek at this fine body without any clothes on it?"

Jojola felt his cheeks burning, as if he'd stood too close to a fire. "No, I don't want to do that," he stammered. "I mean, I'm sure you have a very nice body. But I just meant . . . well, I could show you a place, a little inlet, where you could have privacy . . . and I . . ." He stopped and looked at her for mercy.

Which she granted. "Hold on, oh brave and noble warrior of the Taos Pueblo. I was just teasing. I am sure you realize that there is nothing much to look at on this old woman, but I accept your offer. Who knows, maybe I'll be cleansed of my past sins."

Jojola thought Marlene was wrong about whether there was anything worth looking at in regard to her body. But he was smart enough to keep his mouth shut before he put his boot in it again. He'd showed her the inlet and then walked over the hill. She'd emerged from her dip looking refreshed, if not healed. "Thanks, John," she said, giving him a quick peck on the cheek, which got the blush burning again. "I know this was irregular, and I appreciate the gesture, but I'm afraid even a place this beautiful can't cure what ails me."

Jojola understood her comment. Many times in his dark days he'd bathed in the waters of Blue Lake hoping for a miracle, but none had appeared. At least not all at once. But he also understood that miracles sometimes took time, and they weren't always dramatic. He thought the same would be true with Marlene, so he smiled and said, "No, but you probably made some trout happy."

They'd seen each other often during the month. He'd found her abilities as the former head of a security firm and assistant district attorney helped him sort through the child abduction/murder cases, and agreed with Gates's assessment that they were dealing with a serial killer. She'd also contacted her friend, Father Dugan, and asked where he purchased the rosary beads he'd given Lucy. He said he'd received them from Archbishop Fey at some celebration at St. Patrick's but otherwise didn't know where to find more like them, though he'd ask around.

Jojola appreciated the sounding board as he became increasingly frustrated with the lack of progress in the case. But his time with Marlene wasn't all about work. He played tour guide, but in another sense found himself in the role of spiritual guide as well.

After Blue Lake, he'd taken her later one afternoon to what was one of his favorite spots on the rim of the gorge, above where a pair of golden eagles were nesting. They sat on the edge of a precipice with only the outcropping of the aerie between them and the river bed nearly eight hundred feet below. He explained that he often went there when troubled to burn sage to cleanse himself while appeasing the spirits and asking for their guidance.

As the sun lowered itself in the western sky toward the low dark line of the Nacimiento Mountains, their conversation turned to their pasts. Feeling that Marlene—who he noticed normally brushed over her deeper issues with humor—would need to be drawn out if he was to help her, Jojola began by telling her of his days in Vietnam leading up to the massacre of the Hmong village.

"Despite what the New Agers, and even some Indians, try to project about the native populations before the Europeans arrived," he said, "much of the Americas were embroiled in constant warfare. In North America, raids on other tribes were the way a young man proved himself and how older men showed that they were still capable of leading. It also served other purposes. One was to establish hunting territory and take slaves, who did the menial jobs in a village. Another was that the raids often resulted in capturing women, which helped keep the genetic pool from stagnating. Yes, we in the pueblos were more settled and had agriculture, but we supplemented it with hunting buffalo, which required going onto the plains and led to confrontations with the tribes there. We also did our share of raiding for women, slaves, and—after the Spanish brought them to the area—horses."

Jojola paused, thinking back all those years to when he and Charlie Many Horses received their draft notices in the same week. "But Vietnam was different," he said. "We seemed to have no purpose there. We weren't protecting our homes, or even the homes of the people who lived there. We weren't even trying to conquer new territory. There seemed to be no purpose . . . other than to kill and try to prevent being killed . . . until a Vietcong leader we knew only as Cop, which means *tiger*, and his men wiped out a village of Hmong who were our friends. Then, at least Charlie and I had a purpose . . . revenge. And when Cop lured Charlie into an ambush, I swore a blood oath that no matter how long it took, I would find him and kill him."

"Still?" Marlene asked. "After all these years? If you met him on the streets of Taos, you would still seek revenge?"

Jojola nodded. "It was a blood oath. I can't take it back."

The pair were silent for several minutes watching a thunderstorm building up in the west, casting a shadow over the land in front of them. Then Marlene asked in a quiet, almost-timid voice, "How did you forget about the men you killed?"

"I don't try," he shrugged. "Oh, I did for a time. Tried to block them out by becoming a hermit. Then it was with booze—not so much during the day at first; I could work and focus on a job, whether it was digging a ditch or riding on a garbage truck. But the nights were when the ghosts could not be ignored. So I tried to drink them away, but they only gained strength. . . . I've never told anyone this, but there were nights when I considered joining those ghosts permanently."

Again Marlene nodded without saying anything; however, tears formed in her eyes and trickled down her cheeks. In her mind, she could still feel her husband prying the bottle of Hennessey and the gun out of her hands. Butch tried so hard to help her, but he didn't know, couldn't know about the ghosts . . . not like John Jojola.

"I got married, but it turned out to be a bad thing for her, too," Jojola went on. "A very painful time in my life."

Marlene put a hand on his shoulder. "I heard your wife died. I'm sorry."

Jojola looked at her oddly. "Did Charlie tell you that?"

"Yes."

Jojola shook his head sadly and was silent. "She didn't die," he said after a moment. "She left me." He told her the story of their downward spiral into the cesspool of alcoholism and how, after he'd pulled out of the dive, she'd continued and then that night he found her with her lover and the heroin.

"Then I'm even more sorry," Marlene said. "I know

what it's like to blame yourself for what we do to people we love."

"Thank you," he said. "But I realized that I could not keep blaming myself entirely. She had her own path to follow." He sighed. "And at least she left me Charlie. No matter what we do wrong, as long as we do right by our children, we've done a good thing in this world."

Marlene bowed her head. "I can't even say that," she said. "I've been so busy trying to shut out my past, shut out the world, that I not only shut all that and my husband out, but my children, too."

Jojola smiled. "It's the shutting out part that's the problem," he said and told her about the medicine man and the dream in which the coyote suggested that he had to learn to accept his past, "and let the ghosts become part of my memories, not enemies I have to confront every day in order to vanquish them."

"Did it work?" she said looking sideways at him.

"Yeah," he said and laughed as he pointed to his head. "Sometimes it is like having a whole other village up here. At first, it seemed a little crowded, but now it's more like coming out of your house and seeing a neighbor some distance away working in a field. Unless there is a reason that you want to make the effort to go talk to them, it's enough to just know that they are there, part of the community."

"Yeah but what about the ones you'd rather not be neighbors with?" she said with a laugh. She told him more of her past. "I've killed out of vengeance, and I've killed out of anger. And I've killed men who I still believe deserved it. But who was I to decide who lives and dies? Maybe that's why I have such a hard time dealing with the guilt."

Jojola shrugged. "Like any city or town, there are good

people and bad people in my memory village. The good people do not become better just because you overemphasize their place in your life, and the bad ones don't go away simply because you wish it was so. They're there; you just need to put them in their place, not give them more importance than they deserve. After all, they are just memories."

Again they fell silent. The thunderheads to the west rose tens of thousands of feet into the sky, their tops boiling with pent-up energy, the main bodies brooding shades of deep blues and purples. They blocked out the sun and the land was covered in shadow.

Marlene wondered if she would ever be able to create a village for her ghosts as Jojola had done and learn to live with her memories instead of trying to forget them. It wasn't so different from what she was getting at the Taos Institute of Art Healing.

Much to her own surprise, she was truly enjoying the classes at the art school. However, it was one thing to paint pretty pictures of mesas and sunsets during the day, and then have her sleep filled with images more reminiscent of Dante's *Inferno* at night.

Surprisingly, she found that she actually looked forward to the therapy sessions. Even the group meetings weren't the big cry fests she thought they would be, filled with pathetic victims who'd let men run roughshod over them and done nothing about it. There were plenty of tears in these sessions, even a couple of the "patients" she'd anticipated, but she was impressed by the strength and resiliency of most of the other women.

Marlene was coming to accept that like most of these women, she suffered from post-traumatic stress disorder. In her case, one of the counselors told her, "Not unlike what soldiers suffer who have had to do some pretty horrible things to stay alive or protect their comrades. Good, decent people, ordinary people, who have been forced by extraordinary circumstance to behave in a way that grinds up against their moral code and the way they've been taught to believe. No wonder people with PTSD suffer from depression and fits of anger and suicidal ideation. They're in direct conflict with their consciences. Some try to self-medicate with drugs and alcohol; others simply withdraw from the world from the shame, whether they recognize it or not.

"The fact that you're here—that this violence has troubled you so deeply that you would seek help—is a healthy sign that you want to get past it. Now we just need to find a way that will let you do that."

Jojola seemed to recognize that, too, as he cleared his throat and said, "There was something else the medicine man told me . . . something that was even more difficult to accomplish in some ways. He said that I needed to forgive myself."

"What about forgiving yourself for Charlie's death?" Marlene asked. "If you still want to kill the men responsible, isn't that because you feel guilt for not being there when he died?"

Jojola looked back at her, thought that Butch Karp was a very lucky man, and nodded. "You are a wise woman, Marlene Ciampi," he said. "I suppose you are right, and maybe that is why Charlie is the most restless ghost in my village. In fact, he told me the day I met you that it was time to let it go."

Marlene snorted. "I'm hardly a wise woman," she said. "Otherwise, I would not be here. I just can't get past feeling like I'm going to end up one of the bad people in everyone else's village." She began to cry.

Shrugging off his shyness, Jojola placed his arm around the sobbing woman. "In my tribe, we are born into one of two main clans. You are either in a spiritual clan or a warrior clan. It is simply recognition that not every problem can be solved by prayer and good thoughts, just as every problem cannot be solved by fighting and war. Like the Bible says, there is a time and place for everything. I guess one way to look at it is that if you had not committed these acts that trouble you, it is unlikely that we would have met. And considering the terrible thing that is now happening to my people, and the help that you have given me, I cannot help but wonder if there is a reason for our meeting."

Marlene wiped at her tears and smiled at him. "Is that more of the ancient wisdom of your people?"

Jojola shook his head. "No, just a friend talking to a friend who has shared a similar path."

Marlene thought of her husband and children. She realized at that moment how very much she wanted to share her life with them. Not by going back and trying to change the past, but by looking forward to the future. She at last even saw a glimmer of hope that such a thing was possible, and that she owed this revelation to the good man who sat beside her and opened her heart by exposing his own.

At that moment, the sun broke through a gap in the thunderclouds, bathing the part of the rim they sat on with the golden light of the end of the day. Perhaps disturbed by the sudden change, one of the eagles took off from the aerie below with a piercing cry, and flapping its wings, climbed up past them into the sky.

Marlene laughed delightedly like a schoolgirl. "You planned that," she accused Jojola. "That's some sort of Indian trickery to fool the gullible tourists."

Jojola laughed, too. "No," he said. "But perhaps it was part of a plan we don't know about yet. My people believe that eagles are the messengers who carry our prayers to the Creator."

Marlene watched the eagle soar on the updrafts until it was a tiny spot high above them. "I hope he is a strong eagle," she said. "I gave him a lot of weight to carry."

"He is strong enough," Jojola said. "And look, he will have help." He pointed to the second eagle taking off to join her mate. He chuckled and Marlene joined him until they were laughing so hard that the tears were pouring down their cheeks.

Remembering that day, Jojola now said to Marlene, "Maybe Charlie's information means that the eagles got to the Creator with my prayers." But he felt the rage rising in his throat as he digested the fact that the best suspect in the murder of four little boys was a priest. And that the church had a hand in hiding the killer and others who had apparently preyed on their flocks from the law and allowing them to continue putting more innocents at risk.

One thing that galled him was that this wasn't the first time. Twelve years earlier, a story broke in the New Mexico media that pedophile priests had been sent to a secret sex offender treatment program in Deming, a quiet town in the southwest corner of the state. Then after their "cures," the men had been assigned to parishes throughout the state where they again had contact with children. The church had done it without notifying anyone, but the story came to light when the priests began reoffending and ruining more lives.

Now the church was doing it again. The breach of trust

and what it had meant to four boys he had known since birth made him so angry that he swore the same oath he had when he held Charlie Many Horses in his arms. He would find the killer and, police officer or not, he would kill whoever was responsible.

Marlene seemed to sense this. "What's your next move?" she asked.

"I'm going to go to the sheriff and see if he will ask a judge for a warrant to search St. Ignatius. Maybe see if I can ask the priest who frightened Charlie a few questions. He seems to fit the physical description of the guy seen talking to one of the victims . . . and he limps," Jojola said explaining the tracks he had seen at the first gravesite. "I have to move fast because it sounds like the administrator and whoever it was with him plan to get whoever it is they suspect out of town. But I also want to keep Charlie out of this for as long as I can; he could be in danger if they knew he'd heard them talking."

"Tell the sheriff that you got the information from a confidential informant," Marlene suggested.

"Yeah, but I have to be careful. If I give too many details, and Tobias hears about it, he may remember the discussion and that Charlie was in his office right after that. Got any better ideas?"

Marlene shook her head. "No. But I'll think on it while you go talk to Asher."

Jojola climbed in his truck and left for the sheriff's office in Taos. There he was kept waiting by a deputy who clearly shared his boss's disdain for the Indian police chief.

Finally tired of the game, Jojola walked past the deputy and burst into Asher's office with the protesting underling in tow. "Sheriff, we need to talk. I believe I have a suspect in the murder of four children from the Taos Pueblo."

Asher scowled and made no attempt to hide his irritation that Jojola was within shouting distance. "I thought I told you that this is the Taos County Sheriff investigation, Jojola, and to stay the hell out of it."

Jojola put his hands on the front of Asher's desk and leaned forward. "I have information from a reliable confidential informant that the man responsible for two, and probably four, boys may be a priest residing at the St. Ignatius Retreat." He leaned a little closer, noting that Asher's hand drifted toward the small button above the drawer. "Now sheriff, before you summon help to assist Barney Fife here, I've been doing my best to let you handle this investigation. But if you're not going to act on my information, I will. What's more I will call the governor's office and tell them what I just told you. Now maybe you don't remember, but the governor and I served in Vietnam together, and I think he'll listen to me when I tell him you're a big, fat, ineffective pig who is dragging his feet on the investigation into the murder of four of the governor's constituents. And I'm absolutely positive the media will be just as interested."

Asher turned redder than normal and held up his hands. "Hold on, Jojola, don't get your nuts all tied up in knots," he said. "I appreciate the information. I was just trying to point out that there needs to be one central command for this investigation or else we'll be trippin' all over our fuckin' feet. It's Saturday and I'm not going to be able to find an amiable enough judge to come away from whatever barbecue he's at to give us a warrant to search a Catholic retreat and question a priest, for God's sake, on the word of a fuckin' confidential informant. And tomorra's Sunday . . . ain't no way we're gonna get a judge to disturb a Catholic institution in *this* state on a Sunday. But tell you what I'll do. First thing Monday morning, I'll go see a friendly judge I know—he goes to my church—and see if I can't get him to spring for a warrant."

"Monday!" Jojola shouted. "This guy could be gone already, much less two days from now."

"Look, if he leaves, we'll extradite his ass back here," Asher said. "Provided, of course, we got a case and this CI of yours doesn't just have a hard-on for the Catholic Church."

"If he leaves the state, we'll never get him back here for questioning, and you know that as well as I do," Jojola replied. "And if we don't question him, we might never make a case to extradite him."

"Well, if we don't have a case, we don't have a case," Asher shrugged. "Now if you don't have anything better to do than tell me how to conduct an investigation . . ." He went back to looking at the papers on his desk.

Jojola remained leaning on the desk. He considered what it would be like to cut the bastard's heart out and show it to him while he was still breathing.

The sheriff looked up, his face contorting in anger. "You still here? Deputy, show Mr. Jojola the door, and don't let it hit you in the ass on your way out."

When the deputy hesitated, his eyes on the big hunting knife, Jojola smirked. "Don't bother, Barney. I'm leaving before this gets messy."

Outside, Jojola jumped back in his truck, but he wasn't about to wait until Monday. Instead he drove to the retreat. He arrived at the gated entrance and told the guard, "I'd like to talk to Tobias."

When the administrator showed up several minutes

later, Jojola didn't wait for any pleasantries. "I want to talk to you about a priest who may be involved in a murder investigation I'm conducting. I have reason to believe he resides here."

"I'm sorry," Tobias replied, "but we do not allow anyone to talk to our residents. Unless, of course, you have a warrant. Do you have a warrant, Mr. Jojola?"

"No, I don't have a warrant. I was hoping you would be willing to assist me with the investigation of the murder of four little boys."

Tobias gave his best sympathetic shake of the head. "Well, I don't see how I could help. And until you do have a warrant, I'm afraid my hands are tied. . . . And if that time does come, I'm afraid I'm going to have to ask you to contact our attorney first. Shall I give you his name and telephone number? I believe he's the former attorney general for the state of New Mexico."

Jojola stared at Tobias and fought to control his anger. *He knew I was coming . . . that's why he made the big deal about the warrant. . . . Asher, that bastard!* He lost the battle of control. "If I get a warrant, you smug little prick, I will kick the door down and drag whoever you're protecting out into the road."

Tobias's face twisted in anger. "Well, until then, I think I've tired of this macho display, Mr. Jojola. You'll excuse me."

"There is no excuse for you," Jojola called after the administrator, "or for what the church is doing out here. . . . Oh, Dr. Tobias, one last question."

The doctor stopped walking but didn't turn around. "What is it?"

"Does one of your clients walk with a limp, you know, the big guy?" Jojola asked. He couldn't be sure but it seemed that Tobias flinched. However, the psychiatrist quickly recovered and began to walk again as he called over his shoulder. "I have no idea what you're talking about. Now I really must get to my afternoon prayers."

"Yes, you do that," Jojola replied. "Pray for the bastard who killed my kids because when I catch him, there will be a reckoning for him and for anybody who protected him."

The last comment got the reaction Jojola had hoped for . . . the doctor's forward momentum slowed, he seemed to consider saying something, but then kept going. Pray doctor, Jojola thought, that someday I don't come back for you.

22

THE BLOWSY BLONDE TOTTERED UP TO ANDREW Kane with her older husband in tow. Lost somewhere in her late forties, she was wearing a low-cut blue Versace that exposed ample portions of her store-bought breasts. However, she'd poured far too much body into far too small a dress; it did not flatter the mound of her belly or the saddlebags that clung to her upper thighs, but she was too drunk and too wealthy to care.

Although she had her eyes on Kane, she managed a slurred greeting to Archbishop Fey, who was once again beaming benignly at his side, only this time it was at Kane's penthouse for a highbrow cocktail party/fundraiser for his mayoral campaign. After all, the television spots showing him with his coat slung over a shoulder and his shirtsleeves rolled up talking to construction workers having lunch on the wall outside of Rockefeller Center, or escorting small black children into their gang-infested schools, cost money. Lots of it, he thought, and I'll be damned if I'm going to spend one cent of my own on them.

While the woman's husband turned to speak with the

archbishop, Kane let his eyes rest on the woman's cleavage and inwardly smirked when he saw the marble-size points of her nipples grow larger in response to his gaze. Slut, he thought, as she pretended not to notice and babbled on about the last time she'd seen him. "The Barbra Streisand Farewell Tour at Carnegie I believe, such a wonderful evening."

They fall on the floor and spread their legs at the slightest whiff of money or power, he thought, as outwardly he allowed the other Andrew Kane to chuckle with delight at the recollection of Barbra's jazzed-up "Hello, Dolly," which the real Kane found repulsive. Hell, this one would do me now with the archbishop and her husband watching if she thought there might be a bright bauble in it for her. Maybe thinks she could be the next Mrs. Kane. Fat chance. Something younger, toned, perhaps. Of course that would mean the archbishop would have to be so kind as to grant yet another annulment, this one from the third, I believe, Mrs. Kane. She who is recovering from a love affair with cocaine at an undisclosed location in the Bahamas, though the press believes it's a humanitarian effort to work with underprivileged Third World children. Still, I might be persuaded to bounce Mrs. Whitehead around for a large campaign contribution . . . better at least keep her on the line.

"Ah, yes, a wonderful evening, Mrs. Whitehead," he gushed, taking her small, sweaty hand in both of his curiously effeminate and long-fingered ones. Stepping back a little as though to take in the fullness of her beauty, he added, "My, you look like Aphrodite herself this evening." He let the reference to the Greek goddess of love sink in for a moment, before continuing. "I hope we're going to be able to count on the Whiteheads' legendary generosity for my campaign to put this city back on top where it belongs."

Mrs. Whitehead's usual facial expression looked as if it had been paralyzed into a permanent mask of happy surprise by too many injections of Botox. Now, her face nearly split like a ripe melon as she effusively assured Kane that he could count on their financial support.

"And if there's anything I can do personally to help," she said huskily, leaning forward to give him a better view of the shadowed valley between her breasts, "you know, *stuff* a few envelopes, *lick* a few stamps . . . all you need do is ask." She giggled at what she considered her clever innuendo, her hazel eyes swimming in champagne.

The real Andrew Kane sneered and allowed himself a quick vision of Mrs. Whitehead tied to his bed with dark red welts rising on her generous bottom. Naughty girl deserves a spanking. "I can always use another *eager* volunteer," his alter ego said with a wink, and turned to her husband. "Do you think you could spare her?"

Mr. Whitehead grunted. He'd followed Kane's gaze and noted his wife's reaction to it. Slut, he thought, hell, she'd fuck him right now if he asked. But except for the natural jealousy of any wealthy man when a rival dared mess with one of his possessions—even one he had no further use for—he wasn't particularly disturbed by the current Mrs. Bernard Whitehead IV's willing infidelity. She was his second wife, a trophy twenty years his junior when he first seduced her fifteen years earlier and decided it was time to trade in the first Mrs. Whitehead, the mother of his ungrateful son and daughter. But all the plastic surgery—the boob job, the butt implants, the tummy tucks, Botox injections, and face peelings— couldn't dam the sands of time from running out on this model. If Kane wanted to occupy her attention, it would leave him more time for his "secretary," a lovely twenty-year-old Latina. She could neither type nor spell, but she could suck a tennis ball through a garden hose, so who cared about clerical duties. In the meantime, it didn't really matter to him whom his wife was screwing. Besides, it wouldn't hurt to pave the way for greater access to the runaway favorite to become the next mayor of New York.

Whitehead came from a long line of bankers going back to the days when New York was a British colony. They'd become one of the largest family-owned banks in the world and larger still after merging with a national chain in exchange for a seat on the board and a large percentage of the stock. The Whiteheads had, however, not achieved their status in the banking community without skirting some of the rules. For instance, at his direction, his bank practiced redlining home and business loans to exclude certain neighborhoods. Applications from those who wanted to live or establish a business in those areas—defined on a map by a red Magic Marker line drawn around them—were rarely approved. Of course, these were predominantly black, Latin, Asian, and recent immigrant neighborhoods.

Whitehead thought of it as protecting his bank from people who couldn't be depended upon to repay their loans. But when it came right down to it, he simply didn't like "those people, especially the niggers." Forget that they were all criminals and drug addicts; he hated the way they looked and dressed and smelled. He didn't appreciate the insolent way the males had of swaggering down the crowded Manhattan sidewalks, making better men move aside or risk a confrontation. He personally avoided ever walking on the Avenue of the Americas because it drove him insane to listen to all that jabbering in foreign languages, as well as their butchering of the English language. Most of all, he hated seeing some darky walking with his arm around a white woman.

Redlining was, of course, a violation of federal and state banking laws. But it was difficult to prove and enforcement was generally relaxed unless some new mayor, in a misguided attempt to garner the race vote, got a burr up his ass and insisted on an investigation. So if Kane wanted to fuck his wife, let him; that should later entitle her understanding husband to some sort of gentlemen's agreement about his banking practices. And if that wasn't enough for a small favor or two, Kane could be made to understand that it wouldn't do his political ambitions any good if the press found out that he was boning the wife of one of his faithful campaign contributors. He made a mental note to have Mrs. Whitehead followed by a certain private investigator who did the occasional dirty job for him. Photographs might come in handy.

"Hey, Andy," Whitehead said, extending a hand while the other patted Kane on the shoulder. "You son of a gun, saw the *Times* article that practically had you moving into Gracie Mansion tomorrow. Apparently, we don't even need to bother going to the polls to vote for you . . . though I dare say my wife would love to do what she can to help."

"Ha, ha," Kane laughed. He detested being called Andy or touched without his permission. Smarmy bastard, he thought, practically bending his wife over for me, and then plans to use it after I'm in office, maybe even to blackmail me.

The acknowledgment made him smile even more warmly than before at the man in front of him. He'd made it a point to know the secrets of powerful men and was aware of Whitehead's secretary and what value that information might be to Mrs. Whitehead in a divorce. He also knew about the redlining, as well as certain other bank practices, such as those that allowed drug dealers to launder large amounts of unreported cash in violation of a half-dozen state and federal statutes. When the time came, he planned to add Mr. Whitehead and his bank to his own holdings, like a new butterfly to the collection of an entomologist. He could use the laundering services for his own enterprises. He already had all the photographs he needed. And just for fun, I might force him to watch me fuck his wife *and* his secretary at the same time.

"Well, you never know about the voters. That's why they play the game, ha ha," Kane said in his between-friends voice. "And I'm quite sure I'll be able to find some important position for your lovely wife." He turned to look at Mrs. Whitehead. "You are indeed a lucky man . . . no need to stray from the fold with a fine woman like this waiting for you at home."

Mr. Whitehead frowned at the last statement. Son of a bitch, could he know? But Mrs. Whitehead didn't notice her husband's discomfiture; she was too busy thinking of a question of her own. I wonder if he's got a big . . .

"Come along, my dear," Mr. Whitehead said, taking her by the elbow before she could finish the thought. "Time for this old boy to get home and perform his husbandly duties, ha ha."

Mrs. Whitehead rolled her eyes and waved a dismissive hand at Kane. "That'll be a first. Ouch! Bernard, don't pinch!"

• • •

As the Whiteheads left, Father O'Callahan entered the front door of the apartment wearing civilian clothes, a Brooks Brothers button-down and tan slacks, which still made him hopelessly out of place in a room full of people who actually shopped at Saks Fifth Avenue on Fifth Avenue, and were on a first-name basis with the sales staff at Bergdorf Goodman. His eyes immediately sought out Kane, who motioned him toward a hallway leading to his study. The priest followed his boss with his mind racing, still trying to find a satisfactory way to put the proper spin on recent events.

It was hard to say exactly when the gyroscope of Kane's plans started to wobble. Certainly the ill wind was blowing back when the terrorists bombed the courthouse and the files disappeared. But there'd been a number of smaller issues that also conspired to rob him of a good night's sleep.

For instance, several of the protected priests who had their sexual abuse of members of their parishes covered up by payoffs and promises to treat and/or dismiss them, had disappeared since January. The police suspected foul play, and O'Callahan wondered if some of the offended families of the victims were learning of the priests' return to duty and exacting revenge.

If that wasn't worrisome enough, now the Lichner issue was threatening to blow up in their faces. Once that morning, and then twice that afternoon, he'd received troublesome calls from New Mexico.

The first had come from Tobias, who told him to stand by for a fax, as he did not want to talk on the telephone. A few minutes later, the fax arrived stating that Tobias believed that Hans Lichner

   is too dangerous for this facility to deal with. He is a
   severely disturbed individual exhibiting antisocial

tendencies, possibly psychopathic, and belongs in a secure mental health institution or, perhaps, even a prison with a psychiatric ward. I have reason to believe that he may be involved in the disappearance and murder of local children. The chief of police of the Taos Pueblo was here two weeks ago, asking about a man who fit Lichner's physical description in connection with the disappearance of one child. I sent him on his way, but he has continued to nose around, and of late in the company of a woman named Marlene Ciampi, who you may know as the wife of the New York district attorney. I have a hard time believing that her appearance in Taos is purely coincidental.

As a man of God and as a physician, I am finding it increasingly difficult to retain compassion for what is obviously a very sick individual, and to morally condone keeping him in a situation where he continues to present a danger to the public. In that light, I am sending Fr. Lichner back to New York by the first available flight out of Albuquerque. Flight details to follow.

O'Callahan sneered at Tobias's reference to himself as a man of God. You're as black as the rest of us, he thought, just hiding behind your Hippocratic, or should I say, hypocritic, oath and doctor-client privilege. He tried to call Tobias but only got an answering machine. The little fuck doesn't want me to change his plans. We're going to have to have a little talk about who's the boss. But that can wait.

The news about the Ciampi woman was disturbing. He didn't know much about her although he remembered something in the New York papers in January about her receiving a medal for bravery. Apparently, she had gunned down the terrorists who were trying to blow up the courthouse. She was obviously a dangerous woman, but even more so because of whom she was married to, the frigging DA. However, the boss was going to have to decide what should be done with her and the Indian police chief. In the meantime, he'd placed a call and arranged to have Lichner picked up when he arrived at La Guardia and taken to a safe house the archdiocese owned in the hills along the Hudson River north of the city. "Do not let him out of your sight," he said into the telephone.

The second call had come that afternoon from Sheriff Asher. The sheriff had been on Kane's payroll for a dozen years and told to keep his eye on the St. Ignatius Retreat, including heading off any investigations into the clientele. But now he was worried because the Indian police chief had come across information that St. Ignatius was harboring a killer.

"We got your friend's ass out of here this morning, and you know who I mean," the sheriff growled. "But that don't mean it's over. You do know that Jojola's been nosing around with the wife of your district attorney? Now maybe they're just spanking the monkey, but my guess is she's here for another reason."

"Yes, yes, I know," O'Callahan said with a sigh. He was getting sick of hearing that name. Marlene Ciampi—the more he heard it, the more it sounded like the tolling of a bell. Although he'd never been particularly superstitious in the past, that thought made the hair on the back of his neck stand up. "Look, whatever Lichner did or didn't do, he's out of there now," he told Asher. "They have no proof of anything, and they won't be locating him anytime soon."

"Well, they better not because if I go down, I ain't goin' down alone," the sheriff blustered.

O'Callahan made his voice as cold as he could manage. "Was that a threat, sheriff? Perhaps, you'd like to make that directly to your employer?"

There was silence on the other end of the line, and then the sheriff answered, his voice apologetic. "No. No need to bother him. You're right, we'll jest sit tight and ride this one out."

"That's right, sheriff, ride 'em cowboy," O'Callahan said. He'd hardly hung up when he got another call from Tobias, who had forgotten his qualms about talking on the telephone and was close to hysterical. "That Indian police chief was just here, asking about a priest who limps, and you know who he means. I told him nothing, except that he would have to come back with a warrant and speak to our attorney first. He threatened me, actually called me a smug little prick . . . me . . . a priest! I don't know what to do . . . this has all gotten out of hand . . . I . . ."

"Tobias you *are* a little prick, now get a grip," O'Callahan said, pleased when the rejoinder silenced the psychiatrist. "Again, there is no proof that Lichner committed these crimes, and he is no longer your concern. You can rest assured that we will take care of Father Lichner."

"He's a sick man," Tobias interjected. "We did not have the time to properly treat a man as troubled as he is—"

O'Callahan interrupted him with a hiss. "You listen to me, you piece of shit. How did someone as stupid as you ever get to be a psychiatrist? Guys like Lichner don't get treated. Guys like him talk to idiots like you out of one side of their face as they're daydreaming of screwing and slicing up the next little boy."

"You've got no right to talk to me like that—" Tobias whined, but again the other priest cut him off.

"I'll talk to you however the fuck I want," O'Callahan said. "All I need you to do is listen. With Lichner gone, I'm sure this Indian will become interested in some other avenue of investigation."

"Do you think so?" Tobias asked, sounding like a little boy who'd been told that Santa Claus was indeed real.

"Yes, doctor. In the meantime, you return to assisting the poor, troubled men we send to you. It is important now for you to go about your business as normal. And you keep your mouth shut, understand?"

"Yes. But what about Marlene Ciampi?"

"What about her?"

"Don't you think . . ."

"I think you are worrying about things best left to others," O'Callahan said. "Don't you agree, doctor?"

"Well, yes," Tobias said, now sounding much relieved. "Yes, of course, you're right. Business as usual. Leave Marlene Ciampi and that Indian to you. I wash my hands of the whole mess."

O'Callahan smiled and wondered if Tobias got the irony of his last statement. "Yes, doctor, scrub away," he said and hung up.

Despite the confidence he'd tried to impart to Asher and Tobias, O'Callahan was afraid. In his opinion, Lichner was more trouble than he was worth. His little mission took precedence over even his loyalty to Kane, and he was putting them all at risk. O'Callahan didn't understand Kane's refusal to be done with the giant priest. If it had been up to him, O'Callahan would have had Lichner killed and dumped in the Atlantic, but Kane would not hear of it. "He's part of my plan. You have some objection?"

"No, of course not," O'Callahan answered quickly, feeling a chill go up his spine. He'd seen the results when people objected to some plan of Andrew Kane's, and he wanted no personal experience with it. If there was a fault with his master, it was that sometimes he was a little impetuous when it came to violence. In O'Callahan's opinion, the decision to kill Martin Johnson had been an overreaction to the rapper's betrayal. Better to have sued him and taken the money, O'Callahan thought. But Kane wanted him dead and made it integral to accomplishing the more important goal of framing Alejandro Garcia.

O'Callahan had nothing against murder. It was often an effective tool. But the plan to frame Garcia was complex to begin with—too complex in his opinion, but the boss did enjoy his little strategies and gamesmanship. Now, as he headed back to Kane's office with the news from New Mexico, he was not so sure that the boss wasn't losing his grip.

Kane entered the study and motioned for O'Callahan to have a seat in the low-backed chair in front of his desk, the same desk where his father sat years before and blew his brains out. He thought of the study as his cave, a place removed from the world—done in rich mahogany and soft leathers, the heavy drapes rarely opened to allow the sun in. He closed the door and began wandering around the room as O'Callahan began to speak, giving every impression that he was listening carefully but without undue alarm. He drifted past the wall that held his extensive book collection, absently picking up from the elephant-foot umbrella stand an old riding crop that he tapped on his shoe as he paced.

As O'Callahan talked about the calls from New Mexico, Kane thought about how Lichner fit into his plan to destroy the Catholic Church in New York. Of course, the man was a murderous pedophile who was going to keep on screwing and killing young boys once a month until he got caught. And that was his last little secret. Someday not only would the press discover how the church, in the person of the archbishop, had covered up sexual assaults by its priests by paying off the victims' families. The knife would slip in deeper still when it was revealed that Fey and his predecessor (as this had been going on for some time) signed off on a plan to send the offenders to treatment centers and then allow them to return to prey on more of their flock. But the coup de grâce would be Lichner, the pedophile priest protected by the church who turns out to be a serial killer.

The problem was, of course, the missing files. The files would show that Kane himself had arranged for the payments to the families of the victims who had been lucky enough to survive meeting Lichner. The letters in his files recommending against prosecution had been signed by Kane and stamped No Prosecution.

Still, he'd believed that his plan to retrieve the files was still unfolding as it should, with a few nuances. Yes, the death of Vincent Paglia, as yet undiscovered by the authorities, was unfortunate. But he couldn't take a chance that the star witness had been found out or that he would crack under questioning.

There was the videotaped interview and one more piece of evidence to come. A couple thousand dollars was all it had taken to liberate the .45 caliber handgun

Alejandro Garcia had used to shoot the rival gang member two years earlier from the police evidence locker. The gun, which bore the youth's fingerprints, had then been used to kill ML Rex and subsequently kicked under the car to be found by the police. The case against Garcia was still solid.

However, this new problem in New Mexico was not to his liking. If this Indian and the DA's wife were working together and had focused on Lichner, it could ruin his plans, especially if he didn't get those files soon. He hated it when his plans went awry; it made him really angry. So angry that as he walked behind O'Callahan, he suddenly raised the riding crop and brought it down swiftly and hard across the shoulders of the priest.

O'Callahan grabbed the desk in front of him to keep himself from falling. The shock and pain of the blow had stopped him in midsentence and all he could do was try to suck in air. A second blow drove it all back out of him as a scream.

"I thought I told you to make sure there were never any problems at St. Ignatius," Kane said calmly as the priest bleated in pain. "I want you to call that idiot sheriff and tell him to take care of that Indian cop and this Ciampi woman. Make it look like an accident or someone had it in for the cop and she was just in the wrong place at the wrong time. But get it done, do you understand me?"

Whack! A scream. "Yes, yes, please no more," O'Callahan pleaded from his knees, where the third stroke had driven him.

Kane was rather enjoying himself and was about to add one last stroke when a loud voice interrupted him. "My God, Andy, what in the name of Jesus is going on here?" said Archbishop Fey from the doorway. He had seen his secretary and Kane disappear from the hall and thought he would follow when they didn't immediately return to the party.

"Oh, Archbishop Fey. Please do come in and shut the door," Kane said as though inviting him to tea.

Fey did as told, but demanded in a stern voice, "Why are you striking this good man?"

Kane looked down at the fallen priest. "Riley, tell this old geezer to shut the fuck up and listen," he ordered.

Shakily picking himself up off the floor, O'Callahan turned to the archbishop and snarled, "Shut the fuck up and listen."

Fey stood still for a moment with his mouth opening and closing. Rather like a fish, Kane thought. The old man looked as if he might faint, but Kane walked up to him and slapped him twice. "Now sit down," he snapped and the old man complied meekly on the couch.

Thirty minutes later, Fey sat with his face in his hands weeping. Kane had revealed the true extent of the cover-up regarding the pedophile priests, the No Prosecution files, and that his name was on the payoff paperwork, as well as the papers reassigning the offending priests to new parishes.

"Oh my God, what have I done?" Fey cried.

"Well," Kane laughed, "for starters probably committed any number of crimes. But I think worse, as far as the faithful are concerned, pretty much destroyed any faith they might have in the Church once this comes out. If it comes out."

"But I didn't know," Fey pleaded.

"Oh please, you self-righteous piece of shit," Kane said,

"you signed off on the payoffs and you knew in that pious little heart of yours that there was more going on. You didn't *want* to know what that might be. All you cared about was building a new cathedral so that all those droll little people out there would remember that you even ever existed."

Kane walked over behind the archbishop who kept a nervous eye on the riding crop. But instead of a blow, Kane rubbed the old man's shoulder.

"There, there, it doesn't have to end badly," he consoled. "You can still have your cathedral and the adoration of millions for all eternity. But I may need you to do something for me. . . . If certain things don't go the way I expect them to, I may need you to grant this Father Dugan an audience and demand those files from him. No one ever need know about any of this."

Fey kept his face in his hands. "Oh God, I have sinned . . . how could I have done this to my church . . . to the children?" he whispered.

"Pride, your eminence," Kane said and laughed. "Pride goeth before a fall, remember that one? Now be a good old fart and dry those tears so that we can go join my guests. Riley, I'm sorry, but I'm afraid you had better remain here until my guests leave, your back seems to be bleeding. Besides, you have a telephone call to make."

With that he reached down and pulled the archbishop up by his elbow to help him stand. "Come, come now, your holiness," he said, "stiff upper lip. You just didn't realize that you were playing for the other team. It's not as bad as all that."

"No," the archbishop replied. "It's worse. But I have no choice but to go along with your evil. I must protect the church from my failings."

"Yes, yes," Kane said. "Glad you see it my way." He linked arms with Fey and they left.

Moving gingerly so as not to further incite the screaming demons clawing at his back, O'Callahan sat back down in the chair and reached for the telephone. He called a number in Taos. "Sheriff Asher, please," he said politely, trying not to cry.

"Asher," a voice said a minute later.

"Listen, you fuck," O'Callahan snarled. "This is coming from the top. The Indian cop and the woman have to go . . . make it look like an accident or something unrelated to St. Ignatius." He reached behind and touched one of the burning welts and felt the wetness. "But make it happen or expect a one-way ticket to New York to see the boss."

23

JOHN JOJOLA STOOD IN THE PREDAWN HALF-LIGHT on the edge of the cliff above the eagles' aerie gazing into the depths of the Rio Grande Gorge. The river slithered through the narrow canyon below, a topaz-green snake winding its way south, the rush of its waters over and around the large rocks in its path reaching his ears as a continuous murmur.

He'd been meditating for two hours, arriving while the stars were still at their brightest and the sky around them at its darkest. It was one of his favorite times to be alone in the desert, but it wasn't for the quiet. If one listened carefully there was always some sound: the raspy whisper of a rattlesnake crossing sand in search of prey . . . the cautious hopping of a jackrabbit . . . . the distant yipping of a family of coyotes greeting each other to begin the hunt. But it was peaceful—a time when the natural world was in harmony with itself and his troubles were revealed to him as an infinitesimally small part of an infinite universe.

However, he had not driven out that morning just to enjoy the landscape or the solitude. He was there to meet Sheriff Asher and Marlene Ciampi.

After returning home from his run-in with Tobias at the St. Ignatius Retreat the night before, he'd checked his messages at the Taos Pueblo Police Office. He almost spilled his coffee on his lap when one of the messages was from the sheriff, asking for his help. "I know I haven't been the model of interagency cooperation, but I've been giving it some thought and wanted to see if we can't put this behind us. So I figured you might want to know that I received a tip after you left, 'sposed to be the location of another grave on the east side of the gorge, just north of reservation lands. If you want to meet me tomorra' mornin', say eight about ten miles north of the turnoff before the bridge, I'd be obliged to have your assistance. If it checks out, I think we could use that to go see my friend the judge and ask for a warrant to search St. Ignatius. . . . Oh, and if you want, invite that Ciampi woman. I understand she used to be a prosecutor back in New York; maybe she'll have something to add that us two hicks can't see. Otherwise, sort of as a sign of our new workin' relationship, I'd appreciate it if you kept this information between us." Asher chuckled. "I'd like to get there before the press does this time."

Jojola had listened to the tape with his mouth hanging open like an attic door. Then he'd called Marlene and, after telling her all of what had transpired earlier with Asher and Tobias, asked what she thought.

"Well, at first sniff, something doesn't smell right," she said. "Obviously, he's traced my license plate to figure out who I am. Nobody out here knows much except for you, the people at the art center, and, maybe, Father Eduardo. Then again, he wouldn't be the first cop to use his technology to check out the new girl in town, especially if she's hanging out with a hated rival. Maybe you put the fear of

God, or at least of bad press, into him, and he's decided to turn over a new leaf for the time being. Or maybe he just wants to have a scapegoat if these murders go unsolved. I've seen that happen plenty in New York. Shouldn't hurt to find out what he's up to, anyway."

"Yeah, but there is something that's bugging me," he said.

"What?"

"When I went to St. Ignatius I got the feeling that Tobias knew I was coming."

"So you think Asher called him?"

"Yep. But maybe the sheriff was trying to get out in front of me on the investigation. You know, solve the case himself."

"Yeah, maybe." There was a pause then Marlene added, "Just be careful, John."

Jojola had gone to the eagles' aerie alone because he'd wanted the time to himself to let the anger drain from his body. He was grateful for the release, as the more he thought about what Charlie told him, the more enraged he'd become.

He noticed the eastern sky beginning to turn gray and was suddenly aware of a shadow at his side. If he tried to look at it directly, it was gone . . . just a memory, a breeze rustling the silver-green sage. But if he looked straight ahead at the far side of the gorge, the shadow remained and he felt the presence of Charlie Many Horses.

"You're going to have to let me go, John," said a voice in his head.

"I cannot."

"You must and soon. Lives may depend on it."

"I cannot, you were my brother," he repeated and turned toward the shadow. But it was gone, leaving him to guess if his mind, or the desert, was playing tricks on him.

Jojola wondered how Marlene was doing with her ghosts. She is strong, he thought. She'll be all right with them once she learns how to forgive herself. He actually had greater concerns for the daughter, Lucy. Outwardly, she seemed a normal young woman, enjoying the attentions of the young ranch hand, Ned, and the growing affection of his people. But she was like her mother in that she seemed to attract evil like a flame attracts moths. And she is more likely to be burned than Marlene. He wondered if the women realized that the violent patterns of their lives were not just a series of misadventures or bad luck. Some people seemed destined to walk paths that would bring them into conflict with darkness.

As the morning sun at last peeked over the Sangre de Cristo range behind him, he watched the rays chase the shadows down the rugged rock wall opposite his position and thought, No matter how long the night, light eventually conquers dark. The sun rose higher, warming his shoulders as he raised his palms to the sky. I pray this night will not last much longer for my people.

He turned his head to look down the road in the direction Marlene would be coming from, having asked her to join him at the aerie after the sun rose. Then they'd meet up with the sheriff another five miles farther north. Marlene wasn't coming alone. She'd called back to ask if she could bring Lucy. "She insists and I'd like her to see the eagles." He'd agreed, but now he wished he'd told them both to stay home. Something wasn't right, and he knew it in his heart.

Looking back across the gorge, he caught a quick

movement of gray out of the corner of his right eye. Instinctively, he ducked into a crouch, whipping the big knife from its sheath in one fluid motion to face the coyote that had emerged from a stand of junipers five feet away. Any other time, he might have congratulated the animal on its stealth; he was a man who prided himself on being able to distinguish the scurrying of a lizard over pebbles, or the click of a deer's hoof on stone a hundred yards away. But there was no time, as something that sounded like an enormous bee whizzed by his head so close that he felt its passing. The buzz was immediately followed by the distant report of a rifle, but he was already falling to the ground. He lay still, waiting to see if there would be a second shot, but he'd landed in a small hollow just below where he'd been standing and realized that he was out of sight of his would-be assassin.

Jojola turned over on his stomach and found himself almost face to muzzle with the coyote, which had sunk to its stomach at the sound of the bullet passing overhead. The animal seemed mildly amused by the whole scene, its yellow eyes bright and its mouth open in a mischievous grin.

"Thanks, brother," Jojola whispered. "I'll owe you a rabbit every week for the rest of my life." The coyote grinned wider still, then staying low, slunk off into the junipers.

Jojola snaked his way up behind a clump of dry grass to look out in the direction from which the bullet had come. He had no doubt it was intended for him. The morning was clear, no one could have mistaken him for an animal, and besides, it wasn't hunting season. He wondered if he had stumbled upon the boys' killer out digging another grave. But that didn't make sense, the timing wasn't right, the moon wasn't full anymore. So maybe someone trying to protect the killer, or, he thought wryly, just any one of a couple dozen others who don't like me.

He had not noticed any other vehicles on the way in, or any headlights in the dark of one approaching. That meant the assassin had secreted himself before he'd arrived. Jojola suspected that he was hiding behind a cairn of rocks about a half mile back down the road. You should have noticed where his tire tracks left the main road, he thought, chiding himself for getting lax. Then again, no one told you today was open season on Indian police officers.

Looking beyond the assassin's lair, Jojola tensed when he saw a plume of dust rising from the road another mile farther back. It had to be Asher or Marlene and her daughter. They would have to drive right past the shooter. He sprang up and ran for his truck at the bottom of the hill, knowing he was already too late.

Sheriff Asher saw the plume, too, causing him to turn his attention away from the cliff Jojola had been standing on. But he smiled; after all his plan—with a couple of adaptations—was working to perfection. One down, one to go, he thought. The boss will be pleased.

Asher had always been a bully, as a child and an adult. In fact, he'd gone into law enforcement nearly thirty years earlier because he saw the badge as a way of being able to have power over other people. There was nothing quite as satisfying as beating some perpetrator to a pulp while handcuffed in the back of his squad car, unless it was coercing sexual favors from women picked up on shoplifting or bad-check charges in exchange for leniency. As a patrol deputy, he'd readily accepted bribes to tear up speeding tickets, or look the other way to let a drunk driver go. The only difference when he became sheriff twenty years earlier was that he expected larger bribes for ignoring bigger crimes, like drug dealing and car theft. "Them is just the perks of the job," he'd say when he handed his most trusted deputies their share of the take.

So when first approached by the men from New York a dozen years earlier to keep an eye on the St. Ignatius Retreat—"make sure there's no messy investigations if one of our, ahem, clients happens to make a mistake in the community"—he'd asked only one question. "What's in it for me?" Reporting to O'Callahan, Asher had found, meant easy money—five thousand a month for baby-sitting a bunch of perverts—until this Lichner psycho arrived and started butchering "the little red niggers." Personally he could have given a shit about the missing boys. "They would have all just grown up to be drunks and troublemakers like their fathers. Nits make lice," he joked with his deputies. But Lichner hardly bothered to cover his tracks and now the Indian police chief was breathing down his neck.

Why the man in New York wanted to protect the grotesque priest he had no idea. But while he'd never met the man, or even knew his name, he wasn't about to question him. He'd had a deputy once who threatened to take his suspicions about the connection between the clients at St. Ignatius and reports of children being sexually assaulted to the media if an investigation wasn't launched. Two days after Asher warned New York about the threat, the deputy was found at the bottom of the gorge, having apparently jumped from the bridge. The fact that New York had not asked him to take care of the deputy, Asher believed, was a message from the boss . . . a demonstration of how long his arm could reach.

The day before when he called O'Callahan, however, the message had been for him to take care of the problem, and he didn't complain. In fact, he was rather pleased with himself when the components of his plan had fallen together like the pieces of a jigsaw puzzle.

First, early in the evening he'd released from the county jail a Taos Pueblo man named Leroy Cinque, a violent alcoholic who'd been arrested by Jojola a month earlier for beating his wife in a drunken rage. Cinque had been on the losing end of a number of run-ins with Jojola in the past and had sworn on more than one occasion to kill the police chief. The latest had been immediately after his incarceration and within hearing of two deputies, who could be counted on to testify to that fact.

Upon his release, Cinque had been surprised when he got outside and found Asher waiting in his SUV with an offer to give him a ride back to the pueblo. He didn't like the sheriff or trust him; then again, he didn't want to offend him either. Cinque opened the passenger side door, but had to move a deer rifle out of the way to get in. "Sorry about that, Leroy, just put it in the rack," the sheriff apologized.

Once Cinque was in the car, the sheriff offered him a bottle of tequila "for what that bastard Jojola did to you . . . interfering between a man and his wife . . . sorry there was nothin' I could do 'cept get you out a week early." The former prisoner had accepted the apology and chugged a quarter of the bottle, not sure how long the sheriff's largess would last. He'd reluctantly offered the sheriff a drink, but Asher turned him down. "Nah, I'm on duty. That one's all yours."

As they drove, Asher explained that he was working on a case to implicate Jojola for "stealing from the tribe." Where Cinque came in, he said, "is I need someone on the inside, so to speak, to keep an eye on him, see if he makes any large purchases."

Cinque smiled, although he had only a few teeth so that it mostly looked like a gaping hole in his head. He liked the idea of getting back at Jojola, and took another long swig on the bottle, then another, until he'd finished it and passed out as was his habit.

Asher drove him out into the middle of the desert on the western side of the gorge and rolled him out of the vehicle. The sheriff had then driven his SUV to where he'd left Cinque's old white Ford pickup truck hidden in a gulley several miles away. He pulled on a pair of gloves, took the rifle back out of the rack, and then switched vehicles. Driving back across the gorge bridge to the eastern side he'd turned north on the road that ran parallel to the gorge.

Picking his spot for an ambush several miles onto reservation land, he'd hidden Cinque's truck behind the rock cairn so that it wasn't visible from the road. Then he'd found himself a comfortable spot to hunker down with his Thermos of coffee and the old deer rifle that now had Cinque's fingerprints all over it.

The original plan was to wait there until Jojola drove up the road in the morning with the Ciampi woman. Then, when he couldn't miss, he'd blow the Indian's brains out. The woman would try to run, but there was no place she could hide. He laughed out loud at the vision of her terrified dash down the road in the moments before the bullet hit her, too.

Asher would then return in Cinque's truck to where he

left his own vehicle and switch again. Next, he would "discover" the murders as he arrived—just like his message to the police station had said—to work with Jojola on the homicide cases. With his help, his deputies would note the tire tracks of the killer's vehicle leaving the scene, tire tracks later traceable to Cinque's truck. The then-disabled truck would be discovered on the other side of the gorge, along with the deer rifle with the fingerprints confirming Cinque's guilt.

A massive manhunt would ensue led by the fearless sheriff of Taos County, who would personally come upon the crazed Indian trying to escape across the desert. Cinque could be expected, though it hardly mattered, to have the worthless piece of shit .22 caliber pistol Asher had tucked into his belt. Whether he pulled it or not, as there would be no witnesses, he would die in a hail of bullets from the sheriff's own Colt .45 Peacemaker. Why the governor would probably give him a medal for catching the murderer of his former comrade in arms.

Asher was pleasantly fantasizing about the award ceremony and the speech he would give when Jojola nearly ruined the whole thing by arriving early. It was too dark to risk a shot and then try to find the woman. Asher had no choice but to let the vehicle pass. He was therefore relieved when it turned off the road a half mile beyond his position.

As the sky grew light enough to see, he'd watched Jojola on the cliff—doing some sort of Injun mumbo-jumbo—for a while unsure of the Ciampi woman's location. But as the day grew brighter still, he could see his target's vehicle parked down near the road, and it was soon apparent that no one else was in the car or with the police chief. That's when he decided he would shoot now, and figure out what to do about the woman later. Maybe with Jojola gone, she'd run back to New York. Let them take care of her.

It was a perfect setup, he thought, as he settled the gun on a rock and looked through the scope. The Indian was silhouetted against the sky as he put the crosshairs on Jojola's head, let out his breath slowly, and squeezed the trigger. The 30.06 had a powerful kick and so he couldn't be sure, but it almost seemed to him that just as the gun bucked, his target moved. But then he'd seen Jojola fall and was sure he'd hit him. He was about to rise and go check on his victim when he turned and saw the plume of dust from an approaching vehicle. Got to be the woman, he thought. He trained the scope on the cab and saw that there were two figures. Isn't that sweet, she brought her ugly daughter. He shifted his position so that he would have the shot he'd anticipated the night before.

As he watched the truck drive toward the spot closest to the edge of the gorge, Asher had a new thought. Refocusing the scope on the front driver's side tire, he squeezed off his second shot and was rewarded when the tire disintegrated and the truck veered for the cliff's edge.

The driver fought for control, taking the truck into a skid that had it facing 180 degrees from the direction it had been traveling when it came to a stop. But the passenger side tires were too close to the edge, which gave way, and the truck slowly rolled over into the gorge.

Although pleased with his shooting, Asher couldn't see what happened to the truck once it fell. He figured the occupants would be dead at the bottom of the cliff—two more of Cinque's victims—but decided he would make sure before returning to finish off Jojola if necessary.

• • •

It was close, but Marlene and Lucy weren't dead quite yet. The truck had rolled over one and a half times on a steep slope but came to rest—at least for the moment—against an ancient low-lying piñon tree that had chosen a small rock outcropping above a sheer eight-hundred-foot plunge on which to live its life. The truck was tilted on the slope at such an angle that Marlene was hanging from her seat belt, while Lucy was pressed against the passenger side door. For the moment they were okay; however, the piñon was already losing the battle against gravity and the pressure of the half-ton truck. It creaked and popped under the weight while a steady stream of rocks and pebbles eroded around its base and fell into the chasm.

The predicament was a far cry from the pleasant early morning drive they'd embarked on an hour before. They'd been bouncing along in a comfortable silence, content to watch the sunrise and enjoying just being near each other while lost in thoughts regarding the men in their lives.

As the sun bathed the desert in a soft gold, Marlene realized how much she'd grown to love that country. Absently, she wondered what chance she'd have of dragging Butch out of Manhattan and replanting him in Taos. She tried to imagine him the gentleman rancher, or maybe a country lawyer, while she painted and grew more gray, wrinkled, and eccentric with each passing year. But the image of him in a cowboy hat and boots quickly dissolved into the more familiar picture she had of him in a suit and tie, off to do battle with New York's criminal defense lawyers, and she knew any ideas of him relocating were futile.

It was a sad thought. There was a time she'd thought

her particular brand of insanity would drive them apart. But now that she felt she might be climbing up a little farther on the ladder to mental health, she wondered if the positive change would be just as dangerous to their marriage. So much of her healing she attributed to what she'd discovered in New Mexico, and she wasn't sure she could ever live in Manhattan again.

She had taken Jojola's advice and no longer tried to make the ghosts of her past go away, and in doing so, found them to be easier to live with. Sometimes they glared at her from the streets and corners of the village she'd created, but at least she was no longer exhausted by the effort to keep their faces out of her mind. If they made their presence too immediate, she simply passed them by as she would have unsavory characters on the streets of New York.

The strategy wasn't fail-safe, especially at night when she was troubled by a recurrent dream that her sons were being stalked by an enormous shadow while the bad men of her village smirked and laughed. But the New Mexico sunrise had a way of making even the worst dreams recede and seem less threatening. She'd even started to learn to forgive herself for acts that had troubled the conscience of the former Sacred Heart schoolgirl, recognizing that in many instances if she hadn't acted, greater evil would have been done. In other cases, where the use of force had been less well defined, all she could do was accept that there might have been another way, but there was no going back, only forward with the resolve to do better. But in one odd way, coming to terms with her conscience regarding her past made it that much more clear that the greatest hurdle was ahead, seeking forgiveness from herself and her husband for what she had done to their marriage.

Thinking of Butch made her also consider her feelings for the other adult male currently starring in her life, John Jojola. She found it strange to feel so close to a man without a desire to go to bed with him. With Billy, the sexy dog handler of Long Island, the attraction was purely physical. But with Jojola the attraction was friendship and something beyond.

It was interesting to her that between Jojola and Father Dugan, the priest she was closest to in her own faith, she found the former to be almost more spiritual. Dugan was a great friend, as well as a good and moral man whom she'd entrusted with millions of dollars without a second thought that he might be tempted to take the money and run. But perhaps due to the location, Jojola seemed more in touch with that side of himself, even if she didn't buy into everything about talking coyotes and eagles that carried prayers to heaven. Then again, if she was ever going to believe that such things could happen, it would have had to have been in New Mexico with such a guide.

He just had such a different way of looking at the world. Once, while hiking along the rim of the gorge, they'd been overtaken by a passing rain shower. When it was gone, she'd looked at what she thought of as a gray and brown desert and noted how barren it remained. He'd told her to look again. "Think small," he said. That's when she noticed the tiny flowers that seemed to have magically appeared with the rain. White ones, yellow, purple, and pink—most so little, hardly the size of her pinkie fingernail, that she hadn't noticed them against the immensity of the rest of the landscape. Yet now that she knew they were there, she saw how they carpeted the ground in soft colors for miles in every direction.

"They're so delicate," she said with delight.

"Think so?" he answered again. "Pick one."

Marlene stooped to do as told, but carefully drew her fingers back when pricked by the plant's thorns. "Another Indian trick," she grumped, sucking on the injured digit.

Jojola laughed. "The price we pay for misperceptions," he said. "Sometimes we don't see beauty because it's not slapping us in the face and demanding we pay attention. And sometimes, those things we find beautiful, or think of as fragile, may not be as harmless as they look."

"Couldn't you have just told me that," she sulked, "my finger hurts."

"Some lessons are best learned the hard way," he replied with a smile. "The point is that each person creates their own reality for the world. You saw a harsh, barren landscape, until you really looked; then it was filled with tiny delicate flowers, which then turned out to be quite capable of protecting themselves. It's sort of like those photographs you saw of President Nixon in the village. To you, and maybe most of the United States, he was a villain, but to us he was a hero. And in that light, maybe you perceive yourself to be a bad person, but someone else—like me, or maybe someone who would have been hurt if you weren't who you are—sees you as heroic."

Marlene had paused and smiled when he said that, amazed as always that his compliments were so sincere and without expecting anything in return. But a troubled look passed over her face. "I wonder if this killer perceives himself as being on the right side. The rituals and the rosary beads . . . maybe he thinks he's working for God. Just like I've been able to tell myself that the men I've killed deserved to die because they were on the wrong side."

Jojola looked thoughtful for a moment, then shrugged. "Perhaps, but what is right and what is wrong isn't determined by the individual but the community that he lives in. The community says that murdering children is wrong—it doesn't matter what his perception of it is."

"But society says that if I shot a man, even if I knew he'd committed a crime, without due process and without feeling that I was in immediate danger, that I am wrong, too."

"In theory, yes," Jojola said. "We all understand that a community cannot function with a vigilante justice system. But that's on paper . . . and how we want things to be in a perfect world. But who among us protests when the CIA sends a drone plane to fly a missile into some alleged terrorist's tent. He's certainly not been given due process by our legal standards; he may not have even been designated as an enemy combatant. But someone played judge, jury, and executioner. But does anyone complain? No . . . because we are afraid, especially since 9/11. We might pay lip service to the Constitution, but we sometimes actually *want* someone to take charge. We want someone to skirt the edge of the law, and take care of a problem that everyone knows is a danger, but that the legal system—with all its checks and balances—has not been able to cope with. As a law officer, I cannot say I condone it. But I certainly understand it, and if I find this man who kills my people's children then I will be such a person, too."

Marlene had looked at her friend. I've used the same reasoning, and it nearly destroyed me, she thought, and yet he seems so comfortable with his beliefs. What is the difference? "So when you've killed him," she said, "where will he fit in your village?"

That time Jojola's laugh was bitter. "I have fashioned a special place for him down a very deep, very dark hole near the garbage dump from which he will never escape."

• • •

Lucy was also thinking about men as her mother pointed to a distant cliff and said that was where they would meet one of them, John Jojola. "The eagles' nest is right below, about fifty feet from the top."

Only a couple of weeks earlier, Lucy had been worried about her mother's reaction to Jojola. Marlene's conversations were filled with what she and the Indian had done that day, the things they'd talked about, and how he was helping her deal with her past. Lucy had noted when she saw them together that he made her laugh and that they shared an obvious affection for one another. She was afraid that an affair was in the making. Such a turn of events would have been even worse than finding out her mother had jumped into bed with Billy—at least that would have only been about sex. But an affair with Jojola, she realized, would have been so much deeper, more meaningful, and therefore more dangerous.

The thought saddened her for her father. She knew he enjoyed a certain amount of sexual banter with Stupenagel and that other women looked at him with lust in their eyes, even if he was oblivious to their hints. But his daughter also knew that he wasn't the sort to have an affair. He was dedicated to his wife and family, which for one thing, along with his choice of careers, left him no time for a mistress. Instead, he faithfully came home every night to an empty bed, and the last face he saw before he turned out the light was a framed photograph of his wife on his nightstand.

Lucy now understood that the relationship between her mother and Jojola was not sexual. They were friends, and if there was something more, it was along the lines of student and teacher, which surprised her as she'd always thought of her mother as self-possessed, if troubled.

The recognition that there was nothing untoward between the two did not, however, put her at ease regarding the long-range forecast for her parents' marriage. Her mother and father didn't see that as different as they were in their means, their roles in the world were complementary—Marlene as the sword of justice, and Butch as the scales. They thought they were coming from different ends of the spectrum when there were only two ends. The Good and the Bad.

The likelihood that he was going to run for office, in Lucy's opinion, would only further exacerbate the split. Before she and her mother left for New Mexico, her father sat the family down and told them that he was considering running for district attorney. He didn't try to sugarcoat it. It would mean even more time away from them. The family would be under greater scrutiny from the press. "And there's another very real issue," he said. "The level of potential danger . . . to me and to you . . . will rise. We will have increased police protection, but as you are all aware more than most families, that is not a guarantee of safety. You need to understand one important difference with the past. Then, the danger was always personal—directed at me and you because of something I did, like put someone in prison. But if elected, I would represent an important institution of our government—a big, impersonal target for anyone with a cause or gripe."

He ended by saying he wanted to give them time to think about it, but it wasn't necessary. Her mother had excused herself from the vote with the copout that she'd been in and out of their lives too much to qualify. But the twins and Lucy had encouraged him to run, although for different reasons.

Giancarlo worshipped him and thought that he deserved

the recognition of the voters. "And what you do is important to everyone," he said in his usual precocious manner that had his brother rolling his eyes. "You're sort of like a comic book hero. You take on the bad guy so that other people don't have to."

Zak adored his father, too, but it was the added danger that he liked, just the ticket to spice up what he considered an otherwise humdrum life. He was, however, greatly disappointed that while his father would be the chief elected law enforcement officer for the county of New York, he was not inclined to start carrying some heat.

Lucy initially had her reservations. Like her mother, she worried that the system would wear him down and leave him frustrated and bitter. But she also believed in a world in which the forces of good and evil were battling daily, even if most people were too wrapped up in their daily lives to see the overall pattern as anything more than isolated incidents. A bombing here. A murder there. War and famine and terrorists in airplanes and with dynamite strapped to their bodies. Men who killed in the name of God.

Lucy had framed a saying that hung above her desk at home: "All that is necessary for evil to triumph is for good men to do nothing." Her father had demonstrated through his entire career that he would lay it on the line to prevent evil from triumphing. The world needed more men like him, not fewer; she had no choice but to give him her blessing.

Still, she'd felt guilty leaving him in New York to fend for himself and the twins. As capable as he was in the courtroom, he was lost in a kitchen and around an ironing board. She shuddered as she imagined the stacks of frozen food containers probably lining the counters at that moment and piles of crumpled laundry.

Yet, she knew she would have been of little use to him in the condition she was in. The encounter with Felix Tighe had damaged her far more than she let on. When she was with the psychopath—naked, spread-eagled, and tormented by his knife and the delight he took in her pain—she had accepted the fact that she was going to be raped and murdered. Then David Grale appeared, and she'd been rescued. But ever since then, she felt as if she were living on borrowed time. And if that was true, she'd wanted to be near her mother to mend their rift and support her efforts to come to grips with her moral dilemmas.

Lucy had not really expected to find healing for herself in the Southwest. She believed that she was too far gone to look forward to the future as she once had. But like her mother, she'd discovered that there was something cleansing about New Mexico. Small wonder that three of the world's great religions sprang from the desert, she thought. Out where little could be hidden beneath the sun, it was easier to be honest with God and with oneself.

It was on a late afternoon horseback ride with Ned Blanchet that she finally had admitted to herself that another reason she left New York was that she was also running away from thoughts she'd been having about her boyfriend, Dan Heeney. After she got out of the hospital and went to see him, he'd been kind and understanding. But while she'd made it clear that she didn't want him to try to touch her "that way," she also was a little disappointed that he didn't try. She wondered if that meant he now considered her damaged goods.

Her lack of interest in sex was only partly tied to the heinous things Tighe had done to her. If she was living on borrowed time, she did not want to start something that might not have a future; and if there was romance in her future, she admitted to the New Mexico sky, she was no longer sure she wanted it with Dan. But she was troubled by her reasons. She loved him and knew that it was not his fault that she'd fallen into the clutches of a deranged killer. Yet, while ashamed to admit it even to herself, she blamed him for not being there to save her. Nor did she feel safe while lying in his arms.

On the other hand, there's Ned, she thought dreamily as the road swung toward the edge of the gorge. Not the best-looking cowboy in the West—*then again, you're not exactly Shania Twain*—but he was certainly what any straight romantic girl dreamed of in other respects. He courted her in a way that at any other time or place in her life she would have considered impossibly corny. Flowers left outside her room. Small gifts for dumb little occasions like their fifth week anniversary. Poorly spelled love poems written in his nearly illegible handwriting but made up for with emotion. Nor did she feel like she was holding out as she had with Dan, at least before Tighe.

Ned was exactly what she'd needed and took only what she was willing to give. Early on, he confessed that he hadn't had much experience with women. "As a matter of fact," he'd blushed, "I was taught to dance by my sisters." He even admitted that he was a good deal more comfortable around his horse than with members of the opposite sex. " 'Cept you, Lucy, you're different, more like my horse," a statement she'd let pass. She knew that he wanted more, which made her feel beautiful and desirable, but his shyness got in the way of progress in that arena . . . but not because he was trying to be careful around poor fragile Lucy . . . the damaged goods.

At first whenever he seemed on the verge of professing his undying devotion and love, she'd hushed him up and changed the subject. But as time passed, she found herself enjoying the feel of his hard, flat chest muscles beneath his shirt against her breasts when they danced slow, and the strength of his arms when he helped her down from a horse. In the dark of her room at night, she'd even allowed herself the occasional fantasy of what he might look like with just his jeans and boots on . . . *or maybe just the boots.*

As her mother pointed out the cliff above the eagles' aerie ("I think that may be John standing up there"), Lucy spotted a man on horseback through her side window. He was some distance away, but she looked at the rider's thin frame and the relaxed way he sat in the saddle and thought it might be Ned. Suddenly, the horseman stood up in his stirrups as he looked north in the direction they were driving. He spurred his horse into a run.

Lucy was still watching him when there was a loud *bang* and the truck swerved toward the edge of the gorge.

If Marlene hadn't been looking ahead at the rock outcropping and seen a flash when the sun hit the rifle scope and noted the small puff of smoke, she would have thought from the sound that she had a blowout. Not that it made any difference in the few seconds she had to try to save herself and Lucy. Turning hard in the direction of the skid, she almost made it. The truck stopped parallel to the edge of the cliff, now facing south. Then with a sickening lurch, the truck tilted and rolled over the side.

"Mom!" Lucy cried.

"Lucy!" she'd replied. And that's all the time they had—or would have had if the piñon pine had been growing anywhere else.

"Are you okay?" Marlene asked. Looking past where Lucy was pinned against the passenger door, she could see that there were no more outcroppings or trees to prevent them from plunging the remaining distance to the canyon floor.

"For the moment," Lucy said. She'd looked down once and decided not to do that again. "Mom, I'm scared."

"That's all right, baby. Crawl over me and out my window," Marlene said as calmly as she could.

"No way," Lucy said. "You have to go first. Just climbing over you will jiggle us loose."

Just then there was the sound of a vehicle pulling up above them. A door opened and shut and then there were footsteps in the gravel.

"Sheriff!" Marlene exclaimed when she saw the man look over the edge at them. "Hurry, get a rope!"

Instead, Asher squatted and smiled. "Looks like you gals is in a pickle," he said, then pointed. "Doesn't appear that old piñon is going to be able to hold you much longer. . . . Then again, maybe I should help hurry the process; after all, time's a wastin'."

Asher stood and shouldered his rifle, but he never got a shot off. Realizing his intentions, Marlene had reached under her seat, flipped the safety catch, and pulled out the Glock. Even as the sheriff brought his rifle up, she fired two quick shots. The first caught him in the belly and doubled him over, rendering him incapable of straightening to use his weapon. The next caught him in the top of the head. He pitched forward and landed belly down on the hood of the truck, further burdening the tree. His face was turned toward the women, his eyes still open and conscious as he slid helplessly off the hood and into the canyon below.

"You promised you weren't going to bring your gun," Lucy scolded.

"Can this lecture wait until we find out if we're going to live or die?" Marlene answered. "I'd rather not argue with you if this is our last few minutes together."

Lucy's reply was cut off by the sound of another vehicle arriving in a rush and then a male voice calling down. "Marlene! Lucy!"

Jojola peered over the edge but only long enough to assess the situation before running back to his truck to grab a length of rope. He fashioned a loop as he ran to the canyon rim and tossed it down to Marlene, who was half out of the window standing on the steering wheel. "It won't hold the truck if she goes," he yelled. "Get it under your arms, and I'll haul you up."

Marlene tried to hand the rope below to her daughter. "You first," she ordered.

"It won't work, Mom," Lucy replied. "We've been through this."

Marlene knew that her daughter was right and stopped arguing. With the rope around her, she carefully climbed out of the window, conscious of the increased rattle of stones as the truck shifted.

She was about to take the rope off and insist that her daughter come up. But as soon as Jojola saw that she was clear of the window, he started to haul on the rope, and she had no choice but to climb up the steep slope as quickly as possible.

At the top, she loosened the rope and stepped out of the loop. From below came Lucy's voice. "Hurry, Mom."

Looking down as she picked up the loop, Marlene saw that Lucy had climbed out of the window and was standing precariously on the side of the truck. She threw the rope, but a sudden lurch by the truck forced Lucy to fight for her balance and she missed it. With a popping like firecrackers, the pine finally gave way and the truck slid toward the chasm, and Marlene knew her daughter was gone.

24

KARP EXITED THE LOFT BUILDING ON CROSBY Street, nodding to Mr. Le, the proprietor of the Thai-Vietnamese restaurant supply store on the lower level. They had been neighbors for nearly a decade.

Unfailingly polite and cheerful, Thien Le was an industrious middle-aged man who had fled the fall of Saigon with his family in 1973. Every day he dressed in the same attire—a dark gray business coat, gray slacks, a crisply starched white shirt, and a narrow dark tie. He and his sons, who were apparently allowed to wear whatever was hip for the younger crowd, and what was an apparently extensive family—every male had been introduced as a cousin or nephew or uncle—often could be heard working well into the night.

"Chao buoi sang, Mr. Karp," said Le, who was standing in the doorway of his store surveying the pedestrian traffic. "It looks like a beautiful day. Are Missy Lucy and your lovely wife home yet?"

"Good morning, Mr. Le. Yes, beautiful, but unfortunately, my wife and daughter are not home," Karp replied, glancing up and down the street. He didn't know if it was a career spent as a prosecutor, or living with Marlene Ciampi, but he was a little more alert for trouble in his middle years. He wished Mr. Le a pleasant morning and headed off.

Walking to the south end of the block, Karp turned left on Grand Street and paused. There was a little game he played at the start of his walk to work of mentally dividing the city he was facing: Little Italy to the north, the Bowery straight ahead to the east, and Chinatown to the south. He liked to think of New York as a quilt, each patch with its own history, its own culture and eccentricities.

He reached Centre Street and crossed Grand, heading south along the edge of Chinatown. The open-air markets with their fresh, colorful displays of fruits and vegetables were already bustling. Shop owners alternately harangued their employees in vitriolic Cantonese and smiled at the pedestrians. One held up a head of leaf lettuce, "Very fresh, Butch. Just arrive this morning." Nothing had convinced him of the resiliency of the city after 9/11 as much as how quickly the grocers and souvenir shop owners swept up the dust and resumed business. You can kill us, he thought, but you can't keep us closed for business.

Although not quite seven thirty, the day already promised to be warm even for June. The air carried a hint of the summer to come—fermenting garbage and the smell of eight million people living in close proximity to one another, not all of whom shared the same dedication to personal hygiene.

"Good mornink," one of those on the riper end of the scale greeted him from the corner as he crossed Canal Street. The man was immensely fat and immensely filthy, dressed in what appeared to be many layers of clothes of indistinguishable color and vintage. He had a large, dirt-encrusted finger jammed up his nose and was scratching his voluminous buttocks with the other hand as if something was wandering around back there that he was trying to catch.

"Hello, Booger," Karp replied. The Walking Booger, so named for his nearly constant extraction attempts, was a regular part of the human flotsam and jetsam who considered the streets, alleys, and Dumpsters around Foley Square and City Hall to be their home turf. Of course, on any given day they might be found, as if magically transported, from Battery Park on the south end of the island to Central Park in the middle. Anything north of the park was left to a different crowd.

Booger showered and washed his clothes only when it rained and not through any conscious effort to do so. Thus, he could usually be smelled long before he was seen. His appearance and stench had one advantage: tourists and businesspeople gave him a wide berth when he wanted to move through a crowd, as he was doing now in the direction of Karp. "Hopin' or sometink to eat," he replied, withdrawing the probing finger to hold out his hand.

Karp deftly handed over a dollar without actually touching the man. "Don't spend it all in one place."

Even though he worked for the district attorney's office, which occasionally sent some of their colleagues off to prison, Karp was popular with most of the harmless variety of street people like Booger. In part, he was appreciated because he didn't practice the New Yorker habit of either refusing to make eye contact, or seeing through whoever might not meet the standards of social acceptability, as though nothing or no one was there. Karp wasn't like that; as was his custom, he engaged eye to eye, chatted, and was usually a soft touch.

Beginning with former mayor Ed Koch and continuing through Rudolph Giuliani, the mayor's office had done a lot for New York's image with tourists by insisting that the police focus on so-called quality of life crimes. That meant clamping down on such desperate criminal enterprises as urinating in public, panhandling, sex show solicitation, sleeping in the open, street prostitution, and the small-time crooks who made their living as pickpockets or con men. The theory put forth publicly was that these misdemeanors were committed by the same people responsible for the felonies. But the real motive was to clean up the environs that the tourists saw—such as Times Square and the Village—which it did, but the policy also just pushed the human blemishes off the main avenues and into surrounding neighborhoods where real New Yorkers actually lived.

Karp understood the reasoning, even had to admit that it was pleasant not being accosted by beggars at every corner or having to step over heroin junkies lying on the sidewalks in puddles of piss. Times Square was no longer the squalid cesspool of drug dealings and raunchy sex; it was, in fact, family-friendly and more reminiscent of Walt Disney than Herbert Huncke, the Times Square junkie made famous by the Beat Generation of writers. But Karp felt that if all the various street people of New York disappeared, he would miss at least some of them. They were part of the quilt, too, and therefore he was happy that not all had allowed themselves to be ushered off into the sunset.

"Thank choo," Booger sneezed, smiling to reveal ragged rows of brown teeth. He turned and began to shuffle up Canal, the crowd parting around him like a school of herring escaping a hungry sea lion.

As Karp approached the newsstand on the sidewalk in front of the courthouse, he was greeted by another character who added to the adventure of his daily walk to work. "Good morning, Butch, fucking piece of shit," the man who ran the newsstand called out.

"Good morning, Warren," Karp replied.

"Ass wipe," the man with the watery blue eyes and thick lips replied. "Doing well, thank you, turd eater."

Karp smiled. He took no offense at the man's language. Dirty Warren, as he was known at the courthouse, had Tourette's syndrome, a short circuit in his brain that caused him to frequently let loose stentorian streams of profanity unsurpassed in the western hemisphere for color and variety.

"What have you got for me today?" Karp said as he paid for the *Times* and the *Post*.

"Jennifer Aniston's real fuck you last name, piss me off douche bag."

"Trying to trip me up with the youngsters?" Karp said. Guessing the real names of movie stars was a game they'd played almost as long as they'd known each other, which was more than twenty years. Warren had yet to stump Karp and was apparently running out of vintage material.

The man now gave him a smug look and crossed his arms across his concave chest. "No piss shit rules against it, butt hole."

Karp shrugged. "Okay then, Anistonapoulos. Greek I believe."

"Fuck bitch pussy," Warren moaned as Karp began to move away. "Wait!" he yelled in desperation. "What about Madonna?"

Karp pulled up short. "Madonna? That's not fair. She's not a movie star."

"Sure ass wipe she is," Warren announced triumphantly. "She was in *Evita* and *A League of Their Own*. Her first blow job name is Madonna, but what scumbag vagina is the rest?" He noted the stymied look on Karp's face and began to dance a little jig that rocked his newsstand. "I fuck hell got him slut!" he yelled, startling a blue-haired older woman walking her Pekingese past the stand in her nightgown. "I fucking got him!"

"Moron," the woman yelled back, one of her false eyelashes shaking loose from the effort. The Pekingese snarled, and they tottered off down the sidewalk as fast as their short legs could carry them.

Warren ignored the woman, but his smile disappeared when he saw Karp's perplexed look change to a wicked grin. "Doesn't make her an actress. But just to ruin your day, it's Madonna Louise Veronica Ciccone."

"Ah, you fucker," Warren swore.

"Hey, that wasn't TS-inspired," Karp laughed.

"How would sphincter clit you know, shithead," the man groused.

"I *know* the difference," Karp said. "And you know you're at least supposed to try to watch your language."

"Can't help it, twat-nosed monkey fucker eat me," Warren giggled.

"Yeah, right," Karp said, giving him a sideways glance. He was never quite sure that all of Dirty Warren's X-rated vocabulary was attributable to his disease. Karp knew that TS had many other less extreme manifestations, but there was no proof that Warren was putting him on. Innocent until fuck shit piss proven guilty, beyond a reasonable doubt, he thought.

He wove his way through the foot traffic on the remaining hundred feet to the courthouse entrance—glancing to either side to assure himself that the inscriptions remained—and entered through the door marked for "employees with identification badges only." Over to his right, the usual crowd was standing in line to empty their pockets, throw their purses and cell phones into the X-ray machines, then step through the metal detectors where, if they set off a beep, they were told to raise their hands while a bored-looking New York City police officer frisked them with a wand.

Karp wondered what good such efforts actually were, considering that terrorists, who'd posed as heating and air-conditioning repairmen, managed to import the components of a large bomb into the basement just seven months earlier. He guessed that people just wanted to feel safer after September 2001 and had in an amazingly short amount of time from his point of view accepted any inconvenience, or abridgement of privacy rights, that gave even the appearance of a more secure world.

Walking into the lobby of 100 Centre Street was like flying into a beehive. The air droned with hundreds, nay thousands, of voices adding to the sound of people walking, shuffling papers, elevators ringing, and an orchestra of cell phones rendering a myriad of tunes from "Take Me Out to the Ballgame" to the *William Tell* "Overture." Meanwhile, all the little worker bees ignored everything else to hurry to their assigned tasks, while visitors buzzed around in a daze trying to figure out how to get to whatever courtroom or office they were late in arriving at.

For perhaps the billionth time, he reflected that a cultural anthropologist would have had a doctoral dissertation handed to him or her on a platter by observing the human interactions of genus *Homo New Yorki Criminalcourtus* within the polished stone walls of 100 Centre Street.

Approaching slowly and avoiding eye contact like Jane Goodall with her chimps, a scientist could move close to killers and con men, as well as expectant teenagers seeking restraining orders against the multiple fathers of their children. Making no sudden moves that might disturb them, the careful observer might place himself dangerously close to sullen alpha male gangbangers eyeballing each other as they waited for their court-appointed lawyers while their haggard and tearful mothers stood next to them wondering where they went wrong.

Heck, he thought, there was probably a chair at Syracuse University for the brave soul who conducted a study on the subset *Homo New Yorki Criminalcourtus lawyera*. He mused over what the proper term for a gathering of attorneys would be. A gaggle? A herd or a pack? Or maybe—and most appropriately, like cows—a murder of lawyers.

The lawyers tended to come in three basic species. The least numerous were the assistant district attorneys, who marched through the crowds in working-stiff suits with the grim countenances of the true defenders of justice and the American way. That or bored out of their gourds and biding their time until they went over to the dark side of the force and entered into private practice.

Then there was the top echelon of defense lawyers— the partners and associates from big firms whose clients could actually pay for legal representation. They were the ones in the Armani suits who protected their cherished clients by walking with one arm around their shoulders and the other out to shield them from the rabble.

Lastly, there were the two subspecies of public defenders. Those who—like the young district attorneys, and usually young themselves—wore the poverty of their wardrobe and their still-untainted idealism like badges of honor. And secondly, those who had been at it for a few years and now mostly wore tired, pained expressions. Their shoulders tended to sag when they entered the courthouse, sighing at the thought of another day in hell defending Satan's minions.

As Karp walked up to the elevators, a young black public defender in a pink bow tie and horn-rim glasses was lecturing a man old enough to be his father. "This is it, Henry," he said, dipping his head and peering over his glasses to force Henry to look him in the eye. "You've had a couple of weeks to see what jail's like . . . and it's going to be a lot worse up at Attica if you don't quit drinkin' and hittin' your wife. That what you want, Henry? A few years locked up with killers, and gangsters, and rapists? Men who would sell their own mothers for the change in your pocket?"

"No," Henry said sullenly, his eyes darting in all directions to avoid the lawyer's gaze.

"Well, you remember that when the judge asks if you've got anything to say before sentencing," the young lawyer said. "You're going to promise that you will never ever drink again or hit your wife. And then we are going to beg, and I mean down on our knees and sobbing for mercy, for the judge to put you on home detention and weekly urine tests. And if he goes for it, every time you feel like having a little drink, I want you to imagine what it's going to be like at night in your cell when they turn out the lights and the screaming starts."

Couldn't have said it better, Karp thought. He pushed the button to summon the elevator, but suddenly there was a commotion in the lobby behind him. A loud voice rang out, bouncing off the marble walls and causing several women to shriek as if they'd been personally assaulted. "AND I LOOKED," the voice boomed, "AND BEHOLD, A BLACK HORSE . . ."

The owner of the voice pawed his way through the crowd toward Karp like a man swimming against the current. He swept aside gangsters and secretaries, lawyers and bail bondsmen, until he stood alone ten feet from Karp. An odiferous match for Booger, the man was wearing an army field jacket and tie-dyed T-shirt that stated Grateful Dead World Tour 1976 over the image of a smiling, dancing skeleton. His stained khaki pants appeared to be supported by a rope belt, and his sandals were held together with duct tape. Long, frizzy gray hair stood out from his head as though at some point in the past he'd licked his finger and stuck it in a light socket. He now looked at Karp with blue eyes that jutted from their sockets as if something was squeezing him around his chest, pointed a crooked finger, and said in a shower of spittle: "AND HE WHO SAT ON IT HAD A PAIR OF SCALES IN HIS HANDS . . ."

Whatever the man intended to say next was cut off by the choke hold applied to him from behind by a police officer, who took him to the ground and held him while another slapped handcuffs on his wrists. "Sorry, Mr. Karp," the officer with the choke hold apologized. "He wasn't acting strange or nothin' when he came through security. Not until he saw you. You know him?"

Karp looked hard, trying to see the face without all the hair and the patchy beard; maybe he'd prosecuted him at some point in the past. The man was not struggling or trying to say anything else; in fact, he almost appeared to be catatonic, staring into the floor as though he were looking into some other universe. Karp shook his head. "Can't say I do."

"His name's Edward Treacher," said a raspy, muffled voice behind him.

Karp jumped and turned toward the voice, relieved to see its owner. "Jesus, Guma, you sound more like Marlon Brando in *The Godfather* every day," he said.

Ray Guma grabbed the lapels of his pin-striped suit and struck a mob pose. "Hey *paisan*, just getting back to my roots after so many years on the wrong side of the law."

Laughing, Karp said, "There have been times we've wondered which side you thought was the right one. But you were saying about our friend here, Mr. Treacher?"

Guma shrugged. "Actually, I don't know much. Once prosecuted him on a lewd conduct back in the midseventies, when that little incident with the hooker in the interview room got me demoted to Misdemeanors and Miscreants for six months. If I remember correctly, he was offering five-dollar blow jobs in the men's room at Shea Stadium. Had a pretty good little business going, too, and the Mets were winning, until the cops nabbed him . . . season over for him and the team. Anyway, I was told by our investigators that he used to be a professor of religious studies over at NYU until he dropped some bad acid in the late 1960s, went to go find God, and never really came back. Apparently a pal of Timothy Leary, and spent some time in San Francisco with the Merry Pranksters of *The Electric Kool-Aid Acid Test* fame. Now apparently believes he's God's messenger boy, Heaven's own FedEx deliveryman. He's been around here off and on for the past twenty years when not recuperating at Bellevue; surprised you haven't seen him before. Some of the regulars, like Warren, call him The Prophet because of his biblical rantings, but mostly they think he's just another harmless brain-fried hippy."

The pair watched the police pick up Treacher and half-carry, half-guide him back to a security lockup until they could decide what to do with him. "Well, that was as good as a cup of coffee," Karp said.

"Yeah, you never know when one of these guys will raise a gun, or maybe a knife, instead of a finger," Guma said enthusiastically. "Gets the old ticker pumping."

"Thanks for the encouraging news," Karp replied as they moved past a row of gum-chomping, miniskirted prostitutes sitting on one of the wood benches outside of AR1, the arraignment courtroom. His arrival precipitated a cacophony of whistles and catcalls.

"Hey, Butch," cooed a large black hooker with hair the color of a tangerine. "How about I come back to your office and show you a good time in exchange for time off for good behavior?"

"You must have me mixed up with my friend Guma here," he said. "Better talk to him about any plea bargains taken in trade."

Guma had never let scruples stand in the way of a piece of ass. A native son of New Jersey, the Italian Stallion, as he'd billed himself for years, wasn't quite the stud of his younger years because of the cancer that had caused the surgeons to remove most of his intestines. But apparently that hadn't stopped him from trying.

At the mention of Guma, the carrot-topped hooker sneered. "Screw him. He only wants somethin' fer nuttin'. . . . And I mean nuttin'," she said, holding up a bent pinkie finger. The other whores all burst into knowing cackles.

"Hey, I resemble that," Guma lamented as the elevator arrived and they stepped on. Guma got out his cell phone and started dialing. Karp quickly scanned the front page of the papers and then the cover of the Metro Section in the *Times*. He breathed a sigh of relief not to find what he'd been dreading—any suggestion of a story about the two bodies found in the Rambles area of Central Park on Friday morning. He hated to admit it, but he owed Stupenagel. She'd been contacted by some informant who'd led her to the graves, and to her credit—or her avarice, he wasn't sure which—she'd called in the police without raising a fuss that would have brought the rest of the media swarming.

Two days earlier when he learned about the bodies and her involvement, he'd swallowed his pride and called to ask if she would hold off on the story for a couple of days until the police could identify the bodies and get a jump on the investigation. He suspected that she did it more so that she would have a scoop in the *Village Voice* when the first installment on her series about him came out on Tuesday, but she'd agreed after whining a little about "the public's right to know and my responsibilities as a journalist" just to make sure he understood that he owed her big. "And on the condition that I get to beat you with a baseball bat if something gets leaked to one of my competitors before then."

"The people of the city and county of New York thank you for your civic-minded response," he said sarcastically.

"Fuck that," she answered right back. "I'm half hoping Murrow tells the *Post* just so I can get my forty whacks."

So far, Stupenagel had honored the agreement. And as of the morning's *Times* and *Post*, he was in no danger of a thrashing.

The time had allowed the police to move forward without the press nosing around. After the investigators located the graves, they called in forensic anthropologist

Dr. Nathan Perriwinkle of NYU to excavate the bodies. Then Saturday afternoon, Karp, Rebecca DeAntonio, one of the sharp young ADAs in the homicide bureau who would be handling the case, and the police detectives in charge of the investigation met with Perriwinkle and three other scientists he'd invited along at the grave sites.

"Both victims were male, approximately ten to twelve years old, judging from bone growth and dentition," said Perriwinkle, a thin, grandfatherly man with a shock of white hair that stood out on his head like a snowdrift. "The skulls identified them as either Asian or American-Indian. We noted what appeared to be very severe lacerations to the flesh at the front of the throat consistent with having been cut with a sharp instrument; as you know, the New York Medical Examiner's Office has confirmed that the loss of blood from those wounds was the probable cause of death. No weapons or evidence of weapons, such as bullet fragments, were located in the graves or the bodies. Based on the level of decomposition, within a reasonable degree of scientific certainty, I believe that they were buried four to eight weeks apart, and from nine to twelve months ago. I believe this estimate will be borne out by my colleagues."

Perriwinkle gave way to the other scientists, who all added their bit. The first was a forensic botanist, Dr. Hannah Olivinski, who reported that she'd studied the clipping of roots that had been cut and left behind when the killer dug the graves, as well as new shoots that had pierced the walls since. "The clippings vere still in an active growth stage when they vere cut, one more so than the other, which precludes vinter," Olivinski, a short, thick woman with a trace of a Russian accent, said. "Most of the new growth into the graves occurred simultaneously and since the spring thaw, as opposed to prior to vinter. That would mean the graves vere dug sometime in late summer, or more likely early fall, just before the plants vent dormant. That, of course, does not mean the bodies vere deposited there at that time. For that I defer to Dr. Hobbes."

Dr. Calvin Hobbes introduced himself as an entomologist, "someone who studies bugs." He looked somewhat like an insect himself with thick glasses and a high-domed forehead accentuated by a receding hairline; he even had a curiously pinched mouth that reminded Karp of a grasshopper's mandibles, but the man knew his critters. The lack of all but three fly larvae on the bodies, Hobbes said, suggested that the victims were buried immediately after their murders and before more of the insects could lay eggs. "During the summer and on warm fall days, even a few hours aboveground and I would have expected to see many more larvae, perhaps even maggots," he said while Karp fought a queasy feeling in his stomach.

Karp recognized the fourth scientist, Jack Ludlow, as a weatherman on one of the local television news programs. Tanned and movie-star pretty, Ludlow explained that he helped with forensic cases "as a sort of hobby . . . goes back to my boyhood days as a Sherlock Holmes buff." His contribution at first seemed superfluous when he noted that the murders "probably occurred at night to avoid detection." Well, duh, Karp thought but his interest picked up when the meteorologist, also added that the killing probably occurred "during a full or nearly full moon; otherwise the killer would have had to have used a flashlight and risked detection in order to find his way through that particular part of the park with his victims. Given that my colleagues believe that the murders occurred a month or so apart, I would venture to guess that you have what we call a werewolf killer—he feels compelled to murder by the light of the full moon for either practical or ritual purposes."

While Karp was still digesting Ludlow's dramatic conclusion, Perriwinkle finished up by saying the children had been identified through dental records as two boys missing from Chinatown's Vietnamese-American community. "One disappeared in August of last year," he said. "The other in September. Which, of course, fits with what we've told you."

Karp pondered the ramifications. If this "werewolf" killed every full moon, had he only begun in August? And if so, had he stopped in September? Or were there other bodies out there, one for every full moon? He thought it likely. The guy was too practiced, too purposeful to have murdered twice and then gone back to his day job. Heck, he left the rosary bead calling cards, as if taunting the authorities.

Karp also knew something that the scientists had not been told. The coroner had found foreign DNA in the boys, the result of sexual assaults. Someday, he hoped, the genetic markers would help identify the killer. The scientists were thanked and reminded that they were sworn to secrecy, "especially in regard to the rosary beads."

Leaving any mention of the rosary beads out of her story was another chit he owed Stupenagel. She had at first balked, but he explained: "That's something only the killer would know about. We'll get a thousand crank calls on something like this once your story hits the streets. All the loonies who want to confess to murder for the publicity and attention, plus the assorted nuts, whackos who may or may not have any real information, will be all over it. We have to have some detail to help us weed them out. The rosary beads are it."

Stupenagel complained bitterly that he was "taking half of the most dramatic stuff" out of her story, but again she'd agreed. "So long as when you do get ready to reveal that little fact, you wait until I can get it in first. In the meantime, you owe me twice as much as before, which was a lot. In fact, I'm going to have to think long and hard—get it?—about what I might want in return. But I'll let you know."

Karp was trying not to think about what pound of flesh, or worse, Stupenagel would want when he and Guma arrived at his office on the eighth floor. As they exited the elevator, he stole an appraising look at his old friend and colleague. Guma only worked part-time as a special prosecutor when Karp needed someone with experience and Guma needed something to keep his mind off his deteriorating body. "How are ya these days, Goom?"

"Well, other than having to listen to unfair and untrue remarks about my physical prowess," he said, "I am well, thank you very much."

You don't look well, my friend, Karp thought. In the old days, Guma had been built like a bulldog—low, squat, hairy, and heavily muscled. He could shave at eight in the morning and by five his beard would have sanded the paint off a ship. His goal in life had been to bed as many women as possible—and it never seemed to matter to him if they were beautiful or ugly, thin or fat, balloon-breasted or two peas on a plank. However, the cancer had turned him into an old man almost overnight. He was bent and frail, often using a cane or umbrella to support a decidedly wavering walk. The Mediterranean hair that once would have put a young Dean Martin to shame was now a thinning hedgerow of salt and pepper; likewise the beard, which seemed in a constant state of one-day's growth. The swarthy complexion had faded into a sallow one, and the muscles had abandoned him, leaving behind nothing but skin and bones. But the mind was still sharp, the smirking smile still Guma, and the legal advice better with age.

Guma caught the look as they walked into Karp's outer office. "Yeah, I know, I look like shit," he growled. "But I can still bang with the best of 'em . . . ain't that right, Mrs. Boccino," he added as he walked past Karp's new secretary, who gave the stallion a dirty look.

"Bug off, Guma," the buxom fortyish woman said in the colloquial of her native Long Island. "You only wish."

Karp hurriedly ushered Guma into his office before there was a chance for a reply that might have ignited a federal sexual harassment lawsuit. "We never change, do we," Karp said, then whirled at the sound of someone clearing her throat.

"He is genetically incapable of it," said Stupenagel, who was sitting in one of the overstuffed leather seats left over from the previous administration. "Comes from having his brain located in his penis."

"There was a time when you liked the way my penis thought," Guma shot back.

Stupenagel snorted. "If I remember correctly, and believe me I've tried to forget, most of the time your penis was thinking about sleeping."

Karp let the two former lovers go at it. He had other things on his mind. For the moment, he even had to put the two bodies in Central Park on a back burner. The Alejandro Garcia murder case was more pressing,

There was scheduled to be a preliminary hearing after lunch in front of Judge Alan Friedman. The purpose of such probable-cause hearings was to officially ascertain that a crime had been committed and that there was reasonable grounds to believe that the defendant was to blame.

If the judge agreed that probable cause existed, then the case would be officially marked HGJ, which stood for Held for the Grand Jury. New York state law required that in order to try a defendant for a felony charge in the Supreme Court—the felony trial court—the prosecution must proceed by way of grand jury indictment, unless the defendant waived that procedure.

When he was the homicide bureau chief, Karp had almost always skipped preliminary hearings and gone straight to the grand jury with murder cases. There was an economy to that practice. Why duplicate the presentation at prelim and then again in the GJ? Move the case expeditiously directly to the GJ, get the indictment, and then on to trial in the Supreme Court.

However, this time Karp had told the new homicide chief, Lilli Sakamoto—a tough, Japanese-American Yale Law grad who fought and scrapped her way to the top—to direct assistant district attorney Terrell Collins (the lead ADA assigned to the Garcia case) to ask the judge to schedule a preliminary hearing. The hearing was scheduled for Monday and he still wasn't sure what to do. He didn't usually micromanage the bureaus, but he had a reason this time—one he hadn't passed on to Sakamoto or Collins—and that was he wanted to stall for time.

A week ago, the case against Alejandro Garcia had seemed like a slam dunk. The defendant had been overheard making death threats to the victim, and an eyewitness had identified him as one of the shooters. He had an alibi—his meeting with Father Dugan—but it wasn't bulletproof.

Yes, there had been problems with the case, chiefly

that he thought that Vincent Paglia was a lying piece of shit, which put his people in the odd position of trying to prove that against their own witness. But then Detective Flanagan called on Thursday afternoon to say that the crime lab report on the .45 found underneath the limo was in. "According to the ballistics, it was definitely the gun used to kill Johnson and one of the hookers," he said. "And they got one real good print that's a match for Garcia and a couple other probables."

Playing devil's advocate, Fulton pointed out that Paglia's lies didn't mean that Garcia wasn't one of the shooters. "Maybe there was a falling out among killers," he said. "Or maybe it was a setup to have Garcia do the hit and then take the fall all alone, especially when Paglia learns about the reward."

Vinnie was the only one Karp knew who could answer those questions, but the police had been unable to find him. Flanagan and Leary had reported that he wasn't at the fish market on Wednesday afternoon when they went to pick him up at Fulton's request. Nor did he go home that night, and he wasn't at the fish market again on Thursday. His wife said he'd called to say he was spending the night with a cousin, but a check at the cousin's house didn't turn up the fat man.

When Flanagan had asked why they wanted to talk to Paglia, Karp had given him a lame excuse about wanting the witness to walk Terrell Collins through the shooting at the crime scene. "Where were the shooters when he first saw them, and then when he took off running? What street was he on when he heard the shooting? You know, all the stuff to make it clear for the jury."

Flanagan seemed to accept the answer. But Karp didn't know why he felt the subterfuge was necessary. Maybe I

don't like sloppy police work, he thought. The cops should
have checked Paglia's story better—found out about the
thousand-dollar payoff to get the job, seen if anybody could
connect him to Garcia or Pentagram Records. It was purely
an accident that Helen's cousin just happened to be the guy
who was supposed to be driving that night, or we'd be trotting Paglia out in front of a grand jury to lie through his teeth.

Still, there was something troubling him beyond
Paglia's lies and subsequent disappearance, or the conviction of Dugan and the twins that Garcia wasn't good for
the murders. His gut was telling him there was something
wrong, and it got even wronger when Fulton called him at
home Sunday evening.

"You're starting to make a habit of these Sunday surprises," Karp said, "and I'm not sure I like them."

"What?" Fulton asked in mock surprise. "You mean
you don't want to hang with the brother 24/7? Well, that's
okay; the kids are over at my mom's for the night and me
and the wife have more important things to do, too, if you
catch my drift. But I thought this was pretty important—
almost as important as your little gangsters becoming witnesses in a murder investigation."

"Okay, okay," Karp laughed. "You made your point.
Now what could have possibly pried you away from the
warm attentions of the lovely Mrs. Helen Fulton?
Perhaps, you've gone out of your mind, leaving a woman
like that waiting. She might call the pizza delivery boy
over to keep your place warm."

Fulton chuckled. "She might at that if the look on her face
was any indication when I got a phone call from Flanagan."
But then his voice grew serious. "They fished Vincent Paglia's
body off the rocks at Hell's Gate this afternoon."

"Any evidence of foul play?"

"Not so far," Fulton replied. "No obvious gunshot or knife wounds or signs of blunt trauma. But that's just the preliminary from the paramedics who fished him out of the water, according to Flanagan. They figured he drowned, but it's still uncertain as to the surrounding circumstances. The ME's going to do the autopsy in a couple of hours and maybe we'll know more then. What I know now is that our boy was fully clothed, had his wallet, a watch, and his wedding band on him."

Karp thought about it for a moment, then said, "I know this is asking a lot, and I'll owe you big, but do me a favor, Clay, and sit in on the autopsy. Ask the ME, nicely, to be extra meticulous. Something bothers me about a witness who decides to go swimming with all his clothes on right after we hear he may be yanking our chain."

"Knew the jig was up and committed suicide?" Fulton tossed out as a question.

"I don't think so. This guy was a gambler," Karp said, "not a good one, but willing to lay down big numbers with some pretty rough people. He couldn't have known for sure that we thought he was lying. I mean, we told him we'd be talking to him from time to time about the case. What he does know is that if he sticks to his story, maybe he walks away with the fifty grand that Pentagram offered. You think a gambler walks away from that without knowing for sure that he's been made?"

"So maybe someone was worried that he might say something," Fulton ventured.

"Yeah, maybe," Karp said. "But that's been a possibility since the whole scheme was dreamed up. Why change their mind all of a sudden and knock off the witness who makes it all click, unless they thought we knew something for sure? And how would they know that?"

"Maybe somebody tipped them off. It's a little suspicious that he didn't show up for work on Wednesday or Thursday. And he didn't go home Wednesday night. But only a few of us were privy to that, and I know it wasn't me, and I'm pretty sure it wasn't you."

"Possibly. But let's not assume it was a spy. It could be just coincidence that someone panicked or maybe Vinnie started making threats, and they figure they can do without him."

"Still, it doesn't clear Garcia on the murder, not with that gun and the fingerprints," Fulton pointed out.

"No, it doesn't," Karp agreed. "But what I still don't get is why kill Johnson and then set up this elaborate frame job to get Garcia. Why not just kill Garcia, too? It's obvious that someone wants him to take the fall instead of just whacking him." He thought for a moment about the anonymous caller. "It's also obvious that someone else knows what's going on and is trying just as hard to prevent Garcia from going down."

Karp didn't say the next part of what he was thinking. *Once again, everyone else seems to know their part in this little theatrical production but me.* Instead, he said, "Whether he's guilty or not, I want to keep the pressure on the kid; maybe he'll come around and tell us what's going on behind the scenes. But let's keep all this between us. That caller said I couldn't trust anyone outside of family and friends—I include you in that group, but that doesn't mean the rest of the NYPD unless you can tell me which ones you'd trust to watch your back."

Fulton grunted his agreement. "Okay, I'm out of here," he added. "I got to go upstairs and tell a beautiful, naked woman that I have to leave her all hot and bothered so that I can watch some medical school dropout cut up a fat guy. Man, Butch, if I didn't love you like a brother . . ."

"Love you, too," Karp said, making a kissing sound into the receiver before hanging up.

Afterward, Karp called Collins and gave him the bad news about his star witness. The ADA took it well. They chatted briefly about the next procedural step in the case, particularly in light of the absence of their star witness. Collins left Karp planning to file a motion to get Paglia's videotaped ID of Garcia admitted into evidence, knowing it would be a long shot. He thought the defense had the better of the argument since the Sixth Amendment still required, even in New York, the right of the defendant to be confronted by witnesses against him who were alive and in court.

The bickering between his two friends brought Karp back to the immediate task.

"It's not the size of the ship," Guma was saying, "it's the motion of the ocean. So maybe if you hadn't just laid there like the Dead Sea . . ."

"Ship? Ship?" Stupenagel guffawed. "Since when does a rowboat qualify as a ship?"

"Enough!" Karp barked. He was about to go on when the private line on his telephone rang. "Karp," he said.

"So maybe things aren't as they at first seemed," said the muffled voice of the anonymous caller. "And now someone else is dead."

25

"You again," Karp growled. He gestured to Guma, making hand signals to get a trace going on the call. Guma quit his midsentence comeback aimed at Stupenagel and hurried from the room.

"Yes, me again. But don't sound so disappointed. I believe my last tidbit about the priest and Garcia was worth a few moments of your time."

"Didn't prove anything," Karp said, stalling.

"You forget, Mr. Karp, the defendant doesn't have to prove anything. Surely even the New York district attorney believes in the concept that the accused is considered innocent until proven guilty beyond a reasonable doubt."

"Okay, I know it by heart. Do you have anything important to say?"

"Well, yes, I ought to get to it before your people wear themselves out trying to figure out where I'm calling from—but I could save them the effort, if you'd like. I'm at a pay phone in Union Square Station surrounded by a few thousand of my closest friends. All I really wanted to say was that you passed the first test and will shortly be receiving a second, much more difficult challenge."

"Test? What test?" Karp asked, writing the words "Union Station" on a notepad and handing it to Stupenagel to take to Guma. "I didn't know I was taking a test."

"Well, you were, Mr. Karp," said the voice. "And all you had to do to pass was show that you cared enough about justice to actually go check out what I had to say. But that was an easy one. It cost you nothing but a little time and energy. We'll see how you do on the next one, when you realize the possible consequences. But I want you to understand, Mr. Karp, that as difficult as the second test may be, there is a third and final exam that will make the second look like remedial reading. What's more, the third exam can't be administered while Alejandro Garcia is in jail."

"Let me get this straight. If I pass this second test and whatever it entails makes me want to take the third, I have to release the defendant in a homicide case?"

"Yes."

"Well, I hate to disappoint you but I don't make deals with the number one suspect in a murder case . . . unless he wants to plead to the top count? Now if you, and he, want to quit playing games and let me in on what's really going on and that somehow helps him, then I'm all ears."

"Sorry, Mr. Karp," the voice said. "I'm not at liberty to divulge that information at this time. To be honest, Mr. Garcia does not entirely trust you to do the right thing. That's why these tests are being administered piecemeal. Unfortunately, the materials for the third test will not be handed out until Mr. Garcia is out of jail. This is not an attempt to coerce the justice system, but a reflection that while he is in the Tombs, his life is in danger. And make no mistake, Mr. Karp, if you even see the third test, all of our lives will hang in the balance. You have no idea who or what you're dealing with, but I can tell you this—your career, your political aspirations, everything you care about will be at risk."

So what else is new, Karp thought dryly. "I've been threatened before," he said. "But I don't make decisions based on spy games and ambiguous threats."

"Ignore my warning at your own peril, and if something happens to that boy . . . it will be on your head," the caller said. "Now I really must go; your people are coming. But we'll be watching."

"Wait, dammit," Karp shouted but got only a dial tone in response. He slammed the receiver down.

"Mind sharing with your favorite reporter?" Stupenagel said, smiling sweetly.

"Walter Cronkite's dead," Karp groused. But the reporter's response was cut off by the intercom's buzz. "There's a UPS package out here," Mrs. Boccino said. "Security brought it up after it was X-rayed."

"Is it a heavy box?" he asked.

"No, sir."

"Then would you please bring it in here?"

The secretary appeared, followed closely by Guma, whose eyes were firmly fixed on her ass. Karp had to admit that she was one of those women who walked as if she was constantly thinking about having sex, but he wondered if the extra little shimmy was to further incite the Italian Stallion.

Karp turned to the box that she placed on the desk before exiting the room with another dirty look directed at Guma. He let it sit on the desk for a moment. He knew it wasn't a bomb, but he wondered if the contents might not be more explosive.

"Well," Stupenagel complained, "aren't you going to open it?"

Karp stood and began to slice through the packing tape with his letter opener. He took his time just to irk the reporter and Guma, who also sat on the edge of his chair, having momentarily forgotten the charms of Mrs. Boccino. But at last he had it open and looked inside. There, surrounded by foam peanuts, was an accordion file that held a half-dozen manila file folders bearing on the outside what he recognized as the case numbering system used by the NYPD. A quick glance told him that the files were from a number of different years, but the most interesting marking was a large red stamp on the outside that stated No Prosecution. A sticky note attached to the outside of the accordion file read: "This is just a sample."

Karp pulled out the first file with the feeling that he was the little Dutch boy who pulled his finger out of the dike. Somehow he was not surprised to see that the header read Little, Jumain. Ignoring the various sighs and throat-clearing emanating from Stupenagel and Guma, he opened the file and began to read.

Several minutes later, he closed the file and shut his eyes. The file contained the report of the police Internal Affairs Division's investigation into the shooting of Jumain Little. It didn't contain all of the details, such as the actual police and witness statements, ballistics tests, and autopsy; he assumed they would be contained in a larger file kept at IA. The report was more of an overview, an executive summary, assembled so that those in charge could make a decision on how to proceed. But it had enough.

Several things had jumped out at him. First, there were the statements. The contention by the detective that Jumain Little was armed and had threatened him with a gun when ordered to throw down his weapon. But also the assertion of the witness, who told the investigators

what Bernard Little had repeated for him at the church—
Jumain was shot in the back as he was running home on a
cold winter night. Nor were there fingerprints on the gun
found on Jumain's body. How many teenagers with a gun
wouldn't have handled the thing, even just to show it off
for friends? he thought.

Something else that jumped out at him was that the IA
investigators had recommended that the case be handed
over to the district attorney's office for "further investigation" and possible charges against the detective who did
the shooting, and possibly his partner for lying. More
important was the name of the detective, which had
caused the knot in the pit of his stomach to tighten into a
rock: Michael Flanagan.

Capping it all was a letter that had been attached to the
outside of the IA report. It was a recommendation by the
private law firm of Plucker, Bucknell and Kane, apparently hired by the NYPD to review the report, overruling
the IA recommendation and insisting that no criminal
charges against "the officers involved" be pursued. "A
proposed civil settlement with the family of the deceased
has, at this time, been postponed. However, no further
action is deemed necessary." It was signed by the future
mayor of New York City, Andrew Kane.

Karp quickly glanced through the remaining files in the
box. They contained more of the same—different instances
of police malfeasance, recommendations by the IA to pass
the buck to the DA for further investigation, all of them
overruled by the law firm of Plucker, Bucknell and Kane,
and either signed by Kane or one of his associates. In most
of the other cases, the law firm noted that the victims or
their families had been paid off out of the city coffers to the
tune of nearly a hundred million dollars.

Whoever sent the files wanted him to see more than just the overall picture. Another of the files involved Detective Robert Leary, who had apparently applied the prohibited "sleeper" choke hold on a belligerent intoxicated man until well after the man was unconscious. At least according to witnesses. His partner, however, Michael Flanagan, swore that the victim—who'd never regained consciousness and died several days later in a hospital—had continued to pose a threat "to the officers involved, as well as citizens" even after he had apparently stopped struggling. The man's family had accepted $750,000 to sign papers that they would hold the city and the department harmless.

Karp wondered absently when and how the files had disappeared from his office. Probably in all the confusion after the bombing.

"So what have we got?" Stupenagel said, craning her neck and trying to read the files upside down.

Karp looked at her and a plan began to form in his mind. Obviously, in addition to the general corruption, the anonymous caller was trying to draw a connection between past misdeeds by Flanagan, and his partner Leary, and their involvement in the Garcia homicide investigation. The reasonable inference was, of course, that these were two bad cops who for one reason or another had it in for the defendant.

He thought about the caller's warning that the third test would be more difficult and more perilous. If this was the second, he wondered if the third would be more No Prosecution police files or—as he'd gathered from the intimation that the ante was going to go up—something worse. If so, he couldn't imagine what it could be. Just in the box that had arrived that morning there was the making of a scandal for the NYPD to match the Serpico revelations. The department was engaging in covering up alleged criminal and unethical conduct by its officers, and using tax dollars for hush money.

However, the guilt lay not just with the police department. It was evident that the district attorney's office had failed in its obligation to review the reports and not just accept the recommendation of Plucker, Bucknell and Kane.

As such, the fallout would be pervasive. He knew that just as a matter of habit, the police department would circle the wagons if its members believed that the department was being picked on. Then there was the small matter of Flanagan being a certified hero in the eyes of the public and his own department for his actions when the World Trade Center was bombed. Nobody liked their heroes to be tarnished.

Yet there were bigger fish than Flanagan who wouldn't appreciate winding up in the same frying pan as a disgraced cop. The Jumain Little case and several others in the accordion file occurred during the reign of Sanford Bloom. But that wasn't what worried him—everyone already knew he was a crook.

Karp was more concerned about the fallout from the cases that had been mishandled under the watch of Jack X. Keegan. He respected his former boss, and was greatly disappointed to see that he'd ignored his duty. But he also knew that Keegan would look at an investigation as a personal attack, done for political gain. An ambitious federal district court judge could be a powerful enemy, especially one caught by a scandal that might ruin any future aspirations for a seat on the Second Circuit Court of Appeals and thereafter—who knows, maybe the big enchilada, the U.S. Supreme Court.

Yet there was one shadow that loomed over the rest. It belonged to one of the richest, most powerful movers and shakers in Manhattan—the man who would be mayor, Andrew Kane.

Karp passed a hand over his eyes, feeling the warning of an off-the-charts headache. Now he knew why the caller insisted on calling these revelations tests. To pass, he would have to pursue this blatant abrogation of the public trust and risk his chances of getting elected district attorney. His dream of returning integrity to the office might be ruined by the integrity it would take to reveal what was in the files and put a stop to the practice. However, if he failed the test by ignoring the files, he might as well not run for the office anyway. He had only one choice.

His decision made, he grabbed a green Magic Marker from his desk and crossed out the No Prosecution stamp on the Jumain Little file. Next to it, he wrote FI for FURTHER INVESTIGATION in four-inch-tall letters that he circled. There was no statute of limitations on the grief of Bernard Little and his wife, but there was also no statute of limitations on murder. If they could find the witness who'd disappeared, the case against Michael Flanagan might be reopened.

Karp then called Newbury and Murrow and asked them to come to his office. When they arrived, Karp directed them to sit down and turned his attention back to Stupenagel, who was bouncing up and down like a child about to receive a birthday present.

He smiled . . . a wicked, competitive grin. It was time to take control of this little drama. Time to stop acting the puppet and start pulling strings of his own choosing. Still, he wasn't ready to just lay it all out there. He didn't understand all the connections yet—especially between Flanagan and Garcia and the files. Nor did he know how much worse the third test might be. Other people were operating behind the scenes and he didn't understand their motives or their identities. Until he did, he wanted to keep his cards close to the vest so that his adversaries would not know that he was watching, and maybe they could be lured into making mistakes and showing their hands.

Karp rested a big hand on top of the accordion file. "What I have here are files that contain reports of police misconduct and payoffs by the city to make the problems go away," he told the salivating reporter and his two colleagues. "I believe these reports—as well as others that may be out there—reveal not just instances of police malfeasance and criminal behavior, up to and including murder, but a pattern of deception by a prominent Manhattan law firm that smacks of racketeering."

Stupenagel couldn't contain herself a moment longer and squealed with excitement. "Okay, okay, I know what I want for playing nice," she said, reaching for the files.

Karp pulled them back and just out of reach. "I'm going to let you see these, before turning them over to V.T. for further review," he said. "However, here's the deal. These cases are now officially under investigation and it is the policy of this office not to reveal specifics of ongoing investigations. At least for your story tomorrow, you cannot cite the details, including the names of the parties involved, or that you have actually seen these files. When you read these, you will understand why I need to be careful here." He laughed to see how his statement let the air out of the reporter. "However, you may take any notes you want in preparation for a future story, the publication of which you and I will discuss later."

"Ah, come on, Butch," Stupenagel whined. "I've been doing all the giving, and as Mick Jagger once sang, I can't get no satisfaction. . . ."

Karp held up his hand to shut her up. "You may, however, reveal the generalities of what these contain. That is, this office has come into possession of materials indicating that for at least a dozen years, possibly longer, allegations of police misconduct—including major felonies—have been ignored by the department and this office in collusion with one another. What's more, scores of millions of dollars of taxpayer monies have been paid to the victims and/or their families of this police misconduct. In exchange for getting to look at these, you will pass this portion of your story through Murrow, who will bring any concerns about inappropriate material to me."

"That's prior censorship," she scowled.

Karp shrugged. "Take it or leave it. Take it and I promise, none of your competitors get anything more out of this office than that, and you'll have it first. You'll also have first crack when it's appropriate to reveal the details of these cases. It'll cost me with your so-called mainstream competitors, but what else is new—in any event, you'll get your exclusive."

"You're using me," she said. "And not in a way I like. There's something else going on here, what gives?"

Karp pulled the files closer. "I have my reasons and that's all I can say on the matter. Think of it more as a matter of timing instead of censorship. You'll get the story, but not all at once. I'd also suggest, in case you were thinking of missing it for a bar date, that you attend the preliminary hearing for Alejandro Garcia this afternoon."

Stupenagel squinted at him, as if to see through his camouflage. But she said, "Okay, it's a deal." Even with the restrictions she was already giddy with visions of Pulitzers and Nobels. Her story on the DA's office for the next day's *Village Voice* was already finished and with the editor. She couldn't believe that just two weeks earlier, she'd been complaining that she would be killing thousands of trees to make the newsprint on which to publish "the most boring crime story ever." Then suddenly she had an embarrassment of riches: missing priests; the gangland style murder of a reasonably famous musician and three others; the subsequent disappearance and mysterious demise of the state's star witness in the case; and the ritual slaying and burial of two boys from the Vietnamese community in the heart of Central Park. Now to top it off, she got to break the news of pervasive corruption involving the police and the district attorney's office. Christmas had indeed come early.

Stupenagel picked up the Jumain Little file and read the cover letter from the law firm. "Oh, God, Butch, I'm absolutely wet," she purred. "This was signed off on by none other than Andrew Kane. . . ." She quickly looked at the other files. "And this one . . . and that one by an associate . . . Oh, Butch, can I have your baby, or maybe we can just practice making babies?"

Murrow, whose mouth had assumed its recent habit of hanging open, woke up out of the stupor that taking Andrew Kane's name in vain seemed to have created. "Absolutely not," he said. "Can't have Butch Karp making bastard children while he's running for district attorney." He looked at his boss. "And are we sure we want to trust a member of the press with this sort of sensitive information. It could damage a lot of people."

"You mean me," Karp acknowledged. "You're right, taking on Kane—not to mention some of the others involved in this—could blow the good ship USS Karp right out of the political waters. She can't use that name right now, but sooner or later we're going to lock horns."

"Why, Murry," Stupenagel purred, "I do believe you're jealous of my offer to have Butch's baby."

Murrow crossed his index fingers in the sign of a cross as if to ward off the Undead. "Back Vampira! I'm just trying to protect my employer from negative publicity."

Karp seized the moment to tell Newbury to take the files, Murrow, and the reporter with him back to his office. As she got up, Stupenagel pulled out her cell phone and called her editor. "Hold the story," she said. There was an angry buzzing from the editor, which she waited to subside before adding, "Believe me, when you see what I got, you will piss all over yourself to thank me."

With the three gone, Karp sat at his desk a little longer to gather his thoughts. He looked at Guma, who was leaning back in his chair with his eyes closed. "What do you think, Goom?" he asked.

For a second his friend didn't answer. Karp sat up with a start, thinking that his friend might have died quietly while all the excitement was taking place. But then Guma opened his eyes.

"What do I think?" he said. "I think you've got a tiger by the tail, but how big a tiger and whether you'll be able to hold on and keep him from sinking his teeth into your ass, that's the real question. But I don't think—knowing you—that there's any other way to go than the one you just took."

Karp nodded and looked at his watch. "Shit!" he exclaimed. It was almost one o'clock; the Garcia case was scheduled to be called right after the lunch break. He remembered the caller's warning that he wouldn't receive the third test until the defendant was out of jail and away from danger. He didn't like that the first part of that sounded like blackmail, but he could understand why the second might be true. One did not cross the NYPD lightly, especially when imprisoned on their turf in the Tombs. "Care to take a walk?" he asked.

"Sure," Guma said, rising stiffly with the pain of it written clearly on his face. "Where we off to?"

"To buy some more time," Karp replied. "And maybe stir up a hornet's nest?"

Guma smiled. "I think the stirring has already occurred," he said. "Now, we'll see who gets stung."

A few minutes later, Karp and Guma entered the courtroom of Judge Friedman. Guma took a seat in a back pew, while his boss proceeded forward and sat down next to the surprised Terrell Collins at the prosecution table.

"Where we at?" Karp asked, leaning close so he could speak quietly.

"We just got started, but the judge suddenly called a recess," the assistant district attorney whispered. "By the way he was moving, I think he was hearing the call of Mother Nature. However, we've already won the first skirmish . . . without firing a shot."

Collins nodded toward the pear-shaped public defender sitting next to Alejandro Garcia. "If you can believe it, Garcia's lawyer, McMichaels, didn't oppose my motion to allow the videotape of Paglia's interview to be shown to the jury. I explained that the witness was no longer with us, but that we would put Detective Flanagan on the stand to testify about the veracity of the tape. But McMichaels actually said that he agreed that there were extenuating circumstances and he didn't want to, and I quote, 'waste this court's time fighting a motion I'm going to lose.' The judge thanked him for his consideration, and I'm thinking about sending him a get-well card. But any way you look at it, the whole damn thing is in."

Karp ignored his prosecutor's gloating and looked over at the defense lawyer. Since when does a PD worry about wasting the court's time? he thought. Half of their practice is creating a mountain of motions and causing delays—especially in murder cases—for the express purpose of wasting time to try to wear us down and hope we'll offer a good deal just to be done with it. Something stinks like the city during an August garbage strike. He turned his attention back to the ADA. "Doesn't it bother you that our witness may have lied about his involvement?"

Collins looked hurt by the question. A tall, graceful, coffee-colored man, he had been the lead on the case against the two cops accused of shooting the immigrant the previous fall until he was injured by a car bomb. At the time, Karp had wondered if he would return to the DA's office when he recovered, or if he'd decide the frustrations—not to mention the danger—weren't worth the low pay and backbreaking hours.

It took a special sort of attorney to stay in the New York District Attorney's Office. As he told each incoming batch of newbies fresh out of law school, "Welcome to the priesthood. Why do I say that? Because like a priest, you have to really want to be here to put up with all the deprivation and sacrifice. No one gets rich—legally—in public service and there will be times when you will curse this job and me and probably the mother who bore you but didn't talk you into private practice. But stay and I can promise you the perks of job satisfaction, learning how to evaluate and try a case, and do something that matters to a whole lot of people. If that's not enough, you don't belong here."

For most of them, it wasn't enough. They'd spend a couple of years buffing up their résumés, all the while trying to catch the eye of private firms, and that was okay with him. Those who stayed, for the most part, were the ones he hoped would. So he was glad when Collins returned and asked for his former position with the homicide bureau. He was a thorough, dedicated prosecutor, and when he lobbied for the high-profile Garcia case, Karp had talked it over with Sakamoto and tossed him the plum.

However, Collins was also the sort who bridled at any hint that the boss was looking over his shoulder. He was already feeling the stress of having a slam-dunk case showing signs of unraveling. It had made him that much more determined to dig his heels in to show that he could win the tough case, too.

When the boss had asked if the witness's questionable honesty bothered him, he had replied somewhat testily. "I'm not here to try Vincent Paglia. Of course, I don't like that the defense attorney—if one shows up—will have all sorts of innuendo to try to discredit my witness. But I have a defendant who made threats against the victim. I have, at least on videotape, a witness who was at the scene and says he saw the defendant with a gun. I also have the .45 with Garcia's fingerprints. . . . I think we get this to trial, and maybe see what shakes out on the witness stand. Heck, with the death penalty hanging over his head, perhaps Garcia rolls over and gives us the other shooter, and maybe we learn the truth about who did what to whom and why."

Karp patted Collins on the arm. "I'm not questioning your abilities or decisions," he whispered. "Just playing devil's advocate." From a purely tactical standpoint, the assistant district attorney was right. He could win a conviction in this case, especially if McMichaels was as much of a nonentity as he'd demonstrated so far.

Karp looked around. The courtroom was filled to standing room only, most of it by the press. Normally a preliminary hearing, even in a murder case, didn't receive much attention. But this one involved a celebrity, plus the added sex appeal of the murdered hookers, and all of it iced with the death of the prosecution's star witness. He recognized the usual pack that hunted for the city's dailies, plus the talking heads from the television stations, as well as representatives of the media from Los Angeles and even a reporter from Court TV.

As they'd filed in, the spectators had indicated their allegiances by where they sat. In the pews behind the prosecution table were personnel from the district attorney's office—some of whom were squirming as they wondered if the boss of bosses was checking up on them. There were a few civilians he assumed were fans of the dead rapper, some of them wearing red gang clothing and staring daggers at the defendant. He saw no one he recognized as belonging to Johnson's family, although he assumed one or both parents would be brought to New York during the trial to testify, especially if Garcia was convicted and the court moved to a death penalty phase.

As he was surveying the scene, Karp saw Flanagan and Leary enter the courtroom and sit down in the same pew as Guma, though they didn't seem to notice him. The older detective, however, nodded at Karp, and he nodded back, being careful not to let his face reveal the revulsion he felt.

Directly behind the defense table were Garcia's supporters, most of whom appeared to have made the long trip down from Spanish Harlem. A half dozen of the younger men were dressed in the Latino gang uniforms of plaid shirts, baggy pants, and wide bandanas bound around their foreheads. They were staring back across the courtroom at the gangsters looking at them and Garcia. He wondered if one of them could have been the second shooter.

Leaning close to the wooden barrier between the pews and the defense table was Father Dugan, who was chatting with Garcia. The defendant was dressed in an orange jail jumpsuit, his manacled hands attached to a chain that ran around his middle. Karp felt somewhat unsettled when Garcia and Dugan stopped talking and turned their heads to look at him.

Karp's attention snapped back to the front of the courtroom when the court clerk entered and announced the imminent arrival of the honorable judge Alan Friedman. The audience, lawyers, and defendant sprang to their feet, at which point the judge showed up and told them they could return to their seats.

Friedman was a short, balding man with bushy black eyebrows and a scowl to match intense brown eyes. "All right people," he said. "Sorry about the interruption. Now I believe we are here in the matter of the people versus Alejandro Garcia for a preliminary hearing to determine if probable cause exists to charge the defendant with murder. Is there anything either side would like to bring up before we go forward?"

Karp leaned over to Collins. "I want you to tell the judge that we are not ready to proceed," he said. "Tell him we'd like to take this to the grand jury."

"What?" Collins whispered incredulously. "We have enough for probable cause. Why wait?"

"Because for as long as I am running this office," Karp replied, "we will not bring a case unless we truly believe that the defendant is 1000 percent factually guilty, and we have legally admissible evidence to convict beyond a reasonable doubt. I have concerns about that right now. We need time."

"Gentlemen of the prosecution, would you care to let me in on your little confab?" Friedman glowered at them. "And good afternoon, Mr. Karp, will you be assuming the lead in this case?"

"Good afternoon, your honor," Karp said, rising to his feet. "I want to assure the court that this case will be presented to the grand jury. Accordingly, your honor, the People request that this preliminary hearing be put over for one week as a control date. We will report back at that time or sooner with respect to how the case is proceeding before the grand jury."

The courtroom immediately started buzzing with a hundred voices, causing the judge to bang his gavel down hard. Karp glanced over at the defense table where McMichaels sat stunned with what looked to him like an expression of panic or fear. Looking past the defense attorney, Karp locked eyes with Garcia who frowned slightly but inclined his head.

"SILENCE!" the judge roared, which had the desired effect. "You will conduct yourselves with decorum or you will be removed bodily from this courtroom." He turned back to the prosecutors. "Would you care to explain why we left it to the last possible moment to make this decision, Mr. Collins, or perhaps, Mr. Karp, as it seems the confusion arrived with you."

Karp again stood. "No, your honor," he said. "I apologize for taking your time. Within the last twenty-four hours we learned of the death of one of our witnesses as well as other facts that require a full and complete presentation to the grand jury." He sat back down and resisted the urge to glance over his shoulder to see Flanagan's reaction.

The judge checked his calendar. "Very well, we'll put the case over to the time you request. What about bail, Mr. Karp?"

In response, Karp stood and spoke loud enough for everyone in the court to hear. "Your honor, the People do not oppose a reasonable bail on the condition that the defendant, Mr. Garcia, not leave the city and be remanded to the custody of Father Michael Dugan, whom I believe this court knows and who is present here in the court." He motioned toward Dugan.

Judge Friedman with pen in hand noted instructions on the court file and then stated matter-of-factly, "Bail is set at fifty thousand dollars—10 percent of it payable before release, the rest forfeit should Mr. Garcia not appear when this court so orders—with the conditions as set forth by the prosecution. Is that all right with you, Father Dugan?"

Dugan practically jumped to his feet. "Yes, your honor. He will not be out of my sight."

Friedman stood and intoned, "This court is now in recess."

With the judge gone, the courtroom once again exploded in a cacophony of voices. The press tried to crowd toward Karp, but with a head signal from the DA, the court security officers cleared the room.

With the crowd dispersed, Karp looked over at the defense table where a pale-looking McMichaels was gathering his papers. Must have hoped for a big show on' television, he thought. He noticed that Garcia was standing next to the barrier where Dugan had placed an arm around his shoulders. He couldn't be certain, but the boy appeared to be crying. Then the court security led Garcia off. "We'll post bail right away," Dugan called after him.

Suddenly, Karp was aware of another presence behind him. He turned to see Flanagan. "Can I have a word with you?" the detective said through clenched teeth.

"Certainly," Karp replied calmly. "How can I help?"

"What in Jesus' name was that about?" the detective hissed, barely in control of his anger. "We don't need no grand jury. We got this guy dead to rights. And you let him go? He'll be out of town by sunset."

"I guess now you're in the business of telling us how to prosecute cases," Karp replied coldly. "I think I have a pretty good track record on homicide cases, detective." He let his voice warm up a little. "I would just like to see how the grand jury reacts to the videotape—let them tell us what parts are strong and what we can leave out. When we go to trial, I don't want to bore the trial jury or overdo it. Whatever he didn't do today, the defense is sure to raise the issue of the defendant's right to cross-examine—if not at trial, then on appeal. The less we use—while using enough—the less an appeals court will think we tried to base our whole case on Paglia's testimony."

"What about not opposing bail?"

"Well, detective," Karp said, summoning a conspiratorial grin, "have you ever heard of the expression, 'Give him enough rope and he'll hang himself'? I figure that if you and your guys stay with him, maybe he'll lead us to the second shooter. If we got both of them, one of them is bound to roll over on the other. Mystery solved and maybe Paglia's testimony won't be such a big deal. Eh? Meanwhile, if he tries to leave the island you pick him up."

Flanagan bit his lip and considered what he'd been told. Then he nodded. "Yeah, maybe. I kind of think the second guy might have been this pal of his, Pancho Ramirez; the guy's a bad actor from the word go. Still, you might have let me in on the strategizing. I'm feeling a little lost out here."

Karp slapped him on the shoulder. "Hey, man, ol' Vinnie just got fished out of the drink yesterday, and I didn't know the public defender was going to pass on fighting admission of the videotape. It just occurred to me that he might be doing that to set up an appellate lawyer to argue later that Garcia did not have adequate counsel. These PDs can be pretty damn sneaky. Let's do this right, go to the grand jury, get an indictment, and come back and convict his ass."

He noticed that Flanagan flinched uncomfortably with the use of the words *damn* and *ass* . . . a real Bible banger, he thought. "I wish I could have let you in on it sooner, but there wasn't time. We'll try to communicate better in the future."

Mollified, Flanagan managed a half smile. "Yeah, guess I should keep my big yap out of your business. Like you said, me and my partner," he nodded to where Leary was standing in the back of the courtroom, "will keep an eye on him, see if he leads us to the second shooter or maybe talks to someone who'll squeal."

"That's the spirit," Karp said, leading the way to the aisle and out of the doors in the back of the courtroom. "Now I got to get back to the office where the sky is falling. I take it you've heard about these bodies in Central Park."

Flanagan grimaced, "Yeah, a real sicko, from what they're

saying down at the shop. If there's one thing I can't stand, it's some sex pervert who hurts kids. You sort of hope that when they catch him, he resists arrest, if you know what I mean."

"Oh, I do indeed," Karp said. He walked away with the plastic grin on his face until he got into his office and returned to his more normal scowl, which is how Collins found him.

"Is there something you want to tell me?" Collins asked, obviously angry.

"Yeah, I just couldn't right there," Karp replied, and told him in general about the caller and the box of files that had showed up. "Garcia's lawyer threw me for a loop, and I wanted some time for us to get this thought out. So we go forward with the grand jury, even if it's just for the trial run. Look, it can't hurt."

Collins sighed but nodded his head. "You're right, of course," he said. "Something stinks. But damn, I was looking forward to getting back on the horse and winning one."

"I understand," Karp said. "And I also appreciate what you bring to the job; it's a rare commodity. I promise, if this one doesn't go the way we want, you get the next really juicy one. In the meantime, you get to practice your technique in front of the GJ. Okay?"

Collins grinned. "Yeah, okay."

As the ADA left the office, Karp thought, Good boy, Collins, know when to cut your losses and get what you can in exchange.

A minute later, Mrs. Boccino announced the arrival of Clay Fulton. "Heard about what happened," the detective said. "The files and the courtroom thing. What's the next move?"

Karp pursed his lips. "Good question, have a seat while

I call V.T.," he said. A moment later he had Newbury on the phone and asked for a preliminary report.

"Well, just shooting from the hip," Newbury said, "I think we've just been handed the tip of the iceberg that sank the *Titanic*."

"Why just the tip?"

"'There are too many years between the first and last cases. They all follow the same pattern too much for me to believe that this is all there is over that amount of time. But I guess the big clue is the note saying 'More to follow,' and the caller's warning that it's only going to get worse. Right now, I recommend that we ask for the complete Internal Affairs files on the cases we have. Some of them have passed the statute of limitations as far as criminal charges, but others have not and bear at least further investigation and maybe prosecution. I'm sure you saw that the common denominator with all these files is that they were all signed off on by Kane or one of his hired guns, which means the caller wants us to draw the same conclusion. But why not just spell it out? Why the games?"

"Good questions," Karp said. "Is it just some political enemy of Kane wanting us to do the hitting before the election? I'm sure Kane will say that his firm was just doing its job—protecting the city and the NYPD from lawsuits. As far as any conspiracy to cover up criminal conduct, he can argue that interpretation is subjective and that his recommendations were forwarded on to this office. I spouted off about racketeering, but it would be tough to prove. Now I feel like I'm sitting here with my head on the chopping block as I wait for the ax to fall with this third test."

"Yep, I don't envy you . . . well, except that you get to sleep with the divine Ms. Ciampi," Newbury said. "But isn't that why you get paid the big bucks? The tough decisions I mean, not Marlene."

"I get paid big bucks?" Karp asked, glad that he could count on V.T.'s humor to calm him down.

"Well, maybe not, but there's that job satisfaction speech you give all the rookies," Newbury said. "Or is that just for the cannon fodder?"

"Yeah, yeah." Karp sighed. "I may not have a job to be satisfied with when this is over. By the way, speaking of jobs, what have you got for me on Pentagram Records?"

"I was getting to that," Newbury said. "I may have boasted a little too soon about how easy it would be to find out who owns the company, at least without them knowing that I'm trying to find out. But I have good news and bad news. The bad news is that ownership is hidden behind so many layers of talking-head executives and sham corporations—most of them legal if suspect—that I'm still not at the end of the line. Even my spies who've managed to infiltrate some of the dummy corporations say that no one really seems to know who they are working for other than their immediate bosses."

"What's the good news?"

"The good news is the same thing. Anybody who goes through this much trouble to disguise owning a small record label has to have something worth hiding. But what I don't get is how all of this is tied to the No Prosecution files."

"Me either, V.T.," Karp admitted. "But keep digging; hopefully we'll find out."

Karp hung up and turned back to Fulton. "Clay, I want you to send your most trusted guys to go back over all the evidence in this case. That includes taking that limo apart to see if anything was missed. And take a drive to the

Bronx and see if Mrs. Paglia has anything to add. Express your condolences, but ask if you can look around for any suicide notes or whatever."

Fulton stood to go, but Karp stopped him at the door. "And Clay, let's keep this between me, you, and your guys. Leave Flanagan out of it."

"You know a lot of people think of him as a hero," he said. "And the department is still hurting from our losses, as is everyone in this city."

"You think I should forget this?" Karp asked.

Fulton shook his head. "No, I'm just hoping that this isn't going where it seems to be going. And that maybe the Jumain Little thing was a big mix-up, and it went down like he said it did."

"So what do I do?"

"What else? You do what's right." With that the detective turned and left the room.

26

JOHN JOJOLA OPENED THE OLD ARMY DUFFEL BAG and pulled out a moth-eaten, long-sleeved black turtleneck and loose-fitting black pants—or at least they had been thirty years earlier. He had to strain to button the pants and looked ruefully in the mirror at the way the turtleneck bulged around his middle.

Then he remembered why he was standing in a room at the Sagebrush Inn the night after nearly being killed by an assassin masquerading as a lawman, and the anger returned.

The scars of the betrayal in Deming had never completely healed in New Mexico. In fact, they'd been torn open again when the stories about the pedophile priests in the big cities back east began getting a lot of attention in the media. The press in New Mexico had, of course, dredged up the memories of Deming to make a connection to the day's breaking news. They'd interviewed the victims about their experiences a decade and more earlier; even talked to the psychiatrist who ran the Deming retreat, which he admitted still treated "troubled priests" but, he assured the press, the men would never be allowed to return to public service as had occurred in the Boston archdiocese.

Jojola's anger wasn't just directed at the priests who betrayed the trust given to them—he believed that there would eventually be justice in this world and the next for them. It was the church hierarchy's ignoring or covering up these outrages that troubled him more. He especially hated the excuses made by sad-faced cardinals and bishops that priests were merely human and subject to the same pitfalls and urges as the rest of humanity. Yes, he thought, but the rest of humanity is not entrusted with such a precious gift. There is a higher standard for people who choose such professions, just as there should be for police officers and presidents.

Jojola knew that these betrayals didn't lie just within the Catholic clergy. Protestant ministers, Buddhist monks, Hindu yogi, and Islamic mullahs had predators among them. Men who used their positions of trust, even the supposed concurrence of God, to sexually assault their constituents.

He'd heard that among the tribes there were those who left the reservations and went to the cities, where they billed themselves as medicine men, whether they were recognized as such by their tribes or not. Complaints were common that these so-called medicine men used their so-called spirituality to seduce gullible white women who thought that they were being shown "the Native American way." According to what he'd heard, some of these women at first felt, or were told, that they should feel honored by these special favors, only to realize later that they'd been used when the medicine man moved on to his next victim.

Most American Indians he knew were deeply ashamed

of these men, who were often shunned when they returned to the reservation. But right now, his anger was focused on the Catholic Church, which seemed to have created a culture of tolerance and secrecy surrounding these criminal acts. And if his run-in with Tobias was any indication, that culture had now gone so far toward the far end of the spectrum as to protect a man who raped and killed little boys.

Jojola breathed deeply and let the air pass out slowly. He knew he needed to let the anger dissipate, so that he could think clearly.

He was tucking his hair up under a black stocking cap when Marlene came out of the bathroom wearing a similar getup. Seeing her lithe, athletic body, he was suddenly self-conscious about the roll around his waistband.

"Not exactly Arnold Schwarzenegger," he lamented.

"Cuter with a better accent," she laughed. "Look, I'm no Charlie's Angel either, but we're all we got."

"And Lucy," he pointed out.

"Yes," Marlene sighed. "And Lucy."

The day before, Marlene had screamed as her daughter fell toward the abyss, but her voice was drowned out by the thundering of what she at first believed was the breaking of her heart. Then she became aware of the large, brown, two-headed animal next to her. A horse, she realized, and on it sat a rider in blue denim swinging a rope above his head. The animal was planting its hooves to stop from going over the edge as the cowboy threw his lariat.

As the truck plunged past the dangling tree, Marlene watched the hoop circle down as though in slow motion around Lucy. Then the tree, truck, and girl fell out of sight below the outcropping. Quick as a rattlesnake striking, the cowboy cinched his rope twice around the saddle horn, then held on when the rope went taut.

Down below, Lucy fell hard against the cliff, bruising her face and scraping her arms. She would have screamed but the rope was too tight around her chest.

Ned Blanchet gave a short whistle and Sally, his best roping horse, began to back steadily away from the cliff. Lucy, a bit bloodied and shaken, appeared at the top of the outcropping where she was able to crouch and climb to the top of the slope with the help of the rope and the horse. At the rim, she reached out and was grabbed on one side by Jojola and the other by her mother, into whose arms she collapsed as both women cried.

As soon as he saw that Lucy was safe, Ned was out of the saddle in a single motion as smooth as the pouncing of a cat, and running toward them, his chaps flapping and spurs jingling like tiny bells. Lucy turned to meet him and he picked her up in his arms and swung her around.

"Ow!" she exclaimed. "You're squeezing the rope burn you gave me, you dolt!"

Ned immediately set her down and began apologizing profusely. He stopped, confused, when Lucy started laughing. A moment later, he was blushing red as a chili pepper when the girl of his dreams grabbed his face with her two hands and planted a long, wet kiss on his mouth. For a boy who'd happily dreamed of the day he would get more than a peck on the cheek, he thought he'd done died and gone to Montana.

"My hero," Lucy gushed, which made him blush even pinker. He was scratching at the gravel with his boot and hiding his face beneath his hat when Marlene added to the praise and his embarrassment. "I wouldn't have believed it if I wasn't there to see it," she said, giving him another kiss, fortunately this one on the cheek or he might have fainted. "That was better than the movies."

Ned shrugged and waved his hat toward his horse. "It was Sally did all the work," he said. "I just threw the rope." He explained how he'd heard the first shot and started to move in that direction, concerned that someone was poaching one of the steers he was supposed to be watching.

"Then I come over the rise a half mile back and heard the second shot and was just in time to see you go over the edge. After that, Sally and I went hell-bent for leather to get here, especially after I saw that fella shoulder his rifle like he was going to finish you off. But then there was a couple more shots and he fell in."

"That fella was Sheriff Asher," Marlene said. "I shot him. He's dead."

Ned looked at her hard for a moment, then nodded his head. "Well, I expect he needed shootin' then, 'cause he was sure takin' aim at you. And unless I miss my guess, he fired those first two shots."

"The first one was at me," Jojola said.

"The second took out our tire," Marlene added.

"Well, I can see that there's more goin' on here than I know," said the young cowboy. "But I knowed that I needed to get here pronto. I saw John haul Marlene up and figured Luce needed help. Still, I can't say I had much of a chance to think about what I was doing when I saw . . . when I saw"—he started to choke up and looked up at the sun to stop the tears—"when I saw her falling. I just threw. It was luck."

"Luck schmuck," Lucy interrupted, kissing him again. "You're my hero whether you like it or not."

Alarmed that Lucy might think that he wasn't pleased

to be her hero, he quickly responded, "Oh, I like it, I jest don't rightly know what I'm supposed to do now."

"Why ride off into the sunset, dummy," Lucy said in mock exasperation. "Don't you know nothin', you darling cowpoke?"

Ned looked even more confused. "Well, I know it's only an hour or so after sunrise," he pointed out. "And between now and sunset, I'm 'sposed to move fifty head over to the south pasture and mend that fence by the highway where that tourist went off the road and took out a section. I guess I might be able to ride into the sunset after I get all that done. Why? You want to go for a ride this evening?"

"Ned . . ."

"Yeah, Luce?"

"Shut up and kiss me again. But be careful of the rope burn."

Ned did as he was told, carefully. He even remembered to remove his hat this time like he'd seen John Wayne do once in an old movie.

Jojola and Marlene moved away from the young couple and over to his truck where he radioed for help. "Larry," he said, addressing Officer Small Hands, "this was on reservation property, so call the FBI. But do it on the telephone. Tell them there's been a shooting and Sheriff Asher is presumed dead."

"Sheriff Asher is dead?" Small Hands repeated. "You all right?"

"I'm fine," Jojola replied. "Now no more questions, just do it."

With that accomplished, he turned to Marlene. "You figure we were maybe getting too close for somebody's comfort?"

Marlene had grown quiet now that the adrenaline from her daughter's rescue had subsided but she nodded. Another one for the village, she thought. It's going to be more crowded.

Jojola noticed the mood change and knew what it meant. "You did what you had to do, Marlene," he said, reaching out to touch her shoulder. "Your life and your daughter's life were at stake."

Marlene wiped at her eyes. "I know," she said. "But why do I have to be the executioner everywhere I go?"

"I don't know," Jojola replied. "We can't always see where the path ends, but we have to keep walking to find out. Maybe things happen to cause an ending we can't know yet. Now back to business—are you thinkin' what I'm thinkin'?"

Marlene looked up and managed a small smile, grateful for the psychological slap across the face to stop the swan dive into self-pity. "Yeah," she said. "I think we need to take a look around St. Ignatius. Somebody put Asher up to this, and it wasn't just because he didn't like our looks. We need to figure out who and why. And if your hunch about the missing boys and the retreat are correct, why they would be protecting a killer. This whole little gambit seems . . . oh, I don't know . . . desperate?"

"My thoughts exactly," Jojola said. "The good thing is desperate people make mistakes."

"The bad thing is," she reminded him, "desperate people are more dangerous."

It took only an hour before an FBI agent showed up at the scene. A local search-and-rescue team was rappelling down the cliff to retrieve the body of Sheriff Asher, which had hung up on a ledge five hundred feet below the rim, when Lloyd Bear walked up to Jojola and identified himself as an FBI special agent on an undercover assignment for the bureau.

"You work for the feds?" Jojola said with a scowl, after he and the others gave their accounts of Asher's attempted ambush and subsequent death.

Bear nodded. "Yeah, sorry about the subterfuge," he said. "They recruited me right out of college. This was my first undercover assignment."

"And exactly what were you supposed to be uncovering?" Jojola asked.

"Well, I'm not really supposed to tell you this, but we've been working on a tip that priests who'd committed sexual assaults on children in New York were sent to St. Ignatius in an attempt to cover up the commission of the acts. As you know, interstate flight to avoid prosecution is a federal crime, and the rest of it falls under racketeering statutes." He looked over to where the rescue team was using a winch to pull a stretcher containing Asher's body onto the edge of the canyon.

"We figured Asher might be connected. Every time we tried to ask him anything about St. Ignatius, we got the runaround and the usual local jurisdiction/anti-fed crap. But we didn't have enough for a case yet. Of course, I'm telling you this in confidence and in the spirit of cooperation with your agency. Now, how about a little give-and-take. Does this morning's little adventure have something to do with St. Ignatius and the disappearance of the kids from the pueblo?"

Jojola thought about the question for a moment, and thought about telling Bear what he knew. But first he answered the agent with a question of his own. "Why'd you ask for a boy to help you with cleaning out at the retreat?"

Bear shrugged. "Better cover," he said. "Easier to look around while the kid was doing the work."

"You used my son as part of an FBI undercover operation without asking me, his father?" Jojola asked. "And what's more, took him to a place where the clients make a habit of sexually assaulting children?"

Bear held his hands up and chuckled nervously. "Hey, no worries. I had my eye on him the whole time. Sometimes you have to risk a little to gain a lot, and I—"

The agent never finished his sentence. In fact, he hit the ground before he could utter another word because Jojola's fist had shut his mouth for him. Bear rubbed his jaw. "Okay, guess I deserved that," he said.

"Damn right you did."

"So now you want to tell me why the sheriff wanted you and two women dead?" the agent asked, getting back on his feet.

Jojola shook his head. "I could tell you," he said, "but it's a secret so I'd have to kill you. And as you probably know, killing an FBI agent is a federal offense."

With that Jojola stalked off toward his truck where Marlene and Lucy were waiting. "You get a chance to let Ned in on what we need?" he asked the women. Lucy nodded. "He's game. A little before midnight tomorrow."

Jojola told the women to take his truck and head back to town. He was going to stay and help the sore-jawed agent Bear, and the men who'd arrived in a federal crime-scene van, go over the truck Asher was driving.

"Looks like Leroy Cinque's truck," Jojola noted. "Wonder where he is?"

He found out two hours later when he stopped in the

pueblo police office and heard someone singing a *Tiwa* death prayer from the small holding cell in the back of the building. "Who's that," he asked Officer Small Hands, who was on duty.

Small Hands looked toward the door leading to the cell with annoyance. "It's that damn Leroy Cinque," he said. "He's driving me nuts with his chanting, says he's going to die soon. Some geologist found him wandering around out in the desert west of the gorge, half out of his head and smelling like he took a bath in tequila. He claimed Sheriff Asher got him drunk last night and then dumped him out there. Says he was visited by an evil spirit who told him that death was coming for him. . . . And that's just the junk you can understand. In between prayers, he's also spouting a bunch of other nonsense that sounds like stuff out of the Bible."

A high keening interrupted the officer, who shuddered. "We were going to let him go but got the message you were looking for him. Sorry but I guess I forgot to get on the horn and tell you he'd showed up."

"That's okay, I was busy," Jojola said. He grabbed keys off a peg on the wall and unlocked the door leading to the holding cells. He walked to the end of the semidark corridor and peered in the last cell.

Leroy Cinque was never an attractive man. His face had been deeply pitted by smallpox and his large nose resembled a sunburned orange peel in texture and appearance. His disheveled hair looked grayer than before, and when he looked up at Jojola there was insanity hovering in his eyes. He stood and walked over to the bars, which he grabbed with both hands.

"And I looked," he said quietly, "and behold a pale horse . . ." The man looked like he was about to say something more, when he clutched at his throat and fell to the floor of the cell.

"Deputy Small Hands, call for an ambulance!" Jojola shouted and fumbled for the key to the cell.

White froth mixed with flecks of blood was bubbling out of Cinque's mouth with strange strangling noises. His eyes rolled into the back of his head as his body went stiff and then a moment later went limp.

Jojola felt for a pulse. *Nothing*. The froth at Cinque's mouth remained as it was when he went limp. *Not breathing*. The man was dead.

"What happened?" Small Hands asked as he came up behind Jojola.

"Not sure. Looked like some sort of fit. Leroy have a history of epilepsy?"

Small Hands looked blank. "Don't know . . . not that I ever heard."

The ambulance arrived and a paramedics rushed in to check for vital signs. He shook his head. "He's gone. Looks like maybe a massive coronary blew out the old pump." The paramedic's partner came back with a rolling stretcher, picked up the dead man, and left. "We'll let you know what the coroner says."

They had just pulled out of the parking lot when Charlie showed up on his bicycle. "Hi, Dad," he said, watching the vehicle drive off. "What happened?"

"I don't really know, Charlie," Jojola said, guiding his son back to his private office. "Except that Leroy Cinque died just now."

Charlie was quiet for a moment. "Well, at least he won't hit his wife anymore."

Jojola nodded. "I guess there's that. So anyway what brings you here?"

Charlie sat down at his father's desk on which he proudly propped two feet sheathed in brand-new Air Jordans. "So what do you think?"

"They look like they were made for you. Ought to be good for another ten, maybe twenty points a game." Jojola was rewarded with a smile from Charlie. "Hold on a second and we'll go home." He pushed the play button on his telephone answering machine, wondering if he missed something in Asher's message that might have warned him about the man's intentions.

When Asher reached the part "If it checks out, I think we could use that to go see my friend the judge . . ." Jojola happened to look up at his son, who had fallen silent. Charlie's face was pale, and he was staring at the machine.

"What is it, son?" Jojola asked, concerned, considering that a man had just dropped over dead in his holding cell, that Charlie had taken ill.

"That voice," his son said quietly. "That's the voice of the other man who was in the room with Tobias. He's the one who told Tobias to call New York because you were snooping around and that the lid was . . ."

". . . coming off the pack of fuckin' perverts," Jojola repeated for Marlene and Lucy that night when they met at the Sagebrush Inn.

"Well, I guess that pretty much cements that he was working for whoever it is in New York who's trying to keep this under wraps," Marlene said. "I doubt Tobias is going to be any help. The good doctor was ready to lawyer up just because you wanted to ask a few questions; he and Asher both seem to be afraid of whoever's pulling the strings back east. I'd assume they've moved whoever it was they were worried about—maybe this big priest Charlie met and you suspect—away from St. Ignatius. It sounded like they wanted to send him to New York, but we're not sure, and we need to know the guy's name."

"That's what we're going to try to find out," Jojola said. He was quiet for a moment, then added, "But I've been thinkin' and maybe I should do this on my own. It's breakin' the law, and it's my problem."

Marlene snorted. "After all I've told you, you're worried that I might get caught breaking the law?" She shook her head. "Uh-uh, John, you don't get to have all the fun. Besides, I think you might need some of my more . . . umm, unusual . . . skills. Now quit with the noble hero stuff, Ned Blanchet already monopolized that one up for the day. Let's get ready."

Lucy rose. "I want to check my email real quick before we leave," she said and headed for her room. "I'll wait for you two outside."

When she was gone, Marlene picked up a large Wal-Mart bag. "Got your stuff?" she asked Jojola, who raised his army duffel. "My worldly possessions," he replied.

"Then see you in a minute," she said, walking into the bathroom and closing the door.

"Not exactly Arnold Schwarzenegger," he had lamented when she came out of the bathroom. . . .

They left the room and quickly headed down a back stairs to the parking lot, where Lucy was already behind the wheel of a truck Jojola had borrowed. The plan nearly went awry from the beginning because they couldn't get her to stop giggling when she saw them. "You two look ridiculous," she chortled.

When at last the indignant pair got her to get serious and drive, they left Taos and drove north to St. Ignatius.

They knew that they had a problem in that the only road past the retreat was easily visible from both the front and rear entrances. They also knew from Ned that there would be guards patrolling the grounds, but he had an idea of how to enter the compound.

"It's probably how your guy, that priest, got in and out without nobody seein' him," Ned had said earlier when they were formulating their plans out at the gorge. "The retreat used to be part of an old mission, built way back when this was all still part of Mexico. Anyways, apparently them old monks built themselves an escape tunnel— maybe in case the Indians overran the place—that goes from a root cellar in the main building to what looks like an old mine but is really another entrance."

"How do you know about it?" Marlene had asked.

"I was raised on a ranch that ran cattle on the property before the church in New York bought it and fixed it all up," he said. "I guess like most kids I was curious and checked out what I thought was a mine. I got to warn you, though, it's not a real nice tunnel, and you'll still have to cover fifty yards of open ground to reach it from the road."

"I wonder how the priest pulled it off," Jojola had asked.

Ned had pursed his lips, then said, "If he waited until after bed check at eleven, the guards get pretty relaxed. There's really not a whole lot to do . . . have to admit, I've dozed off a couple of times myself."

"Can't count on it tonight," Marlene had said. "With the run-in with Asher today, Tobias might have things stirred up a bit more than usual. He's bound to be a little paranoid."

Still, they'd agreed that the tunnel was their best hope for gaining access to the main building. Ned, who was more of a roving patrol at night, had volunteered to distract the guard at the front gate when he saw the truck drive past. But that still left the guard at the back gate. So before they came into view of the retreat, Jojola had Lucy stop the truck while he and Marlene hopped into the bed. "Now keep your lights on and drive slow but steady down the road past the retreat," he said through the back window. "Keep driving up and out of sight, wait an hour and come back for us but don't stop, just slow down."

Jojola explained to Marlene that the tactic was an old deer-hunting trick. The animals would watch the truck's headlights and not notice when a hunter jumped out of the back to creep up on them from another direction. "Hopefully, the diversion will work on the guards as well," he said.

When the truck was nearly at a small ravine that Ned had told them to follow to reach the tunnel entrance, Jojola and Marlene lowered themselves from the back of the truck, took two steps, and rolled into the ditch at the side of the road.

"Well, that was fun," Marlene whispered rubbing a sore elbow.

"Just like James Bond," Jojola whispered back.

"A very old, easily bruised, and no-longer-agile James Bond."

"Shaken, not stirred."

"Exactly."

They quickly moved up the ravine and, staying low, reached the tunnel entrance without raising an alarm. Inside the entrance, they turned on their small flashlights with the red bulbs, to make it more difficult to see them in the dark, but it also gave the musty, cobwebbed tunnel an eerie ambiance.

Jojola went first, uncomfortably reminded of the tunnels he and Charlie Many Horses had hunted Vietcong in. "Sure you want to come?" he said, turning to Marlene.

"You going to stand in the way all night," she replied, imagining what it would be like to suddenly meet a huge hairy priest in the darkness ahead.

They had to move at a crouch, trying not to worry about the loose gravel falling in from the ceiling and sides, or the occasional cobweb that clung to their faces. At last, they reached an old wooden door that opened into a root cellar as Ned had described. It was obvious at a glance that the cellar wasn't used much, a relic that was no longer needed with the invention of refrigerators. But someone had been there in the not-so-distant past—when Jojola's light fell on the staircase leading to the floor above, there in the dust were the imprints of giant sandals.

They paused at the top of the stairs, listening for any sounds of someone stirring. But all was quiet, and so tensing at the smallest creaking, Jojola opened the trapdoor and they found themselves in the retreat's kitchen. Based on their discussions with Charlie and Ned, they quickly found the hallway that led to Tobias's office.

Jojola tried the door. "Locked," he whispered.

Marlene moved him aside and shined her light on the door handle. Reaching into a small pack she carried around her waist, she brought out a leather case that she flipped open to reveal a number of curious instruments.

Jojola chuckled quietly. "You always carry burglar tools on your vacations?"

"A lady never knows when she might need to use the bathroom, only to find out some male idiot locked the door," she whispered back. A moment later there was a soft click and she opened the door.

Jojola moved to the desk, while Marlene went for a small safe in the corner of the room.

"Find anything?" she asked a few minutes later when he came up behind her.

"Nothing," he said. "Charlie's magazine but otherwise it's almost like it's been cleared out. A few pencils, an empty notepad, paper clips. Not a working man's desk."

Marlene nodded and returned to her task. She had some sort of long steel needle inserted in the tumbler. Her fingers made several sure, quick movements; then with her other hand she grabbed the latch and opened the safe. It, too, was almost empty, except for Tobias's passport and banking receipts and a checkbook for the St. Ignatius Retreat. "If there was anything here, it looks like we're too late," she said, disappointed.

Jojola looked around and then tapped her on the shoulder and pointed. "Not by much," he said. Against one wall was a paper shredder and next to it a large plastic lawn bag filled with strips of paper. He went over to the bag and was considering whether to take it with him, when Marlene whispered to him.

"Well, looky here." She'd gone over to another office machine, the fax, and was now reading a paper she'd found there.

"What is it?" he asked.

"The key to the city," she replied and handed him the document, which the sender had forgotten to retrieve.

It was a faxed letter that had been sent to the Archdiocese of New York, Office of the Archbishop, attention Father Secretary. Jojola began to read it and felt the anger returning.

Hans Lichner . . . is a severely disturbed individual exhibiting antisocial tendencies, possibly psychopathic, and belongs in a secure mental health institution or, perhaps, even a prison with a psychiatric ward. I have reason to believe that he may be involved in the disappearance and murder of local children. The chief of police of the Taos Pueblo was here two weeks ago, asking about a man who fit Lichner's physical description in connection with the disappearance of one child. I sent him on his way, but he has continued to nose around, and of late in the company of a woman named Marlene Ciampi, who you may know as the wife of the New York district attorney. I have a hard time believing that her appearance in Taos is purely coincidental.

"I think we got what we need," whispered Marlene, interrupting his reading. "Let's get out of here. I don't think he'll miss that."

They made it back to the tunnel and out to the road where Lucy was waiting for them without any incidents. Once in the truck, Jojola removed his stocking cap and swore. "I don't believe this," he said. "The archbishop of New York?"

Marlene swallowed hard. "Yeah, hard to believe," she said quietly. She was thinking of the power they were now up against, and the ramifications for thousands, even millions of people, if this information led where it appeared to be going.

"Remember the scene in the movie *Jaws*, where the sheriff sees the shark for the first time and goes and tells the captain, 'You're going to need a bigger boat'?" she said.

"Yeah, but what . . . ," Jojola replied, confused by the analogy.

"Well, we're going to need a bigger boat," she said. "Get ready, Mr. Jojola, you're about to be introduced to the Big Apple."

27

"THIS IS THE PLACE," GUMA SAID, AS IF THE flashing pink-and-purple neon sign proclaiming Hip-Hop Nightclub on the outside of the former warehouse wasn't enough. Or the pulsing beat that was already giving Karp a headache although they were standing on the sidewalk a good ten feet from the entrance.

In fact, the whole day had been a headache, if not an unexpected one. Stupenagel's story, of course, had been the talk of the town and started the initial throbbing in his temples. He actually thought that she'd done a balanced job of reflecting life in the DA's office, as well as accurately portraying his day at the Harlem church, including the confrontation with Bernard Little, and their discussions about why he was considering running for office. He was a little uncomfortable with the part in the story about his mom—not because it wasn't true and hadn't affected him the way he'd described, but because he felt as though he'd exposed some vulnerable part of himself.

Murrow had certainly been pleased, walking into the office with an armload of the *Voice* he'd looted from one of the sidewalk racks, and babbling about "a tour de force." However, there was no denying the fact that much of the article read in some ways like a bad detective novel with missing priests, bodies buried in a public park, and a prosecution witness washing up on the rocks at Hell's Gate.

The kicker, of course, was that "according to highly placed sources, the New York District Attorney's Office is investigating allegations of a widespread cover-up of misconduct and criminal acts committed by officers and detectives of the New York Police Department. The cover-up has apparently cost taxpayers millions of dollars in hush money paid to victims and victims' families. And the scheme has, according to the sources, been going on for at least a dozen years and may eventually implicate the administrations of two previous district attorneys, Sanford Bloom and Jack X. Keegan."

Stupenagel had not been able to reach Bloom, who had been transferred out of state to serve his sentence, due to threats made against his life by other inmates. She had contacted Keegan at the federal courthouse down the block from 100 Centre Street, but he had declined to comment. "Except," he said, "to say that this whole thing smacks of crude political maneuvering. I'm sure any *legitimate* investigation will show that there were no such improprieties involving the office of the district attorney, at least not on my watch."

Seeing the name of his former boss in the newspaper, the man who'd recommended him as his replacement, had been more of a shock to Karp than he'd anticipated. He knew that eventually any probe into the No Prosecution files would have to examine the conduct of the DA's office, but having it in black and white reminded him of the caller's warning that exposing this sore was bound to garner repercussions from men in high places.

They'd already started with a call first thing that morning from an obviously perturbed Jack Keegan. "What's this crap, Butch?" he demanded. "Trying to run for office by stepping on my back?"

"No one in this office has accused anybody of anything," Karp replied. "We're just following up on some allegations . . . as I'm sure you would have done." It hurt his stomach to say that last part, but it had come tumbling out of his disappointment in the man. "I have always respected you, Jack, and you should know me well enough to realize that it's not my style to advance myself by stepping on someone else's back."

"Styles change," Keegan growled. "Politics and power do funny things to people."

You're a fine one to talk, Karp thought. "Well, let's see how this plays out," he said. "It's probably nothing. I have passed the word to my staff that any further news leaks will be dealt with appropriately."

"Yeah, well, just remember who got you into that office and behind that desk," Keegan warned. "That little bit about this maybe implicating folks in the government and politics has a lot of important people stirred up, Butch. I'd think real hard before I opened every can of worms in the cupboard."

Keegan was talking about an unauthorized statement in Stupenagel's story that she had apparently slipped in after Murrow's review. It said that the investigation might eventually implicate "well-known and powerful figures in city government and in the political arena." He'd been upset that she went behind his back on that one, but Keegan's thinly veiled threat now made him glad she did. After all, if the goal is to smoke out the bad guys, she'd certainly put a match to the gasoline. He wondered what the reaction had been over at Plucker, Bucknell and Kane, and if the next mayor of New York was the important person Keegan was referring to.

"Thanks, Jack, I'll keep that in mind," he said. "Now I have a few fires to put out. We'll talk more about this later, I'm sure."

The one statement was the only place in the story that Stupenagel had crossed the line of their agreement. Otherwise, she'd left out or danced around those things that he'd asked not be printed, including the twins' role in the Garcia case. "They're listed in court records as confidential informants, and that's what they stay unless they're called as witnesses. Then they're fair game," he'd warned her.

As he'd predicted, the rest of the media had come howling to his door, complaining that he was playing favorites. They wanted to know why she was the only reporter in town to know about the bodies buried in Central Park. "Simple," Karp replied at a hastily called press conference. "She knew about them before we did. You're going to have to ask her how."

However, Karp angrily refused to comment on the part of her story claiming that his office was conducting an investigation into the allegations of police misconduct and a cover-up. "I am neither confirming nor denying that there is any such investigation," he sputtered with righteous indignation. "But if there were, it would not be appropriate for any member of this office to comment on the existence of an ongoing investigation and would be subject to dismissal. Do I make myself clear?"

"Not really," said one of the journalists. But the Karp Stare silenced him and the others from any more gratuitous comments, and they had gone away grumbling. He did make a note to himself to make sure that V.T. handled any future press conferences on the investigation so that it would not appear that he was using it to grandstand for political purposes. He wasn't going to give Keegan that bone to chew.

After the press conference, Karp returned to his office, where a few minutes later Newbury and Murrow entered to tender their joint written resignation for "consorting with a member of the press, to wit Adriadne Stupenagel." He laughed and pushed the resignation back across his desk to them. "Consider it your punishment that you will have to continue working in this office at the pleasure of the district attorney."

"I'd like to pleasure the district attorney," Stupenagel announced as she walked into the office past the harried Mrs. Boccino, who'd been fielding the angry calls from the press and had given up trying to guard his door.

Karp pointed at Newbury and Murrow. "They were feeling guilty about consorting with you. Even offered to resign as a result."

"Consort?" Stupenagel asked. "Don't I wish I could interest these two hunka-hunka burning loves into an Adriadne sandwich. But alas, you've surrounded yourself with Boy Scouts, Karp."

"I thought you liked them brave, clean, and reverent," he responded.

"You have that mixed up with creative, smells good, and willing to worship me on their knees."

"I'll get down on my knees if you'll get down on your elbows," Newbury said, entering the fray.

"You're on, big boy, I—" Stupenagel began to say, but was cut off by a shout from Murrow.

"ENOUGH ALREADY!" he yelled. "Must everything you say be an invitation to carnality?"

The others looked at Murrow in surprise, which caused him to turn red. Without another word, he stood up and stomped out of the office. Newbury and Karp looked at each other and said, "What got into him?"

Stupenagel smiled knowingly. "I do believe I just saw the green monster known as jealousy raise his sexually repressed little head."

Karp scoffed. "Murrow? Jealous of you," he said, then shook his head. "You're not his sort. I've met his girl-friends—nice, respectable debutantes from Mount Vernon. All of them sworn to virginity until their wedding nights, maybe longer."

"Are you suggesting that I'm not a virgin?" Stupenagel sniffed. "And how would you know? Perhaps, I'm all talk."

"Yeah, and I'm a rock and roll star," Karp said. "You forget that my beloved was the one sleeping in the student lounge while you were carving notches on the bedposts of the dorm room you were supposed to be sharing with her."

Stupenagel stuck her tongue out at him. "There weren't any bedposts, so there's no physical evidence of such behavior. Besides, she could have always kicked me out if she hadn't been such a prude."

The conversation had made him think of Marlene, which also contributed to his headache. He'd tried to call her all day Monday, leaving several messages at the Sagebrush Inn front desk saying he needed to talk to her ASAP about Giancarlo. With all the excitement of the past week or so, he hadn't followed up on Dr. Zacham and his offer to remove the shotgun pellet from their son's brain. What kind of father am I, anyway? he thought.

Then their family doctor called to remind him. "I got good news and I got bad news. The good news is that Dr. Zacham still has a spot open; the bad news—it has to be Friday," he said.

"Friday! That's impossible. I haven't been able to speak to Marlene yet . . . ," Karp complained.

The doctor commiserated but added, "You don't understand how in demand this guy is. He's willing to do Giancarlo Friday, has two more scheduled for the weekend. Then it's off to Russia to show their doctors where the brain is located. You have to let me know tomorrow. He'd have to be in the hospital by Thursday afternoon to be prepped."

Karp's first inclination was to say no. But he decided it was only fair to ask Giancarlo, whom he'd told about the offer when he first heard about Dr. Zacham.

"I've already thought about it, Dad," he said. "I've been doing a lot of reading on the Internet, or actually Zak has been reading to me. And Dr. Zacham is like a generation ahead of other brain surgeons, and I want him to do it. I'm okay being blind, and in a way I think it was meant to happen; I learned a lot about stuff I wouldn't have if my eyes still worked. But I want to see again. I want to see your face and Mom's; I want to know what Zak looks like when he signs with the Yankees, and Lucy's face when she becomes a mom. And there's another thing—I don't think Zak's going to go on with his own life as long as I am blind. So I sort of need to do this for him, too. That make sense?"

Karp nodded. "You make a lot of sense. I just don't think I could live with myself if something happened to you, and I know your mom would self-destruct because she'd blame herself."

"But it's my life, my choice," Giancarlo said.

Karp ran a big hand through his beautiful son's curly hair. "Yes, it's your choice." He found himself staring into Giancarlo's eyes, while his own were dripping tears.

So he'd been desperately trying to find Marlene. She'd want to be back for the surgery.

Marlene had called back Monday afternoon when he was in court with Collins and left a message with Mrs. Boccino, who read it with a great deal of dramatic flair. "I'm involved in something but can't talk 'bout it on the telephone. Returnin' to NYC soon. Love, M."

Oh no, here we go again, he thought when he'd translated his secretary's accent. His honey had apparently once again attracted killer bees and would be on her way home to the hive. But what had she stirred up and when would she and their daughter arrive? Oh well, I guess she'll be back in time to go with us to the hospital.

When he called the Sagebrush Inn again that morning, he was told that she and his daughter had checked out early but had not said where they were going. The headache had intensified. He was glad she was coming home—the little man who lived in his groin was turning cartwheels and already making plans—but he didn't need any more trouble on top of what he was already dealing with.

He was searching his desk drawer for aspirin when his private line rang. Everyone in the room froze, their eyes locked on the flashing red button. He picked up the receiver. "Karp."

"Good story in the *Voice* this morning," the anonymous caller said.

"I didn't write it," Karp growled. "You'd have to talk to the reporter."

"Is she still there?"

"Look, let's dispense with the games. I'm not in a good mood," he said. He looked up as Guma entered the room and took a seat on the couch next to Stupenagel, who removed the hand he placed on her knee.

"Well, I thought you'd like to know that you passed the second test—at least for now; we'll see if you have the backbone to butt heads with the NYPD and the inestimable Mr. Kane."

"Yeah, I guess we'll see. Now is that all? Or can we move on to test three. Or maybe we can just quit the 007 stuff altogether and talk like real people."

"It's all about trust, Mr. Karp. Before you get all self-righteous with me, maybe you should take another look at those No Prosecution files and ask whether there might be some reason to doubt the integrity of the men who've sat in that office over the past dozen years or so."

Karp sighed; the caller had a point. "Okay. But I'm not them."

"Yeah, well, I might believe you, but I'm not the only one who you need to convince. You didn't help your cause with that photograph in the *Times* a few weeks back of you chumming it up with Citizen Kane."

I knew that would come back to haunt me, he thought. "Lots of people have their photographs in the newspaper with people they don't necessarily like," he said

"Again, I'm not who you have to convince," the caller said.

"Okay, who then?"

"You might try asking Alejandro Garcia that question. You did the right thing yesterday, Mr. Karp. I know you believe that I might have some dark ulterior motive, and I guess I did, and still do, want something. But it was only to prevent a gross miscarriage of justice in the case of

Alejandro Garcia, and now it's to help you put an end to an even greater travesty."

"I don't like being manipulated," Karp said.

"I'm sorry if you feel that way, Mr. Karp. It just seems that in this case, justice needs a little shove."

"I have a family member who thinks like that," Karp responded dryly. "It's caused us a lot of grief."

The caller laughed. "Yes, I am aware of some of the . . . um, eccentricities . . . of your family. But you know, Mr. Karp, there is a reason that Lady Justice holds a sword in one hand to go with the scales in the other."

"I would concede your point so long as the sword follows the application of due process and that we agree that it's a metaphor for just punishment . . . not vigilante terrorism, Mr. . . . hmmm, I seem to have forgotten your name."

Another laugh. "Nice try. But on your point, we are at least philosophically in the same family, if not twin brothers."

Karp smiled grimly. "Well, I always wanted another sibling. So what's the next step? Where are the 'more to come' files? And when can I expect the third test?"

"The remaining No Prosecution files are being delivered at this moment, I believe, to Mr. Newbury's office. Forgive me if I usurped your authority, but I thought I'd save you the trouble of carting the boxes hither and thither—they contain considerably more files than you already received."

"You seem to be well informed about what goes on in my office," Karp said, giving the high sign to V.T. to read the note he was scribbling: *More files arriving your office NOW!* Newbury trotted out of the room.

"Yes, well, I would like to say something enigmatic like 'a sparrow does not fall from the sky that he does not notice.' But really, I'm sure it's pretty hard to keep a secret in an agency as large as yours. According to your comments in the *Voice* this morning, you apparently can't keep your staff from revealing state secrets to Ms. Stupenagel. Or were you play-acting for the rest of the media?"

Karp ignored the gambit. "And the third test?"

The caller was quiet for a moment, and when he spoke, his voice had grown somber. "I'm not sure, Mr. Karp . . . soon I would think," he said. "But again, I feel that I should warn you about the consequences of even taking the final exam. If you've considered the repercussions of the police files on the NYPD, one of its heroes, and the already shaken psyche of the public, I can only say that impact will be magnified many times over. Although I believe this is the only course, I even hesitate to hope that you succeed, as it could do great harm to the lives of many innocent people. And there is you individually. Whether you pass or fail, it might still ruin your political career and quite likely place you and your family at a greater risk than anything you've faced in the past. But having said that, Mr. Karp, I really must go. I wish you luck and courage; you're going to need both."

Then the caller was gone. Karp leaned back in his chair and blew an imaginary smoke ring at the ceiling. Leaning forward again, he pressed the intercom button for Mrs. Boccino.

"Grace, get me Father Michael Dugan on the phone. His number should be in your Rolodex," he said. Releasing the button, he turned to the others. "Ariadne, not a word of this until I say it's okay. But I think it's time I had a private talk with Alejandro Garcia."

"Don't bother calling Father Mike," Guma said. "It's

Tuesday, open mike night down at the Hip-Hop. Garcia will be there."

"Well then," Karp said, "anybody up for a little rap?"

Stupenagel cheered and clapped her hands. "Oh goody, the second in the series begins with me going clubbing with the DA."

Actually, as he stood on the sidewalk outside the nightclub, Karp was thinking how much he detested rap music. He didn't get the point. It was repetitious—the same few bars played over and over—and not even original music but something swiped from other musicians who actually played their own instruments. From what little he'd heard when he'd catch the twins illicitly watching MTV, being able to sing wasn't a requirement—just the ability to grab one's crotch and distort the language until *whore* rhymed with *show*, by shortening the former to *ho*. But his chief complaint was that it all seemed to be a graphic glorification of violence and promiscuity, as well as the denigration of women.

He'd even argued those points with Marlene when he discovered a clandestine Snoop Dogg CD in the boys' music collection. "So Bob Dylan had a good voice?" she asked. "And you might remember that the Rolling Stones put out a little tune called 'Under My Thumb,' which is about as misogynist as it gets."

"Dylan was a poet who wrote about issues that were important to society, like stopping an ill-thought-out and immoral war," he said. "And 'Under My Thumb' was more the exception than the rule for songs back then. Even the female rappers seem to accept how the males talk about women. You think Janis Joplin or Grace Slick would have let the Stones get away with referring to them as bitches and whores without kicking Mick's ass?"

"No," Marlene agreed. "And I'm not defending some of the crap that passes for hip-hop these days. But rap had its roots in a different culture, one under siege from guns and drugs before rap was born. There's also a proximity issue. In the sixties the musicians were singing about a war in Southeast Asia; the guys today are rapping about wars in their neighborhoods. It's bound to be angrier, more personal. But even at that, all you know is a stereotype: that all hip-hop is gangsta rap. If you actually listened to artists like Common and Tribe Called Quest, you'd hear a great variety that runs the gamut from thoughtful commentary on social issues from single-parent households to antidrug messages that are every bit as intelligent as 'Blowin' in the Wind.' Even some of the so-called gangsta rap is really pretty clever satire and even downright funny, though you get the feeling the artists are laughing to keep from crying."

Outside the Hip-Hop Nightclub, Karp wondered if he'd be able to distinguish the satire from the rest over the booming background music. His hearing wasn't the same as it had been in his youth, and he was sure that after tonight it would be worse. But he hoped it would be worth it, if he could get to the source of the No Prosecution files.

Before they left the office, Newbury had called to say that he was right about the tip of the iceberg. The boxes delivered to his office that afternoon contained nearly three dozen more suspicious No Prosecution files involving the NYPD.

"Added up, they cost the taxpayers nearly a hundred million smackers to make the problems go away," Newbury said. "Some of these cases easily rise to the level of unindicted felonies just on a cursory examination, yet

Kane and Associates overturned the IA recommendations in every instance. Something else interesting is that a lot of the same guys' names keep popping up, including one in which Messrs. Flanagan and Leary were accused of arresting and beating a Jew who was out in front of St. Patrick's protesting the Catholic Church's failure to act during the Holocaust. According to the victim, they told him he had no right to complain about the church because 'the Jews killed Jesus.' "

Outside the club, Karp glanced up at the immense bouncer at the door giving them a baleful look as they waited for Guma, who'd insisted on driving his own car. Maybe the bouncer won't let us in, he thought hopefully.

"You sure this is safe?" Murrow asked, nervously adjusting his forest green bow tie as several rough-looking customers exited the nightclub and upon seeing the group on the sidewalk started laughing.

"Don't worry, Murry, Momma's here and she won't let anything bad happen to you," Stupenagel assured him.

"Oh, I wasn't worried about me," Murrow said, trying to make his voice lower. "I was concerned about your safety, a civilian and all the while we're here on official business."

Karp rolled his eyes and considered canceling the whole thing on the grounds of felonious flirtation. Then Guma arrived from around the corner, and the bouncer's expression changed to one of delight. "GOOO-MAAA," he chortled in a baritone that sounded like the rumbling of distant thunder.

"Brotha Jim," Guma exclaimed. He climbed the steps to the entrance, where he and the bouncer exchanged a complicated handshake and embraced. "It's been too long, my man."

"Way too long, dog," Jim agreed. He looked at the rest of the entourage. "These your friends?"

Guma stood on his tiptoes and whispered in the big man's ear. They both then laughed in a way that suggested to Karp that he'd just been made the subject of some joke. Jim looked at him and said, "Welcome to the Hip-Hop, Mr. Karp. Please come in, no cover charge for y'all tonight."

They were all passing into the club when Jim stopped Fulton. "Sorry," he said, nodding at the bulge of his shoulder holster. "Club rules. No firearms."

"I'm a police officer," Fulton growled, and started to walk past.

Jim moved and blocked his way. "I don't care if you is the Reverend Jesse Jackson, no one goes in there with a gun."

The scene was about to get ugly when Karp intervened. "Clay, we're only going to be a few minutes," he said. "Would you stay with the car?"

Fulton glared at the bouncer and shook his head. "I'm responsible for your safety." He'd agreed to take the job when Karp asked, on two conditions: he got to handpick the detectives who would be working under him, and that he would serve as the main bodyguard/chauffeur assigned to the district attorney. He took that responsibility seriously.

"We'll be responsible for his safety while he's in the Hip-Hop," Jim said as his twin brother emerged to see what the commotion at the door might be.

Fulton looked at Karp, who gave him a pleading look. The detective was about to say something that might have ignited Armageddon but then the bouncers smiled, the diamonds in their teeth gleaming in the light of the naked bulb that hung above the entrance. Jim held out his hand, his voice soft. "We'll take good care of him, I promise."

The detective looked disgusted but shook the offered hand. He nodded to Karp and walked back to the Lincoln, which he'd parked down the block.

Karp and company entered the nightclub and stood for a moment to let their eyes adjust to the dark. "You a regular here?" he asked Guma, who shrugged.

"I catch the occasional new act," he said. "Long story, tell you about it some other time."

Karp sniffed the air. "I think I'm getting high just standing here."

"Just make like Clinton and don't inhale." Guma laughed. He nodded toward a far corner of the bar. "Let's go this way."

They skirted the dance floor, where dozens of dark bodies seemed to be engaged in what appeared to Karp as mating rituals. The party was acutely conscious that theirs were the only white faces in the bar, but while some of the looks they received were openly hostile, most seemed only curious, and a few even smiled and nodded. They were halfway to the back of the bar when a tall, good-looking, mocha-colored man ran up and took Stupenagel in his arms, planting a long kiss on her lips that she returned with equal vigor.

"Ari, baby. Where you been, Momma?" the man complained. "I been taking my vitamin E, and I think I'm up to the challenge of another booty call whenever you are."

Stupenagel laughed, one hand caressing the smooth brown skin that appeared between his shirt, which was open to his navel. "That's what you said last time, Rene, but then after a few short hours you left a girl hanging. But my, my, you sure are looking good; I might have even been tempted to give you a second chance, but tonight I'm with a real man. Rene, meet Gilbert Murrow."

Murrow almost squeaked at the introduction. But he recovered enough to hold out his hand. "Pleased to meet you."

"A real man, huh?" Rene said, looking him up and down. "Dynamite must come in small packages if you can keep this woman satisfied."

"But I . . . ," Murrow stammered. "I mean, I never . . ."

"That's okay, Murry honey," Stupenagel said, linking her arm through his. "No need to brag. Now, let's dance." Before the poor man knew it, she'd nearly ripped him out of his loafers as she tugged him toward the mass of writhing bodies.

Murrow looked back at Karp and mouthed the word *Help!* But Karp, who was actually glad to have the reporter otherwise occupied, merely waved and continued on after Guma, who led him to the corner where a group of young men and women were sitting at three couches surrounding a table.

As they approached, a large Hispanic youth stood and moved in front of the others with his arms crossed. "We're here to speak to Alejandro," Guma said.

"Maybe he don't want to talk to you, *pendajo,*" the youth replied.

"Call me a penis again and I'll feed yours to the pigeons in Union Square," Guma said evenly.

The youth's eyes hardened but he backed down when a voice behind him said, "Chill, Panch. They're just here to talk, ain't that right, Mr. DA?"

Karp nodded to the speaker. "If you wouldn't mind, I'd like to ask you a few questions."

Alejandro shrugged and invited him to take a seat across from him. "Aren't you going to read me my rights. Or maybe now you believe I didn't kill nobody?"

"That hasn't been determined," Karp replied. "And if you want me to read you your rights, I will. But I thought we might make this an informal chat. Nothing on the record."

"Shoot, homes. Or I guess maybe that was a poor choice of words. Go ahead and ask your questions."

"I wanted to ask you about certain files that recently came into my possession . . . or I guess I should say, were returned to my office."

"And what files might these be?" Garcia asked innocently.

"Oh, I thought maybe you might have seen today's story in the *Village Voice* that mentioned information we've received regarding allegations of police misconduct," Karp said.

Garcia laughed. "The *Village Voice*. Shoot, that rag's for white yuppies and artsy types, not homeboys from Spanish Harlem. But don't matter. I don't know nothin' 'bout no files. But say I did, and say there was worse to come . . . much worse . . . the real question here, Mr. DA, is whether you have the *cojones* to do the right thing."

Karp glared at Garcia. *This isn't getting me anywhere.* "You can take this to the bank; I've spent my career trying to do the right thing, fighting bad guys who'd make you and your friends look like Mary Poppins."

Pancho leaped to his feet. He was several inches shorter but heavier . . . and younger, Karp thought as he weighed his options if things got physical.

"Fuck this, bro," Pancho said over his shoulder to Alejandro. "The only people you can trust are your homies, the 106th Street Inca Boyz." His vitriol was accompanied by nods and words of encouragement from the young men and women sitting on the couches.

Karp wondered if the meeting was going to degenerate into a bad Ice Cube gang movie. But then Garcia spoke up again. "Panch, sit the fuck down." He then addressed Karp. "Excuse my friend. He's sort of like a junkyard dog. He'll die for you, but he's hard to take anywhere there's polite company." Pancho looked hurt until Garcia added. "But I love this dog as my brother."

Karp nodded. "Loyalty is an admirable trait," he said. "My sons are loyal to you, too. I'm hoping that loyalty hasn't been misplaced. But I've been told that I'm about to be tested and that pass or fail, a lot of people might get hurt. I'd rather not be blindsided if that's the case—given enough time, maybe I can mitigate the damage. So I was just hoping maybe you could give me a heads-up."

Garcia looked at him, and for the first time Karp saw the kid's self-confidence waver. The moment passed when another young Hispanic walked up to the table accompanied by Father Dugan.

Bouncing out of his seat with a glad shout, Garcia embraced the other young man. After a minute, he turned his friend around to face Karp.

"Francisco, this is Roger Karp, the district attorney of New York City. He's a big fan of rap music."

Francisco Apodaca held out his hand, which Karp shook, and then asked, "So are you another rapper?"

Apodaca laughed. "Me? No way. I can't put three words together in front of an audience without stuttering. And to be perfectly honest, I prefer Vivaldi to Fifty-Cent, though I make an exception for my friend Alejandro."

Garcia interjected himself into the conversation like a proud father. "Francisco is a first year premed student at Syracuse. He's going to grow up to be a famous brain surgeon or maybe a gynecologist, hey, dog?"

Francisco blushed. "Well, I've got a long ways to go just to get into medical school," he said. "But I have high hopes."

"Good luck," Karp said. "That's a long road, but sounds like you're on it and moving ahead." Nice kid, he thought, a good reminder to you that the same neighborhoods that breed gangsters have kids like this who deserve their shot.

Karp turned back to Garcia and told him that when he was ready to talk to get in touch.

Partway back to the door, Guma nudged Karp and nodded toward the dance floor, where Murrow was gyrating like a contestant on *Soul Train*. Stupenagel was dancing next to him with an amused smile on her face as her partner threw a little moon walking into what might have been the Funky Chicken and followed it up with break dancing.

Karp caught his special assistant's attention and motioned toward the exit. Murrow joined them there, his clothes drenched in sweat.

"You hurt anything, Murrow?" Karp asked.

"Now, Butch," Stupenagel chided, "just because you've grown into an old fogey doesn't mean your staff has to join you in the Retirement Home for Cranky Curmudgeons. Murry was just showing these jokers how to impress a woman. Any man who can move like that . . . well, let's just say, I'm not the only girl in here with the hots for the Bow-Tied Bandit of Love."

Murrow smiled stupidly at Stupenagel until he looked over and saw his boss grinning. "I'm feeling just fine," he said, composing himself. "If you've concluded your business, I'm ready to blow this joint."

• • •

Karp and his entourage got to the door first and walked down the steps to the sidewalk, where they gathered to wait for the car.

"Y'all come back now, y'hear," the bouncer, Jim, said with a grin.

"We will," Murrow said and waved just as Garcia and his group appeared at the door. "Great tunes!"

Karp shook his head and laughed as he turned to look down the block. He saw Fulton get out of the Lincoln and start to move around the car to open the doors on the passenger side. But Karp's attention was drawn to a big black Toyota Land Cruiser beyond Fulton. The car was moving slowly down the street toward them. Then he noticed the back window on the driver's side of the SUV opening.

Suddenly, the car sped up and the barrel of a submachine gun protruded from the open window. Still, he felt frozen in place and would have remained standing there, except that he was struck hard from behind and knocked to the cement by something heavy that landed on top of him. He had no time to react to the assault before he was aware of the staccato sound of the submachine gun, and the angry whine of bullets ricocheting off the sidewalk and the building behind him.

There were screams and curses, the roar of the Land Cruiser speeding past, and then the popping of a handgun from the street. He turned his head and saw Fulton running down the middle of the street after the SUV, firing his gun. Then there was return fire from the vehicle directed at the detective, who ran several more steps, staggered, and fell to the ground.

As luck would have it, an unmarked police car had apparently been sitting in the alley across the street from the nightclub. It came roaring out now, a red bubble light on its roof, and took off in pursuit of the assassin's car.

Karp felt the weight that had been lying on his back remove itself and he sat up. Guma, who'd seen the SUV and realized what it meant, had knocked him to the ground and covered him with his own body. His old friend was now standing above him, offering a hand up. He took the hand and stood, wincing at the pain in his bum knee that had been wrenched in the fall.

Then he became aware of a voice yelling a name. "Francisco! Francisco! Talk to me, homes!" He looked toward the stairway leading into the club. At the bottom, Alejandro Garcia was cradling the head of his friend Francisco Apodaca as a dark wet spot blossomed on the latter's shirt.

Garcia looked up and screamed, "Somebody call an ambulance, please!"

"Already done, Alejandro," Jim called down from the doorway with a cell phone to his ear. "Help's on the way, man."

Karp looked back to the street, where Fulton was sitting up holding his leg. He expected the detective to stand, but when he didn't, he hobbled over to him as fast as the red-hot ingots in his knee would allow, followed by Guma.

Fulton had lowered his pants and taken his belt off which he was trying to fasten around his upper thigh, above the bloody wound just above his knee. "God damn . . . God damn . . . God damn," the detective hissed through clenched teeth. He stopped cursing when Karp limped up. "You can have my resignation in the morning for not seeing that motherfucker coming, but in the meantime would you mind helping me cinch up this

tourniquet good and tight. I'm feeling a little peaked. . . .
God damn."

Karp leaned down and pulled the belt as tight as he
could, alarmed by the amount of blood that had already
pumped out of the hole and glad to see that the tourniquet
cut it to a trickle. "Wasn't your fault," he said. "No one could
have seen that coming. Probably somebody out to get
Garcia for the ML Rex shooting. We were just in the wrong
place at the wrong time, including that poor boy over there."

Fulton shook his head and spit out the words through
the pain. "They were after you, boss," he said. "I was looking back for you and saw Guma's face when he realized
what was going down. I turned in time to see the motherfucker in the backseat draw a bead on you before he
pulled the trigger. If he was after Garcia, he wouldn't have
waited, not given him a chance to duck."

The detective nodded to where Garcia was still holding
his friend while Father Dugan knelt at his side. "Whoever
that is, he caught the tail end of the burst meant for you."

As the sirens of the approaching ambulances split the
night, Karp nodded and limped back to the stairway.
Every step felt as if someone was pounding nails into the
joint, but the pain he was feeling was nothing compared
to Garcia's as he cried over the limp body of his friend as
Dugan administered last rites.

When the ambulances arrived a few moments later, Guma
waved one down for Fulton, while the other sped to the
curb nearest the front of the nightclub. The paramedics
inserted themselves between Garcia and Francisco, whom
they scooped up and placed in their vehicle, and roared off.
The ambulance bearing Fulton left soon after.

Several police cars had arrived in the meantime with the officers going about the business of securing the crime scene and taking witness statements. The sergeant on the scene recognized Karp and walked up. "I just heard on the scanner that some of our guys got those scumbags who did this holed up in an abandoned warehouse over near the docks off Christopher Street."

"What was the unmarked doing across the street?" Guma asked as he walked up.

"No idea," the cop said. "Sleeping, for all I know. All we got on the scanner was a report of an officer down and that the district attorney may have been hit, too. Glad to see you're all right, sir."

Karp thanked the officer and turned aside to talk to Guma. "How'd they know it was me?"

Guma stared at the street a moment before answering. "I guess they could have made you in the streetlight. You're not exactly easy to miss, and Fulton is a legend in the department; everybody knows him. They could have seen him, a tall white guy, and put two and two together."

"Yeah, you're right," Karp acknowledged. "It just seems weird with it all happening so fast. Hey, by the way, thanks for saving my life."

"You owe me," Guma agreed with a grin. "You don't grow up in my old neighborhood without smelling a hit in the air before it happens. The moment I saw the car I knew we had to get to the ground."

Karp looked around. "Where's Murrow?" Then he saw his special assistant sitting on the curb at the corner with Stupenagel kneeling in front of him, dabbing at a cut above his eyes that was bleeding pretty badly.

"You okay, Murrow?" Karp asked as he walked up.

"Are you kidding? Look at all this blood," Stupenagel

said. "He deserves a Purple Heart or the Medal of Honor or something. Yours truly would have been Swiss cheese except that at the last moment, this brave man pushed me behind that Dumpster back there and those bastards shot him."

Murrow gently pushed her hand away. "I wasn't really shot," he said. "I was running for my life when I tripped over my own feet, pushed her behind the Dumpster, and hit my head on the side. So I'm afraid I was nether brave nor was my wound the result of enemy fire. I don't qualify for the Purple Heart or Medal of Honor."

"Hush, sweetie," Stupenagel commanded as she resumed patting at his wound. "You're so modest. It was an act of bravery above and beyond the call of duty and you did it to save little old me. You deserve a medal . . . or maybe something better."

Feeling suddenly nauseous, Karp looked back to where Dugan had his arm around Garcia, whose shoulders shook with his sobs. The priest looked up as he walked over to offer his condolences.

"It's always the way," Dugan said sadly. "We lose the best of them. Francisco was so important to his community. Not just because he promised to return after medical school and work in Spanish Harlem, but as proof to the younger kids that if you work hard, you can beat the circumstances of your birth. But now he's gone."

Karp patted Garcia on the shoulder. "I know it doesn't bring him back, but they have the guys cornered who did this. At least there will be justice for Francisco."

Garcia shook his hand off. "You still don't get it, do you?" he said angrily. "Whoever the cops have cornered, they're working for somebody who will never pay for what they did to Francisco. Somebody who is not going to stop at anything to get what he wants or to keep himself safe, including putting out a hit on the district attorney. You do know it was you they were after, don't you?"

"So I've been told," Karp replied. "But perhaps that should convince you that maybe the time has come to stop playing games and giving tests. School's out, it's welcome to the real world."

Garcia looked at him hard and was about to say something when someone began shouting across the street.

"AND I LOOKED," said a man with frizzy hair wearing a Grateful Dead T-shirt standing on the sidewalk bathed in the flashing blue and red lights of the police cars. "AND BEHOLD, A PALE HORSE. AND THE NAME OF HIM WHO SAT ON IT WAS DEATH, AND HADES FOLLOWED WITH HIM. AND POWER WAS GIVEN TO THEM OVER A FOURTH OF THE EARTH TO KILL WITH SWORD, WITH HUNGER, WITH DEATH, AND BY THE BEASTS OF THE EARTH."

With that Edward Treacher fell silent and shuffled back into the shadows from which he had emerged. Garcia and Karp looked at one another as Dugan crossed himself and whispered a prayer in Latin.

"Say one for all of us, Father," Karp said. "I have a feeling we're going to need all the help we can get."

28

DETECTIVE MICHAEL FLANAGAN TAPPED THE SIDE of the black Toyota Land Cruiser with his gun and looked inside to make sure there was nobody hiding in the vehicle. Advancing toward the warehouse, he signaled Leary and the two uniformed officers who'd joined in the pursuit to move in with him.

He and his partner had been sitting in the alley across from the Hip-Hop Nightclub when the shooting went down. "Let's go," he'd shouted as the Land Cruiser roared past them. Leary hit the gas and he placed the red bubble light on the roof and called in: "Ten-Thirteen. Shots fired. Officer down, Thirty-eighth and Tenth Avenue. One other possible vic, the district attorney, maybe more."

"Butch Karp?" the incredulous dispatcher asked.

"Yeah, dammit, Butch Karp, send ambulances. We're in pursuit of the suspects heading south on . . . Eleventh Avenue," he said as they wheeled violently around the corner of Thirty-eighth.

The patrol car joined the chase at Fourteenth Street and together they'd followed the SUV when it turned into an area of old warehouses off Christopher. The Land Cruiser had continued around behind one of the abandoned buildings until coming to a stop on the Hudson River side.

As the two police cars pulled up, the suspects jumped out of the SUV and ran inside through a sliding freight door that had been left ajar. The detectives and officers entered the same way.

Flanagan listened carefully. But there were no sounds except the usual hum of the city, the occasional hooting of boat traffic on the river, and the sirens of other police cars continuing south on West Street past their location.

Without apparent regard for his safety, Flanagan stepped out into an open area and shouted, "Okay, boys, time to come out." He waited a moment and was about to yell again, but then there was a stirring in the shadows.

"Shee-it, dog," said a young black man, stepping into the light, followed by his two companions. "We didn' knowed you'd was inviting the entire En-Why-Pee-Dee. Now where's our cash and a ride out a here?"

Flanagan inclined his head toward the entrance. "Behind the warehouse next door. Money's in a bag on the front seat; key's on top of the right front tire."

"Good. So how'd we do? We get the big white muthafucka?"

Flanagan frowned and shook his head. "Nah, you're a lousy shot. The radio said you got a cop and a kid. So now I'm going to have to go to Plan B."

"Sorry 'bout that, but you said, 'Spray the fucker down and run,'" the gunman pointed out. "So we wasn't hangin' 'round to finish the job."

"Well, that's not quite accurate," Flanagan replied. "For one thing, I never use those sort of words. But hey, that's neither here nor there. You can go, but first I need you and your friends to do something for me."

"Yeah, what's that?" the gunman said, gripping the Mac-10 submachine gun a little tighter. His two companions were holding what looked like 9mm handguns down at their sides.

"I need you to fire off a clip in our direction . . . after we get out of the way, of course," Flanagan replied.

"Why?"

"Our story is that you guys shot it out with us and got away. Officer Calloway here"—he waved his gun toward one of the uniformed officers—"has even volunteered to get grazed by a bullet—that I'm going to shoot—to make it look real."

"Oooh, that's cold," the gunman laughed and spoke to his companions. "Five-oh's gonna shoot one of his own homeboys." He turned back to Flanagan, "Man, you sumpin' else."

"It's for a good cause."

"Well, thas cool," the gunman said as he lifted his weapon. "Okay, step out the way, homes, we be blastin'."

The police officers and detectives moved off to the side. Flanagan plugged his ears and waited grimly as the air inside the warehouse was suddenly filled with the sound of small arms fire and gunpowder smoke.

Detective Michael Flanagan did not consider himself a bad cop. Quite the opposite, he thought of himself as an exceptionally dedicated officer of the law. One who had risked his life on numerous occasions for the citizens of New York City, including that day in September two years earlier when he ran into the World Trade Center to help evacuate the buildings. He'd only just made it out before the towers came down, killing his partner, who was still inside.

However, he was sick and tired of the way the world was heading, starting with Manhattan. Everywhere he looked, there was sin and depravity, homosexuals parading around in public, atheists mocking the church, a general decline in moral values. The criminals were in charge of the justice system and victims were not even given a second thought. But almost nobody seemed willing to do anything about it.

It wasn't like that when he was a boy. He'd been raised in a devoutly Catholic home, attending Mass at least twice a week, and memorizing his Bible while other boys his age were polluting their minds on comic books and, later, *Playboys*. Other decent Catholic boys complained about the rigors of their faith, but not Mikey Flanagan. He actually made up sinful behavior so that he would have something to say to the priest at confession; he always felt cleaner, fresher, even if the sins were not his.

In the Flanagan household, there was zero tolerance for cursing and using the Lord's name in vain. A minor offense would be cause for having one's mouth plugged with a bar of Dial soap; repeated or larger offenses, met with a whipping that made it difficult to sit down for a week.

The Holy Roman Church was all knowing and all powerful, its representatives—from the parish priest to the pope himself—infallible in both deed and mind. There was only one institution that came close to that kind of respect in the Flanagan household, and it wasn't the United States government, which his father informed him "everybody knows is run by Jews bent on creating a One

World Order." No, the only other institution worthy of nearly as much devotion was the NYPD.

He was the son of a good Irish Catholic cop, and learned to be like him the hard way. Liam Flanagan believed in running his household with a firm hand. He didn't take lip from his wife or his kids, not without them seeing the back of his hand or, if he'd been drinking, that hand balled into a big grapefruit-size fist.

But all Michael Flanagan ever wanted to be was a cop like his dad and uncles. His favorite memories were of the Saturday evenings when they'd gather in the basement of the family home in the Inwood section of northern Manhattan to drink beer, play poker, and review the past week's adventures on the job. They'd roar with laughter over tales of busting the niggers' heads, or chasing some queer in drag across the George Washington Bridge ("And keep your fag ass in Jersey where it belongs!"). All of it under the noble banner of keeping the streets safe for decent folks. Every once in a while, his father would let him have a sip of beer, which made him feel like one of the guys, then remind him, "Loose lips, sink ships, Mikey. What gets said among the men in blue stays with the men in blue."

However, he also learned that his father didn't mean all the men in blue. He learned that the only ones he could really trust were the Irish Catholic cops, a core group that for more than a hundred years had been the real power on the force. Even with the influx of the "kikes, niggers, wops, chinks, spics, Polacks, faggots, and Protestants" onto the force, the men whose first allegiance was to the pope and the archdiocese of New York still dictated the way things would run and who would be in charge.

Despite the sometimes harsh upbringing, Flanagan

loved his dad. The day the old man with tears in his eyes pinned a badge onto his rookie uniform was the proudest day of his life. The worst day of his life was two years later when he learned that a nigger drug dealer had gut-shot his father and left him to die in an alley off 151st and Broadway. But his pride had swelled at the funeral as he sang "Amazing Grace" along with hundreds of other cops, each with a piece of black tape across his badge, accompanied by Irish bagpipes. That's how he wanted to go someday with, perhaps, a chorus or two of "Danny Boy" thrown in to get everybody weeping.

Flanagan's mother had died soon after the funeral and was laid to rest beside her husband. In a way, her son was glad she'd passed on and didn't live to hear the killer testify at his trial that Liam Flanagan had been shaking down dealers in that area for years and meted out gratuitous beatings. "I finally got tired of it and capped his white ass—in self-defense!"

Michael Flanagan never believed that his father would have done such things. It was one thing to be on the take, accepting a little payola, to swing by a business a little more often than usual so the local thugs knew to stay away, or even to look the other way when it came to some back-of-the restaurant bookie operation. Flanagan had even taken the plain white envelope with the hundred-dollar bills that showed up in his locker, and was grateful for the dough. Especially after his first wife started whining about wanting a boob job, and even working overtime wasn't getting it done. But gambling was a harmless vice; drug money was dirty and not something Liam Flanagan would have accepted, his son was absolutely, positively sure of it. And anyone he kicked the shit out of damn well deserved it.

So Michael Flanagan didn't take kindly to the aspersions on his sainted father, and when the nigger got out of prison—a mere six years later after District Attorney Sanford Bloom, may his soul roast on a spit in hell, signed off on a manslaughter plea agreement—he didn't last a week back home in Harlem. One night he'd been picked up by a half-dozen men and taken to the Brooklyn Bridge where he "committed suicide" by falling 135 feet into the East River and drowning (the Irish Catholic deputy medical examiner ruled that he'd received the large purple bruise on his temple when he knocked his head on the way over the railing).

By then, Michael Flanagan had received his detective's gold shield and had already embarked on a crusade of his own to bring a little balance to an out-of-whack system. The criminals and perverts had been on a roll for too long—aided by the bleeding heart liberals and bullshit Miranda warnings to make the already dangerous job of policing that much more difficult. But Flanagan and a few of the other boys he'd recruited over the years were out to set things right again, like in the days when his dad joined the force.

He'd started by bending the rules, such as "finding" small packets of dope on the front seats of cars he pulled over—most driven by people of color—which gave him probable cause to search the rest of the vehicle. Could he help it if a lot of his collars tried to resist arrest and had to be taken to the hospital, sometimes for days or weeks, before being transported to the Tombs? But those were the sorts of things his superiors looked the other way on; no cop who'd ever been on the streets wanted to second-guess another.

Yet it was all penny-ante stuff and unorganized until he met Andrew Kane. It all started a dozen years earlier on that winter day when a liquor store was robbed and the owner was killed up on 153rd and Broadway. Granted, Flanagan probably shouldn't have been on the job that afternoon. It had only been two weeks since his first whore of a wife had left him and moved with her Jew doctor to Los Angeles, and he'd been hitting the bottle pretty heavy. He might have been a little distracted and missed the dispatcher's description of the perpetrator—five foot ten and wearing a blue coat, not a red Bulls jacket.

Still, the kid should have stopped running when Flanagan got out of the car and ordered him to halt. The snow was blowing around pretty good, but he was sure that he saw a gun in the kid's hand when he turned slightly at the sound of his voice. But then he kept running, and Flanagan was not in the mood for a foot chase. They were only a couple of blocks from the alley where his father had died and that always put him on edge. Still, he'd only intended to fire a warning shot and wasn't sure why he felt it necessary to shoot the fleeing suspect three times in the back.

Flanagan had run up and turned him over. Bloody bubbles were forming around the kid's lips, but he still managed to ask, "Why'd you shoot me?"

" 'Cause you ran," Flanagan answered, though he was never sure the boy heard him as the eyes had already dimmed. He looked around on the ground and felt in the boy's pockets but couldn't find the gun he was sure he'd seen. But he could hear the sirens of an approaching patrol car and an ambulance, so he quickly reached for the little .380 he carried in an ankle holster. He wiped it clean and thought about pressing it into the corpse's hands to get his prints on it, but the damn kid was wearing dark blue mittens that looked like something his mother had knitted for him. So he stuck the gun in a pocket of the Bulls jacket and stood up just as the ambulance arrived.

While the paramedics checked on the body, he went back and told his partner, Big Bill McKeowan, what he'd done. He knew he could count on McKeowan to back him up; the older detective had once ridden shotgun with Flanagan's father back in the good old days. As expected, his partner assured him that he'd stick by him, but he was worried about a woman he'd seen looking out her window. "I'm not sure what she saw," he said, "but don't worry, it'll be her word against ours."

And that's how it had been when Internal Affairs investigated the shooting. The woman said she saw him shoot an unarmed man, and the two detectives swore the boy had a gun and briefly turned as if to shoot. Flanagan should have known there might be trouble when he saw that the IA officer assigned to the case was a chink, Walter Chin, and was sure of it after he repeated his story about the suspect holding a gun.

"With mittens on?" Chin asked.

The next thing he knew, his lieutenant told him to go talk to some hotshot lawyer the department hired to review IA cases named Andrew Kane. It was Kane who informed him that the traitors in Internal Affairs wanted to pass his file on to the district attorney with a recommendation that charges be filed in the shooting death of Jumain Little.

"You may be looking at manslaughter, even homicide," Kane said.

"The nig . . . the perp pointed a gun, I swear to God," Flanagan told the lawyer. "But then he turned around and ran just as I fired; that's why he got hit in the back."

"Three times?" Kane asked.

"You ever faced an armed man?" Flanagan replied angrily. "It's not like in the Lone Ranger where you shoot the gun out of his hand. In real life, when you pull the trigger, you keep pullin' till the guy goes down."

Kane didn't answer but instead seemed to be appraising him with those unsettling blue eyes. When at last he spoke, his tone was smooth and creamy as milk. "Yes, well, you're in luck. I'm not inclined to see a good officer take a bad fall because of an unfortunate case of mistaken identification. The victim *could* have been the robber; you *might* have been at risk. You are a good cop, aren't you Detective Flanagan?"

"Yes, I believe I am, thank you, sir," he replied proudly.

"A good Catholic, too," Kane said studying the file in front of him.

"A better Catholic even than I am a cop, I hope."

"Well, then, perhaps there are ways you can be of service to one of my other clients, the Archdiocese of New York, and together you can help make this a better world," Kane said, clasping his hands in front of him on his desk.

"I'd do anything for the church," Flanagan said. "And the department."

Kane smiled and explained that he was prepared to overrule the IA recommendations and could guarantee that there would be no charges in the case. But there was something Flanagan could do, too. He was not alone in believing that the world was going to hell in a handbasket. In fact, none other than Archbishop Fey, for whom Kane worked as legal counsel, had recently decided that the church needed to take a more, "how should I say this . . . proactive role," in halting the moral decay of Manhattan.

"He's interested in forming what you might call an Army

of Christian Soldiers within the police force—good Irish Catholic officers such as yourself; after all, who else could you trust—to perform occasional acts at the direction of the church . . . through its representative," he said with a smile. "Me, or someone the archbishop may appoint."

So Flanagan and his boys found themselves with a new purpose, which wasn't all that much different from their old. But he blessed the day he met Kane and started mixing his service to the Lord with his service to the department. The courts and the politicians had failed to protect—or, hell, like Clinton, were part of the problem—the public from the criminals, communists, faggots, terrorists, and other subversive elements. So as far as he was concerned it was about time for the Catholic Church, and a few of her chosen servants on the New York City Police Department, to step up to the plate.

Sometimes that meant dealing firmly with people who sought to damage the church itself through their scurrilous lies and exaggerations against her priests. More often, however, the characters he and his lads dealt with were sinners who had been identified by Kane, and later Father O'Callahan, who was introduced as his "intermediary with the archbishop."

While he knew that the general population might consider what he and his boys were doing was criminal, Flanagan felt that he was answering to a higher law, God's law. For him, without question, the ends did truly justify the means.

The archbishop had repaid the service and loyalty by instructing Kane to protect Flanagan and Co. from Internal Affairs whenever some reprobate complained about his treatment. Or the occasional problem when a victim died, such as when his new partner, Bob Leary, choked that drunk to death; the smelly bastard had taken a swing at Bobby, who lost it and had to be dragged off the corpse.

Granted, there were times when Flanagan wondered how the church chose some of its targets. That business with knocking the archbishop's old secretary senseless in a fake mugging had troubled him. The man was a priest, but Kane had assured him that the secretary was one of those perverts who sometimes snuck into a religious order so that they could molest little boys. Apparently the old perv had wormed his way close to Fey, which would have caused a huge scandal if it ever came out, Kane told him. So he'd hit him upside the head with a blackjack and called it a good deed well done. It was shortly after that he was introduced to Father O'Callahan.

He understood that some of his orders might not be specifically at Fey's request, such as harassing reporters who seemed to be working on uncomplimentary stories about Kane, or raiding record company offices looking for small amounts of cocaine. But he had no problem showing loyalty where he'd received it in kind.

Still, he wondered sometimes why they were asked to put a strong arm on some business that didn't seem to be hurting anyone. Or for that matter, why they'd be instructed to shoot one drug dealer but not another, or put this pimp in the hospital but not that one. When he asked O'Callahan, "Why not take them all down?" the priest replied that it would look too suspicious.

The inconsistencies and gray areas nagged at him when he lay awake at night staring at the dark ceiling with Lena snoring next to him. But whenever he raised a question, O'Callahan reminded him that "the Lord works in mysterious ways" and that even things he didn't understand were all part of "his eminence's grand plan to put the fear of a Christian God back into this city's populace."

Of course, he'd never actually received any direct orders from the archbishop; however, he'd been around the politics of the department long enough to understand the concept of plausible deniability. Kane and O'Callahan had explained that the archbishop had to keep a buffer between him and these good deeds "for the sake of the church if something was to go wrong."

That wasn't to say he hadn't protected himself just in case someone got caught and left Mike Flanagan's neck in the noose to hang. Mrs. Flanagan, God rest her soul, did not raise a fool for a son. So he'd tape-recorded several of his meetings, both with Kane and O'Callahan, but even that he considered just an insurance policy against an unlikely catastrophe.

Flanagan realized that O'Callahan was just a messenger boy and that Kane was probably the tactical commander carrying out Fey's plan. That had been fine with him until O'Callahan approached him with the plan to kill ML Rex. The mission had been presented to him by the priest as striking a blow for decency and to send a message to other rappers who denigrated women and promoted the shooting of police officers.

However, O'Callahan added that the killing had to be done in such a way as to frame Alejandro Garcia. The little greaser apparently had something the archbishop wanted—some sort of files the punk was using to blackmail the church. "As well as the police department," the priest warned.

Simply killing Garcia, which was Flanagan's first choice, wasn't possible. The priest said that the archbishop did not know where the files were hidden or who else might know about them. They needed something to hang over his head—like a murder charge with the possibility of a death sentence.

It was all getting too complicated. Flanagan decided he needed more assurance that he was truly working for the church. "How do I know that the archbishop wants this to happen? I don't mean to doubt you, or Mr. Kane—I owe him and I never forget a debt—but this is steppin' in some pretty deep horse poop. I would just like some sort of sign from his eminence."

O' Callahan had told him he would see what he could do. Several days later, he was asked to report to the archdiocese offices, where he was escorted by the priest into a small receiving room where Kane was already waiting. A few minutes later, Fey came into the room with O'Callahan and offered his hand and ring for Flanagan to kiss. "I'm sorry to have so little time with you, Detective Flanagan. I knew your father and he was a great friend of the church, as you well know. But I wanted to thank you personally for the work you have done on behalf of the Holy Church and this community."

Tears had sprung to Flanagan's eyes at the mention of his father. He could hardly speak after the archbishop's kind words other than to blurt out, "It has been my honor and duty to serve you."

Fey looked confused, but O'Callahan had moved in quickly and firmly grabbed the archbishop by the elbow as though to support him. "Your service is much appreciated, detective," he said. "I want to apologize personally that his eminence has so little time today, but we really must hurry." With that the two churchmen left the room.

"Sorry he couldn't say more," Kane apologized, too. "You know how it is . . . he's got to protect the church in case anything ever goes wrong. But he wanted to personally let you know that he appreciates your sacrifices. Satisfied?"

Flanagan nodded. At that moment, if given the word he would have thrown himself off the tallest spire of St. Patrick's. He even felt bad about carrying the transceiver that looked like a pen. When he got in the car, he told Leary to give him the tape of the conversation. "It's something that I'm always going to cherish."

Leary furrowed his brow in response. "He didn't say much."

"He didn't have to," Flanagan replied, irritated that the young man was such a wet blanket on one of the best days of his life. "Some things you just got to accept on faith, Bobby. Once you get that through that thick Irish skull of yours, you'll be a happier man."

"I guess," Leary said with a shrug.

After that, Flanagan had thrown himself into the plot to kill ML Rex and frame Garcia with a vengeance. It was a stroke of luck that he recalled Garcia's shooting conviction. He figured the .45 would have his fingerprints all over the gun. A few thousand dollars and the gun was in his possession; a few thousand more after the killing and a friend in the latent prints unit switched the tags.

Vincent Paglia was a lowlife who owed some of Kane's friends a lot of money. Flanagan didn't like threatening the guy's wife and kid to get him to cooperate, but sometimes a little fear would keep idiots from making stupid mistakes. The guy was just bright enough to follow instructions—one of which had been to burn the business card with Flanagan's cell phone number and the mug shot taken of Garcia after his juvenile arrest.

They'd picked up the limo when it turned into East Harlem and followed it to the desolate area where they knew it was unlikely there'd be any witnesses. At least nobody who would willingly come forward to rat somebody out. Still, they'd pulled on black ski masks, and when Paglia jumped out and started to run, they walked up to the limo and did what needed to be done.

A few minutes later, as they were driving away, Leary pulled off his mask and laughed. "Good hunting for one night," he said. "Two nigger gangbangers and a couple of spic whores."

"Can it, Bobby," he'd replied. "Doing the Lord's work ain't nothin' to laugh about."

Chagrined, Leary turned red and apologized, "Sorry, Mikey. I didn' mean nothin' by it." But Flanagan, who'd placed a call on his cell phone, waved off the apology and gave him a reassuring smile. He spoke a few words into the telephone, then hung up.

Despite chastising his partner, Flanagan had actually enjoyed putting a bullet in ML Rex's mouth. It was a fitting end to all that filthy language and perversion of American values.

They'd driven to McDonald's, picked up a bite to eat, and headed to Central Park to wait until Paglia reported the shooting and a patrol car discovered the crime scene. After that, everything just fell into place like O'Callahan said it would. They'd waited a few days, "found" Paglia, who "confessed" and became the state's star witness.

After that, according to instructions, they'd taken their time and let it all play out naturally. Leary had called in the tip to the NYPD Crimestoppers hotline that Garcia had made death threats to ML Rex, which had then been passed to Flanagan. They then picked up Garcia and put him in a lineup where the star witness Paglia picked him out, thanks to the mug shot.

It was all working so perfectly. But then Clay Fulton called and said the district attorney himself wanted to talk to Paglia. "He may be more involved than he told you." Flanagan immediately called O'Callahan.

Flanagan was surprised when the priest called back a few minutes later and said that the archbishop had decided that Paglia had to be removed. "Permanently. He's a danger to the church and all of us, especially you," he said.

"He won't say anything. He'd be up for homicide, too," Flanagan pointed out.

"You think he won't see that rolling over is his only chance if they're onto something," O'Callahan replied. "You think you can trust an Italian to keep his mouth shut to protect a couple of Irish cops, not to mention an Irish archbishop?"

Flanagan thought about it for a moment. The priest had a point. The Irish had to stick together. But he knew that this order had to be coming from Kane, and he demanded to meet with the lawyer.

Instead of driving to the fish market to pick up Paglia at Fulton's request, Flanagan had been invited to Kane's penthouse, where the priest escorted him down a hallway to the library. Kane entered from another door, and O'Callahan left them alone. "What can I do for you, detective?" the lawyer said, sitting down at a big mahogany desk and indicating that he take a seat in a low-backed leather chair.

"I just wanted to be sure that getting rid of Paglia wasn't just O'Callahan's idea."

"Has he ever steered you wrong in the past?" Kane said, gazing at his fingernails.

"Well, no . . ."

"You know that he has the archbishop's complete confidence, don't you? And, by the way, Mike . . . ," Kane said, sitting forward, "he has my complete confidence as well, and that should count for something after all this time."

"It does . . . it does, it's just that we had a plan and now . . ."

Kane held up his hand to silence him. "Plans change, Mike. You have to be flexible. It's the inflexible stick that snaps in two when there's pressure. Now are you going to snap on me, Mike?"

Flanagan wasn't sure if that was a threat, but it sounded like one. He suddenly felt uneasy. "No. Nobody's snapping, Mr. Kane. I just wanted to make sure that Paglia's no longer important to the plan."

"Well, are you sure now?"

"Yes, sir."

"Good, then I believe that this meeting is adjourned. I assume you can show yourself out?"

When he reached his car, Flanagan got in and sat for a moment. He took the pen transceiver out of his coat pocket. "You get all of that, Bobby?"

Leary held up the tape. "Clear as a bell. Is there something wrong between you and Kane?"

Flanagan thought about that, then shook his head. "Nah, just an insurance policy. After all, Kane is Catholic, but he ain't Irish Catholic."

He'd taken the tape home and put it in the kitchen floor safe along with the others, covering the cut in the linoleum with a rug. Then he'd called Paglia and told him to stay away from his home and work.

Tossing Vinnie off the footbridge had not troubled him. But he did feel sorry for the guy's wife and little girl. They were Catholics, even if they were Italians. He resolved

that he'd do what he could to get them the fifty grand—
minus ten for Kane's friends—when this was all over.

Then things went from bad to worse when the article
in the *Village Voice* appeared. An emergency meeting at
Kane's penthouse had been called. He noticed that
O'Callahan seemed to be moving rather stiffly, as if he'd
pulled a muscle in his back. But most surprising of all was
the expression he saw in Kane's face—he could have
sworn it was fear.

However, the lawyer pulled himself together and
explained that a spy in Karp's office had called to say that a
box containing some of the police No Prosecution files
had been delivered the day before. "And several more
boxes containing similar files showed up today," he said.
"So far the files involving spurious allegations against the
church are still missing . . . but they must not fall into
Karp's hands. In fact . . . ," the lawyer said directly to
Flanagan, "I'm afraid that Karp has to die."

The detective wasn't sure he heard right. "You want me
to kill the district attorney of New York?" he asked incredulously. "Do you know what sort of storm that will cause?"

Kane jerked up out of his chair, his blue eyes bugging out
of his face, as he pointed a finger at the detective. "Do you
know what sort of storm it will cause if he continues his
investigation into the files he has, much less those he
doesn't? Don't you understand? The man is onto us . . . and
if one of us goes down, we all go down."

Seeing the hesitation on Flanagan's face, Kane tried a
new tact. "The man's a Jew. You do understand that the
Jews want to destroy the Christian church, especially the
one true church?"

"What's in those files?" Flanagan asked.

"A Jew plot," Kane shouted. "For years they've been

planting perverts into the priesthood, men who engage in sexual assaults on their congregations knowing that they will be caught. Don't you see, they plan to destroy the church by destroying the faith upon which it's built."

"Is that what happened in Boston?" Flanagan asked.

"Yes, yes, exactly," Kane said nodding emphatically. "But we were onto them here. We found ways of getting rid of these horrible men and removing all traces of their sins before they could bring their evil plot to fruition."

Flanagan's mind was reeling. He heard his father's voice—"You can't trust the government, it's all run by Jews and their One World Order." Could it be true? Karp was a Jew. "What prevents the next district attorney from doing the same thing?" he asked, knowing the dice had already been rolled.

"By that time I will already have the files in my possession," Kane said, calming down. "They are the only proof that can doom us, doom the church, and the NYPD. And next time, I will make sure that someone who is sympathetic to our cause is in that office. Someone who is not a Jew."

Flanagan was wondering how he was going to get to the district attorney, when the spy called again. Kane listened and hung up. "Karp and his pals are going to the Hip-Hop Nightclub tonight to speak to Garcia," he said. "That will be your opportunity. A dangerous part of town, not safe to be walking around there."

Kane had already worked out the details. Kane had arranged for three LA thugs from ML Rex's old gang to fly to New York City in case he'd needed to amp up the rap war scenario. "They're waiting in a hotel in Brooklyn," he said.

So it had been arranged to deliver a stolen Land

Cruiser as well as the Mac-10 and handguns to the gangsters, who were given their instructions on how to find the Hip-Hop Nightclub and the warehouse off Christopher. "The guy you're supposed to whack is real tall, easily the tallest white guy on the sidewalk," Flanagan told them over the telephone. "When he comes out of the club, make sure you got a good shot and then take it. Spray him down real good, then take off. We'll meet you at the warehouse with the money and another car. Then you go home to Los Angeles and don't come back."

As he and Leary, and then the patrol car carrying two more of his boys, followed the SUV into the warehouse area, he called in on the radio and said the suspects were still headed south, giving a wrong location. He'd explain it later as having made a mistake in the heat of the chase.

The gangsters finished shooting their weapons. "That it?" Flanagan asked. "I want the crime-scene guys busy looking for a lot of bullet holes."

"Shee-it, yeah," the leader said, pulling the bolt back and squeezing the trigger. There was a dry click. "Y'all was just in a hell of a shootout. Lucky y'all wasn't gunned down in the line of duty." He laughed as did his companions, who also demonstrated that their guns were empty.

Flanagan laughed, too. "Yeah, well, like I said, you're a lousy shot." Then he stopped laughing. "Now, let me show you how it's done." He raised his .44 Magnum and blew the top half of the surprised gangster's skull off.

As instructed, Flanagan's team let the others run for cover. He knew there was no way out, and they were soon hunted down where they fled behind some packing crates and shot, still clutching their useless handguns.

Leary went out to the car and radioed that they had the gang trapped in a warehouse at Christopher and West. "They doubled back on us but we lost radio contact there for a minute."

Meanwhile, Flanagan looked around. It certainly looked like the gangsters had tried to shoot it out and lost. He could hear the sirens of their backup approaching. "Officer Calloway, are you ready?" he asked.

The big young man stepped up. "Yes, sir."

"Where do you want it, left arm or right?"

"I'm right-handed, so the left I guess."

Flanagan smiled. "I'll have to put you in for a commendation for this," he said, picking up one of the gangster's 9mms, and inserted a single round in the chamber.

"Thank you, sir, but that won't be necessary. Glad to do it for the church and the force . . . not to mention a nice payday."

"Good lad," Flanagan said, taking careful aim. "But really, you deserve it. Now hold still so I only nick you a little."

An hour later, Kane took the call in his library. He cursed. "Find another way," he said and hung up.

Karp wasn't dead, but it wasn't the end of the world. He might have been frightened enough to back off, decide that prudence was the better part of valor when going up against the NYPD and the Catholic Church in New York. If not, well there would be other chances.

What Karp didn't know yet was during all the evening's excitement, several well-trained men had broken into the office of V.T. Newbury by posing as a cleaning crew, whose original members were now dead in the parking garage of 100 Centre Street. They'd removed the police No Prosecution files, which he was now burning in the fireplace of his library.

As he tossed another file on the fire, Kane reflected on how he met Flanagan. The archbishop had come to him after the shooting of Jumain Little and asked him to take on the case of Michael Flanagan personally.

"I knew his father, Liam," the archbishop said. " A good man, faithful . . . worked endlessly with us through the Sons of St. Patrick that helped us minister to our flock. Too bad about the allegations after his death. Never believed them, of course. His son's a good boy and an excellent officer, from what I understand. It would be a shame if his career and life was ruined because of an error made with the best intentions."

The archbishop cleared his throat, evidently ill at ease making such a request but determined to go on. "I'd consider it a personal favor to me if you'd do whatever you can to help Michael. And if there's any way the church can help with his defense—financially or otherwise—please call me."

So he'd rescued Flanagan and Fey had certainly been helpful. It had been only a minor irritation when the detective demanded to meet with the archbishop. O'Callahan had called in a panic. "What if he talks to Fey?"

Kane, however, calmed him. He thought about it for a moment and came up with the idea for what he considered one of the great con jobs of his life. He told O'Callahan to arrange a private audience with Fey for Flanagan. "We'll keep it brief—no time for questions and answers—and here's how to explain it to the old man," he said.

The archbishop had been told by his secretary that the police detective was being honored by the Catholic

Benevolence League for his work with troubled young-sters. "It would really mean a lot to him if you'd say some-thing in appreciation. Just a few words, as we have a meeting to attend immediately afterward with the archi-tects for the new cathedral."

So Fey had thanked Flanagan for his work on behalf of the church and the community. Then O'Callahan hustled the archbishop back out the door. The detective had been a willing minion ever since.

29

IT WAS NEARLY 1:00 AM WHEN KARP AND COMPANY were finally ready to leave the scene. As Karp talked to one of the detectives outside the club, Guma had been on the cell phone to the hospital to check in on Fulton. He now walked over and gave his report. "Just talked to Helen, who just spoke to the surgeon. Apparently the bullet just missed the major artery in his thigh, though it hit a couple of other smaller veins and such. Without the tourniquet, he would have probably bled to death. But the doc says he thinks they've saved the leg. Clay's going to be laid up for a while and probably faces more surgery, but otherwise a full recovery is expected. Helen sends her love."

Karp grimaced as much for the medical personnel on the floor of the hospital, who were going to have to put up with a man who never stopped moving and was now immobilized, as for the wounded detective himself. "I guess only the good die young," he said and started to smile until he looked at the puddle of drying blood at the foot of the stairs and remembered Francisco Apodaca. Unfortunately, the saying probably has more than a bit of truth to it. He sighed, wishing he could just go home and Marlene would be there. He'd take out all the frustrations and tensions of the past two months on her body, but she'd understand and throw herself into the project until he was exhausted and drained of all the bad things. But she was a thousand miles away in New Mexico and in God only knew what kind of trouble herself. He did not want to go home and lie in bed thinking about her, so he uncharacteristically suggested that they all go have a drink to unwind.

He'd called the twins to let them know that everything was okay, but he wouldn't be home until really late. "I have some catching up to do down at the office. Bolt the door and I'm sure Gog will be happy to sleep in your room tonight if you want her to," he said, referring to Marlene's huge Neapolitan mastiff guard dog. The boys had all sorts of questions they wanted to ask about the story in the *Voice*, starting with whether Paglia's death would have any bearing on their friend Alejandro Garcia.

"Yes, but I don't know what," he said. "We'll talk later, okay?" He got off the telephone quickly, not just because he didn't want to answer any more questions, but he was suddenly aware that maybe he couldn't trust the telephone line. If Fulton was right and the shooters were after him, did that mean someone had tipped them off to his presence at the club? And if so, who? Someone at the club? That would have been pretty quick; we weren't inside more than twenty minutes. Or was it someone at the DA's office? Did that mean his telephone was tapped? Was his home being watched?

Not so fast, now you're getting paranoid. It might have been a crime of opportunity. He'd made a lot of enemies in his career, any one of whom wouldn't have minded driving by and taking a potshot. Heck, it might not have had anything to do with the Garcia case, he thought, but didn't believe it. He called Chip McIntyre, the detective who was Fulton's second in command, and filled him in on what had happened.

"Hold on, I'll be down there in ten minutes," said McIntyre, who came from five generations of Irish Catholic cops, the first one having hardly stepped off the boat from County Cork before he joined the force.

"That's okay, Chip, stay home. I don't think anybody would try to shoot me twice in one night, except my wife and she's not in the state," he said. "But send a car over to park in front of my place, okay? My twins are sleeping up in the loft, but I'm not going home for a while."

"My guys will be there in five," McIntyre promised. "Clay going to be okay?"

"Yeah, sounds like he'll be fine," Karp assured him, glad to hear the loyalty in the man's voice. "Oh, by the way, tell your guys not to go to the door of my place. If the boys open it and don't recognize them, there's a dog in there that eats entire cows for supper . . . preferably live cows it has to chase down and kill."

McIntyre laughed. "Okay, avoid the Hound of the Baskervilles. See you in about six hours down at the office. I'll be picking up the slack for that candy ass Fulton . . . one little bullet and he calls in sick."

Guma had to outfight Stupenagel to drive the Lincoln, but they finally all piled in and headed to the White Horse Tavern in the West Village. The White Horse was famous as the bar where, Stupenagel reverently announced, the writer Dylan Thomas "drank himself into a fatal coma, may we all be lucky enough to share a similar fate." The bar featured drafts of local beers, and there were soon pitchers of amber liquid crowding their table.

They'd consumed several of the pitchers when Guma, who had been off checking with "some friends from the old neighborhood," returned. "You'll never guess who the plainclothes guys were across the street from the Hip-Hop," he said.

Karp scowled at him over the rim of his upturned beer mug. He wiped the foam off his mouth and said, "I'm tired of games, Guma, just tell me.

"Okay, spoilsport, it was Detective Flanagan and his sidekick, Bob Leary," he said, letting it sink in before adding, "Them and a patrol car were the ones who pinned the shooters down in a warehouse off Christopher and West."

"We have an ID on the shooters?"

"Yeah, three members of the Crenshaw Mafia Gangster Bloods out of LA—ML Rex's old running buddies—each of them with a rap sheet as long as my leg. So maybe they were after Garcia and you just looked like the biggest target to start with."

"I take it they're now under arrest?" Karp asked.

Guma cleared his throat and shook his head. "Not exactly," he said. "They apparently decided to resist arrest and didn't live to talk about it."

"All dead?"

"Yeah. All of 'em. The guys at the crime scene say it was quite the battle—dozens of rounds fired by the bad guys. But I guess our guys are just better shots; one of the uniformed guys was nicked in the arm, but that's about it."

When the White Horse bartender kicked them out at 3:00 AM, the troupe trooped back into the Lincoln. This time there was no argument from Stupenagel about Guma, who couldn't drink anymore because of his cancer, driving. She apparently had other things on her mind as she slid in next to—or more accurately, on top of—Murrow, who was closing one eye and then the other in a vain attempt to focus.

"Watch out, Murrow, Stupe thinks she's poured enough beer in you and her to contemplate robbing the cradle," Karp warned as he got in the front passenger seat.

"He's of legal age. God, you've got to love a man with battle scars," she purred and brushed the hair from the bandage on his forehead.

"I'm not *that* drunk, and I'll thank you to unhand me, you cad," Murrow slurred, proving that he was *that* drunk but, Karp noticed, making no attempt to put any space between himself and the avaricious journalist.

They dropped Stupenagel off at her apartment in the East Village. "I've just got to get some sleep before I start writing up our latest little adventure," she said. "Murrow you want to play wartime censor? You could tie me up and . . ." But Murrow was asleep with his face pressed firmly against the window, his mouth wide open and making a sort of quacking noise as he breathed. She patted him on the cheek. "Good night, sweet prince," she said, and got out.

"I think I'm going to throw up," Karp said.

"It's people like you who kill romance," Stupenagel pouted.

"No, I mean it, I think I'm going to throw up," Karp repeated before opening the door and letting go in the gutter.

"Oh, great," Stupenagel said, rolling her eyes. "We'll be smelling the inner workings of the New York DA around here until the next rain."

"Sorry," Karp replied, wiping his chin. "Not used to

drinking beer." Along with all the excitement, fear, and anger that had curdled the contents of his stomach like cottage cheese.

A half hour later, Karp was asleep in his chair, his size-sixteen oxfords propped up on the desk, as Murrow curled up on the couch. They were still in that position when V.T. Newbury knocked and entered five hours later.

"Oh my God, it smells like a brewery in here," he said, leaving the door open to ventilate the fumes that boiled up from the stomachs of the sleeping men. "Mrs. Boccino, I suggest you remain outside while I check for vital signs."

"Whaaaa?" Karp managed, although his tongue had swollen to the size and consistency of a roll of toilet paper.

"Don't mind me, Sleeping Beauty, I just came to find the files," Newbury said. "You should have left me a note. I about had a heart attack when I walked into the office this morning and discovered I'd been cleaned out."

Karp was instantly awake. "I don't have the files."

Newbury's pale complexion turned pasty white. "Tell me you tied one on and are now experiencing a blackout. Tell me they are here somewhere, or you took them home. Because they are not in my office."

An hour later, after a frantic search of all the possibilities, it was clear to one and all that the No Prosecution files were gone. Karp was describing the previous night's debacle to Newbury when Guma walked in. The district attorney knew right away that something was wrong when the Italian Stallion didn't bother to proposition Mrs. Boccino.

"What's up Goom, but be forewarned I don't want to hear any more bad news," Karp said.

"Then you better turn off the hearing aids," Guma replied. "They just found the bodies of two members of the

cleaning crew stuffed in the trunk of their car in the parking garage. One shot to the back of the head each, close-
range, small caliber, probably a .22. Very professional."

Karp didn't hear the rest because of the roaring in his
ears that he recognized as the sound of rage. With an
effort he fought the urge to hurl his desk across the room
where it might well have struck the still-sleeping Gilbert
Murrow. "What now?"

"We can start from scratch by using the police department files," Newbury said. "Between me and the gang,
we'll probably recall many of the names, certainly the
most egregious cases. Let's ask Internal Affairs for the
files on those cases first."

"That's okay for going after the bad cops," Karp said.
"But it doesn't give us any evidence of who signed off on
this crap. I don't want to just round up the soldiers who
were only following orders; I want the generals who gave
the orders."

"It's a start," Guma pointed out. "You don't wave a wand
over this kind of shit and it's all taken care of . . . POOF!
It's like when I was a kid cleaning stalls out at the
Meadowlands. The first day I got in there and started shov-
eling to beat the band, but I didn't seem to be getting anywhere; I'd just dug myself into the middle of a bunch of
horseshit. But the old black guy who was in charge of us stable boys took me over to a corner of the stall and said, 'Start
here. A shovelful at a time, scoop by scoop, don't move
on until that spot is clean. That way you'll be able to see
your progress, instead of just tossing shit all over the place.
Then, maybe, that big pile of shit at the back of the stall
won't look so bad.' So it's the same thing here; we start shov-
eling with the little guys and work our way back to the big
shit at the back."

Karp shook his head. "God love you, Guma. I knew you'd shoveled a lot of horseshit in your time, but didn't know you got your start with the real thing." He was quiet for a moment as he thought about the next step. "Okay, let's go over to One Police Plaza to talk to my old pal Bill Denton and see if I can get him to release those files. They'll be talking to Flanagan, Leary, and the rest, and I'd sure like to know what they have to say about last night's events."

"So you figure Flanagan set you up?"

"Well, do you believe in coincidences?"

"Depends."

"How about him just happening to be the first detective on the scene of the ML Rex homicides? Then when he's told to find Vincent Paglia, the fat man goes for a long swim. After which, his name just happens to be at the top of the heap of the No Prosecution files sent to us by someone trying to save Garcia's neck. Next, we find him loitering in front of the Hip-Hop Nightclub, just in time to chase down some gangster killers, none of whom survive to say who put them up to it . . . or how three guys from LA knew where to find me."

"Oh, well, put it like that and I guess, no, I don't believe in coincidences."

"Neither do I. We know the guy's a bad actor from the Jumain Little case. What we don't have is proof that he's involved in this up to his eyeballs or enough to go after the guy who's pulling his strings."

"Who?" Murrow said, sitting up and both looking and sounding like an injured owl.

"Somebody with the wherewithal to pull off a burglary at the New York fuckin' criminal courthouse and willing to kill two innocent people to do it. Somebody we would have never suspected in a million years if we hadn't seen his signature, or the signature of one of his cronies, on every one of those No Prosecution files."

"Andrew Kane," Newbury said, "the next mayor of Gotham."

"Correct," Karp said. "But with those files gone, we got diddly-squat on him."

"But we will, and soon I think," Guma said.

"What?" Karp said, racking his brain, which was suffering a hangover relapse and was sloshing around in his head like sponge in a bucket.

"The third test."

Karp sighed, "I can hardly wait."

A half hour later, Karp was sitting in the office of Bill Denton, the chief of the NYPD. They'd known each other for most of their professional careers; they'd even been in charge of the homicide bureaus of their respective agencies during the same period of time. While they weren't exactly bosom buddies, they shared a healthy dose of mutual respect for one another. However, Denton wasn't particularly pleased to see him.

Karp quickly realized that it was because of the story in the *Voice*. Put the words *police misconduct* in a newspaper and even a cop as honest as Denton would close ranks with the rest of the thin blue line. He had a right to be pissed, too, as he pointed out to Karp. "You could have at least given me a call to let me know the story was coming. Instead, I don't even see it before I get to the office, and there's already two-dozen calls from the bastards in the press wanting me to comment."

Karp apologized and meant it. "I didn't know exactly

what she was going to write, but I knew something was going to come out," he said. "Let me fill you in on the details now, and then I hope you'll understand what I've been dealing with . . . to be honest, all I've been doing for the past few weeks is reacting to stimuli like a rat in a science experiment."

He then spent the next forty-five minutes going through his life since the murder of ML Rex—to the discrediting of Vincent Paglia, the man's disappearance and death, up to the drive-by shooting the night before. "I'm sorry to have to tell you this," he said, "but I think Michael Flanagan, and probably his partner, Robert Leary, are dirty."

Sitting at his desk, Denton rubbed his big ruddy face with thick fingers while his breath escaped like a teapot boiling over. "Goddammit," he swore.

Karp commiserated, "I know he's a hero in the department—"

"He's a hero to this whole damn city," Denton interjected.

"Yes, the whole damn city, and I know this city needs its heroes, and wish this wasn't so," he said. "But something's going on here and it's bad, really bad . . . much worse and much bigger than dirty cops, even dirty cops who commit murder. At least eight people are dead, and I don't even know why yet. Only that someone is willing to throw lives away like sacks of garbage to get something he wants. And it's been going on a long time. But it's not just the NYPD; two previous administrations over in my building have had a hand in it. And what really bothers me is that I was there while this cancer was growing all around me, but I was too blind to see it, or too wrapped up in my own little world, fixated on my own assigned caseload."

As Karp spoke, Denton got out of his chair and wandered over to the window where he could look down on the crowded sidewalks. "Believe me or not, the vast majority of cops are good apples, but it's wrong to know about corruption and do nothing about it," Denton reflected.

"It seems to be endemic to our line of work," Karp said. "We sense that it exists, but without evidence what can we do about it?" He was thinking that he'd let plenty of little wrongs slide by in his years with the DA. There was always someone to blame—Bloom or his efficiency experts or Keegan and his lack of interest. He and his friends had always told themselves and each other that as long as they were fighting the good fight, picking and choosing when to go to war and when to remain quiet, they were not responsible for what went on in the office as a whole.

"So what do we do about it?" he asked the police chief but looking over at Guma. He hoped Denton would make the right move so that he wouldn't have to nail him as well.

Denton looked at Karp and Guma hard for a minute, then smiled. "We do our jobs. Where do you want to start?"

Karp asked for the IA files pertaining to the case names that Newbury and his staff had recalled and written down. "And you might ask the guys if they can remember any cases over the last, oh, dozen years or so in which they recommended further investigation or even charges brought by the district attorney. Everybody's fair game in this, okay; the police department is not going to take a rap that my office is not willing to share the blame—maybe even a lion's share as my predecessors apparently were the ones who could have stopped it and did nothing."

"Consider it done," Denton said. "But after the little incident last night, I would prefer it if Newbury looked at the files over here. We'll set him up with his own secure room, and put a cop outside the door 24/7. You can choose the cop if you want."

Karp waved off the implication that he didn't trust whomever Denton would choose. "You pick. I'll send Newbury and his gang over."

Denton looked at his watch. "I think IA is debriefing Flanagan now. Let's go."

"You bet," Karp said. "I'm always interested when somebody's trying to shoot me and puts a big hole in one of my best friends, not to mention murders a young medical student unlucky to be within shouting distance of yours truly. . . . Now, what can you tell me about Flanagan that I don't already know?"

As they walked, Denton filled him in. Flanagan, he said, was the latest of several generations who had spent their lives on the force. His father had been killed by a black drug dealer in Harlem, and was buried even as allegations that he was dirty were surfacing.

"The thing of it is, the guy *was* dirty," Denton said. "The guys in Narcotics knew it; in fact, the brainiac was shaking down some of their own undercover people. He probably would have been busted before too much longer—even cops on the take don't like cops who sell out for drug money. But then the guy was dead, and there was no point in hurting his family. As you know, we don't like airing our laundry in public."

"And the son?"

Denton scratched his head and said, "Now that's the strange thing in all of this. I've always pegged him as a straight arrow; a real Boy Scout to the point of being anal about it. He's requested transfers in the past because he didn't want to work with partners who cussed or liked to check out the pornography shops when they were still active in Times Square. He goes to church religiously, pun intended, a Catholic somewhere to the right of the pope on the political spectrum. His first wife left him a while back, and he was pretty bitter about it, boozing a lot, including on the job.

"But he's also been decorated for bravery three times, twice in shootouts with armed felons. As you know, he and his partner ran into the WTC towers and started hauling people out, until the last time when he made it back but his partner didn't. To be honest, whatever he may or may not be getting out of this, I would bet my gold shield that it ain't money. He lives in the same small house in Inwood that he grew up in, drives an old Ford with bald tires, doesn't seem to go anywhere on his vacations, doesn't go out drinking or whoring like some of the guys. Just does his job, then goes home to his second wife, Lena, a real nice gal if nothing to write home to Mom in the looks category, if you catch my drift.

"He does have a pretty short fuse. I remember that in his younger days especially, there were a lot of complaints about guys he arrested coming in pretty beat up. The rest I think you know."

An hour later, when the red light on his private line lit up, Karp was waiting. "Thought you'd call sooner," he said without waiting to hear the voice. "When do I get the next test?"

"After giving them back test number two?" the caller said angrily.

"My *bad*," Karp admitted. "But if you know so much about what's going on over here, then you know we're not giving up on those. The files we lost let us know where to look. But I concede that it also lets the big fish off the hook unless you have more."

"We do," the caller said. "But one last time, I'm warning you that what you'll be seeing in the next twenty-four hours or so will rock this city in a way that even 9/11 couldn't. At least there, we never lost our faith, but I fear that will not be the case when you pass the third test."

"So you're assuming I will be willing to accept the challenge."

"Yes," the caller said. "You do not strike me as one of those cold and timid souls who knows neither victory nor defeat."

Karp listened carefully. It sounded to him as though the caller was weeping. "Father Mike?" he said.

The line was quiet and for a moment he thought the caller had hung up, but then he answered. "Yeah, Butch . . ."

"Next time, just drop by and we'll talk like friends."

"If there is a next time."

30

KARP STOPPED BY THE HOSPITAL ON THE WAY HOME to check on Fulton. As soon as he got off the elevator, he could hear the detective arguing with someone down the hall.

"I'm fine," he was lecturing a young man dressed in surgical scrubs. "I got a little hole in my leg. You patched it up, now I'm good to go." He saw Karp poke his head in and added, "Tell him, Butch."

"He says he's good to go," Karp informed the doctor, who was unimpressed.

"The bullet that caused that 'little hole' missed severing a major artery by two millimeters," the doctor said. "There was still significant damage to the muscles of the leg, as well as loss of blood. He's not going anywhere for a week, maybe more if I need to go back in there and clean things up; it may have chipped the bone but it was tough to see on the X-rays because of the bleeding."

"Missed, missed . . that's the operative word," Fulton said. "I'll promise to take it easy."

"No," said the doctor. "If I have to put you in a full body cast to keep you in that bed, I will. And if I hear any more about it, I'll make sure that cast covers your mouth."

"Butch, come on man, I *hate* hospitals," Fulton complained. He sniffed the air. "They smell bad. Like dead people."

Karp looked at the doctor, who shook his head and said, "We'll get him an air freshener, but he stays."

"Looks like I'm outranked," Karp told his friend, patting him on his injured leg to remind him that bullets hurt, even on pain killers. "We'll try to avoid letting the bad guys take over the city while you're relaxing here. In the meantime, try not to drive the doctors and nurses crazy or they may decide to shoot you in the other leg."

"Now Butch, don't you leave me here with these ghouls," Fulton begged. "Butch. BUTCH!"

As Chip McIntyre drove him home, Karp laughed at the memory of the detective's plaintive pleadings that had followed him all the way back to the elevator. He was still chuckling when he opened the door to his loft and was greeted by a petite, sultry woman who jumped into his arms, wrapped her legs around his waist, and planted a long, slow, wet kiss on his mouth.

"Geez, you guys, get a room," Zak said with a big smile on his face, which mirrored that of his brother and sister, who were standing behind him.

"Close your eyes if you can't handle a little unadulterated lust," Marlene told her son and kissed her husband again. "Welcome home, baby."

"Welcome home yourself, gorgeous," he replied conscious of the urgency with which his wife was pressing her hips into his.

Suddenly the sound of the refrigerator door slammed shut, which brought Karp out of his blissful fantasy of what might happen next. He counted heads again and decided that unless Gog had been especially trained in the past twenty-four hours, someone else was in the house.

Someone else in the form of a short, thick man with long black hair and bronze skin, wearing blue jeans with a big silver belt buckle the size of a salad plate and cowboy boots, walked out of the kitchen.

Marlene smiled mischievously. "Butch, I'd like you to meet the chief of police of the Taos Pueblo, John Jojola. John, this is my husband, Roger 'But Everybody Calls Him Butch' Karp, the district attorney of New York City."

"He's a real Indian!" Zak shouted. "You should see his knife . . . it's huge!"

Jojola stepped forward and extended his hand. "Pleased to meet you," he said. "Marlene's told me a lot about you."

"All good I hope," Karp heard himself say with a false half-laugh that he recognized had its roots in jealousy. *Now who had she dragged home.* "You're a long way from your jurisdiction, chief," he said, then immediately wondered if he'd made a politically incorrect faux pas calling him chief; the *man* was an Indian.

"People keep telling me that," Jojola said, "about out of my jurisdiction." But it was Marlene who finished the sentence. "We'll talk about it later," she said giving her husband their secret "young ears are listening" high sign.

"She means, 'When the boys are asleep,'" Giancarlo interpreted for everyone.

"Aw crap," Zak swore, "we always get left out of the loop."

Karp grabbed his eldest son and despite the lingering pain in his knee hoisted him over his head. "I swear your mouth," he laughed. His mood shifted, however, when a hard dark object fell from Zak's pant leg and clattered to the floor. It was another switchblade.

"Damn it, Zak . . . ," Karp began.

"I was just showing it to Mr. Jojola," the boy protested.

"You're not supposed to even own a switchblade," Karp sighed. "Are you ever going to get that through your head?"

Tears welled in Zak's eyes. "No, I guess not," he said wiggling out of his father's arms. "I'll just always be a big fuckup." He ran off to his room as his father called after him.

"Let him go, Butch," Marlene said. "He's humiliated and not going to listen right now."

Karp looked at his wife. "I guess I'm the big fuckup," he said. "I just can't seem to get through to him that this isn't the Balkans. He doesn't need to be constantly armed and dangerous. . . ."

"No, just New York City," Marlene said, "which at various times in its history has been the murder capital of the world."

Karp sensed the old tension between the two of them starting to build like a snowstorm in late December. With the little man in his groin starting to panic, he decided to de-escalate before the Big Chill. "Sorry about that," he said to Jojola.

"Hey, no problem, I shouldn't have been showing him my knife," he said, pointing to a long, wicked-looking hunting knife lying on the kitchen table.

"Not your fault," Karp replied. "I think all boys are genetically predisposed to gravitate toward knives and guns and anything else dangerous. This one seems a little more inclined in that direction than most."

"Hey, tell me about it," Jojola replied. "I got a kid just a little older and let's just say he's been more than a handful."

Lucy got them through the awkward moment by

announcing that she was preparing dinner and that it would be served momentarily. "Spaghetti with meat sauce à la Ciampi," she said. "I could tell by the stacks of empty boxes of Kids Cuisine Macaroni and Hungry Man Salisbury Steaks on the counter when we came in that a real meal hasn't been cooked here since the night we crossed under the Hudson."

"We ate out sometimes," Karp offered hopefully. "Whenever we felt like having a salad."

"And pizza, Chinese food, burgers, and, judging from the wrappers that made it home, a steady diet of candy."

Karp took the opportunity to excuse himself and head back to the twins' room, where he found Zak facedown on his bed. "Can we talk?" he asked.

"Go afray," was the muffled reply.

"What?"

Zak turned his tear-streaked face to him. "I said, Go Away!"

"Can't do it," Karp said. "When I asked if we could talk, what I really meant is we need to talk and because I'm the dad and I outweigh you by a hundred and fifty pounds and could mash you into a bloody pulp just by sitting on you, it gives me the right to revoke your right to remain silent."

"Nice talk from a so-called officer of the law," his son snipped, but only with great effort that made the sides of his mouth quiver was he able to keep a smile from his face.

"Hey," Karp said gently, "I'm sorry for humiliating you out there. If I had a problem, I should have respected you enough to talk about it privately."

Zak nodded his head. "Damn straight."

"However," his dad continued in a more serious tone to

ensure that a budding self-righteousness did not distract his son from the message, "this felonious possession of a weapon is getting to be a real problem. I understand you want to protect your brother—and God knows you've been through a lot these past years—but it can't continue. I want you to promise me you'll stop carrying."

Zak looked at him long enough for his father to see his brain working on various schemes to get out of this one and then finally gave up. "I promise," he said.

Karp hugged and squeezed his son, then kissed his head, feeling lousy about the pain he caused. "No fingers or toes crossed? Now let's go have dinner."

The rest of the evening went much better with the aid of a thick, musty Chianti and good company. Karp found himself regretting his initial jealous reaction to Jojola. He'd watched his wife interacting with the man, and while it was evident there was great affection there, it reminded him more of a close brother and sister relationship than anything else. More than that, he sensed a moral certainty about the man that left no doubt that his intentions were honorable in all phases of his life. He also seemed to have a calming affect on Marlene, and Karp hoped that it would be permanent.

To the twins' great disappointment, they were sent off to bed before the adults got into anything exciting, although the air was charged with it, making the hair on the back of their arms stand up like just before a lightning strike. Marlene accompanied the complaining boys back to their room and first kissed Zak, who had gone on strike and almost refused to kiss her back for spoiling the fun, goodnight. She then sat on Giancarlo's bed stroking his cheek.

"So your dad tells me that there's this fancy-schmancy surgeon who thinks he can make the blind see," she said.

"Yep, I want to do it this Friday," he said.

"You know it's dangerous, and there's no guarantee it will work." She felt the tears starting to slip out onto her cheeks and for once was glad he could not see.

He sensed them anyway. "Don't cry, Mom. I'll be okay. Heck, I could be hit by a truck crossing Broadway tomorrow because I messed up at the traffic light that I couldn't see. But it's more than that. I used to feel sorry for people who are blind from birth because they'd never seen the world, but now I think maybe it's better not to know what you're missing. I want to see what I miss again."

Marlene leaned over and kissed the angel who had accidentally been placed in her womb through some celestial mix-up. If I could only be half as wise, she thought. "Friday it is then," she said.

When she returned to the living area, Lucy had gone off to her room. The two men were still sitting at the kitchen table talking amicably, Butch with a glass of Chianti in his hand and Jojola with a can of Coke. Looking at her husband she felt a longing stir starting at her navel and drifting down. He still rings my chimes, she thought and found herself hoping that the evening's conversation wouldn't last too long; she had other plans for her man.

Still, Marlene hesitated to turn the discussion to more serious matters. He wasn't going to be happy that she was mixed up in yet another bloody adventure. How do I explain killer pedophile priests and murderous sheriffs and cowboys who arrive in the nick of time? She had to admit that it all sounded like a bad movie. And he's never going to understand that I wasn't looking for trouble. It found me . . . again.

Butch looked up at her and smiled. His eyes drifted to her body and the warm slow feeling started all up again. Bubble, bubble, toil and trouble. It did give her hope. As long as he was horny, he wouldn't start lecturing her or giving her the cold shoulder. She sat down next to him and let her knee fall over against his leg and tried to send him her thoughts through osmosis.

In the end, it was Butch who steered the conversation to the less inviting by asking Jojola, "So what brings you to our fair city?"

"I heard that some guy gave some relatives of mine a down payment of about twenty-four dollars in beads for this island, and I thought I'd try to collect the late mortgage payments," Jojola joked. "Or I might have to foreclose on behalf of the owners."

Karp laughed. "Believe me, you don't want it. As a matter of fact, since you're representing the landlord, I have a leaky sink, the air conditioner doesn't cool in the summer, and the heater doesn't heat in the winter."

"In that case, I defer to your wife." Both men turned to Marlene, who suddenly felt like a deer in the headlights. Marlene gave Jojola a dirty look and said, "So what would you like to know?"

"Well, the message I got was you were . . . ahem . . . 'involved in something.' And since you couldn't talk about it, I'm reasonably sure it's not 'involved' as in 'involved in my art classes.' As much as I hesitate to ask, what gives?"

Marlene looked at Jojola. "I told you he'd be suspicious." But she took a deep breath and launched into the Ciampi version of "What I did on my summer vacation." As she laid out the tale, she watched her husband's expression turn pale and then drain of all color when she mentioned the rosary beads in the graves.

"Did these beads have a medallion attached?" he asked. "A gold St. Patrick's?"

Now it was Marlene's and Jojola's turn to stare at him. "How did you know," they asked in tandem.

"I recently saw two sets just like that," he said. "They were found in the graves of two boys buried sometime last summer in Central Park."

"Could there be two such killers?" Jojola wondered.

"Not likely," Marlene said. "Unless, I guess, this was some sort of cult thing. But since we believe that Hans Lichner flew back to New York, meaning he was probably from here in the first place, there's no reason to think it was anybody else."

"Lichner?" Karp asked.

Marlene explained the rest of their story, including breaking into the St. Ignatius Retreat. "We found a fax transmission dated last Sunday to some priest at the New York archdiocese that pretty much spelled out how dangerous Lichner is and that this quack psychiatrist Tobias was sending him home from summer camp."

"And you said he kills once every full moon?" Karp asked. "Because that's what the scientists who are helping us with the Central Park case think, too. Which means we have less than two weeks to find him before he does it again. What was the name of the priest the fax was sent to?"

"O'Callahan."

For the second time since the conversation began, Marlene saw her husband look like someone had punched him in the stomach. "What's the matter?"

"I think I met a Father O'Callahan at a recent fundraiser. He's with the archdiocese."

"So what's the rub? You get the cops to pick him up and we ask him about Lichner."

"It may be a more delicate situation than that," Karp said. "He's the archbishop's secretary." He stopped and rubbed his eyes. "Damn, this has not been a good month for making friends with the powers that be in New York City. Next thing you know, George Steinbrenner will be on my case, too."

"What do you mean?" Marlene asked.

"Well, since you've been gone, and in addition to my usual forays into alienating most people I meet, I've managed to antagonize, aggravate, or anger the New York Police Department, a former DA-turned-federal judge, one of our hero cops from 9/11 who is dirty and probably a murderer, and topped it all off with becoming a threat to maybe the most wealthy and powerful man in the city of New York, a man who will probably also be our next mayor." He let that mouthful sink in for a moment. Then it was his turn to fill in his wife and her friend on his summer so far.

Marlene whistled. "Whew, you have been busy. Guess I don't have to worry that you've had time to carry on an affair or get into drugs."

"Both would have been safer courses to pursue," he replied. "But at least, thanks to you, we have a lead for our Central Park case, as well as your homicides, John. It would be nice to have one of these headaches dissolve with an arrest and adjudication. Then I could concentrate on the No Prosecution files."

"I hope you'll be careful handling the Lichner case," Marlene blurted out.

"Why, thank you for the concern, my love," Karp said smiling.

"You're welcome, but that's not how I meant it this time. A case like this could hurt a lot of innocent people.

If it's true that someone close to the archbishop is participating in covering up the existence of a possible serial killer in the priesthood, it would scandalize the church and cause serious pain to a population of devout and decent people."

"And?" Karp was trying to understand where Marlene was going with this. Normally, she was the one who went in guns ablazing while he preferred the slow, thoughtful approach.

"Aannnnd . . . you don't understand because you're not Catholic," she said. "It's not like with a Protestant minister—although I concede someone like Jimmy Baker can do a lot of damage to people's faith. But Archbishop Fey is the pope's representative in New York, which means he is God's representative here, too, for more than a million Catholics just in the greater metropolitan area of New York. And that number is conservative. I'm just saying you need to think about how this is going to go down."

"We'll do the right thing," Karp replied.

"That's what I'm afraid of."

The conversation ended when Lucy emerged from her bedroom and announced that she was going for a walk as soon as she got off the telephone with Ned Blanchet back in New Mexico. "He says he misses me and that at least two stars fell from the sky last night after we left," she gushed to her mother.

"That's nauseatingly romantic," Marlene replied. But her daughter had already retreated back to her bedroom.

"Isn't it dangerous for her to go out at night in New York?" Jojola asked.

"Yes, just like it was dangerous for her to be with me last Sunday morning," Marlene said. "Different kind of danger. But Lucy was born and raised in this city, she knows what to avoid. Besides, after all she's been through, it's kind of pointless to try to tell her it's a hazardous world and to be careful."

Jojola nodded and rose from his seat. "In that case, I think I'll go for a walk, too," he said. "I'm not used to spending so much time indoors at once; I got here at three and haven't been out since. If I'm going to be in New York, I'd like to see a little of it."

Marlene gave him the security code to the outside door and a key to get into the loft. She also instructed him on the general guidelines for finding his way around their part of downtown, and then stuffed a note with their home telephone number in his shirt. "In case you get lost, you can call and we'll get a cab to bring you back," she said. "Now be in for curfew, don't associate with the riffraff, and if a woman walks up and propositions you who looks sort of like a pretty man, she/he is a pretty man."

"Thanks, Mom," he said.

"I'd go with you to keep you safe, my son," she said, "but I have something I . . . ummm . . . want to discuss with my husband . . . a personal matter that can't wait."

"That's more than I needed to know. Have fun," he said and left.

Ten minutes later, Lucy bounded out of her room looking like someone had scrubbed her cheeks with steel wool, did a single pirouette, and sailed out the door with a "Ta-ta, see you in an hour or so."

"What was that?" Karp asked. "She looked like she has a fever."

"That, my tall, dark, and handsome, was the rosy blush of love," Marlene said. "Tell you about it some other time."

"What about Dan?"

"What about him? She's not engaged. And do you want to talk about boys, or do you want to talk about these," she said, pulling her sweatshirt over her head to expose her breasts.

"Those," he freely admitted.

"Well, then, let's get busy, we only have an hour until she gets back."

"Only an hour?" he pouted.

"Only an hour in which I will feel free to scream my fool head off with pleasure. The boys are sound sleepers."

"Oh."

"So what are you waiting for?"

"I want to watch you take off the rest."

"Oh."

Lucy was sure that by the time she reached the lobby, her parents would already be in bed making those noises that she'd grown up with, which to her meant they were still in love and therefore all was right with the world. Until recently, she'd thought she would never want to be placed in a position—pun intended, she giggled—to be making those noises herself. But there was nothing quite like a romantic young cowboy riding to the rescue to put a romantic young woman in the mood for love.

As she dressed to go out that night, she'd paused with her shirt off to look in the mirror. She was proud of the red marks his rope had left on her sides and wished they wouldn't fade; she considered having the image of a rope tattooed around her body. Oh my God, where did that come from, she thought and laughed out loud. But I do think my breasts are getting bigger. She remembered how carefully he had touched them when she encouraged it the night of her rescue. "They're not eggs, you dolt, give 'em a squeeze . . . and you may kiss them if you'd like," she'd told him. He had certainly liked, but that was as far as she let him go—or actually as far as she told him to go, as he would never have attempted such liberties on his own. She was surprised how much she'd liked it, too, even more that not a single thought of Felix Tighe crossed her mind. Not until later.

As she stared in the mirror and tried to imagine what a little more weight would do for her figure, her mind flashed on her old boyfriend, Dan Heeney. But she shoved him back out of her thoughts just as quickly. *Right now, I need a cowboy not a rocket scientist.*

However, neither Ned nor Dan was on her mind as she made her way down Grand to the subway station. She didn't notice that two men began following her after she left the loft building; the first man, an older but well-knit Asian intent on her, the second man, close in size and musculature, intent on him.

At the station, Lucy walked down the flight of stairs to the turnstiles where she purchased a new Metro card and pushed on through. She skipped down another flight of stairs and caught the number 9 train to the south end of the island. There, she climbed back out into the open air and headed south until crossing the street into Battery Park. Her two shadows—one behind the other, hardly noticeable, except to a trained observer—slipped into the shadows of the trees and kept pace.

John Jojola had been standing across Grand Street when Lucy left the building. He considered hailing her to see if she wanted company, but she immediately set off at a brisk pace that implied she had something going on besides a stroll. He was about to turn and go his own way, but then he saw the other man leave the restaurant supply store on the first floor of the building and walk in the same direction as Lucy.

Jojola considered the man for a moment. He seemed vaguely familiar, which surprised him as he did not know any Asian men in New Mexico. Perhaps it is just that he walks like someone I used to know. But who he could not recall, so he wrote the feeling off to coincidence in a strange place.

After deciding to go to New York to try to find Lichner, Jojola and the two women had split up in case someone was watching. The women had checked out of the Sagebrush Inn early Tuesday morning and drove a rental car to Denver, where they caught a flight on Wednesday morning. He'd waited until Tuesday night and then slipped out of the reservation, staying low in the backseat of a police cruiser driven by Officer Small Hands, who'd taken him to Albuquerque to catch a plane. "If anybody calls the office and asks where I am, tell them I'm at the pueblo for a kiva ceremony and can't be disturbed."

He'd arrived at La Guardia two hours after the women, a stranger in a strange land, indeed. The first thing he noticed when he got into the city was the air; it tasted *used*, as if it had been in and out of hundreds of other mouths by the time it got to his. The second thing was the noise. It ebbed and flowed, changing subtly all the time—like standing next to the Rio Grande River—and loud. And there was always something adding to it; he'd been startled the first time a subway passed beneath the sidewalk he was standing on with a roar and shaking of the ground, like an angry beast trapped beneath the surface. He found it odd that the people walking around him didn't seem to notice the noise, or at least weren't disturbed by it. Personally, he wondered how anyone could hear themselves think with such a racket going on all the time.

Then there were the buildings. He'd felt like such a tourist—a despised species in New Mexico and tolerated only for their money—craning his head back to look up until his neck hurt. Some of them were more beautiful than he had imagined buildings could be, sculptures of steel, stone, and glass competing with their neighbors for space and attention. In a way, they reminded him of the mesas and rock formations of his native land with their terraced sides and massive walls. But he also felt oppressed by how they closed in on him, as if trying to block out the sky and weigh him down.

Yet, to him the most interesting aspect of New York was the people. He'd never seen or imagined—not even recalling his brief sojourn in Los Angeles and the occasional trip to Denver—that so many people could live in one place without driving each other insane. He wondered where they went for privacy, or a little peace and quiet.

When he first arrived at Crosby and Grand, he didn't immediately go to the building where Marlene and her family lived. He was waiting for a signal they prearranged, so he'd used the time to people-watch and there was certainly plenty to choose from.

They moved in human rivers down the sidewalks, some following swifter currents, while others drifted along. Most, however, seemed to walk like they had someplace important to go, except the obvious tourists—who stood around looking up at the tall buildings or simply looking lost—and the obvious homeless people, who were lost but in a different way. The purposeful people kept their eyes straight ahead; they did not smile or try to engage their fellow New Yorkers. He experimented by trying to catch their eyes and then smiling, but if they looked at him at all, they quickly looked down or away again, as if they'd been caught doing something illegal.

The sheer number of vehicles impressed him, too, as they roared, honked, and swarmed like herd animals along the streets. It reminded him of Canadian geese heading south for the winter, as he watched great flocks of yellow taxis move as one, sticking close as if there was safety in numbers.

Eventually Lucy had emerged from the building carrying a shopping bag. She gave him a knowing look and then walked two blocks before entering a bookstore, where she went into the restroom. When she emerged, she wasn't carrying the bag. He went in after her and found a ball cap and a pair of gray coveralls with what appeared to be a hand-stenciled logo on the back that read Soho Heating and Air. He got the idea—this was his disguise—and put on the coveralls and tucked his hair up under the cap. He went back to the loft building, where he buzzed to be let in.

Jojola was surprised when he stepped out of the loft building that night to find that the noise was still there. Perhaps not as intense overall, but punctuated more often by sirens and car horns. He noticed that there was a sort of overarching background sound and wondered if it could be the collective beating of the eight million hearts Marlene had told him lived in the City.

One of those hearts had come running up to him inside

the body of an odd little fellow with coarse brown-and-gray hair, some of which poked up from the neck and sleeves of his T-shirt as if he had fur. "You need help?" he asked, panting. "Something I can find for you. Anything, anything at all . . . drugs, girls, boys . . . perhaps a priest, perhaps you are in need of spiritual guidance?" The man danced around him, skittish of the people who passed near them.

Jojola shook his head, noting the man's curiously yellow eyes. "Not tonight, brother," he said.

"Okay, okay, okay," the man yapped. "Be careful. Be careful. Evil is afoot." The man ran off howling down the sidewalk, dodging in and out of people, who ignored him.

Jojola had also been surprised by the number of people still out at that time of night, which he figured had to be getting close to midnight local time. Only now they were happier, smiling and laughing, still in a hurry to get somewhere, still avoiding looking at anyone who was not with them, but now he assumed from their expressions they were off to bars or the arms of their lovers.

Thinking about lovers was part of the reason he'd decided to go for a walk. He'd wondered how he would react to Marlene's husband, admitting to himself that while he and she were only what they were, he might still be jealous. But he'd liked the man immediately, sensing a fortitude and strength. *He is a warrior, too, though a reluctant one who does not yet understand the role he is playing in the grand workings of the world.* Seeing him together with Marlene and how much they clearly adored each other made him long for something like that again with a woman, and he hoped it would be a woman like Marlene.

• • •

But now he had more serious matters to attend to. The man from the store was apparently stalking Lucy. Aware of some of the family's turbulent history (not to mention having apparently found himself in the middle of another of their adventures) and knowing no good reason for a man to follow the girl, he decided to track them.

At first he thought the man might just be a masher who had taken an interest in a young woman. But he soon realized that the man was too professional at the business of tracking without notice to simply be a pervert; he was hunting Lucy, and Jojola felt glad that habit had caused him to place his knife in its boot sheath.

On the sidewalk, Jojola had no problem keeping up with the pair. But when they got to the subway station, he fumbled about trying to manipulate his Metro card in the turnstiles. Finally, an impatient New Yorker behind him reached over and took the card from his hand, flipped it around, and passed it through the machine. "Go," the man urged. He turned to thank the man after he got through, but his benefactor didn't even bother to acknowledge it.

Jojola ran to the stairs in the direction he had seen Lucy and her tracker go. At the bottom, he hesitated when he spotted her standing next to the track; the man was twenty feet farther along the line. The train pulled up but he waited until the two got on board separate cars before running to catch yet another, arriving just as the door was closing—causing it to slide back open and a mechanical voice to warn against standing too close to the opening. He got several dirty looks for causing the delay.

The ride was unsettling to Jojola, who didn't like the idea of having been stuffed into a tin can and then rushed along at great speeds through a dark tunnel. His people believed that in the beginning of time, they had emerged from a hole that led to the center of the earth. But the thought didn't make him feel any better and he was thankful when the train reached the end of the line and he got out and walked up the stairs into the open.

As he continued to follow the pair, he was surprised when they reached what appeared to be a large park with big trees. He had begun to wonder if the entire island had been covered with buildings and streets. The air smelled better too, salty and wet, and he realized the ocean could not be too far away.

However, he was soon alarmed as Lucy walked into the park and along a dimly lit path surrounded on either side by trees. He saw vagrants and other disreputable-looking sorts staring after her, though they seemed to shy away when Lucy's stalker passed.

As he moved, keeping to the trees and shadows as best he could, he kept estimating how long it would take him to reach Lucy if the man suddenly attacked her. The man seemed to be growing bolder, not bothering to stay out of sight. But then Jojola froze, aware that other shadows were now moving in the same direction as the three of them. They kept to the sides and filled in behind the man, as though protecting him. There are too many, he thought, but perhaps I can buy enough time for her to escape. It was vaguely disappointing to him to have come so far only to die in a park, but if that's the way it was intended, he was ready to give a good accounting of himself. He paused long enough to retrieve his knife.

Lucy reached a clear area surrounded by park benches and stopped. She seemed unsure of herself, but the man who was following now walked rapidly toward her.

Jojola broke from his cover of the trees and swiftly closed in on the man. His target guards were too far out and had not seen that he was in their midst and now it was too late. He was moving so fast that he nearly missed the man's hesitation and the slight dip of the shoulders before the man spun and slashed; but he saw the gleam of the knife that nearly eviscerated him.

Jojola's back slash bought him enough time to launch a roundhouse kick that caught his opponent in the kidneys. If he'd had better footing and had not been caught off guard, he might have done more damage, but his opponent grunted and he knew it had hurt him. But then the man repaid him with his own kick, which caught him in the ribs as he was stabbing forward.

Jojola heard other footsteps running up and knew he didn't have much time. "Lucy, run!" he shouted as he dropped and swept his opponent's feet out from under him, sending the man crashing onto his back. He was on the man and about to cut his throat when Lucy's voice stopped him.

"John! Tran! Stop it!" she screamed. When both men froze, she modulated her voice to calm them. "I don't have many friends and certainly don't need the two of you killing each other."

Jojola and Tran Do Vinh broke apart but kept their knives pointed at each other as a half-dozen other men surrounded them, all with guns pointed at the Indian. "He's your friend?" the two men with the knives asked.

"Yes," she said. "No, please put the knives away and Tran, tell your men not to shoot."

Tran barked a quiet order in Vietnamese and the other men lowered their guns. He laughed. "This must be the air-conditioning repairman we saw loitering outside your home and then going in and never coming out. I am pleased to meet any friend of Lucy's. My name is Tran Do Vinh."

"John Jojola."

Tran turned to Lucy, who spoke to him in Vienamese. *"Em vui ve gap lai Anh."* She then hugged him as she turned to Jojola and said, "I told him . . ."

"That it is good to see him again," Jojola finished for her. "And you called him 'older brother,' *Anh.*"

Lucy looked surprised. "You speak the language?"

"No, not really," he said. "I picked up a little when I was in country and recognized the formal greeting."

"I take it that you spent some time in my country," Tran interjected.

"Yes, 1968 to 1969," Jojola said.

"Ah, then you were with the imperialist American army." Tran smiled.

"The good guys in the white hats," Jojola said. "I take it you were the bad guys with the black pajamas."

"You mean, of course, the courageous Viet freedom fighters. But then, I guess one man's freedom fighters are another man's terrorists."

"Bullshit," Jojola fired back.

"Okay, okay," Lucy said. "You two can relive the good old days some other time. I don't have long before Mom and Dad will miss me."

Tran saluted her. "Then I am at your service. I received your emails with the prearranged signal that you are in danger. I take it, it is not a danger represented by this man who nearly managed to stick that . . . what do you Americans call them . . . oh yes, pigsticker, between my ribs? So what is the danger, and how is your mother?"

"She's fine and I imagine enjoying the benefits of wedded bliss at this very moment; however, we're really in it this time," she said.

"So your father has forgiven her for the 'incident' in West Virginia?" he asked.

"I think it is more a matter of her forgiving herself," Lucy replied. "All he wants is a nice normal family."

Tran blurted out a laugh. "He married the wrong woman then. But on to other subjects, do not tell me that the family of Karp and Ciampi have once again stirred the gods of war."

" 'Fraid so," Lucy said, and for the next thirty minutes gave him an overview of what was going on. When she finished, she sighed. "I love my church and the good it has done far outweighs the bad, but I also recognize that it has a long history of doing what its hierarchy believes is necessary to protect it. Along with the hornet's nest my dad managed to kick, I'm worried that this time my family has taken on more than even my wondrously violent mother and valiant father can handle."

Tran nodded. "We were wondering," he said. "My men noticed that in addition to the usual police protection, there have recently been men watching the building. They try to be discreet, but they are clumsy and obviously cops. But the regular guards do not know they are there, so I believed there was something fishy."

"I'm glad the guys in the store were watching out for Dad and the boys while we were gone," Lucy said.

Tran looked amused. "So you are aware that my cousin, Thien Le, is not just the proprietor of a restaurant supply store."

"Puleeze, with all the comings and goings at night," she said, rolling her eyes. "Only my dad is that naive. I'm sure my mother knows as well that it's yet another lair of the bandit chief Tran Do Vinh."

"Yes," he said thoughtfully. "I would have guessed it might be obvious. But your family needs such constant attention, it only made good economic sense to move one of my operations closer. Besides, who would believe that there would be an antiquities smuggling operation going on, literally right under the nose of the New York district attorney. It is a wonderful irony. Anyway, I think your family is safe while in the building. No one can gain access through my part of the property, and even if they get to the loft, they will have to deal with that hellhound, Gog, your mother and"—here he laughed again—"let us not forget Zak. He may be the most dangerous of you all."

"That's what we're afraid of," Lucy acknowledged. "So will you help me make sure they all stay safe?"

"What's in it for me and my men?" Tran asked. "After all, I am a crime boss and must keep up appearances and bring in the loot, or the younger men will think I've grown soft and think they can challenge me for leadership of our association. And that could be dangerous to me or them."

"Well, Ahn, you can tell them that we will arrange some sort of protection fee from my mother's foundation," she said. "But you will do it because even a bandit chief knows when to stand up to evil."

"Are not good and evil also in the eye of the beholder?" he asked. "John and I were on two different sides of a war, each side believing it was good and the other evil. It is easier to kill a man when you have convinced yourself he is some sort of demon. Isn't that right, John?"

Jojola looked at him and replied, "Perhaps in Vietnam it wasn't always so easy to tell the difference, although there is only one man from those times who I have demonized in my mind. But I think in this case, the line is drawn a little more clearly."

"Yes, but the youth today . . . my young men do not fight for causes, they fight for money and sometimes revenge." Tran shrugged.

"But you will fight for the love of my mother," Lucy told him. "The others will be paid if necessary."

"Good," Tran said with a smile. "Then we have a deal. And I will have a new experience, going to war for love. Now it is time to get you home before your mother comes and finds me."

Tran gave a hand signal and his men melted back into the trees, forming a ring around the two men and the young woman as they walked back to the street where a long black limousine waited. They drove to Crosby and Grand, with the bandit and Lucy catching up since they last saw each other two years earlier in West Virginia.

When they arrived, Lucy popped out of the car while Jojola shook Tran's hand. "Someday we will have to sit down and talk about your time in my country," the latter said.

"Perhaps," Jojola said, "though most of my memories from there are not good ones."

"I have both good and bad," Tran said. "I used to have a family there, but they were murdered by the South Vietnamese government."

"And I used to have friends there, my best friend as well," Jojola replied. "But they were murdered by the Vietcong."

"Ah, again there is that 'eye of the beholder' thing again," Tran said. "Is it murder when it is committed during a war?"

"It depends," Jojola said. "But let's leave it for our next

conversation." He closed the door and entered the building with Lucy.

Tran sat for a moment watching the pair disappear behind the door. His thoughts were interrupted by the driver, an older man, who turned around and asked, "Are you ready to go, Cop?"

"Cop?" Tran said. "That is not a name I go by anymore. It belongs to another time. Please do not use it again. But yes, I am ready to go."

31

ALEJANDRO GARCIA WAITED ON THE EAST BALCONY
of Grand Central Station for the woman to appear. She
said she'd be entering from the Vanderbilt Avenue side and
his vantage gave him an excellent view of those doors, as
well as allowing him to survey the huge lobby for signs of
danger.

At five in the morning, the station was fairly quiet. A few
people milled around the information kiosk in the center,
pairs of police officers joked with men in army uniforms
carrying M-16s—a new sight in New York since 9/11—
some business types trying to beat the bosses in to work,
and a large bearded man in a plaid shirt lounging over by
the subway shuttle tunnel, probably one of the many
nomadic homeless who lived in the tunnels and stations.

In another hour, he knew the concourses would begin
to fill with commuters arriving on the Hudson railroad
line, as well as those making subway connections to dis-
perse throughout the island of Manhattan. An hour after
that, the place would be packed. But he'd chosen this
time to meet with Marlene Ciampi because it would be
easier to spot someone if she was followed.

If she is, I walk, he thought as he looked up at the ceiling. When he was a child, his grandmother used to bring him there for something free to do. She'd point up at the blue dome and show him how the twinkling lights outlined the mythological people and creatures that had been drawn up there. "They're called constellations, *hijo,* and each has a story. The stars look just like that, only brighter and prettier and there are millions more of them, in the real world away from the city." She'd tell him some story from her childhood in Puerto Rico, "where the air was clean and so clear that you could see the stars reflected in the ocean when we walked along the beach."

As he wondered what it would be like to see stars like that it struck him how much he missed her. She had always brought such balance to his life, had saved him from the anger that might have consumed him. They hadn't caught the man who knocked her down, but it no longer made him angry. The guy was probably a junkie and didn't intend to kill her, just feed his disease, which sooner or later would kill him anyway. Hating him wasn't worth his time.

When he considered time, Alejandro had spent a great deal of it in the past few weeks thinking about his future. He loved writing poetry and setting it to music, but he realized that making it in the business was a long shot and wondered if the compromises he'd be required to make to get noticed by record company executives were worth it. He knew that he wanted to write, and had the idea of writing a book. About a gangbanger who turns out to be the hero by taking on the system. The idea made him laugh out loud, as that, too, made him think of his grandmother, who had always encouraged him to dream. But it also made him sad and angry, as any such book would also have to deal with the murder of Francisco Apodaca. In that case, they did intend to kill and now they're going to pay.

Alejandro had come by the No Prosecution files almost by accident. He'd been told to move some filing cabinets into a courtroom that was being used for storage while the building was cleaned up after the bombing. One of the small filing cabinets had popped open when he tweaked his back and dropped it a little hard. He was going to slide the drawer back closed when two words stamped in big red letters on the outside of one of the files caught his attention. No Prosecution.

Curious, he looked inside and began to read the letter attached to the front of the other papers. It was a letter addressed to then-district attorney Jack Keegan, essentially saying that allegations brought to the Archdiocese of New York against a priest for sexually assaulting a young boy "appear to be unfounded." The letter writer noted that to limit the liability of the archdiocese against any future lawsuits, payments had been made to the victim and his family totaling $830,000 to settle the matter out of court. "However, a review by this firm of the material contained with this letter leads us to believe that no prosecution for criminal charges is warranted." The letter was signed by a lawyer, someone even a former gang member from Spanish Harlem would know by name: Andrew Kane.

As he'd read the letter, Alejandro felt a chill go up his spine and his stomach knotted. The accused priest's name started with a G; with dread he flipped through the files until he reached the letter L . . . for Lichner. There were actually three files under Hans Lichner but he quickly found one with the slash mark and the name *Garcia.*

With trembling hands he looked at the letter on the outside of the other material. "The accuser is eight years old and his allegations cannot be substantiated . . . he may be trying to get attention from his parents who have drug- and alcohol-related issues." His parents had settled for fifty thousand dollars—sold me out for nickels and dimes, he thought—in exchange for signing papers agreeing not to bring suit "against the archdiocese as an entity, or its clergy and staff" and, of course, were sworn to confidentiality.

"No prosecution of criminal charges is warranted at this time." Nothing for taking a frightened little boy to Central Park—a little boy who'd been taught to trust priests without question—and raping him. Alejandro had no doubts that Lichner had intended to kill him afterward, too, but fortunately a young couple had come along, looking for a secluded spot for their own amorous intentions, which chased the priest off. But no criminal charges were warranted and his parents had taken the money—his dad disappearing with most of it one day, his mother using the rest to feed her habit until her trust fund finally killed her.

One good thing had come of the whole experience. With his parents gone, he'd been raised by his grandmother; it was almost worth having been raped. Without his grandmother's love and support, he might have turned harder than he did. It hadn't stopped him from joining a gang or doing stupid things—like shooting that other kid—but he'd remained generally good-hearted. He'd joined the Inca Boyz mostly for the feeling of having an extended family, somebody who thought of him as a brother. They thought he was tough because he always carried a gun, even nicknamed him Boom, but only Panch knew it was because he was afraid that the big priest would come back someday and finish the job.

Alejandro doubted whether the victims—mostly boys—mentioned in the other files would have welcomed being rescued from their parents as he had. So he got a dolly and took the filing cabinet to the parking garage and put it in the trunk of his car; no one had even questioned him about it then or since. He wasn't even sure what he was going to do with it, just that he didn't want the district attorney's office to have the files anymore. Andrew Kane had told the DAs that justice wasn't warranted, and they'd apparently agreed . . . or didn't care.

He'd taken the files to Father Dugan and they'd opened the second drawer of the cabinet. It contained No Prosecution files, too, also vetted and signed by Andrew Kane or somebody from his law office; only these involved cases of police abuses. But again no prosecutions had been warranted.

After they'd glanced through most of the files in the two drawers, Dugan rubbed his face. Then he closed his eyes and appeared to be praying.

"So what do I do?" Alejandro asked when the priest opened his eyes again.

"I don't know," Dugan said. "Obviously, a stop has to be put to this outrage, and these predators must be removed from the priesthood and prosecuted where possible. But I worry about the impact of this on the innocent people who look to the church for support and hope."

"Maybe the church doesn't deserve that trust," Alejandro said. "Look what's been happening in Boston. What makes you think it's any different here or in LA for that matter?"

"I don't," Dugan said. "Not after reading those files—though to me these are worse than anything in Boston because here, through the offices of Andrew Kane, the corruption of the church has been coupled with the corruption of the justice system. But at the same time, Alejandro, the evil done by men, even men of the cloth, does not mean that the teachings and example of Jesus Christ are meaningless. Don't blame God for evil deeds."

Dugan suggested that he act as an intermediary and go to Archbishop Fey. "He's a good man. I can't believe that he knows this is going on, or he would have put a stop to it. Maybe there is a way for the church to heal itself without damaging the faith of millions."

Alejandro had his doubts. The church had let him down as a boy. He remembered the young priest who came to visit and told him that it was a mortal sin to lie, "especially about priests. God has a special place in hell for those people." His parents had crossed themselves and agreed. Only his grandmother, whom he told about the incident later, supported him. "You have nothing to fear if truth is on your side."

"You believe me, don't you grandmother?" he'd asked.

"Of course, *hijo,* I know you are telling the truth."

"We have to start somewhere," Dugan said. So Alejandro finally agreed, only his friend was foiled in his attempt to reach Fey by O'Callahan, whom Garcia remembered as the young priest who'd told him not to lie.

"They're all corrupt," he complained bitterly to Dugan, who offered no argument.

There was certainly no debating it when O'Callahan came back to them with the offer to purchase the files for his interested party. They figured that had to mean Kane.

"Fey would have just asked me for the files, so perhaps he doesn't know," Dugan said hopefully. But there was no way to reach Fey except through O'Callahan.

That's when Dugan suggested that he return the files

to the new DA, Butch Karp. "All these cases occurred when either Bloom or Keegan were in office," he said. "Butch isn't like the others. I know the family well, and even consider myself to be on friendly terms with him. I believe him to be an honest man."

Alejandro wouldn't listen. "No way. He's part of the system and the system had its chance to do the right thing and failed."

Shortly thereafter, the priest had introduced him to Karp's family. He found that he liked them, even started letting the twins hang out with him and collaborating with Giancarlo on his music. But he remained adamant against giving the files to Karp.

"The man's a politician," he said, "and he's going to be running for office soon. Even if he's an honest one, do you think he's going to risk his career, maybe his life to take on Five-Oh, the Arch, *and* Andrew Kane? Fuck no, not for a bunch of 'Ricans and uptown nobodies he doesn't know."

"I think you're wrong about Karp," Dugan said. "What if we gave him a few files at a time, starting with the police files because it would be less of a shock? Test him to see how he reacts?"

Alejandro still wouldn't listen. They'd even argued about it again the night that ML Rex was murdered. He'd gone over to see Dugan after the fight at the Hip-Hop Nightclub and told him that he was going to pick up the filing cabinet sometime in the next couple of days. "I want you out of this," he said.

"Why? You don't trust me now?" Dugan asked.

"You know better than that, man," Alejandro said. "I just don't want to see you get hurt. One of these days, they're going to try to reach out and take the files, and whoever's in the way is going to go down."

"I'm not afraid, and I'm not going to let you stand alone on this one," Dugan replied. "It's my church, too, remember? I think, though, that you need to reconsider going to Karp. He's only been in a few months, but he's already making waves with his anticorruption unit. Even taking on black city council members over payments they've received to protect some drug-dealing front in Harlem."

Alejandro shrugged. "Maybe he's a racist and just wants to push a few blacks around."

"Not if he wants to be elected district attorney," Dugan said.

"Exactly my point," Alejandro said. "If he wants to be elected, he might hit on some Harlem nightclub, but the Arch in New York?"

"You have to trust someone, Alejandro."

"I trust you and I trust my homeboys. Now get off this Karp thing; it ain't happening." They'd exchanged a few heated words and Alejandro had stomped off into the night.

When Alejandro left, Dugan looked again through the files, trying to think of a way to get Karp involved that Alejandro would accept. When the priest looked up again, it was 12:15, ML Rex was dead, and a gun with Alejandro's fingerprints had been kicked under the limousine.

The next thing Alejandro knew, he'd been framed for murder. Then he'd had no choice but let Dugan, as the anonymous caller, go through with his plan to test Karp.

Dugan had practically crowed when Karp reacted as he'd predicted. Still, Alejandro wasn't sure. Especially after he saw the photograph in the *Times* where Kane and Karp were standing together, the former with his hand on "his buddy's" shoulder. "Kane and Karp, get another K in there and you'll have the KKK," Alejandro said only half jokingly. "We still haven't seen what he would do with the priest files."

Then Vincent Paglia was found on the rocks at the East River's edge of Hell's Gate, and he didn't know what to think. On one hand, there was no longer a living witness trying to frame him; on the other, there was no living witness to say that there had ever been a frame. He'd been livid when he learned that the police No Prosecution files were taken from the DA's office.

"I told you," he yelled at Dugan. "You going to tell me somebody just walked right into the courthouse and took the files without Karp knowing?" Only reports from Dugan's spies on the police force that the DA was still going after the worst of the offenders by demanding the Internal Affairs files, changed his mind. But he had his doubts about who was going to win—Kane with all his money and connections, or Karp, who couldn't even keep his offices secure. He hesitated handing the DA the third test . . . until his hand was forced.

All the killings had certainly proved that Kane and his people would stop at nothing to get the files. But the lesson was brought home to Alejandro even more bitterly by the murder of his friend Francisco. The only problem for Kane and his killers, however, was that it made up his mind for him. He'd asked Dugan to play "Deep Priest" one more time, "but tell him to send Marlene."

Dugan had called him back at four in the morning. "I just talked to a woman who was not at all pleased to be dragged from her bed after not seeing her husband for several months," he said. "I will have to speak to that woman about her vocabulary, especially when directed at a man of the cloth. However, she will meet you on the East Balcony at 5:15, as you asked."

Alejandro looked at the clock: 5:10. He fiddled with the key to the big locker he'd rented in the concourse near the Hudson Line, normally used for suitcases by travelers, but this one containing two large boxes of No Prosecution files. He'd had to bring them there himself, as Pancho Ramirez would have nothing to do with it after Francisco was killed.

"What the fuck you talkin' about, dog," Pancho had yelled. "Let the system take care of it? What fuckin' system? The one that got Francisco shot? The one that fucked you over when you was a kid? The system is for rich, white muthafuckas, homes. It could care less about you or me, or even a fine upstandin' citizen like Francisco."

"I have to trust somebody, Panch," he'd replied. "I can't do this alone. Karp has done his part so far—"

"How do you know they was shootin' at Karp? Maybe it was a setup and they were trying to kill you," Pancho interrupted. "Maybe Karp set you up."

"I don't think so. The cop that got shot was a friend of his, and those bullets were too close to Karp to have been part of a setup," Alejandro said holding out his hand. "Come on, Panch, help me get the boxes to Grand Central. It's going to take me a long time by myself."

But his angry friend batted his hand away. "You want to play with the man, you go play with the man by yourself. I'm going back to the Inca Boyz, where I know the homies ain't sold out."

Alejandro looked at the clock again: 5:12. He needed to go to the bathroom and decided that there was time. Trotting down the marble stairway, he looked up and noticed that the big bearded man in the plaid shirt was glaring at him. The man looked quickly away, but Alejandro knew that it had not been just idle observation. He turned quickly and went down the concourse to the food court area in the lower level. On the escalator near the bottom, he looked up and saw the man peer over the edge.

Running down the last couple of steps, Alejandro considered finding a police officer though suddenly none seemed to be in sight. Can't trust any of them anyway, he thought. Instead, he ran down the aisle on the left and ducked inside the men's restroom next to the Mexican food kiosk. He went inside a stall, and for want of a better idea, stood on the toilet like they do in the movies, wishing he had not given up carrying a gun. Feeling in his pocket, he took out the key and shoved it up in the plastic box holding the toilet paper.

The door opened and he heard someone enter. He held his breath as he heard the person bend over and look beneath the stalls. Then he glanced out through the crack in the door; an insane red-rimmed eye was looking in at him. The next moment, the door crashed in on him, as the brute came through, knocking him back against the wall.

In his terror, Alejandro recognized his assailant. The beard wasn't there ten years earlier, but it was the same man: the priest who had raped him and was now back to finish the job.

Lichner grabbed Alejandro by the neck and held a big curved knife against his belly. "Vare are the files?" he demanded, his breath smelling like something had rotted inside him.

Alejandro reached into his pocket and pulled out a set of keys. "Here, a locker upstairs in the Hudson terminal."

"Vich key?"

Alejandro chose the key to the janitor's closet at the courthouse. "This one," he croaked due to the pressure of the giant's hand on his throat.

"Then go to hell," Lichner whispered and plunged the knife into Garcia.

Alejandro slumped to the floor where he lay holding his hands over his belly in a vain attempt to stop the bleeding. He saw the big sandaled feet of his attacker walk quickly away and felt himself losing consciousness. Then there seemed to be some sort of confrontation, a yell and a loud crash; there were more footsteps, these coming toward him. A female voice cursed, and then the face of Marlene Ciampi appeared, telling him it would be all right.

"Key," he whispered.

"What?" she asked. "Take it easy, help is on the way."

"Key," he repeated. "Toilet paper." He tried to point with his eyes. The effort cost him, but was worth it when she at last understood and reached into the toilet paper holder and pulled out the locker key.

"The Hudson concourse," he said and passed out.

Late that afternoon, Marlene and Butch were arguing in his office. They'd spent most of the day reading through the files and were fighting over what to do with them. He said he planned to pursue criminal charges "wherever possible, up to and including Archbishop Fey, his man, O'Callahan, and Andrew Kane."

Marlene wanted him to wait and think about the ramifications. "What you have in those two boxes could destroy the Catholic Church in New York City, probably the state and, if the connection to the murders and cover-ups in New Mexico gets out, maybe the country. That's hurting a lot of people who count on the church, who need the church."

"Goddammit Marlene," he exclaimed. "I'm supposed to ignore sexual assault, most of it on children, and murder, as well as a pattern of criminal conduct that goes from the parish priests right up through the archbishop? Not to mention the office of the man who could be this city's next mayor? What kind of a DA, what kind of a person, would that make me?"

"One who understands that there is a bigger picture here," Marlene shot back. "One who can see that there are more lives at stake here than those represented by these files."

Marlene had walked into Grand Central that morning still feeling toasty after several hours of lovemaking, wishing she were still in bed, getting ready for round . . . was it five or six? She was just in time to see Alejandro disappear down the dining concourse, followed by a big man who walked with a limp. Warm and sensuous had been replaced with cold and afraid as she'd raced across the lobby, cursing herself for not bringing her gun. She'd wanted to do things Butch's way, and now she was going to have to stop a man the size of a bear from killing a boy.

She arrived at the restroom too late to prevent the attack. She heard the commotion and the voices and ran in just as Lichner was trying to leave. She struck at him with her fists and tried to get a kick in at his groin, but he had swatted her aside like an insect and left her dazed just inside the door. She was about to get up and give chase, when she saw Alejandro lying in a pool of blood.

Whipping out her cell phone, she called for an ambulance and ran to the boy. He told her where to find the key, after which, she did her best to keep pressure on the wound until the paramedics arrived.

A detective was waiting outside the restroom when she emerged. She gave him a statement, saying she heard yelling from the restroom and saw a large bearded man with a limp emerge holding a bloody knife. "I looked in the restroom and saw the boy."

"Is that it?" the detective asked. "You know the suspect or the victim?"

"Can't say I do," she replied. Can't or won't, she thought. It's probably not fair to you, but I don't trust the NYPD at this moment.

After giving her statement, she casually strolled upstairs where she found John Jojola waiting for her. She had called home after the paramedics arrived and, after explaining to her husband what had happened, she had asked him to have Jojola meet her.

"I'll come down," Butch had said, sounding hurt.

"No baby, nothing against you, but you need to get into the office and put out the fires there and then get Giancarlo over to the hospital, remember? Besides, people would recognize you if you show up here, maybe the wrong people. I think we need to keep this quiet at the moment. Send John. And Butch?"

"Yeah?" he pouted.

"I'm expecting a repeat performance tonight." As anticipated, he sounded much happier when he said good-bye.

Jojola had followed her to the Hudson concourse lockers at a discreet distance just in case the lockers were being watched. But there were no suspicious-looking characters, certainly no large, limping priests. She opened the locker as Jojola pretended to be fiddling with one next door and saw the two big boxes. "Where's that bigger boat I was talking about?"

They borrowed a porter's dolly and got the boxes out to the curb, where they hailed a cab. "100 Centre Street," Marlene said as they got in.

"The courthouse?"

"Yep, and step on it."

Now she was wishing that she'd taken the files somewhere else. They were both bound to be a little tense with Giancarlo in the hospital. Butch had gone home at lunch and then took him to Beth Israel to get checked in and left him with the doctors, who wanted to run a series of tests, including new CAT and MRI scans.

"The docs told me it was going to take all afternoon," he said when he got back to the office where Marlene was plowing through the files. "Might as well work to get my mind off of it."

Several hours later, they'd made at least a cursory examination of all the files. That's when she'd asked him to back off on pressing criminal charges. "I'm not talking about throwing these files away. But maybe you can go to the church council and use them to quietly have the predators removed. Force them to clean up their act."

"And ignore that crimes have been committed? Even murder?"

"That's Kane and Flanagan. Nail them with the police files. Prison walls look the same no matter what crime you're in for."

"What about O'Callahan and Lichner?"

"Some sort of quiet plea bargain that sends O'Callahan away for a long time. Extradite Lichner to New Mexico, let John put him away. Nobody in New York gives a rat's ass what happens west of New Jersey."

"And the archbishop? The fact that sexual predators were allowed to prey on children again and again?"

"Fey obviously looked the other way when this was going on. But that's not his real signature on those papers, that's a rubber stamp of his signature. You can bet O'Callahan's behind it."

"Fey had to know," Butch said. "Maybe not about Lichner, but the payoffs and St. Ignatius and the priests who reoffended. Nobody who rises to that position is that naive or stupid. He was in Kane's hip pocket, consciously or because he didn't want to know—he abused the trust that had been given to him."

"So you force him to quietly retire."

"That's hardly justice for dead boys and ruined lives. It's just compromising, taking the easy way out of this."

"Everybody compromises, Butch," she said. "It's how the world works."

"Maybe that's the problem," he retorted. "Everybody is so busy compromising that nobody knows where the standards are anymore. I'm sorry but you're asking me to do something I cannot do."

"Why not?" she replied. "Why do you always have to be such a stickler for the rules? Why always the Boy Scout?"

Butch was silent for a minute, staring out the window at the crowds on the sidewalk along Centre Street. At last he said, "Because of my mother."

"What? What's your mother got to do with this?"

"Everything," he said. "Because she died of cancer, because this is like that, a cancer."

"You're not making sense."

"Then let me tell you about my mother's death," he said. "I've never talked about it with anyone, but maybe it's time I did with you."

"She was a wonderful woman," he began. "And I know most boys think that of their moms, but she was so full of life, so caring for other people, and yet her death was so senseless, so pointless.

"When she first got cancer, I went into full denial. What, are you kidding me? My mom's never been sick a day in her life. She'll be fine. Even when it was obvious that she was wasting away and not getting better, I wouldn't believe it. I figured that if I just went on with my life, she'd be up and around in no time. There was nothing to worry about.

"Then came that horrible night when my aunt, who'd been living with us to help care for her, called me into my mom's room. I really didn't want to; I was getting ready for a big game that night and didn't want to be bothered with what was going on in the real world. But my aunt insisted.

"Well, I got in there and my aunt handed me a syringe with morphine in it. She was crying and said, 'I can't do this anymore. You have to do it.' . . . I looked at her like, 'You've got to be kidding, I'm not going to do that.' It meant having to admit how sick my mom was; there was no way."

Karp leaned his head against the window. How many of those people down there are suffering? he wondered. How many had lost loved ones to some senseless, pointless death? "But my mom was in such pain, and I finally took the syringe. My aunt made me practice sticking it into an orange a few times first, but nothing prepared me for sticking a hypodermic needle into this woman I loved. Her skin was so warm and dry. I was afraid, but I gave her the shot. The needle went so deep into her arm, she moaned in pain. It shocked me, and all I could think was, My God, I hurt her so badly. Soon the morphine took effect, and she slowly closed her eyes. I then left for my game."

Karp turned and looked right at Marlene. "It's strange where you find compassion sometimes, that touch of humanity at just the right moment that keeps you sane. . . . I got to the game late and expected that it would have already started, but nothing was going on yet. All the players on both teams were on the floor, so I hurried to the locker room to get changed.

"Then my coach walked in and asked how I was doing, which was kind of strange because he was old-school—in your face, give him 100 percent every time or don't bother to show up. And here we're in the locker room, and he's asking how I'm feeling—of course, I never said a word about what was going on at home—but I found out later that my father had tipped him off. At the time, I didn't know how to answer, so I asked him why the game hadn't started yet. And you know what he said . . ."

Karp paused as his eyes welled with tears. "He said he'd talked it over with the other coach and the refs and they'd agreed to let him use up all of our time outs at the beginning of the game to give me more time to show up. We looked at each other and then silently I started to lace my sneakers. But my hands started shaking so badly I froze, so he knelt and tied my sneakers for me. I don't remember how I played that night, but for the rest of my life I will never forget that somebody cared enough about my suffering to go the extra mile for me.

"When I got home after the game, I went to check on

my mother and found that she'd fallen out of bed and was lying on the floor. I picked her up and was shocked by how little she weighed. I could feel her bones through her skin. I held her there in my arms like you would a small child and she looked me in the eyes. That's when I finally let it sink in. She's going to die soon, and there's nothing I can do about it. It was so damn unfair, this monstrous, evil thing was going to happen to this beautiful, loving person."

Karp took a deep breath and let it out slowly. "She died the next morning, and I knew that evil had triumphed. And I swore that I would do everything I could for the rest of my life to fight evil wherever I found it. That's why when I got out of law school, I applied to one place and one place only, the New York District Attorney's Office so that I could work for the best DA in the country, with the best trial lawyers, and eventually I would volunteer to prosecute the most vicious, depraved murderers.

"Maybe it doesn't make sense to you, but I promised my mother's memory that I would never compromise with evil. I would not look the other way for the sake of expediency or politics. Cancer destroys from within—for whatever his reasons, Kane understands that and so do I. You can cut cancers out, attack them with chemotherapy or the New York penal law, but they do not quietly retire without leaving some small part of the disease behind to grow large again when conditions are right."

He stood silently at the window, a big man mourning the loss of his mother, his leonine head bowed, slumping somewhat into his shoulders. And at last Marlene understood what drove the man she loved. She came up behind him and wrapped her arms around his waist and held on as his body tensed and his eyes welled with tears.

When the private line on his desk rang, she picked it

up so that he could compose himself. "Butch Karp's office," she said.

"Hi, Marlene."

"Hi, Father Mike. How's Alejandro?"

"Just got out of surgery. The knife nicked his liver and he lost a lot of blood, but if he can get through the next twenty-four hours or so, he's got a good chance. . . . He put it all on the line, Marlene. I want to know if it was worth it. What does Butch plan to do?"

Marlene looked at her husband, the man who would go the extra mile for people who had no one else to speak for them. "Why he'll do what he's always done," she said with pride. "He's going to kick the shit out of the bad guys. Was there ever any doubt?"

Dugan was quiet for a moment before replying softly, "No. There was never any doubt."

A half hour later, Marlene was still thinking about her husband when she arrived at Crosby and Grand, wanting to freshen up before heading down to the hospital where Lucy and Zak were waiting with Giancarlo. That's probably why she was caught unprepared when the large young man came walking up behind her and stuck a gun in her ribs. "Get in the car or I'll blow your fuckin' heart out," he said as a dark sedan screeched to a stop at the curb and the back door opened. He shoved her in next to another man and climbed in after her, tapping the driver on the shoulder and shouting, "Let's go!"

The whole thing happened in less than ten seconds, which did not give Tran and Jojola time to react. They'd been talking inside the restaurant supply store when a lookout at the window yelled. They ran out onto the sidewalk with their guns drawn, heedless of the screams of startled pedestrians who scuttled like frightened hens to get away.

"Shit!" Jojola cursed. "Nice job we did of protecting her."

"No one stops the determined assassin," Tran said.

"Do you think they'll kill her?" Jojola asked.

Tran thought about it. "No, not yet. If they wanted to kill her, she'd be dead. She's bait to catch a bigger fish."

"Butch."

"Yes, the district attorney. And once they have him, they will kill them both. They will have to if they want to have any chance of getting away with this."

"Any suggestions?"

"Yes, if I may be so bold as to suggest that you keep an eye on Mr. Karp. I have a feeling that they will be contacting him next."

"What are you going to do?"

"Wait by the telephone," Tran said, "and hope I get a call before it's too late." He gave a sharp whistle and a cab that had been sitting down the block pulled forward. "This is my cousin Minh, he'll take you to the courthouse and wherever you need to go from there."

Jojola started to get in and then asked, "Why a taxi?"

Tran smiled. "In case you have not noticed, taxis in this city pretty much do whatever they want. They follow no laws except that of the Great Yellow Cab Company. Goodbye, Mr. Jojola, we may not meet again, but I wish you luck. It is always good to meet an old enemy and realize he was not really the devil."

32

BUTCH KARP ARRIVED AT RAY GUMA'S LOFT BUILD-
ing in Little Italy about 9:00 PM wheeling a dolly on
which two boxes of No Prosecution files sat. He was taking no chances on another break-in at the courthouse, and
his friend's building was a cross between Fort Knox and
Alcatraz.

He'd meant to arrive earlier, but Stupenagel walked
into the office as he was about to leave and wanted to
chat. He didn't want to arouse her curiosity by leaving
with the boxes—he wasn't ready for that part of the story
to come out yet—so he'd excused himself and quickly
walked next door to Murrow's office.

"I want you to go ask Stupenagel out to dinner," he told
his assistant. "She's in my office."

"Why?" Murrow asked. "This may be above and
beyond the call of duty."

"Just do it," Karp replied. "Anyplace you want to go.
It's on me. Just do whatever it takes to keep her out of my
hair tonight."

They walked back into the office together. Karp stifled
a fake yawn. "Well, guess I'll wrap it up and get my ass out

of here. What are you kids up to?" He looked pointedly at Murrow.

"Oh . . . yeah, hey, Ariadne, want to go grab a bite to eat?" Murrow asked.

Stupenagel squinted her eyes and looked from Murrow to Karp. "Something's going on here," she said. "And I don't like it." Then she brightened. "However, since I'm unlikely to find out anyway, and a girl never knows where her next expensive meal with a handsome young man is going to come from, sure, sweet cakes."

Murrow gave him a dirty look, and Stupenagel gave him a wink and left. He waited for the coast to clear, then loaded the boxes on the dolly. Chip McIntyre stopped in as he was leaving. "You need me anymore tonight?" he said.

"Nah," Karp replied. "Going to go drop some old files off at a friend's house and then head to the hospital. My son's having surgery tomorrow."

McIntyre said good-night and left, with Karp following a few minutes later. He cursed when he discovered that it had started to drizzle and tried to keep the files dry by shielding them with his body. He pressed the buzzer for Guma's apartment and looked up at the security camera.

"Who is it?" Guma asked innocently.

"Let me in, asshole," Karp growled. He was in a hurry to drop off the boxes and get to the hospital. He was surprised that Marlene wasn't there yet when he called the kids, nor had she answered at the loft. Probably stopped to pick up something for Giancarlo, he thought.

"I don't know anyone named LetMeInAsshole."

"Guma!"

"All right already. But I was hoping you were the pizza delivery boy." The door buzzed and several locks clicked, allowing him to back his way inside, hauling the dolly in after him.

When he got to Guma's apartment the door was held open with a video tape, *College Coeds Gone Wild*. He rolled his eyes and entered, finding Guma on the telephone.

"Hey, make yourself at home," Guma said, pointing to the apartment, which looked as though it hadn't been cleaned or even picked up in years. Laundry—dirty, clean, who could tell—lay strewn about, as were various boxes, bags, and plates that had once contained food and were now collecting dust, mold, and mouse droppings. "Just chatting to Deep Priest."

Karp gave him a puzzled look, and Guma added, "Father Mike." His conversation was interrupted again by another buzzing at the security door.

Glancing at the monitor mounted on the wall next to the door, Karp saw a teenager with a pizza box standing in the dark on the sidewalk. "Domino's?" he asked with disgust. "In New York?"

Guma shrugged. "It's fast and it's cheap. I figured you might want a bite before heading to the hospital." He punched the door unlock button on his desk.

There was a sound outside the door and Karp got up, figuring Guma had arranged the delivery and telephone call perfectly so that he would have to pay for the pizza. He pulled out his wallet and looked up, directly into the silencer attached to what appeared to be a .380 pistol in the hand of Detective Michael Flanagan.

"Back up," Flanagan said.

Guma started to reach into his desk, but Flanagan warned him. "Hands in the air now or your friend's brains will be all over the wall. Now get over here and the two of you sit down on the couch." He looked at the couch and made a face. "If you can find a place. What a mess."

Guma shrugged as he stood, replacing the receiver but touching the conference call button. He and Karp took a seat. "I wasn't expecting company, Detective Flanagan."

Flanagan ignored him and addressed Karp. "First, we have your wife," he said and pulled out a small tape recorder and hit the play button. A woman's voice was heard: "Go fuck yourself you piece of shit. Give me a chance and I'm going to put a hot one up your asshole, asshole." He grimaced and turned off the tape recorder. "She really should watch the cursing," he said.

"Sure sounds like Marlene," Guma admitted. "But could you play it again, I liked the part about putting a hot one up your asshole."

Karp rolled his eyes. "What do you want?" he asked the detective.

"The files," Flanagan said, glaring at Guma, who smiled back at him. "But we're all going to sit tight for a couple of hours. Then we're all going to take a ride to meet up with some people. If you want to see your wife again, you won't give me any trouble."

Karp was about to say something when he noticed a shadow pass across the opening of the apartment door, which was still held ajar with the videotape. A brown face glanced in and was gone. Need a distraction, he thought and played a hunch.

"You do know what's in the files, don't you, Flanagan?" he said. Everything he'd been told about Flanagan was that he was such a straight arrow, Karp was hoping he was also an ignorant one who still thought he was working for the church. "They're cases about priests who sexually abuse little boys."

"Shut your mouth," the detective responded. "I know all about how you Jews are trying to destroy the church by infiltrating the priesthood with perverts. Now you plan to go to the press, like that sweet little story in that filthy rag the *Voice*."

Karp laughed and didn't even have to fake it, the idea was so ludicrous. "Is that what Kane told you? And you believed him? Go ahead, peek at a few of the files and check out all the Jewish names of the priests who've been accused. You know, Fathers Finnegan, Esperanza, O'Toole . . . all straight out of the Old Testament for sure. Oh, and I almost forgot, Hans Lichner, a real Aryan dirtbag who screws and then slices up little boys. I'm sure you saw the news about the two children found in Central Park?"

"Shut your yap," Flanagan demanded, pointing the gun at Karp's head. "You kikes lie as easily as you breathe."

"Well, don't take my word for it, ask the guy behind you."

Flanagan laughed. "You expect me to fall for that old trick. You watch too much television."

"Boo," Jojola said as he came up behind the detective, who whirled and snapped off a shot. But the Indian had blocked his arm so that the bullet zinged harmlessly into the wall. There were no more shots because Jojola had then dislocated the detective's elbow and the gun clattered to the ground.

Flanagan screamed in pain and rage but reached with his good hand for a second gun he kept in a back holster. Instead, he ended up reaching for the side of his head as Jojola's knife flew up and sliced off one of his ears, which fluttered to the ground like a wounded butterfly. He screamed again.

"Where's Marlene Ciampi?"

"I don't know," the detective snarled, but then screamed again as Jojola sliced open his nose.

"Please, could we do this in the kitchen on the tile," Guma complained. "He's bleeding all over a five-thousand-dollar Persian."

"Sorry," Jojola apologized. "Now would you just tell me where Marlene is, or we're going to have to go for your throat and that would ruin Mr. Guma's carpet."

"I don't know where they're keeping her now," Flanagan cried. "She's with my partner and a couple of other guys. We were supposed to meet up in Central Park, behind the flower gardens off 106th Street . . . and bring the files."

"Why there?" Karp asked.

Flanagan hesitated, then screamed again as Jojola stuck him in the shoulder. "Ah, Jesus help me," he cried looking fearfully at the Indian.

"I think you're asking the wrong boss," Jojola said. "You were working for the other guy. Now answer the question."

Flanagan blinked at him, blood flowing profusely, and turned to Karp. "The plan was take the files and then"—he looked at the knife—". . . and then . . . it's Inca Boyz territory. It was supposed to look like Garcia's gang kidnapped the family and killed them."

"The family?" Karp said alarmed.

"Yeah, that priest you mentioned . . . Lichner . . . he and some guys from the force are on the way to the hospital where they know your kid is," he said. "They're going to pick him up and your daughter and the other boy if they're around, and take them to St. Patrick's. Just in case, you pull something funny at the park. They'll be brought over to the park later."

"You'd go along with killing three children?" Karp said.

Flanagan looked down. "It's to protect the church . . . from a bunch of Jews."

Guma returned with two towels from the kitchen where he'd gone. "Cover your ugly face and ear hole," he said. "You're making a mess."

"When were we supposed to arrive at Central Park?" Karp asked.

"Ten," Flanagan said. "You in one car, then me in mine to make sure we're not followed. It goes down like that or they kill the woman and the kid."

Karp looked at his watch. Thirty minutes, he thought. He looked at Jojola. "Can you warn Lucy at the hospital; we'll call Chip McIntyre on the way and get some cover over there. Make sure this scumbag doesn't go anywhere."

Jojola nodded. "Get going."

"Get that, Father?" Guma said into the speaker of his telephone. There was no reply. "Guess we're on our own."

"Uh-uh, I'm on my own," Karp replied.

"No way, *paisan.* One, you don't get to have all the fun," Guma replied. "Two, you need me. Detective Asshole here said they'd be expecting him driving the second car. He doesn't show and the show is over before they raise the curtain."

Karp and Guma emptied the file boxes onto the living-room table. Then Guma grabbed his raincoat off a coat-rack and put it on.

"You worried about getting wet?" Karp asked.

"No, just bringing a friend," Guma said. "He reached inside the coat and brought out a double-barreled, sawed-off 10-gauge shotgun. The entire weapon was only four-teen inches long. "The great Sicilian equalizer," he said. "Let's go. I want to swing by your place first."

"Why? We've only got a half hour or less."

"Yeah, I know, but we're going to need more muscle."

"Zak's at the hospital."

"Ha, we probably could use him, too," Guma laughed, "but I have someone a little older and more experienced in mind."

Karp nodded and they picked up the boxes and headed out the door. As they reached the elevator, they heard another scream.

"I wonder what piece that was?" Guma said.

"Think anybody will call the police?"

"Are you kidding?" Guma replied. "The entire building is home to a bunch of wiseguys. There's always somebody screaming."

At Beth Israel Hospital, Lucy was entertaining a drugged-up Giancarlo with stupid Zak tricks. But she was wondering why her parents were so late. Her mother had called more than an hour earlier to say she was taking a shower and then would be right down; her dad called a little later and said he was stopping by Ray Guma's and would do the same.

When the telephone in the room rang, she thought it must be them, calling to say they'd be right there. But it was Jojola.

"Lucy, listen carefully," he said. "Your mother's been kidnapped and your father has gone to rescue her. But Lichner and some cops are on the way to the hospital to get Giancarlo and the rest of you. They want to take you to St. Patrick's . . . and Lucy, they mean to kill you and the boys once they have your mother and father and the files. Your dad was going to call McIntyre, and I'm on my way, but I don't think we'll be there in time. You only have a few minutes."

Lucy hung up the telephone and went to look out the window. Four floors below, she saw the big priest followed by two cops and two paramedics wheeling a gurney. She looked at Giancarlo; he was in no condition to run anywhere. She took Zak aside and explained the situation to him.

"We've got to hide," she said.

"No time," Zak countered. "They'll come looking." He looked at his brother. "We need to switch places."

"What?"

"Switch places. Then you hide with Giancarlo and they take me to St. Patrick's."

Lucy shook her head. "I can't let you do that. You take Giancarlo."

"You're not making sense," he told her. "They are looking for a boy. If they find one, they may not look for the two of you. Giancarlo's blind, he doesn't stand a chance. But if they don't know that I can see—and that I'm not drugged up—I may get a chance to escape."

Lucy started crying and shook her head again. Zak reached out and took her hand. "Lucy, it's our only chance. Now let's get Giancarlo into the room next door and you guys stay there until these assholes are gone."

They half-carried, half-walked Giancarlo into the room next door. A dim light showed an old man lying on one of the beds, hooked up to a ventilator. "Hide in the bathroom," Zak suggested.

They placed Giancarlo on the toilet seat and Lucy turned to Zak. "I'll come looking for you as soon as it's safe to move him back to his bed," she said. "In the meantime, take this." She reached in her purse and pulled out a switchblade. "I believe this is yours."

Zak looked at her and smiled. "Luce, you're a peach. I

feel better already," he said, flickering the blade in and out a few times.

Then the elevator bell rang. Zak stood on his toes and kissed his sister. "I'll be okay," he said. "Just don't forget to come looking for me."

Zak ran next door, where he quickly got out of his clothes and into a hospital gown. He barely got into the bed when a large dark figure appeared in the doorway.

"Here," Lichner said. "There's only one, but it vill have to do. Take him." The men posing as paramedics wheeled the gurney in and hoisted Zak onto it.

Next door, Lucy listened to the men take her brother with her hand over Giancarlo's mouth. She waited a minute after she heard the elevator bell ring again and then took Giancarlo back to his room. "Stay here, honey," she said. "Somebody will be back for you soon." Then she ran out of the room.

Ten minutes later, Lucy stood in the shadows of the building across from St. Patrick's. The ambulance that had brought her brother was parked on the dark east side of the cathedral. She figured the two men loitering on the sidewalk over there weren't real paramedics, and she had no idea how she was going to get past them.

Suddenly she was aware of an overpowering stench and the presence of a large dark figure next to her. Lichner! she thought in terror.

"Evenink, Lucee Karp," said the smell.

"Booger!" she whispered happily. "What are you doing here?"

"He's waiting for me," said a familiar voice behind her. "Nice to see you again, Lucy."

"David, oh God, am I glad you're here," she said.

"Really? I thought you did not care for deranged psycho killer demon hunters?" David Grale said.

"Only when I don't need one," she replied with a shy smile. After all, she once had had a schoolgirl crush on that particular psycho killer. "And I need one now." She looked up and was shocked to see how haggard and pale the once-handsome face had become; she thought he looked like paintings she'd seen of Rasputin, the mad Russian priest of the czars. "My brother's been abducted by a priest who's even crazier than you, only he's as evil as they come."

Grale laughed. "Thanks for making the distinction. I have been hunting this particular demon for a long time, though I do not know his human name."

"Hans Lichner."

"Doesn't matter," Grale said. "I have sort of a sixth sense for these fellows, you know, and I knew he was back in town. So I had my friends, like Todd Reedy here"—he pointed to Booger—"watching for him. Todd saw him and sent word."

"Todd?" Lucy said. "I didn't know that was his name."

"Did you ever ask?" Grale said.

"No, I'm ashamed to say I didn't," she acknowledged. "I'm sorry, Todd."

"S'okay, Lucee," Todd the Booger replied. "Mutha fuckah isen side." He pointed a large grimy finger at the cathedral.

"Yes, the mother fucker's inside," Grale said. "The question is how do we join him with those two men standing almost on top of a secret entrance I know. We need a distraction. Think you can do it, Lucy?"

"No way," she replied. "I'm coming with you. That's my brother in there."

"Very well," Grale said. "How about you, Todd?"

"Sure, Fatha, no problem," Reedy replied.

"Then give us enough time to circle the cathedral and come up behind them," he said. "Wait until you see us, then do your thing."

Grale and Lucy emerged from the shadows and walked down the block until they were out of sight from the men next to the cathedral. They then crossed the street and walked rapidly down and around the building until they reached the southeast corner on Fifty-first Street.

Seeing them, Booger walked up to the two men and held out his hand. "Want sometink to eat," he demanded.

"Holy Christ, this guy smells like he crawled out of the sewer," one of the men swore. "Get lost, asshole."

Booger stomped his foot. "You da asshole . . . want sometink a eat now," he yelled. He grabbed at one of the men, who backed up in horror, pulling a gun.

"So much for unarmed paramedics," Grale whispered. "Let's go." He led the way, sliding along the wall, staying low in the shrubs and ivy that grew on that side of the building.

Booger began sneezing, spraying the two men.

"Get the fuck away from me," the first man shouted.

"Don't shoot him," the other man warned. "Or every uniform in the area will come running. He wants money, give him some money."

"Christ, anything to get that smell to go away," the first man replied, reaching for his wallet as he waved the gun at the smiling Booger. "I'm not going to be able to handle eating for a week. Let's get the fuck out of here."

Meanwhile, Grale reached a place along the wall where he instructed Lucy to lie down while he cleared the ivy from the wall. He uncovered a stone that looked like part of the foundation and gave it a hard shove, freezing at the grating noise as it moved to reveal a dark hole. But the two men were still occupied with Booger. Grale and Lucy crawled inside.

The passage led to an opening behind the organ. Peering out from behind, while Grale shoved the stone back into place, Lucy froze, horrified by what she saw. Her brother lay naked on the altar with Lichner standing above him, a large curved knife poised in his hand. Not knowing what else to do, she screamed as Grale rushed past her.

Lichner had decided not to wait until called to bring the boy to Central Park. It had been Kane's idea to take the boy to St. Patrick's, where Lichner had a key to the small side door that led into the sacristy. "The paramedics have a form signed by 'Dr. Zacham' asking that he be transferred because of technical difficulties in the surgery room," he explained. "If anybody notices the boy is gone, they'll never think to look for you at the cathedral. And if something goes wrong with my plan, you have my permission to . . . ummm . . . sacrifice him there."

Kane's remark had planted the idea in Lichner's mind. He decided he could always take the body to the park later; conducting a sacrifice in God's house was simply too good an opportunity to pass up. He thought that God would even understand not waiting for a full moon. The priest was so consumed with the idea and sexually aroused that he had not noticed that his apparently drugged, unconscious victim had palmed a switchblade knife.

Then the woman's scream ruined the ambiance. As did the dark shadow man who was racing toward him. He'd never seen the man before but knew in an instant that he was the one who had been hunting him. Good, he thought, time for the hunter to be hunted. But as he started to move toward his opponent, he felt a sudden searing pain in his right thigh, near the groin. He looked down and was amazed to see a knife protruding from his leg and his victim scrambling to get off the altar. Roaring with pain and anger, he grabbed the boy by the neck and flung him down the steps leading to the altar, where he collapsed and lay still.

Then Lichner turned to meet his hunter. Their blades met as they moved past one another, the steel ringing as both men grunted from the force. Slashing and stabbing, they circled, neither gaining an advantage until the priest stumbled slightly because of the earlier wound and then doubled over when the other man kicked him in the groin.

Grale reached down and grabbed Lichner's hair, pulling his head up and intending to slash across the giant's throat. But Lucy yelled. "No, David, don't kill him. Let Dad bring him to justice."

Ridiculous, he thought. Justice is here and now.

But he'd hesitated just long enough for Lichner to recover. With a scream the giant stood and drove his blade deep into the midsection of Grale, lifting him off the ground. He kicked him off his blade and sent him sprawling. Smiling at the young woman, he bent down to pick up the boy. The sacrifice would go on, and then he would deal with the girl.

Only this was to be a night of interruptions. A new voice shouted at him. "Let the boy go." He looked up and saw a short, stocky brown man walking toward him, a blade also in his hand. "Come and get him." He laughed, intending to cut the child's throat. But again the little brat surprised him by twisting suddenly away.

When Lichner looked up, the brown man was upon him and again he felt the searing pain. Only this time it was on the side of his head. In disbelief he put a hand there and felt the bloody stump of what had been his ear.

"Who are you?" Lichner screamed, only this time in pain.

"John Jojala," the man replied. "Otherwise known as your worst nightmare." The man's blade swung again, so fast Lichner didn't have time to react, and the fingers holding his knife fell to the floor, along with the blade.

He looked up, his mouth forming a dark circle. But that was all, as Jojola's blade rocketed up and caught him under his chin and pierced up into his brain. He was dead before he hit the floor.

At about the same time that Lichner's soul was being dragged down into hell, Karp was staring his own death in the face.

Arriving at the road that circled up behind the flower gardens, Karp was stopped by a man with a gun and a flashlight. "Up the hill," he said. "Park when you get to the top and walk out on the grass."

Karp did as told and was getting out of the car when he saw the sedan that he hoped was being driven by Guma arrive and park behind him. The driver got out and whispered, "Good luck. Got your back."

Who's got my front is what I'm worried about, Karp thought as he walked up to the top of the grassy knoll where he could just make out the figures of three men. When he was six feet away, he stopped. He recognized two of the men: Father O'Callahan and Detective Robert Leary.

"I presume the files are in the car?" O'Callahan asked. He nodded to the third man, who walked in the direction of the cars.

"Where's my wife?"

O'Callahan raised his hand. Thirty feet away, near the edge of the treeline, a flashlight was turned on. The beam illuminated a figure on her knees with her hands tied behind her back. She lifted her head.

Marlene, hold on, baby, I'm coming. On the ride over, he'd thought a lot about how he was going to save her, not knowing if she was already dead. And he didn't want to live if he lost her.

So he had come, prepared to save her or die trying. He faced the two men as light rain began falling on them.

Karp knew that as soon as the third man reached Guma, he would be out of time. He prepared to run for Marlene. Maybe it will distract them enough for her to get away.

Then out of the bushes immediately to his right, there was a rustling and another man emerged and started walking toward them. "Wassup, homes," the stranger said. "This is Inca Boyz territory."

Karp now recognized the form and voice of Pancho Ramirez. He also noted the teen was carrying a handgun.

"Go away," Leary said. "Police business."

"Yeah?" Pancho said. "And was it police business to kill my friend Francisco? And was it police business to stab my bro Alejandro?"

"Who are you?" O'Callahan demanded.

"Me? Oh, I'm just a nobody from the 'hood. But you're on my turf, so I suggest you leave this man alone and let the woman go," Pancho said as he came to a stop next to Karp.

Leary reached into his windbreaker and pulled out a gun. "I don't think so, punk." He started to raise his gun but then several things happened at once. From the direction of Marlene and her captor, a man suddenly screamed. Then over by the cars a shotgun roared. Pancho pushed Karp aside and raised his gun at the same time Leary brought his to bear.

Karp took off running for Marlene with guns erupting behind him and not knowing if any of them were aimed at him. Red-hot pain shot through his bad knee but he ignored it as he ran toward the flashlight beam. There was a gunshot ahead of him. Oh God, please, not Marlene, he begged as he ran. He could see a body lying on the ground, lifeless in the rain. His heart sank and tears sprang to his eyes.

"Took you long enough, lover."

"Marlene?"

"What? You were expecting to meet another woman in the middle of Central Park? Would you prefer to untie me before or after your dirty little secret shows up?"

Karp leaned over and picked up the flashlight that was lying in the grass next to the prone body with its light still on. He shined it on the body. A man lay there with his sightless eyes staring up at the cloudy sky. A star-shaped object protruded several inches from his forehead—one of those ninja things, he thought absently—and the man was quite dead. One other odd thing, the man's fly was open and that area of his pants was covered with blood.

Karp turned to his wife. When the light hit her face, he saw blood around her mouth.

"Don't ask," she said.

"Are you okay?" he said, alarmed.

"I am now."

And at the end . . .

IT WAS ONE OF THOSE LOVELY INDIAN SUMMER evenings in New York City when the leaves on the trees in Central Park looked as if Jackson Pollock splashed cans of red, orange, and yellow paint across the branches, then added bold brushstrokes of plum for accent. Standing near the edge of the trees, Butch Karp squinted to see across the football field where a pack of eleven- and twelve-year-old football players huddled, wearing shoulder pads that looked as wide as they were tall.

"Maybe next year I can play, too," said a young voice next to him.

Karp looked down and ruffled the hair on Giancarlo's head. The spot on the side that had been shaved for the surgery had filled in nicely. The surgery had been an unqualified success in terms of removing the shotgun pellet without further damage. Then it had been a waiting game, a wait well worth the anxious moments when the bandages were removed and his son announced that he could see again.

Giancarlo's vision still wasn't perfect; he described it as "sharp in the middle, fuzzy around the sides, but who's complaining." The surgeon, Dr. Zacham, had called several days earlier from Israel and urged them to be patient.

"We don't really understand the brain all that well," he admitted. "Perhaps his eyes and brain are still relearning how to communicate again. Perhaps with time the fuzzy areas will sharpen."

Giancarlo's quick recovery had allowed Marlene to return to New Mexico, the only truly disappointing result of the conclusion to the No Prosecution case. She explained that while she believed that she was on the road to mental health recovery, "this whole thing sort of interrupted the progress."

Marlene had laughed at the pout on his face as they lay in bed the night before she left. "I won't be gone long, lover," she assured him. "I love New Mexico and may have to return there from time to time when I need to clear my head, and I'd love to show it to you sometime, too. You'd look great in cowboy boots and a straw bull rider's hat, and if you're lucky, that's all I'll let you wear for a few days. But I also know where my home is—this city, but most of all with you and my kids. I promise I'll come back soon a new woman."

"I don't want a new woman," he said. "I want the one I got."

"You're a liar," she said kissing him, "but I appreciate the attempt at gallantry. Now quit pouting. I have to go back for a while; this whole affair left a bad taste in my mouth, if you know what I mean."

Watching Zak come out of the huddle and line up behind the quarterback in his position as running back, Karp grimaced recalling her choice of words. It was an unnecessary reminder of the last time he was in Central Park and its aftermath.

After her abduction by Detective Robert Leary and two of his cohorts, Marlene had been held at the archdiocese offices until brought to the area behind the botanical gardens in the northeast corner of Central Park. There they met up with a man she later learned was O'Callahan who was waiting on top of the grassy knoll and told one of her kidnappers to escort her over to the treeline to his right. Her guard, a thin, acne-scarred man with "a face like a rat . . . long nose, beady eyes, yellow teeth," did as told and then forced her to kneel with his gun pointed at her head.

With a three-quarters-full moon illuminating the scene, it was easy to see that the tall man who emerged from the first of two cars to arrive a few minutes later was her husband. She'd hoped that he'd arrive with the cavalry, and her heart sank when he came alone, believing that her carelessness had doomed them both. He's coming for me, she'd thought as he'd approached the three men on the hill, one of whom split off and walked toward the cars and the man who got out of the sedan. It's my fault he's going to die.

When Rat Face turned his flashlight on and pointed it on her, she knew the moment of truth was fast approaching. She racked her brain desperately to think of some distraction that might give Butch a chance to save himself. Her guard was one of those insecure cops—probably a nerd in high school—who seemed to grow balls only when they were waving a gun in someone's face. Which gave her an idea.

"Please, I don't want to die," she begged. "I'll do anything you want."

The remark earned her a cuff from his free hand. "Shut up, bitch," he said.

She'd persisted. "You could let me run into the woods," she said and looked at his groin.

He'd looked quickly over his shoulder at the confrontation on the hill, then smiled. "Okay, bitch," he said, undoing his zipper and exposing himself. "Suck this and I might let you have a head start."

Marlene closed her eyes and bit. . . . Karp closed his eyes and quickly shut the image out of his mind. Desperate times call for desperate measures, he reminded himself.

The mutilated guard screamed and, enraged, pointed the gun at her head, intending to shoot her. Marlene closed her eyes and waited for the bullet, surprised after she heard the shot to discover she was unharmed. Rat Face's bullet had gone harmlessly into the ground, as he sank to his knees and then fell onto his back with a martial arts throwing star protruding from his forehead.

Then Tran had stepped quickly out of the bushes. He was the muscle Guma called on his cell phone and picked up on Grand and Crosby. When they pulled up to the curb, Tran was already waiting and jumped in the trunk of Flanagan's police sedan that Guma was driving while Karp drove the Cadillac.

Guma later explained how after watching Karp drive past one of Flanagan's boys inside the park, he'd pulled up and shined a flashlight in the guard's eyes. "Flanagan?" the man had asked. A moment later he was unconscious on the ground after Tran slipped out of the open trunk and disabled him with a blow to the throat.

"I'll find Marlene; you look after Butch," Tran said and ran up the hill into the woods.

Tran had seen the man flash his light on Marlene's face and knew he had only seconds to reach her before it was too late. He arrived at the moment she created her "distraction" and only just in time to throw the star even as Rat Face pulled the trigger. "Are you, okay?" he asked and then looked up. "Uh-oh, here comes the good guys, I have to go. Talk later." He'd disappeared back in the trees, just as Butch hobbled up.

Too bad, I would have liked to have met him, Karp thought when he learned who Marlene's rescuer had been. But he understood after Marlene later explained that given Tran's nefarious business dealings, the bandit chief had no desire to meet him.

"He'll probably move his people out of the restaurant supply store now," she'd said.

"Well, if you talk to him, tell him I hope he doesn't," he'd replied. "It's hard to find nice, quiet neighbors."

Karp figured she must have had that discussion with her friend because the store was still there. Every morning as he left for work, Mr. Thien Le greeted him with the same cordial *"Chao buoi sang,* Mr. Karp," although it seemed there was a small glint in his eyes ever since that night.

Guma had filled him in on some of the other details. He'd stayed over by the cars as if guarding the files, hoping that the moonlight would not give away the fact that he wasn't Flanagan until the man approaching him was within range of the 10 gauge.

"We're 'sposed to get the files," the man said, walking up. He'd suddenly pulled up short and reached for his gun. "You're not Flanagan!"

The man might have beat him to the draw, Guma admitted, except that when Marlene screamed, he'd momentarily jerked his head in that direction. "Which gave me the time to raise Teresa and let him have both barrels."

The discharge had knocked both men off their feet: the one, who turned out to be Officer Sean Calloway, wounded only a few days before in a "shootout" with notorious Bloods gang members, with a massive hole in his chest; and, Guma, who fell back into one of the cars and had the wind knocked out of him.

Yet, that didn't mean all the good guys survived the fight. After Karp untied Marlene, she'd picked up her guard's gun and raced back up the knoll where three bodies lay on the ground. Robert Leary was dead. Riley O'Callahan was crawling toward the cars with one hand while the other was pressed against his midsection as blood flowed between his fingers. "Please, call an ambulance," he begged. "I think I'm dying."

"Don't worry," she said, "there's a nice warm bed waiting for you, you know"—she gestured to the ground with the gun—"down there." He'd then pitched forward onto his face and didn't move again.

Marlene turned to the third figure, Pancho Ramirez. He was still alive, too, though from the number of bloody holes in his sweatshirt and the bloody foam at his mouth, she knew it wasn't for long. She'd known him through Alejandro for years and knew how devastating this would be to Garcia.

"Thank you, Pancho, for saving my husband," she said as she began to cry.

"Didn't do it for the man," he said as a spasm of pain passed over his face. "I did it for my homeboys, 'Jandro and Cisco. Besides," he added with a slight smile, "this is Inca Boyz territory, nobody shoots nobody here, unless we say it's okay." After suffering through another spasm, he looked at her with pleading eyes. "Please, get me a priest."

"I'll take it from here, Marlene," said a voice behind her. She turned and recognized the face and figure of Father Dugan. She stood and backed away so that he could kneel in her place to hear Pancho's confession and administer last rites.

"Forgive me, Father, for I have sinned," she heard Pancho say, "I banged Lydia Sanchez in her uncle's car last night . . ."

A few minutes later, Dugan made the sign of a cross over the still body and stood up. He explained that Pancho was with him when Guma switched his telephone over to conference call. "It took me a moment to realize what was going on, but enough to hear the part about the botanical gardens and to know that you two needed help." He looked down at Pancho's body and sighed.

"Pancho insisted on coming," he said. "They killed one of his friends and tried to kill another. There was no stopping him and I didn't trust calling the police."

Pancho Ramirez had only recently come back to the church, Dugan said, from the influence of his friend Alejandro. "He was trying to change," the priest said. "Trying to break free of the gang life. I hope he'll find peace."

The police arrived and after sorting through what had happened with the aid of Karp, they'd arrested the guard—a rookie patrol officer—whom Tran had knocked out near the entrance, and the bodies were hauled off to the morgue. Karp had insisted that another ambulance be called for Pancho. "I don't want him to have to ride with the trash," he said.

Chip McIntyre had called to say that the kids were fine. Giancarlo was sleeping, as was Zak, who'd taken over the bed next to his. Lucy was dozing in the chair but woke up long enough to ask how they were—she'd already heard they were alive from Guma—and inform them that "John Jojola can fill you in on everything. Why don't you two go decompress at home, and we'll see you about noon tomorrow before the surgery."

Nice to have one adult in the family who can be counted on to remain calm, Karp thought as he watched Zak line up in the backfield. His team was playing for the Manhattan Pop Warner Football League Championship, twelve-year-old division, and they were behind five points with two minutes to play. The ball was snapped and the quarterback turned around and handed off to Zak, who was stopped for no gain.

"Face mask!" Giancarlo yelled. "Open your eyes, ref! Are you blind? They grabbed his face mask."

"Simmer down, Lombardi," Karp said, but his mind remained on the aftermath of the shootings.

He and Marlene had done as Lucy suggested and returned to the loft to recuperate. They found Jojola waiting for them and got that side of the story.

After warning Lucy, Jojola had tied Flanagan to a chair in Guma's apartment, then rushed outside to the taxi driven by Tran's nephew and asked him to take him to St. Patrick's. When they arrived, they saw two men standing near an ambulance on the east side arguing with a large filthy man. So they'd circled the building and he'd gotten out and made his way through the bushes without the men seeing him.

Still, he had no way of getting inside the cathedral and was wondering what to do next when his attention was caught by movement in the bushes near him. At first he thought it was a coyote, but then he realized where he was—the island of Manhattan. The German shepherd went on its way as he chuckled.

A few yards farther he'd found a set of tracks made by a very large man who walked with a limp. They led to a small door in an alcove on the side of the building, but when he tried the handle, it was locked. So he backtracked and discovered two more sets of tracks: one made by a man he did not recognize and another set he did. Lucy. They led to a dark hole that he thought at first might lead to the coyote's den beneath the cathedral, but then heard Lucy's scream come from the hole, followed by the sounds of a fight. As quickly as he could, he wiggled through the hole and emerged just as Lucy asked Grale not to kill Lichner.

He recounted his own fight with the giant, shrugging at its brevity. "He was a coward used to attacking children and defenseless people, not fighting men," he said. "Grale would have taken him, except for Lucy's plea for mercy. But I am just as happy that I don't have to extradite him and have him foul the air of my home again."

Lucy had picked up a woozy Zak when she looked around at the shadows in the cathedral and said in a frightened voice, "We have to go."

"I thought she was worried about Flanagan's men," he told the couple. "But then I looked and saw that there were shadows moving within the shadows."

"They want David," she'd told him. "And don't want us to see them. We have to go. It isn't safe."

Jojola knelt and felt for Grale's vital signs. They were weak but he was still alive. "We can't leave him," he said.

"We have no choice," she said. "They are coming. He'll live or die according to what they can do for him. We need to get my brother out of here."

The mention of the boy moved Jojola to leave. They fled through the hole in the wall and were surprised to find that there was no one standing near the ambulance anymore.

"Lucy and Zak thought it best to return to the hospital and pretend nothing happened until they heard from you," he said. "Chip McIntyre showed up with some of his men right after we got there so I felt comfortable leaving them."

Jojola had then gone over to Guma's to check on the prisoner. "Flanagan volunteered that he made several tape recordings that will be of interest to you," he said. "They're in a safe under the kitchen floor."

"Volunteered?" Karp asked.

"Yes," Jojola said. "He seems to have an unnatural fear of knives, and when I brought mine out and laid it on the table, he decided to tell me about the tapes. After that I called McIntyre, who sent a couple of his boys to pick up Flanagan and take him to the hospital, where I believe he is being kept in secret and under guard."

"Thank you, John, for everything," Marlene said.

"That's what friends are for," he said with a shrug. "All in all, New York has been an interesting place to visit, but I think I prefer my peaceful pueblo."

In the morning, Marlene got up early and headed straight for the hospital. But Karp had gone into the office to put out fires and get the ball rolling on what had to happen next. He'd listened to an early newscast on the television about reports of gunfire and the police having cordoned off an area of Central Park behind the botanical gardens. But there was no comment from the police, except to refer all calls to the district attorney's office—something he'd worked out with a stunned Chief Denton at 5:00 AM. He was grateful that no one had made a connection to another small item in the newscast that a priest involved in setting up St. Patrick's for morning Mass had discovered two large pools of blood on the steps leading to the altar. Church officials were blaming vandals "or perhaps a Satanic cult." He noticed that neither Archbishop Fey "nor his spokesman, Father Riley O'Callahan, could be reached for comment."

All morning the telephone had rung nonstop, most of it requests for information from the press. So he was grateful when Mrs. Boccino announced the arrival of Murrow, who unfortunately was accompanied by Stupenagel. He took a deep breath when she walked in, expecting to get an earful for cutting her out of the action. But she was amazingly calm.

"I should be mad as hell," she said, "and will expect a full, and exclusive, report." She winked at Murrow, who blushed and looked quickly at something interesting on the ceiling. "But this time, I'll forgive you because it was your idea to have Gilbert take me out to dinner."

"Gilbert?" Karp said.

"Yes, Gilbert," she replied, "my knight in shining armor who you should show your appreciation for a lot more than you do. I tried to make it up to him last night, but the occasional word of thanks from you would go a long way, too. Isn't that right snookums?"

"Well, I . . . ," Murrow blushed again, finding something even more interesting on the floor. "Maybe I don't do all that much."

"Snookums?" Karp gasped. "I think I'm going to lose my breakfast."

"Now wait just a minute, Butch," Murrow protested in a rather high, squeaky voice. "You said to do whatever it took to keep her out of your hair. And besides, whatever I do in my free time is my affair. So if Ms. Stupenagel . . . aka Honey Buns . . . and I want to engage in mutual congress of a sexual nature, then that is entirely my business."

"God, I love it when he talks like that," Stupenagel sighed. "But speaking of business, I have a story to write . . . so what have you got to tell me."

Karp and Stupenagel haggled over some of the guidelines but soon had a deal in place. Then he instructed Murrow to come up with a short press release to feed to the vultures essentially stating that there had indeed been a shooting in Central Park the night before and that there were several fatalities. "Names withheld pending notification of next of kin. . . . There were also two arrests with more pending."

As soon as he'd approved Murrow's press release, Karp left for the hospital for the rest of the day, holding Marlene's hand and comforting his other two children as they waited. Finally, Dr. Zacham had emerged and held up a tiny dot, the shotgun pellet. "I give you this to hold on to for him. But everything went perfectly. Now we shall see if it has any effect."

The family again spent most of the day, Saturday, at the hospital trying to entertain Giancarlo. Same thing Sunday, except a break Karp took in the afternoon when he'd met at his office with Guma, Newbury, and Terrell Collins representing his office, and Denton and McIntyre from the NYPD.

• • •

Then on Monday morning, he'd called the offices of the New York Archdiocese and requested a meeting with Archbishop Fey. "And please, ask him to have his legal counsel, Mr. Kane, present."

He'd arrived at the archdiocese offices and was escorted into a large meeting room where he was left to contemplate stained-glass windows depicting a bunch of bearded men in colorful robes mounted around the skylight. After several minutes, Fey walked in, followed by Kane. The two men sat on the opposite side of the table from him.

"So what can we do for you, Mr. Karp?" Kane began the conversation.

"I thought the question at this point would have been more along the lines of what I can do for you," Karp replied.

The tension visibly flowed out of Kane. He looked at Fey, who smiled weakly, and said, "See, I knew Butch . . . may I call you, Butch? . . . was a reasonable man." He turned back to Karp, "Yes, you're quite right, what can you do for us? I hope you realize that whole . . . ummm . . . misunderstanding the other night was not authorized. I'm afraid the archbishop's secretary, Father O'Callahan, may God have mercy on his soul, overstepped his authority."

"What about Flanagan, Leary, and the others?"

Kane held his hands apart as if to say it had been beyond his control. "They followed O'Callahan's orders, I'm afraid. We—the archbishop and I—of course, had no idea that he'd be taking this all so seriously. Born, I'm sure, of his desire to protect the church from old news."

"Old news?" Karp asked.

"Yes, the No Prosecution files," Kane said. "Old news . . . everybody's happy."

"Really? I wonder. Have you spoken to Bernard Little lately?" Karp asked.

"Who?"

"Didn't think so. You don't even remember how you tried to pay him and his wife to forget that Flanagan murdered their son."

Kane waved his hand. "Oh that. Let's be honest, one less nigger hasn't been noticed. Why ruin a cop's career over a single trigger-happy incident."

"And what about Francisco Apodaca? He didn't have anything to do with any of this."

"An accident. Again, without getting clearance from anybody, O'Callahan and Flanagan on their own decided that you needed to be out of the picture," Kane said. Then he laughed. "But it seems that O'Callahan and several of his men are dead, and Mr. Flanagan seems to have disappeared. So that should make you about even."

Karp looked at Kane for a long minute, fighting the urge to reach across the table and break the man's neck. "So I guess we just forget all this . . . old news," he said as calmly as he could manage. "A little corruption is the price we pay to keep the barbarians from the gates and ourselves in power, right?"

Kane smiled. "I knew you would understand. We let this blow over and then I'll be mayor and you'll be the district attorney and between the two of us, we'll run this city for the next forty years. So we have a deal? Let me write a check—a campaign contribution—to seal it," he said, pulling a checkbook from his suit pocket. "I'll fill in the zeroes, you put the number you want in front of it . . . say up to nine?" He scribbled on the check and slid it across the table.

Six zeroes, Karp thought, up to nine million dollars. He nodded. "Yes, we have a deal. But it might not be the same deal you're talking about. Let me know what you think."

He turned to the archbishop. "I have to say that you are the biggest disappointment in all of this. I expect vermin like your boss here to think that corruption and lies and abuse of power are all just part of doing business. But you, you were given the most precious thing people have—their trust and faith, their hope for something better, if not in this life, then the next. But you took that and ground it into the dust with such a reckless disregard for the lives of the people who counted on you that it makes me sick. In fact, to quote one wise man I met recently, it was a motherfucking ferocious disregard."

Fey never let his gaze leave the table in front of him. "I had no idea things had degenerated this far," he said weakly.

"But you knew something wasn't right," Karp replied. "You knew about the payoffs."

"It seemed such a small thing—the victims got money, the priests got psychiatric help, the church was safe," Fey replied. "Only later did he tell me about Lichner and those poor children." The old man began to weep. "I should have said something then . . . but the church . . ."

Karp looked up at the saints on the ceiling. He wondered if there were people like that anymore. Lucy maybe. "You knew that once you crossed the line, there was no way back. But yes, when he told you that, you should have said something."

Fey wiped at his tears and nodded. "I know it was

wrong, and I expect to pay for it in this life and the next," he said. "I don't want any deals. In fact, if you need me to make a statement, I waive my right to remain silent and to have counsel present. Mr. Kane no longer represents me."

Kane, who had been looking from one to the other, slammed his hand on the table. "Shut the fuck up. What in the hell are you talking about? Karp understands how the world works. Now, do we have a deal or not?"

Karp gave Kane his famous glare. "Okay, here's the deal. The deal is the archbishop can plead guilty to manslaughter. He engaged in a conscious disregard of the grave risks of abusive and homicidal conduct that Lichner and others meted out. If he wants to make a statement regarding his knowledge of other criminal activities or accomplices, such as you, I'm sure the court will take that into consideration at sentencing."

Kane's eyes bugged out of his head. "What in the hell do you mean at sentencing? You can't arrest the archbishop of New York."

"You're not listening," Karp continued. "You asked me what the deal was and I'm telling you. *Your* deal is you can plead guilty only to the top count, capital murder, or you can go to trial. Either way, you're going to rot in hell. There, that's the deal. Any questions?"

Andrew Kane began to scream out a profanity-laced tirade that would have made Dirty Warren blush, while the veins on his forehead looked as if they might pop. "You can't arrest me," he shrieked. "I'm going to be mayor. I can't be mayor if I'm in prison. What in the hell are you talking about?" The shrieking continued to build in volume. "You're dead, Karp! You, your bitch wife, and your fucking kids. I'll have you killed just like all the others."

Karp shrugged his shoulders, shook his head, and grinned, then pulled a pen out of his shirt pocket. "Thanks that will help in court," he said clicking it twice.

Immediately, McIntyre and several other detectives from the DA's squad burst into the room. As they hand-cuffed Kane and Fey, Karp couldn't help but toss in another jab. "I'll think about what you just said while I'm sleeping in my bed tonight, Kane. I hope you enjoy your cot . . . especially when they turn out the lights, and the screaming starts." He looked at McIntyre. "Get these bastards out of my sight."

That evening he held a joint press conference with Denton, who announced the arrests of Archbishop Timothy Fey and attorney Andrew Kane for homicide "and a variety of other charges yet to be determined." Karp had said only that the cases would be taken before a grand jury. "Otherwise, I am not at liberty to discuss an ongoing investigation at this time." The two men then stepped down from the podium as all hell broke loose, leaving Murrow to answer questions as obliquely as possible.

Returning to his office, Karp found Stupenagel sitting on the couch. The day after the shootings when they made their deal, he'd told her that he couldn't give her an exclusive on the arrests. "The rest of the media would never forgive me," he said, "and while I could live with that, it wouldn't be fair either and smack too much of favoritism." He had agreed—mostly because he needed the time anyway—to delay the announcement until Monday evening so that her story in the *Village Voice* would appear at the same time the other newspapers ran

theirs. And because she had more detail, including refer-
ces to the clergy No Prosecution cases, she said, "My
story will be better anyway. They'll be chasing my tail for a
week."

"You do realize that you may have torpedoed your
chances at getting elected," she said as he sat with his
elbows on his desk and his face in his hands. "Andrew
Kane still has a lot of connections and a lot of money.
Then there's the Catholic reaction to this story; they'll
blame the church, but they may also blame you for bursting their little bubbles of faith. Now if I understand you,
Fey intends to be a witness for the prosecution and tell
everything he knows, which will help."

Stupenagel stood and crossed over to the desk where
she bent over and kissed him on top of the head. He looked
up with a weak smile and asked, "What was that for?"

"Well, I should say something smart-alecky like thanks
for hooking me up with Murrow. Believe it or not, I may
be in love, though at the moment I am settling for lust,"
she said. "But that wouldn't be why I kissed you. I guess
I'm just saying thanks from all of us nobodies out here for
showing us that there are still knights in the world willing
to joust with windmills."

"Why, Stupe," he said gently, "you're not getting all
sentimental on me in your old age?"

"Nah," she said. "I'll be watching, and if you fuck up, I'll
write a story every bit as scathing as this one is laudatory."

"Now, that's the Stupe I love," he laughed.

At Zak's football game several months later, Karp smiled
at the memory. So far he'd done pretty well with the windmills.

Bernard Little and his wife had attended every calendar appearance in the Flanagan case. They were sitting in the back of the courtroom when the court set a firm trial date and Karp informed the court that the People would accept no lesser plea than capital murder for the death of Jumain Little.

"I 'spose you think I should thank you for doing your job," Bernard Little said afterward.

"That's not necessary, Mr. Little," Karp replied. "I'm just sorry that it took this long."

Little started to say something but tears came to his eyes and he choked up. It was his wife who reached forward and touched Karp on the arm. "He does want to thank you," she said. "We want to thank you. The words are just a little tough right now. We miss our boy." Karp looked back to Bernard, who nodded his head and stuck out his hand.

Kane was, of course, fighting the charges tooth and nail. But he'd already been handed a series of setbacks. First, he was remanded without bail. The big blow was when the judge announced that he was denying defense motions to quash Flanagan's tape-recorded messages, as well as the testimony of Fey (based on attorney-client privilege). The writing was on the wall for Kane to see. All of his supposed friends and political allies had long since abandoned him and were now talking to the press about how they'd always suspected "something wasn't quite right with that guy." He'd also been moved into protective custody after receiving several death threats from Catholic inmates at the Tombs.

As a sidebar to the indictments of Kane, Newbury and his merry band of sleuths had indicted a dozen police officers and twice that many clergy members from the No

Prosecution files. Newbury also finally had the means to prove that Kane owned Pentagram records. "A little late," he admitted. "But another piece of the puzzle that will show his connection to the ML Rex murders."

Fulton had also come up with a couple more pieces. He'd shown up at the office one day on crutches and began by giving Karp a full dressing down for not keeping his bodyguard around at all times. But then he'd moved on to the real reason for his visit. His guys had gone through the limousine again and discovered a business card with Paglia's fingerprints all over it. "The phone number on the back is to a cell phone registered to Michael Flanagan. The idiot was too stupid or lazy to use a second untraceable phone. We also did another search of the Paglia home and turned up a mug shot of Alejandro Garcia."

Finally, Karp thought, this little theatrical production is moving to a conclusion I'm directing. And I now know my lines.

There was one last bit role that came to a conclusion when he and Guma made a big show of entering his outer office with a box of files and placing them on Mrs. Boccino's desk. "Well, that's about everything we got on Kane," Guma said.

"Yeah," Karp acknowledged. "We better lock it up in my office until we can move it someplace safe after the meeting this evening."

"Good idea," Guma said, and they'd carried the boxes into Karp's office.

When they were out of the room, Mrs. Boccino carefully picked up her telephone and dialed a number she'd been given. "It's me," she said quietly, listening for the return of the two men. "Get word to him that someone needs to get down here in about an hour. I know where they're keeping all the evidence on Andy. . . . Oh, and tell him that I love him and miss him and . . ."

"And isn't that sweet," Guma said from behind her, pressing a finger down on the receiver. "You really aren't the brightest bulb on the Christmas tree are you, Mrs. Boccino. Not only do you turn down a night of heaven with yours truly, but you're a dirtbag, too." He picked up a pen he'd laid on her desk when he entered the office. "These really are amazing gadgets," he said. "But I guess this means we won't be on for tonight, unless it's dinner in jail."

"Bastard," she said.

"Bitch," he replied and stuck out his tongue.

"Defensive holding!" Giancarlo screamed as an incomplete pass left Zak's team with one final fourth-down play between them and defeat. "Oh my God! Hey, I know a good seeing-eye dog for sale!"

Karp laughed and shook his head; his kids were something else. Tomorrow, he was going to need a little courage himself as he was going to officially announce his candidacy for New York district attorney. The good news was he'd received a call from Marlene in the morning, saying she and Lucy were coming home in time for the press conference. "We just thought your whole family should be there."

Lucy had gone with Marlene, saying she wanted to fulfill her obligation to Father Eduardo. However, he figured there was more to it than that, as she talked nightly to Ned Blanchet. Wonder if she'll end up in a little house on the prairie, he thought, amused by his own joke.

The two women and Jojola also had been accompanied

by a fourth person. They'd invited Alejandro Garcia to go with them to convalesce "out where the air is clean," and he'd jumped at the chance. "Maybe I'll get started on my book," he said. "Though I'm thinking of going to college next year."

"Yeah? What are you thinking about majoring in," Karp asked.

"Prelaw. I think I might want to be a lawyer."

"Great. We can always use a sharp mind in the DA's office," Karp said.

But Garcia shook his head. "Uh-uh, somebody's got to keep the system honest," he said. "I'll be working for the other side. Maybe set up a practice in Spanish Harlem."

Somebody's got to keep the system honest. What a summer, Karp thought as Garcia's words echoed in his mind. But whatever tomorrow brought, today he just wanted to watch his boy play football.

Zak had played his heart out, but it looked as if it was going to be for a losing cause. He hoped Zak wouldn't take it too hard.

The night before Zak had admitted to a case of nerves. He was the best player on his team, and if they lost, he said, it would be his fault. Karp had thought about that and then gone to his closet where he dug out an old shoebox full of mementos. He'd found the fragile piece of folded paper and handed it to his son. "Read this," he said. "Your grandmother gave this to me once when I was doubting myself. It's not magic, but it helped."

Zak read the flowing cursive carefully as Karp thought about how his mother's death had affected him. When she first died, he'd felt sorry for himself. Why did she have to leave me? How am I ever going to make it? Then after a time, he'd stopped feeling sorry for himself and dwelled on the unfairness of it all for his mother. She was so young. Her whole life was ahead of her. But as he looked upon his son, he knew that the real shame of her death was that she never got to meet Marlene and his kids. You would have loved them all, Mom, and they would have adored you, as I did.

"Thanks, Dad," Zak said carefully handing the note back. "I liked that a lot . . . about being in the arena." Then he yawned. "Time for me to go to bed. The team is counting on me."

Karp took the note. "This is yours, now," he said. "But I'm going to go get it framed so that it doesn't fall apart. You may want to give it to your kid someday."

Now, the game was almost over. With a "hut hut," the ball was snapped and the quarterback faded to his left with Zak pulling out in front of him. The play was a swing pass to Zak out in the open and five yards down the field.

Only twenty to go, Karp thought as his son caught the ball and made the first tackler miss. Then Zak was headed for the sideline, sidestepping another defensive player bent on mayhem and turning up field in front of his father. There was only one boy to beat. The other team's middle linebacker, who had battled Zak all day to a draw.

Karp could see that the linebacker had the angle on his son and would catch him somewhere around the ten. He leaned forward to look, not realizing that he'd blocked the sideline ref's view.

Then several things happened. The defensive player launched himself at Zak, who spun out of the other player's grasp, but his momentum clearly carried one foot out of bounds. Zak knew it, too, as he was looking at his foot when it crossed the line.

However, the refs didn't see it although the linebacker immediately pointed to where Zak had stepped out of bounds. Karp groaned and looked at the sky; Zak's team was going to win, but it would be a tainted victory.

Then when he looked down, he saw the most amazing sight. His son was standing a yard from the end zone. All he had to do was fall forward and victory was his; he'd be carried off the field on the arms of his teammates. The hero.

Instead, Zak knelt and put a knee on the ground as the linebacker ran over, still trying to make the game-saving tackle. But the other boy pulled up when he realized what Zak was doing and instead tapped him on the shoulder pad. The game was over; the other team had won. The linebacker held out his hand; Zak took it and was helped to his feet. The boys gave each other a tap on the helmet and walked to their respective sidelines.

As the other side erupted in celebration, Zak walked alone across the field, his teammates and the spectators on his side stunned and quiet. Then the coach stormed onto the field and got in his face. "What in the hell do you think you were doing?'" the man screamed.

"I stepped out of bounds at the ten," Zak said. "The ref should have seen it."

"Should have, but he didn't," the coach ranted. "That's their problem. You blew this for us, Karp."

"It wouldn't have been the right thing to do," Zak replied.

"Right thing to do?" the man swore. "Jesus Christ, who the fuck do you think you are?"

"He's my son," Karp said, walking up and inserting himself between the man and Zak. "And if you so much as open your mouth again with anything other than an apology, I'm going to knock you stone-cold out."

The man started to open his mouth, thought better of it, and stalked off the field.

"I'm proud of you, kiddo," Karp said hugging Zak's helmeted head.

"Yeah," Zak said. "Well, I'm sort of proud of me, too. Hey, Dad?"

"Yeah, Zak?"

"That was really cool when you said you'd kick his . . ."

Atria Hardcover
Proudly Presents

FURY

ROBERT K. TANENBAUM

Available in hardcover September 2005
from Atria

Turn the page for a preview of *Fury*. . . .

Prologue

Then . . .

TWENTY-EIGHT-YEAR-OLD LIZ TYLER WOKE IN *the dark moments before her alarm clock would have chimed. Reaching over to the nightstand, she turned it off. She lingered for a moment, enjoying the warmth of her husband, who slept soundly next to her, half hoping that he'd wake up and make love to her.*

She'd never been more in love with him in their seven years of marriage. There'd been a rough spot three years earlier—a meaningless fling with the cliché tennis instructor to get even with her husband for his workaholic hours as a stock-broker—but he'd forgiven her and understood that he'd played a role in her infidelity. Wading through a flood of tears and self-recriminations, they'd reached a new level in their relationship and were stronger and more loving as a result. They'd conceived a baby, Rhiannon, named in memory of their first meeting at a Fleetwood Mac concert, and the child, now two, had cemented them to each other still further.

Sighing but getting no response, Liz decided to move on. This was her favorite time of day—just before the dawn, a precious few minutes to be alone with her thoughts before the demands of mommyhood and domestic engineering drove all other considerations from her mind until after the last bedtime story.

Liz slid from bed and into a sports bra, baggy sweatshirt, running shorts, socks and running shoes. She walked around to his side of the bed and leaned over to kiss his cheek, rough with a day's growth of beard.

"Going running?" he mumbled, finding and stroking her long muscular leg with the hand that hung off the bed.

"Yeah, lazybones, want to join me?" She didn't really want him to go—this was her time—but knew he wouldn't so it was polite to ask.

"Maybe next time." He sounded more than half asleep but his hand had continued to explore up her leg until it was reaching suggestive levels.

She moved away from his fingers, raising a muffled complaint. "You missed your chance five minutes ago, tiger," she said laughing. "I'm up, dressed, and off for the beach. I'll be back before you go."

Leaving the bedroom, she'd tiptoed into her daughter's room and peeked over the rail of the crib. Rhiannon lay on her stomach, a thumb stuck in her mouth. She was dreaming, judging by the small sounds of discovery and joy she made in between sucks. Liz leaned over until her nose was less than an inch from her toddler's neck and inhaled deeply the sweet and sour smells of childhood.

With an effort, she straightened and left her daughter's room. Time to start or you're going to miss the sunrise, she thought, grabbing the lanyard, with the whistle on it, off the coat rack and heading out of her Brighton Beach apartment.

She quickly made her way over to the boardwalk and down the steps to the beach. Crossing the loose sand over to the shoreline where it was harder and more compact, she then headed up the beach toward Coney Island. She could just make out her destination in the growing gray of the dawn—a big insectlike pier a mile away.

Liz liked running in sand. It gave her a better workout and was largely responsible for her shedding the twenty extra pounds she'd gained during pregnancy. Only five foot six, she was down to a lithe, trim 110 pounds with just enough breast to give her cleavage. She was proud of how she treated her body and had adopted a tan, athletic look with short, spiky black hair that framed her green, almond-shaped eyes nicely.

Pounding up the beach, scattering the seagulls, who complained obscenely about the intrusion, she was mostly alone. She could see the occasional beachcomber in the distance and the early riser or two along the boardwalk, but this stretch of beach was all hers. It gave her a chance to think about an issue that was troubling her—whether to return to work.

She didn't like the idea of leaving Rhiannon with a babysitter. But on the other hand, she'd had a career she enjoyed before she got pregnant—working as a florist after getting an associates degree in horticulture at Brooklyn Community College. She missed the work and she missed getting to socialize with adults during the day. But that just made her feel even more guilty, like she was being a bad mother.

The dilemma consumed her so much that as she approached the pier, she didn't notice the shadows moving beneath the weathered, barnacle-encrusted pylons. That was unusual, because she really didn't like to run beneath the hulking structure. As a little girl, she'd been afraid of dark places—those spaces beneath the bed, in closets, and down in basements where monsters were said to hide.

The dark places beneath the pier frightened her as an adult. But she always forced herself to finish this half of the run by racing beneath its beams, timing the sprint to match the waves receding enough to allow her a clear shot to the other side. In part, the idea was to conquer a childhood fear, but it was also similar to the reason people enjoy watching horror movies . . . they like being scared.

Liz was so caught up in the internal debate over going back to work that she didn't see the real monsters until she was halfway under the pier and one jumped out at her and yelled, "Boo!"

She veered and tried to sprint away but stumbled, giving him time to cut in front of her again. He wasn't horrible-looking for a monster, just a tall, gangly black teenager with mocha skin, nice, white teeth, and hazel-colored eyes. But he talked like a monster. "Say, where you going, bitch? Me and the homeboys was partyin' and thought maybe you should join us."

Standing as a wave came ashore and soaked her running shoes, Liz noticed that she was surrounded by a half-dozen teenagers—some of them leering, others looking uncomfortable. "Leave me alone!" she said forcefully as she'd been taught in a rape-prevention course she'd once taken at the YMCA, but the teenagers just laughed and smirked.

Liz tried to push her way past her tormentors. She could see the light on the other side of the pier and thought if she could just get there, she would be safe. She almost got through them, too, but then one of the boys,, who seemed to be their leader, grabbed her by the arm and spun her around.

Terrified, she reached out and clawed his face. He

looked at her with surprise and then rage. He lifted his hand, which held a piece of steel bar and struck her on the side of the head. It felt as if someone set off a big firecracker inside her skull. There was a flash of white light accompanied by a searing red pain, and she sank to her knees.

"Fucking ho'," the boy snarled and grabbed her by the hair. He began dragging her up the beach, farther into the shadows beneath the pier.

The pain of being pulled by her hair and her fear of what would happen in the dark brought Liz partly to her senses. She stuck the whistle in her mouth and blew as she lunged up, scratching for his eyes.

She saw fear in his eyes and even dared to hope that she might fight her way to freedom. But then someone kicked her in the back, crushing the wind out of her and sending her sprawling head-first into the sand. She pushed herself back up on her hands and knees. Then another firecracker went off in her head.

The next thing she knew she had been turned over on her back and someone was yanking her shorts off. "No, please," she begged. She couldn't see out of her right eye and her left caught only a blur of images as her dazed mind tried to reject what was happening to her.

"Hold her," the first boy shouted. Hands grabbed her shoulders and legs, pinning her to the ground as he got between her legs. She felt him trying to penetrate her and willed her mind to some other place where the world was still safe and good. The sun shone on a field as her daughter ran toward her laughing and her husband looked on.

The firecracker went off again. Then again. She drifted in and out of consciousness. Faces appeared. Some angry. Some frightened. Voices taunted her and urged each other to . . . violate her. "Yo, Des, your turn." Their voices sounded like crows in the cornfields of Iowa where she'd grown up before she'd moved to New York to become a writer, fell in love at a Fleetwood Mac concert, married, had a baby, and named her Rhiannon.

"Fuck her, homes, ain't you a man?" There was a terrible pain on her right breast. She heard herself scream, but it sounded as if it was coming from some other woman.

There was a moment's respite. Then the first boy spoke again. "Hey, ratface, you want some of this bitch?"

Another voice entered her head. An evil voice, laced with malice. "Show you boys how to treat these bitches," the voice said. "If you want to teach them a real lesson, you got to fuck them dirty."

A man with a pockmarked face and foul, rotting breath leaned over and grinned in her face. Someone rolled her over. She felt the cool sand on her shattered face; it felt good and she wondered if these boys would now allow her to die. But the nightmare wasn't over. She felt herself penetrated again, ashamed to be used so horribly. Filthy, dirty, so much shame that she welcomed the new blows to her head, hoping that they would put her out of her misery. Die, she told herself.

In the distance, sirens wailed. The boys shouted words of alarm, indistinguishable from the screams of the seagulls and the whispering condolences of the waves.

Then the monsters were gone. She felt their running footsteps recede across the sand as she waited for death to release her from the humiliation and pain. But death was not so kind.

Slowly, painfully she rose to her knees, then to her feet. She couldn't see much, just a light and a green moving field she knew was the water. Dirty. Filthy. She had only one desire—to cleanse herself before she let the sea take her.

They found her standing in the water up to her waist, scrubbing furiously between her legs, trying to wash away the shame of what the monsters had done to her. Someone summoned a police officer, who waded into the water to escort her back to shore.

When he got close, he had to look away for a moment to compose himself. Her face was covered by a sheet of blood, her left eye swollen shut, her right eye hanging half out of its socket. Her lips were split, a black hole where her front teeth had been.

She screamed when he first reached out for her arm and pulled away from him. "Please, ma'am, let me help you to someplace safe."

Turning a sightless face toward the officer, she'd cried, "Don't you know, there's no such place!"

Not sure what to read next?

Visit Pocket Books online at
www.SimonSays.com

**Reading suggestions for
you and your reading group**

New release news
Author appearances
Online chats with your favorite writers
Special offers
And much, much more!